'As far as the world is concerned, you've slept with a killer.

'Nothing to take pride in. Certainly no one you would stand in front of an altar with.'

Julie sat up, and he couldn't miss the anger in her face. 'I don't think I've mentioned an altar. And how do you know what I take pride in?'

'It can't be me,' he said steadily. 'And you're the kind of woman men marry. Dammit, you're much too trusting. I've cost you money. Friends. Neighbours. I'm not going to take away your self-respect.'

She started to reach for him, but he rose before she could touch him. Without looking at her, he dressed.

'I'm sorry,' he said, and started for the door.

'Ryan?'

He stopped but didn't turn around.

'I *would* take pride in you,' she said.

His insides twisted.

If only…

Dear Reader,

Welcome. We've some wonderful Christmas treats for you in Sensation™ this month, so you can take a little time and indulge yourself—*whenever* you get the opportunity!

Suzanne Brockmann's visiting with another TALL, DARK AND DANGEROUS man in *It Came Upon a Midnight Clear*—I wouldn't mind waking up and finding Crash Hawken under *my* Christmas tree!

Then there's everybody's favourite, Linda Turner, with *Christmas Lone-Star Style*, another story set in the old house in San Antonio where you ENTER SINGLE, and LEAVE WED...

Then historical author Patricia Potter makes a terrific debut with *Home for Christmas*, where our hero's a cop wrongly convicted. It is easy to see why Patricia's had books on the *USA Today* bestseller list!

Finally, award-winning writer Ruth Wind sends a secret agent to visit an ordinary B&B, and when the bullets start to fly, he's suddenly on the run with the pretty landlady. That's *For Christmas, Forever*—it's certainly not your average Christmas.

Don't miss one of them!

The Editor

Home for Christmas
PATRICIA POTTER

™ SILHOUETTE
SENSATION®

*Silhouette, Silhouette Sensation and Colophon are
registered trademarks of Harlequin Books S.A., used under licence.*

*First published in Great Britain 1999
Silhouette Books, Eton House, 18-24 Paradise Road,
Richmond, Surrey TW9 1SR*

© Patricia Potter 1998

ISBN 0 373 07897 8

18-9912

*Printed and bound in Spain
by Litografía Rosés S.A., Barcelona*

PATRICIA POTTER

is a former journalist with a passion for history and books. While working at the *Atlanta Journal*, she met and reported on three presidents and covered news stories from murder to space launches to the Civil Rights movement. An avid reader, Patricia tries to fit a bit of everything into her hectic life-style—anything from reading biographies and espionage books, caring for her animals (of which she has a few) to travelling. She's a multi-published author and her books have reached the *USA Today* bestseller list. A three-time Romance Writers of America RITA finalist, Patricia also earned the *Romantic Times* Storyteller of the Year Award. A former president of the Georgia Romance Writers of America, she now serves on the national board. Patricia currently resides in Memphis, Tennessee.

For Carol Quinto,
whose courage, love and friendship will always be an
inspiration.

Chapter 1

A split second. A lifetime.

From the instant Julie Farrell felt the shock of another car smashing into hers, heard the grinding sound of folding metal, felt the incredible impact of an air bag exploding, she believed she would die.

And, dear God, her son!

I killed my husband; now I've killed my baby. The thought flashed through her consciousness like lightning through a storm. Terror filled her. Stark terror. Not for her. For her son.

Please God, let him live!

Pain ripped through her chest from the impact of the safety bag. Still, her panic focused on her son, Nick, silent in his car seat in the back. Ignoring the chest-crushing agony, she twisted against the seat belt that held her in place. The top of the car had crunched inward. She couldn't reach him. Frantically, she fumbled to unfasten her own seat belt, and tried again to reach out to her son; bent metal blocked her.

She smelled the acrid odor of smoke, felt the heat beginning to crawl into the car, and saw flames dart from the engine. Desperate, she tried to open the door but it was crumpled, jammed.

Nick, my baby! She heard herself scream in her mind. She heard more sounds. More crashing metal. Something that sounded like a shot. Yelling. Screaming. Her own screaming.

How long before the car exploded?

Where was help?

"Nicholas," she screamed. A cry answered her. She squirmed around, trying once more to stretch out her hand to him, but he remained out of reach.

The smoke grew heavier. She could barely breathe. Words strangled in her throat. *Dear God, help Nicholas. He's only four.* Tears mingled with blood blinded her as she frantically tried to reach her son, talk to him, calm the fear in his sobs.

Then she heard a noise from the back. Someone was trying to wrench open the right back door.

"Dammit!" The profanity ripped through the car, and she stretched around to see. Two arms were reaching through the right rear window, working desperately to release Nicholas from the car seat. "Please, God," she whispered. "Please, please, God..."

Then she heard a voice, the same voice that had been swearing a moment earlier. But now it was soothing, soft. "It's all right, son. I have you." Someone was taking Nicholas from the car through the window. He was safe! Safe. *Thank you, God. Thank you.*

The smoke was denser. The heat...dear God, the heat...

Her hand tried the door handle again. *Please. Please. Please. Someone please help.* She did not want to die. Nick needed her. He had no one else. No one...

Then a bloody hand reached inside her window. She heard the same voice she'd heard seconds earlier. Steady and sure. Confident. "Lady, I'll get you out." A hand tugged on the door outside as she tried from the inside. The door did not move.

"Lean back," her rescuer said, "as far as you can."

She trusted that voice. She trusted its confidence. She leaned back, and heard the remainder of the broken glass being cleared from the window. Then she was being pulled out by two bloody arms. She was aware of strength, incredible strength.

Heat singed her. Flames darted out from under the hood.

"Nicholas?" she screamed.

"The boy's safe," the man said as he finished dragging her out. He took her in his arms, and for the first time she felt as if she might live. There was confidence in those arms, in the stark face that looked worriedly down at her. He started toward the side of the road.

Someone yelled, "It's gonna blow."

She was hurtling through the air. He had thrown her, tossed her like a rag doll. She was rolling, rolling down an embankment just as the world exploded into noise and heat and raining particles of metal.

"Nicholas," she whimpered again as she covered her head and felt tiny bits of shrapnel piercing her as she continued rolling. Then from nowhere, she heard herself whisper, "Doug. Doug. Why?"

Then pain faded into darkness.

Killer Cop Saves Mother, Child

The headline raced across the front page in letters large enough for even Julie Farrell's fogged, aching eyes to read.

She squinted and concentrated, trying desperately to read the sub-head:

Prominent Attorney And Son
Pulled From Flaming Car
By Convict

Her eyes went to the paragraph below, but the small words wriggled and dimmed until they were a mass of indecipherable blobs of ink. If only the pain would fade away like the words.

It was useless. She could only read the large type. After a moment's frustration, she gave up, allowing the sheet of newsprint to fall on her lap as she looked up at the senior partner of her law firm, who had brought her the paper. Her eyes hurt. Her head hurt. She could barely move, and when she did, every part of her— external and internal— ached, pounded or burned.

She closed her eyes for a moment, trying desperately to arrange her thinking processes. Her first thought, when she regained consciousness at the hospital, was her son. She was assured that he'd been clear of the explosion and was in much better shape than herself, though that was of small comfort, considering that she felt like a pincushion punctured with a thousand needles.

She had threatened to crawl, if necessary, to see him, and finally a volunteer had brought him to her room. Nick looked terribly small in a wheelchair, and bandages covered some cuts from glass, but his eyes were as bright as ever, and he climbed next to her, putting a chubby hand on her cheek.

"I was afraid," he said tearfully. "I was afraid you was going away."

"No," she said. "I will never, ever leave you."

"I love you," he said with the intensity of a frightened little boy. He was allowed to stay several more minutes before being taken back to the pediatrics ward.

Then she asked about the man who had thrust her away from the burning car.

But no one would tell her anything. They kept dodging her questions, reassuring her instead about her own injuries. But she already knew *she* was going to live. Painfully for a while, but live. What about the stranger who risked his life for Nick and herself? She remembered being thrown away from the car; he wouldn't have had time to escape the brunt of the explosion.

It wasn't until David Caldwell, the managing partner of her law firm, appeared and handed her the newspaper that she received some answers. "You made the news," he said in his usual no-nonsense voice. "The doctors say you should rest for a few weeks, but you're not to worry about it. Mark will take over the Crispen appeal."

She nodded, well aware of the importance of the case to the firm: a battle over a valuable patent the court ruled did not belong to their client. The deadline for the appeal was next week.

He hesitated for a moment, obviously wanting to say something else. She was curious as to why *he* had come rather than a junior partner. David Caldwell was not known for niceties. He was always all business, often curt, even rude to his underlings, of which she was one. Her gaze wandered up and down the impeccably dressed figure, noting the frown that lingered on his lips.

"Well, ummmm, we're all happy that you...and your son...were not injured more severely," David finally said.

"Thank you," she replied, wishing he would leave. Wishing she could close her eyes and forget the pain.

He balanced on one foot, then the other, obviously uncomfortable. She wondered suddenly whether he had ever been in a hospital room before. And then she remembered the brusqueness with which he had given her the newspaper. He did not like publicity. The *firm*—Caldwell, Michaels, Evans and Cagle—did not like publicity. Dammit, *she* didn't like publicity. In fact, she loathed it.

She wanted him to go. She wanted to read more of the story. To heck with the publicity. She wanted information.

"The news media is full of stories," Caldwell continued. "That...police officer was big news ten years ago. Most people believed he should have gone to trial, been sentenced to death. This will stir things up again."

Her head seemed to pound even louder. Police officer? Death penalty? She stared at the large headline again, though she had difficulty absorbing it. "Did you?" she asked curiously.

He raised an eyebrow in question.

"Did *you* think he should have received the death penalty?" she asked, wondering why on earth she was asking such a thing. Caldwell was not someone you questioned. Yet she wanted to know. She wanted to know everything about the man who had saved her son's life. Her own.

"Yes," he said harshly, surprising her. "I think he should have. He was an officer who dealt drugs and killed his own partner."

Condemnation hung in the room, condemnation she understood. She, too, despised dirty cops.

Caldwell looked away from her. "I know the publicity isn't your fault," he said in a voice that did not reassure her at all. "But we would appreciate your discretion on the matter."

Discretion, she thought, meant ignoring the fact that the man in the article, the *killer,* had risked his life for hers. She didn't answer.

He cleared his throat, "If you need anything..."

He really was trying to be kind. He just wasn't very good at it. "Thank you," she said.

"I understand your boy is doing splendidly," he said gruffly.

"We were lucky," Julie said, looking back down at the newspaper. They were lucky that one man had the courage to pull them from a flaming car. *One* man. She swallowed hard as she remembered the headline. She wanted her visitor to leave. She wanted to read more. She wanted to know how badly her savior was injured.

She closed her eyes, then opened them, feigning sleepiness. She did not have to feign much. She was tired, so very tired.

The senior partner cleared his throat. "I should be going," he said. "They told me not to stay long. I just thought you should know about...that." He gestured to the newspaper. "Reporters have already called for information about you. They will probably be swarming all over you."

Another not-so-subtle warning. Disappointment stabbed through her. She'd thought for an instant that perhaps, maybe, he had come because someone cared.

She merely let her eyes close again. She listened to retreating footsteps and a door opening and sliding shut with a small thud. Part of her wanted to keep her eyes closed. Did she really want to learn more about the man who pulled her from the car?

But she opened her eyes and stared at the headlines, then the three accompanying pictures. One was the skeletal remains of her car. Another was a photo of herself. She remembered that picture. It had been taken after she had won her first case as an assistant district attorney eight years ago.

The third was a man. She had no idea when it had been taken. He had a hawk-like face, deep-set eyes and thick eyebrows which made his eyes look sleepy. But that was his only benign feature. His expression was grim. And the grimness looked natural on him. The photo caption identified him as Ryan Murphy.

Her eyes went to the columns of type. She felt the heaviness of sedatives, the dullness they created, and she finally set the paper down on her lap. The headline stared back at her.

Killer Cop Saves Mother, Child

She managed to read the first few paragraphs. The convict, Ryan Murphy, had evidently defied his guards and a warning shot to rescue Nick and herself.

She managed a few more sentences. There had been a chain reaction of crashes, injuries, confusion which apparently was why no one else offered help. No one, other than the convicts, was near enough. Apparently the guards had been indecisive on whether they should assist the wounded or watch their charges.

Murphy had been critically injured and was in a coma, according to the report.

She swallowed hard as she reread the headline. Killer Cop. She had known bad cops. One had lied to her and as a result she had sent an innocent man to prison; she had subsequently resigned from the district attorney's office.

Her hand tightened around the newspaper. Was that why no one would tell her how he was? No one thought the man worth her worry?

A nurse came in the room with a tray. Another blood sample. She knew they worried about infection. Blood pressure and temperature were taken. A few questions were asked about nausea.

Julie answered impatiently, then held up the newspaper. "The man...in the story...is he here?"

The nurse hesitated, obviously reluctant to give out information about another patient.

"Please," Julie said. "He saved my son's life. And mine."

She knew the nurse had to know about her. Nurses knew everything, even in a hospital as large as Memorial. She'd discovered the power of the grapevine when her husband had been brought here years ago.

"He's in intensive care," the nurse said.

"He's still alive then," Julie whispered gratefully.

The nurse nodded.

"Thank God," Julie said, then her mind turned to practical things.

She had to make telephone calls. She had to get someone to take care of her cat, Prissy. Her neighbor, Emily Richards, would do that; she had a key to the house. But there were other details...so many details....

"How long will I be here?" she asked. All her appendages seemed to move, if painfully. Bandages covered her arms and back.

"The doctor will talk to you in the morning," the nurse said. "We'll be checking you frequently through the night because of that bump on your head."

Julie felt an onslaught of pain, then closed her eyes against it.

She felt the paper being tugged from her hand.

"No," she said. "Leave it here."

She heard retreating footsteps, the closing of the door again. She clutched the newspaper and saw the picture of Ryan Murphy in her mind. She heard his voice. "Lady, I'll get you out." She remembered his calmness, the unhurried assurance that had made her believe him.

Julie tried desperately to remember more. She had been concentrating on the heavy traffic before the accident, but she recalled seeing the white-clad prisoners on the side of the road. She had taken little notice since clean-up gangs were frequent sights on the interstates.

Her rescuer had had tanned wrists. She remembered that, too. And a white shirt.

His voice. She couldn't get the voice from her mind. A convicted killer. A confident comforting voice. Two discordant images.

But it was the latter that remained in her mind, even after she drifted away from the pain.

Julie waited restlessly for release from the hospital. Nick had been released yesterday and was staying with Emily, the next-door neighbor with whom Julie exchanged babysitting duties. But because of Julie's recurring headaches, the doctors had wanted to keep her an extra day.

Emily would be here at the hospital in several hours to pick her up. The doctor had already come by with a long list of instructions, and she was ready to go. Emily, however, had already organized her day around a noon release.

Julie dressed in the loose sweat suit Emily had brought the day before when she'd picked up Nick. Her head still ached, yet she couldn't stay still. A need had been building inside her to see for herself the man who had saved her life. After receiving directions to intensive care, she started down the corridor toward the elevator.

Her heart seemed to pound faster as she reached the nurses' station in the intensive care area. A killer. A dirty cop. Everything she hated most. Yet the man had risked his life to save hers. She couldn't forget that. Ever.

She asked the nurse on duty about Ryan Murphy.

"He's still in a coma."

"Will he...make it?"

"I don't know." Julie knew the nurse couldn't give out any more information than she had. But she heard the doubt in the woman's voice. "I can only tell you he's in critical condition."

"Can I see him?"

"I'm sorry. No visitors," said the nurse, a competent-looking woman in her forties.

"I'm the woman he saved," Julie explained, assuming the nurse knew what she was talking about. It certainly had been all over the media. "And he saved my son. I was just released and I wanted to see him, to thank him...even if he's still unconscious," she pleaded. "I have to."

The nurse—her name badge said Sarah Mashburn—hesitated. "You'd have to get by the police officer on duty."

"Which room is it?"

"The fourth on the right. You can't miss it. It's the one with the officer sitting in front."

"Thank you," she said.

"I didn't say anything," the nurse said, turning around to face a board that was suddenly flashing.

Julie went by several rooms, each separated from the hall by a wall of glass. Most had one or two people huddled inside next to a patient. She reached the cubicle where a uniformed officer sat. He stood as she approached.

She noted his name on his shirt.

"I'm Julie Farrell," she said. "I was an assistant district attorney with Dan Watters's office."

He relaxed and nodded. "I recognize your name. You're the one he pulled from the car."

"As well as my son. I was hoping I could see him for a moment, thank him."

"He's unconscious."

"I know," she said. "Still, it's something I need to do. My son is just four years old."

"I have a kid myself," the officer said. "If the nurse said you could, maybe it would be all right. I'll have to go in with you."

"Of course," she said. "You can search me if you want."

He looked embarrassed, but all the same he patted her down. "Okay. Only a moment."

She went inside, aware of the officer behind her like a shadow. She stood next to the bed. Numerous tubes ran in and out of Ryan Murphy. His arm was in a cast, and much of his body was wrapped in bandages. One wrapping partially covered the side of his head. Abrasions marred a face that was all angles and planes. His features should have looked relaxed in sleep, but they didn't. His mouth was grim even in unconsciousness. Yet there was an odd little twist at one end that also gave him a quizzical look. His eyes were closed, covered by thick, black lashes, and what hair escaped the bandage was thick and just as dark as his lashes. He wasn't exactly handsome, but his features were strong, compelling.

She touched his hand. "Thank you," she whispered. "I know you can't hear me, but thank you." She felt the warmth of his hand, and her own fingertips tingled with the touch. He was so still, the beeping of the monitor so ominous. "Live," she said in a low, demanding voice. "Ryan Murphy, live. You have to live. Fight, dammit. Fight."

She willed his fingers to move, but they didn't. She stood still, trying to pass some of her life force into him.

"I'm sorry, Mrs. Farrell, but you have to go. This could cost me my job."

"Of course," she said. She gave Murphy's hand one last squeeze, then turned and walked out the door. Outside, she thanked the officer, then turned back to look through the window. He looked so still. *It's all right, son, I'll get you out.* She thought she would always remember that voice, that reassurance. The feel of his arms as he'd lifted her from the car.

He'd paid a terrible price for it.

She felt her heart constrict as she forced herself to look away and leave.

Fear crawled through him. It was a terrifying, insidious thing that filled every crevice of his mind.

He had grown used to the pain as he slowly emerged from darkness. For a while, the crushing, smothering pain shoved everything else from his consciousness. But as that pain receded ever so slowly, something else filled the void it left: emptiness.

His head pounded. He could barely breathe through the soreness in his throat.

"Mr. Murphy?" He heard the sounds, tried desperately to understand them. Who was Murphy? He'd heard the name before. Over and over as if someone was pounding it into his skull. But it made no sense to him.

He opened his eyes, saw several blurry forms. Slowly, they came into focus, their mouths making noises as they opened and shut. One of the figures—a man in white—leaned over him.

"Can you answer me, Mr. Murphy?"

He tried, but his throat ached and his mouth felt as if it were stuffed with some dry substance. He tried to speak, but nothing came out.

Only with intense effort could he fathom the conversation taking place. "He's conscious." Then the face neared his again and a hand held out a glass with a straw to him, guiding the straw into his mouth. He sipped slowly, using the time to try to understand what was happening. So good. It tasted so good. But then it was taken away.

"Mr. Murphy? Do you remember anything? Can you tell us how you feel?"

There was an expectant silence.

He swallowed with difficulty. His mouth was still dry, hurting. His throat was raw, sore beyond imagining. He ached all over, but his head...his head was agony.

"Mr. Murphy," came the voice again. "You're in a hospital, but you'll be all right."

All right? He felt terrible. He moved slightly, and his chest felt as if someone had pounded his ribs with sledgehammers. His hands and wrists were bandaged, and one arm lay stretched out in a cast. His throat...

And who was Murphy? Suddenly the pain faded as he frantically sought information, explanations, but nothing came.

He could only look up at the source of the voice. He remembered hearing it before when he'd drifted in and out of consciousness. He vaguely remembered questions that had made no sense. Nagging, insistent questions he didn't want to acknowledge.

"The woman and child...they will live, thanks to you." The man was speaking again.

He swallowed, trying to remember. Anything. He couldn't. What woman and child?

But that comment was lost in the torrent of more questions. "What is your name? Do you know where you are? Do you know what month it is?"

The questions kept bouncing around him, always returning to his name. He was asked it over and over again until he wanted to yell at them. Instead, he tried to retreat into himself, trying to escape into the empty, dead silence that was only a little less frightening than the incessant questions he didn't understand and couldn't answer.

They wouldn't leave him alone, though. A steady stream of people came and went, sticking him with needles and thrusting tubes into his mouth. He was washed and shaved as if he were a baby. And then the man in white returned, along with the burly man in a brown uniform.

The questions started again. "Do you know who you are? Do you know where you are? Do you know who the president of the United States is?" Some he thought he knew. Like Nixon. The name just popped into his mind when he was asked again who was president. But the disappointment on faces told him he was wrong. He hated the feeling of searching in empty places.

Once when he was asked his name for yet another time, he recalled the name he'd heard over and over again when he first woke up. "Murphy," he said slyly, expecting the questions to stop.

But they didn't. "What's your first name?"

He remained stubbornly silent.

"Ryan," the man in white said patiently. "Your name is Ryan Murphy. Does that sound familiar?"

No. He wanted to scream a denial at them, but instead he stayed silent.

A large man in brown clothing started yelling at the questioner in the white coat. "Hell, how long do we have to put up with this? He's faking."

He puzzled over the words. He didn't understand them, but he recognized the hostility and contempt in the voice. He closed his eyes again, willing them all to go away. It had worked before.

"He's sleeping again," said the soothing voice.

"Hell, he's been unconscious for two weeks. You would think he had enough sleep."

"He almost died." The soothing voice sharpened above him.

"Too bad he didn't," the angry voice said. "Save the taxpayers from footing the bill for his keep."

"I want you out of here." The mildness was gone from the calm voice.

The rough voice again: "He won't get away with the amnesia act."

"I don't think he's faking it."

"Then you're a fool, Doc. You don't know how many cons try this kind of thing. Don't remember what they did, try to get themselves transferred to some mental institution." His voice dripped his contempt.

"I want you to leave, Mr...."

"Bates. *Sergeant* Bates. And I don't leave until he's secured with an ankle chain since you refuse to send him to the prison ward."

"He needs attention he can't get there, and restraints aren't needed. He just came out of a coma. Brain injury. Broken arm. Broken ribs. Bruised lungs. Burns. He won't be going anywhere for a while."

"Save your sympathy, Doc. He's a lifer. A killer. A dirty cop who killed his own partner, and the rules say he has to be secured."

"I don't care what he did. He's my patient."

"Well, the state does care. He'll be chained, or he goes to the jail ward."

He heard all the words, but the one that pierced the darkness was "killer." He felt the cold, hard word echo crazily in his head, blocking out the others.

The voices above him continued to argue. Then he felt something cold and hard tighten around his leg. He forced himself to remain still. He wanted to fight whatever was being done to him. Yet something inside told him to remain still, to listen.

"A guard will be posted outside the door until he's moved to the jail wing," the harsh, angry voice said.

There was no reply, only retreating, heavy footsteps.

Then silence. Finally, the soothing voice again.

"You can open your eyes."

He did and stared up at the face over him.

The face smiled at him. "Good try."

There was approval in the man's voice, and he felt oddly comforted. Someone understood. There was a brief silence. "Take your time. Do you remember *anything?* A childhood pet? A game? Sports?"

He tried. But the more he concentrated, the worse the pain in his head became, the greater the void. He felt as if he were falling, his body twisting and turning into a great hole. "I can't remember," he said painfully.

A hand settled on his shoulder. "I'm Dr. Dailey, a neurologist. Do you know what that is?"

He searched again in his limited knowledge, but he didn't find anything.

"I'm a specialist in the nervous system, basically injuries or diseases that affect the brain. You received a bad blow, resulting in a concussion and some damage to the brain. We know you suffered injuries to the parietal area of the brain and the frontal area." He paused. "Do you remember anything? Anything at all?"

He could only shake his head. He didn't even know where Nixon had come from. He knew what a doctor was. He knew killer. He knew some words, not others.

"I think you have some sort of amnesia," Dr. Dailey said. "You've lost some of your memory—most of it—apparently."

"When...?" He could barely manage the word.

But the man in white apparently understood. "It could just last a short time," he said.

He tried to understand.

The doctor was talking again. "You have your speech, you understand words. The rest could return. You were lucky."

He didn't feel lucky. He felt lost in nothingness. "Who am I?" He could barely whisper the words.

"Your name is Ryan Murphy," the doctor said.

"Killer?" That word echoed in his head. As did the contempt behind it.

"Don't worry about that now. Just try to remember what you can."

God help him, he was trying. God? He closed his eyes as the pain in his head grew stronger. He swallowed a moan, then felt a prick in his hip. Darkness swallowed him.

When he woke again, he was alone. The pain still nagged him, but the greater torment was the recurring emptiness. His gaze searched the room. White. Bare. A line stretched above him to his arm where a needle was taped to his skin. He tried to move, but his ankle was tethered to the bed and with the movement came waves of pain.

Murphy. He remembered being called that over and over again. But it sounded strange to him. He tried to remember more. Shadows flittered in and out, dissolving when he reached out to capture them. His mind was slow, confused. He reached within it for something familiar, but he found nothing.

Think! *Doctor. Murphy. Killer.*

With a groan of frustration, his hand pressed the button on the small box lying near his hand.

A disembodied voice said, "Can I help you?"

But he couldn't speak. His voice was still a ragged whisper, and he didn't know whether anyone could help him. He didn't even know what he wanted.

In moments, the doctor was back, by his side. "I told the nurse to call me when you woke again," he said in a deep, soothing voice.

But now it didn't soothe him. Pain mixed with panic as he explored his mind again and still found nothing.

"Do you remember your name?" That same question.

"Murphy." He tried to remember more, but things faded in and out.

"Good," the doctor said with satisfaction. "It's not unusual to have short-term memory loss as well as long-term," he said.

He felt…muddled. Woozy. Blank.

Blank. Except for the pain.

He tried to quiet the rising anxiety.

The doctor, though, must have seen something in his eyes, because he put a hand on his shoulder. "Don't worry about it now. We don't know how much memory you've lost or whether parts, or all, will return. Amnesia is rare, rarer than you would think, and we don't know a great deal about it."

He moved, and he felt the steely band pull at his ankle. "I'm not sure I want to remember."

"Yes, you do," Dr. Dailey said. "And if you don't recall anything else, know that you saved a woman and a child from death. You pulled them from a burning car. It exploded, and you were thrown down an embankment."

"He called me…a killer?" That was what had stayed in his mind. That one word.

"I don't know anything about that," the doctor said. But his tone of voice said he did.

He struggled to remember other words said in this room. "Prison. He said I was in prison. I seem to know…" His voice trailed off. He knew the word. Somehow, he knew what it meant, that criminals were sent there. But he didn't remember being there. "How could I save…?"

There was an uncomfortable silence, then the man said, "You were on a prison road gang which was picking up litter from the side of the road. A car was hit by another one, and apparently the gas tank ruptured. You managed to get a child and his mother out before it exploded. Your hands and wrists were cut and burned, and you were thrown over an embankment by the force of the explosion."

He tried to remember that. But he couldn't. Instead, the word killer kept coming back. Why did he remember that, and little else? Yet the word haunted him. "Why…why was I in prison?"

There was another hesitation. "I really don't know much about it, Mr. Murphy," the doctor said. "Do *you* remember *anything* about your past? Anything about the accident?" The doctor's voice was calm but persistent.

He tried. Something, anything, would be better than the pain of nothing. Frustration crowded out everything else. Murphy. His name was Murphy. He hung onto that. Nothing sounded familiar. Not his name. Not anything.

"You'll probably start to remember things slowly," the doctor said. "I'll try to keep you here as long as I can."

His mind moved to the one positive thing he had heard. "The woman and child? You said they are...all right?"

The doctor nodded. "The woman—Mrs. Farrell—has been here several times and has called nearly every day wanting to know how you are."

A woman. Somewhere deep inside, he remembered a woman's voice...calling him.

Someone cared. Apparently he wasn't all bad....

Not all bad.

But he was a killer. A dirty cop, the one man said with contempt, as if he were the lowest thing on earth. Why did it sound wrong to him? Why did the thought send waves of revulsion through him? Why couldn't he remember?

Why? Why? Why?

His head exploded in pain. Involuntarily, he cried out and in a moment felt a needle again. For moments, he fought against the oblivion he knew it would bring. He had to *know,* dammit. But then, exhausted, he closed his eyes again and drifted back into a more welcoming world.

Chapter 2

"He's conscious."

Julie breathed deeply. Three weeks had passed since the accident, two weeks since she'd left the hospital. She'd asked the doctor in charge of Ryan Murphy's case to call her when he was out of danger. The doctors hadn't been at all sure he would emerge from the coma.

She slowly placed the phone back in its cradle. Thank God! She felt as if she were being eaten alive at the thought that Ryan Murphy—whatever he had done in his past—would lose his life saving hers. He hadn't had to come back for her after rescuing Nick.

Not only did she owe him for her son's life, she owed him for her own, and over the past weeks that fact had created a huge burden on her, so great indeed that she'd visited him several additional times in the intensive care unit of the hospital, each time cajoling the guard to let her enter.

His face was now engraved in her mind. His lips were wide, sensuous, but there were no lines around it. It was a mouth unfamiliar with smiles, with laughter, and, indeed, why would it be? He had been in prison ten years, though the usual prison pallor had been replaced by a deep tan obviously obtained while working on the road gang. The taut, drawn face was lightened only by the hint of a dimple in his chin that seemed as out of place as a rose in a field of wild grass. She also

sensed a restless vitality about him, perhaps because of his lean, muscled body.

Was that what had landed him in prison? Impatience?

She knew about a man's impatience to succeed. She knew far too
much about it. She closed her eyes for a moment, thinking about her
dead husband, about all the signs she should have recognized but
hadn't. Had this man's wife gone through the same horror she had?

On her last visit to see Murphy, she had touched his hand again to
offer some human contact, and then had turned blindly toward the door.
She'd thought to go home, but instead she'd driven her rental car five
blocks to the district attorney's office to see her former mentor and
boss, Dan Watters.

Despite his always busy schedule, he'd seen her immediately. He
stood as she entered his large office. "I read about the accident in the
newspaper," he said. "I meant to drop in, but..."

"I got your flowers," she said. "Thank you."

He smiled awkwardly. He wasn't good at small talk, which was
unusual in a man who ran for office. Yet he was uncommonly good
at his job, and the voters appreciated his blunt honesty. Julie admired
him tremendously and liked him even more. He had been the one
reason she regretted leaving her job as an assistant district attorney.

"How's Nick?"

She smiled. Nick had recuperated far faster than she. She worried
that somewhere deep inside he'd buried the terror of the accident.
Memories still haunted her at night, but so far her son had shown no
signs of trauma. "Fine. He was cut when he was pulled from the car,
but now he's as active as ever."

He nodded. "And you?" Her neck still sported stitches where a
flying piece of metal had cut a long gash. There were other bruises,
places that ached. She wasn't even supposed to be up yet.

"I'm better than I look."

"You were lucky. I saw the photo of the car."

"The man who saved me wasn't so lucky."

He fixed her with a stern stare. "Murphy," he said. "I hear he's
still in a coma."

"I want to know about him, Dan," she said. "His case must have
come to you before I joined your office."

"I was afraid you might want to know." He hesitated. "Stay away
from him, Julie. He's bad news."

"He saved my son's life," she said stubbornly. "And mine."

"That doesn't change the facts of his case."

"What *are* the facts?"

"He killed his partner on Christmas Eve ten years ago. Traces of cocaine were found in his car. He took a plea bargain for second-degree murder."

"Why?"

He looked away, his gaze wandering toward the window.

"Why did you plea bargain?" she persisted. "Why didn't you prosecute for first-degree murder?"

"I probably should have," he said. "But until then, Murphy had an unblemished record. There were no witnesses. He first claimed the killing had been in self-defense and that the cocaine had been planted. The odds for a conviction were probably no more than fifty-fifty. To tell the truth, I had some doubts myself until he offered to plead guilty to second degree."

"No premeditation," she said. "No death penalty."

He nodded. "I could buy that. If he had planned it, he would have done a hell of a better job concealing it. That bothered me from the beginning. Murphy was too damned smart to get caught."

"Then why was he?"

"Everyone slips now and then." He hesitated, then continued thoughtfully, "Murphy was a real pain in the ass, but he was one of the best detectives I ever knew. He never gave an inch, never allowed for weaknesses. He didn't know the meaning of the word compromise. If he'd been innocent, he never would have pled guilty. He would have fought it to the end. When he asked for an offer, I knew he must be guilty, but I just didn't have the evidence to go for first degree. I did demand the maximum sentence. You know the way I feel about dirty cops."

"So he got life," she said.

He nodded. "He came up for parole three years ago, but my office opposed it. I doubt he will ever make parole, not until he's an old man."

"Why did he risk his own life to save mine?"

Dan shook his head. "Instinct, maybe. Or maybe he thought it might help get him paroled. Don't go making a hero of him, Julie. He's a dangerous man."

"Does he have a family?"

"Had a wife and daughter. She divorced him not long after the sentencing. I don't think they'd been getting along for a long time. That was in the information compiled for his sentencing hearing."

"You handled it yourself?"

"Yes. And it was painful. As I said, I'd worked with him. He was a loner, a perfectionist. He wasn't the kind of man you'd choose to have a beer with. But I trusted him. I don't like being wrong." His tone hardened, and Julie remembered how very little Dan liked being wrong. He never forgot a betrayal.

She rose. "Thank you for seeing me."

"Stay away from him, Julie," he said again. "I know you're grateful, but I don't want to see you hurt again." He stood, too. "And if you ever want your old job back..."

"And all the bad publicity that would go with it? You're a saint, Dan, but I wouldn't do that to you, or myself."

"You got a rotten deal."

"I brought it on myself. I was so sure I was right...and someone else paid a high price for that mistake."

"You were one of the best assistants I ever had. Don't think convicting the wrong man never happened to anyone else."

She shook her head. "After what happened with Doug, I don't have any faith in my judgment any longer. You need certainty to be a prosecutor."

"You're hiding, Julie."

"No, I'm practicing law, and I'm home for my son. It's what I want, Dan. I need some peace in my life."

"Corporate briefs? That's not law."

"It is for me." She extended her hand to him. For a moment, she remembered the old excitement of being involved in his office, in the idealism she once shared with him and her fellow assistants. She'd been so young and eager and hopeful of changing the world. And she'd been such a bad judge of character....

Remember that, she thought as she headed home.

And now, days after that meeting with Dan, Ryan Murphy was awake.

He's dangerous. He's bad news. Reasons to stay away. She didn't need to be involved with another dangerous man. Her husband should have cured her of that weakness forever. But she *wasn't* getting involved. She was merely doing what anyone would do: thanking the man who had risked his own life to save her son's.

Ryan Murphy. He kept trying the name on his tongue. Part of him wanted desperately for it to become familiar. Another part was repulsed by the idea. He was a criminal. A murderer.

He had been moved from the intensive care unit to a nearby room on the neurology floor two days earlier. He had a television set now, and the doctor urged him to watch, said it might help him remember things.

He found himself fascinated with it, but his memory remained blank, though his mind eagerly soaked up everything he heard and saw. There was still that total vacuum, the terrible frustration of knowing nothing about himself other than what he was told.

And that was all bad. He even watched a portion of a show that mentioned him and showed a picture of him. A woman impersonally described him as a drug dealer. Crooked cop. A man who killed his own partner. He couldn't turn it off, though. He lay there, his gaze glued to the picture, his stomach clenching with a pain worse than any he'd felt before. Proof. Proof that he was what others had said. He hadn't wanted to believe it.

He moved restlessly, desperately wanting to stand, but a chain linked his ankle to the bed. He had pulled at it once when he was alone, but he soon discovered he could do nothing to loosen it. He hated that chain, just as he hated the way none of the nurses would look at him as they hurried in and out of his room. Each time one entered, a man in a brown uniform would enter with them, and stand at the door.

The only friendly faces were those of Dr. Dailey, and a new doctor, a stout, older man who asked many of the same questions Dr. Dailey had. Ryan tried to answer them all because he hoped it would help him remember. Then he would wonder whether he really did want to remember.

He punched a button, and a new picture came on the television. Four people were sitting in chairs talking about a crime. He listened intently. He had been a policeman. Maybe something would make sense, would bring back a memory. Just a few moments into the program, he heard loud voices outside the door. He pulled the sheet over the ankle that was chained and to better cover what the flimsy garment he wore didn't.

The door opened, and a woman appeared at the entrance. Unlike the others who'd been dressed mostly in white, she wore a light blue blouse, dark blue slacks and a matching sweater. Her hair was dark. Cut shoulder length, it swung easily around an attractive face. She hesitated at the door, a tentative smile on her lips, before taking several steps toward the bed.

He waited for the guard to come inside with her, but he did not.

He also waited for the now familiar contempt to crowd out the smile.

"Mr. Murphy," she said softly, "I'm Julie Farrell. You saved my son's life and mine. I wanted to thank you."

His hand tightened around the small box that controlled the television. Confusion rolled over him, then some kind of emotion so strong the area behind his eyes hurt. He didn't know how to answer her. He didn't remember anything about the accident, although he recalled the doctor telling him about it.

She stepped closer, and he noticed her eyes were gray, a soft clear gray like the sky at dawn. The image jumped into his mind as nothing else had. He wondered over it for a moment. A beginning. Did he really want a beginning?

"I know," she said, "that you can't remember, that you have amnesia, but I wanted you to know how grateful I am. My son is all I have and..."

She was pretty. He recognized that. He had seen many women on the television, but there was something about this one that caught his interest, as the others had not. Because she was real? Because she didn't look at him as if he were someone detestable?

"How do you feel?" she asked.

"I don't know," he finally said after a long silence.

"It must be difficult...not to remember anything."

He swallowed hard. If everything they said about him was true, being in the dark was probably not as terrible as remembering.

"You remember nothing about the accident?"

He shook his head. He wanted to. He wanted to remember for her sake. For his own. God help him, he wanted to remember doing something decent.

"Then I'll tell you about it," she said. "Can I sit down?"

He felt inadequate. Awkward. He didn't know what was expected of him. He was very conscious of the steel cuff around his ankle, of the guard outside his room. "How did you get in without...my keeper?"

She hesitated, then said slowly, "The district attorney is a friend of mine. He arranged it. Reluctantly."

"The district attorney?"

"Dan Watters." She waited a moment. "Do you recognize the name?"

He shook his head. "Should I?"

"He prosecuted you," she said matter-of-factly, her gaze studying his face intently.

She obviously expected a response. There was no fluttering of familiarity, no awakening of an emotion. The void was threatening to drown him again. He responded bitterly. "Aren't you afraid?" he asked bitterly. "Everyone else seems to be."

"How could I be, when I remember you pulling me from a burning car, when I keep hearing your words? You told me my son was safe, that you would get me out." Despite his silence, she sat down. "Did anyone tell you anything about it?"

He went still. Suddenly, he wanted to hear. He wanted to hear everything about himself. No, he corrected. Maybe he didn't *want* that. But he *had* to know. Good. Bad. *Everything*.

"Someone ran into my car," she started, obviously taking his silence as an invitation to speak. "The crash jammed the doors of my car and ruptured the gas tank. My son was in the backseat. I was in the front, and I couldn't reach him. Nor could I get the door open. I smelled the smoke. I know I was screaming for someone to help, but no one came. And then I heard your voice as you cleared out glass from the back window and lifted my son out.

"The smoke thickened and flames darted up from the engine. I didn't think there was any way to get out, and then you reappeared. Your arms were already bloody, but you cleared the glass from the window, then somehow pulled me out and threw me away from the car just as it exploded."

It was as if she was speaking of someone else. He couldn't imagine his part in her story. He didn't, couldn't, respond.

"I wish...I could do something for you."

"There's nothing anyone can do for me." His voice was rougher than he'd intended. "You know...what I am?"

"I know what they say you are."

Desolation filled him. The desperate loneliness of not knowing who he was, of feeling so thoroughly alone, rolled over him in waves. He had been told he had no future. He didn't have a past. All he had as of today was this hint of something...worthy, but he couldn't have that, either.

"Get out," he said suddenly.

Her eyes opened wide.

"Please," he said, flinching at the desperation he heard in his voice.

She leaned over, and he caught the scent of something sweet and intoxicating as she touched his arm. "If I can do anything for you, please let me know," she said and shoved a card in his hand.

He looked away, toward the window, toward the blue sky. He felt her gaze on him, then heard the sound of her shoes against the floor and the opening and closing of the door.

His hand crushed the card and he felt even more alone than ever.

Julie had expected her visit to end her...obligation to Ryan Murphy. Dan had called it an obsession, when she'd literally begged him to allow her to see the man alone. She'd listened as he told her his sources said they believed he was faking amnesia. Cons often faked any number of mental disabilities as grounds for parole or a less restrictive prison. Prison authorities were convinced that this was the case with Murphy. They were already demanding that he be sent back to prison, but this time to the maximum security facility at Reidsville where he'd spent his first eight years in virtual isolation because of his status as a former police officer. Apparently it had been difficult even for a man termed a loner because he had requested to go into the general population. He must have managed to stay out of trouble since he was then sent to a medium security institution in Atlanta.

She could barely tolerate the idea that he was to be punished for helping her. As an assistant D.A., she'd been to Reidsville and to the segregation cells where they held high-risk prisoners who, for one reason or another, were in danger from other inmates. Eight years! She couldn't even imagine the toll of such solitary confinement for that length of time.

When she'd heard that, she'd wanted a chance to see him alone, to determine for herself whether or not he was faking.

He hadn't been faking. She would stake her life on it. She stood outside the room, leaning against the wall, then made the trek down the hospital corridor while she thought about Ryan Murphy. The lost, lonely look in his eyes hadn't been calculating. Rather, confused. Bewildered. Emotions she didn't think could be feigned.

Those eyes. She had wondered what color they were. She had not been prepared for the indigo color, a dark blue shade she had never seen before. Nor had she expected to see the depths in them.

And they seemed vulnerable. He had been careful about what he said, even though she recognized the need in his eyes for knowledge, for information. She felt his isolation, his loneliness, and something inside her responded to it. She knew about isolation and loneliness.

She'd hoped for something else altogether. She had hoped that she would see the bad cop. The convict who'd betrayed everything he'd sworn to protect. Dan had thought so, too, and she knew that was why he'd eventually agreed to the visit. He'd approved it on the assumption that it would end her feeling of obligation.

She felt it stronger than ever.

He's a loner. Not the kind of man you would choose to have a beer with. Dan had depended on his recollection of the man to turn her off. Instead of arrogance, she found vulnerability. And because of her, he was to be sent back to what amounted to solitary confinement.

She made her way down the hall to the desk. "Dr. Dailey?"

The nurse at the desk looked at a schedule. "He's probably in his office."

"Do you have a phone number?"

After a moment, she had it in hand and found a telephone. A woman answered and she asked to speak to Dr. Dailey. "It's about Ryan Murphy."

After several moments, he came on the phone. His voice was cautious. "Mrs. Farrell?"

"I would like to talk to you about...Mr. Murphy."

"Is there a problem?"

"The district attorney says prison authorities believe he's faking the amnesia. They want to send him to Reidsville."

There was a long silence at the other end of the phone. "Are you sure you want to become involved?"

She wasn't. "No," she said truthfully. "But if he's really ill because of what he did for me, I...have to help."

"I'm sorry. I can't discuss him unless you obtain a release from him."

"Can you talk hypothetically about amnesia?"

He hesitated again. "All right," he said finally. "I'm in the building next to the hospital. Can you come over now?"

She looked at her watch. Three more hours before Nick returned home. "Yes."

She scolded herself every step she took. She should be spending her time at the law firm, getting up to speed on Mark's brief. She should be baking cookies for Nick. She should be doing anything but hanging around the hospital, worrying about a convicted murderer. But she couldn't let go.

The neurologist opened the door for her after she was announced by the receptionist. He ushered her to a seat, then sat down. His fingers tapped on a brown file folder. "The floor nurse said you spoke to him. Did he seem to remember anything?"

She realized why he'd consented to the meeting. He wanted information from her as badly as she wanted it from him. "No," she said. Remembering his rules, she approached the subject tentatively. "Could someone fake amnesia?"

"Realistically?" he asked. "Probably, but not for long."

"You couldn't know for sure?"

"We know very little about amnesia. There is no way to tell whether parts of the brain have been damaged, or how much. I've never seen a case of prolonged amnesia before, but I've been consulting with some physicians who have. We do know that there are two kinds. Neurological amnesia—injury to the brain—and psychological amnesia in which the mind blocks out memories too painful to tolerate. Sometimes in the former the recent past is erased and the patient might remember his childhood or learned, repetitive skills. The patient might or might not regain memories that he lost. In psychological amnesia, the chances are his memory will return after treatment.''

She searched again for the right words. ''And someone with serious injuries such as those incurred in an explosion?''

''I would say it was probably neurological, but I wouldn't preclude the possibility that psychological amnesia is somehow involved.''

''And someone with neurological amnesia might never get his memory back?''

''Not only that, but the complete personality might be changed. I've read case studies where a formerly mild-mannered subject became violent, and vice versa.''

''In other words, the patient might become an entirely different person?''

He nodded.

''If he's not faking it?''

The doctor nodded.

She mulled over the implication of his words. ''If someone, say a person guilty of a crime, did suffer neurological amnesia, and his personality—his character—*has* changed, then that man would be paying for a crime another man committed.''

He smiled at her as if she were a particularly bright student. ''That's a lot of ifs, but the thought has occurred to me. Interesting scenario.''

''Not for the person involved.''

The doctor's smile faded. ''No. I would think it would be pure hell.''

''There's no way to know for sure?''

He shook his head. ''I wish there were. All I have is instinct. Professional experience. But even that wouldn't be worth a lot if the person has changed in fundamental ways. If I didn't know this person before, I couldn't testify as to changes in his personality. Nor could I say absolutely on a witness stand that I was sure he did have amnesia.''

Julie's mind was already racing ahead, considering the legal implications. She had been attracted to law because she relished the mental gymnastics involved in its practice. She could take almost any case and argue the merits of either side, finding legal precedents to support her position. That ability made her valuable to the law firm that now employed her. It had not been quite as helpful when she was a prosecutor where she'd had to thrust aside her doubts.

She didn't have doubts about Murphy's guilt. He had pleaded guilty.

But what if he was a different man today than he had been three weeks ago? What would be the legal ramifications?

Julie listened intently as the physician recommended several books on amnesia.

"Will he be here much longer?" she finally asked.

He nodded. "He still has terrible headaches and his lungs were badly bruised. We need to keep an eye on him a bit longer until I satisfy myself that we have done all we can to ascertain the extent of the injury to his brain. I don't know how long I can keep him out of the prison ward, though."

"Thank you," she said.

"Will you be back?"

"I don't know," she said.

"He's an interesting man," the doctor said slowly. "He's reading everything. He's full of questions. Although memory might be lost, his mental capacity apparently was not affected."

"How could that be?"

"Are we speaking hypothetically again?"

She nodded.

"The injury would be to the hippocampal system. Damage in that area can cause impairment of long-term memory. Someone with that kind of injury can read without remembering how he learned to read. He can add and subtract without knowing why or how he can perform these skills. His ability to think hasn't been impaired. It's as if the hard drive of a computer has been wiped out. The computer still works, still has all its capacities, but it needs new information to drive it."

She tried to imagine how it might feel if her own mind was emptied of everything that had made her who she was today. Wonderful, warm experiences: the birth of her son, his first step, graduation from college, the pride of her first job. Even the terrible memories: the death of her mother, her husband's death and its aftermath. She couldn't imagine stumbling alone in a maze of emptiness. She felt her heart constrict, her breath catch in her throat at the very thought.

She tried to jerk her mind from its imaginings. "He killed his partner," she said flatly, trying to convince herself that she should follow Dan's advice and forget about Ryan Murphy.

Dr. Dailey shook his head. "That's what they say."

"You don't believe it? He confessed."

"I know." He sighed, obviously prohibited by ethics from saying more, but she heard doubt in his voice. She wondered why.

She stood. "I have to go. My son will be home shortly."

He stood, also. "If you want to see him again, just let me know. I'll try to arrange it."

"Thank you for your time."

He walked her to the door. "Any time, Mrs. Farrell. It's important that he feels he has someone in his corner since there is no family."

"I don't know about that. He just ordered me from his room."

"Still, I think he needs someone like you."

She thanked him again, then left, his words thrumming in her head. She had never questioned Murphy's guilt, not after talking to Dan, but now her mind weighed the conversation with the district attorney. There had been real betrayal in Dan's voice.

Ryan Murphy. Was he more of a mystery than she'd thought?

Chapter 3

Julie sipped her coffee as she studied the computer monitor. She had accessed the archives of the metropolitan newspaper, in particular articles about Ryan Murphy and the sensational case which had rocked the Atlanta Police Department.

The ten-year-old dateline was December 27th. She remembered that Christmas. She had been in California finishing law school. Her mother had died three months earlier, and her one sister lived in Rome, Georgia, too far to travel. She remembered the loneliness.

It was the worst Christmas she had ever spent. She knew it had been even worse for Ryan Murphy. She read the original story once, then printed it out and read it again.

Decorated Cop Charged In Partner's Death

Detective Ryan Murphy, a highly decorated police officer, was charged today in the murder of his partner, Detective Michael Cates.

Murphy, 31, was found standing over his partner's body at 10:00 p.m. on December 24 at 223 Simpson Street. Sources say the bullet which killed Cates came from Murphy's department-issued gun. Traces of cocaine were found in the trunk of Murphy's car.

A police spokesman said Murphy denied any knowledge of the

drugs and claimed that he fired at Cates in self-defense.
Murphy is married and has a five-year-old daughter.

The story continued with more details about both men. Cates had
been with the department fifteen years and left behind a wife and two
children. Murphy, an all-star baseball player at the University of Georgia, was a decorated officer and sharpshooter who'd been shot once in
the line of duty. He had been responsible for cracking several large
narcotic rings before being teamed with Cates several months before
the shooting. Police officials expressed amazement that someone with
his fine record had been involved with drugs.

Several other stories followed, mostly city politicians decrying corruption in the police department and a major police announcement
concerning a drive to root out police corruption.

Then a final story:

Cop Pleads Guilty

Former Atlanta Police Detective Ryan Murphy pleaded guilty
Thursday in Fulton County Superior Court to second-degree murder in the wrongful death of his partner, Michael Cates.

Murphy admitted his guilt as part of a plea agreement made
with the district attorney's office.

Superior Court Judge Alvin Richards sentenced Murphy to life
imprisonment on the recommendation of District Attorney Dan
Watters. Under Georgia law, Murphy could be paroled in seven
years.

Julie read the story over and over again. Dan had said Murphy had
been an extremely competent officer; he most certainly would have
been more than aware that the evidence against him was insufficient.
Even Dan had confided he had doubts.

Until Murphy pled guilty.

Why?

Because he was filled with guilt? In her personal experience with
criminals, few, particularly those who dealt drugs and committed cold-
blooded murders, had much in the way of a conscience.

She heard a knock on the door. She saved the file, then turned off
the computer and went to the door. Emily stood there with Nick in
hand. Her daughter, Abby, attended the same preschool, and Julie and
Emily often exchanged driving duties.

"Coffee?" Julie offered.

Emily shook her head. "Got to get home. We have company coming tonight." Her gaze went to Julie's face. "Everything all right?"

Julie nodded. "I'm just tired. Thank you for taking care of Nick."

"Any time, and don't worry, I'll be asking you to reciprocate with Abby."

Julie closed the door, then walked to the sofa and swallowed Nick in her arms. He allowed a big hug, then cuddled next to her.

"Missed you," she said. "Did you have a good day?"

"Learned a song," he proclaimed proudly.

"You did?"

"'Old MacDonald hath a farm,'" he sung merrily. "'E-i-e-i-o.'"

She grinned at him. Her heart flooded with love and gratitude, and she clasped him tightly. How close she had come to losing him. How very close they had come to losing each other.

She closed her eyes with the joy of holding him, an elation that faded when in her mind's eye she saw the dark blue eyes of Ryan Murphy and recalled the questions in their wounded depths.

His hand touched the telephone. Once, twice. Each time he snatched it away. He had no right to intrude in her life.

But the compulsion to learn more about himself grew stronger and stronger, like some great wave engulfing him. He knew what they said. He knew he was a convict. He knew he was going back to prison. What he didn't understand was why. Why had he killed someone?

Doctors, young and old, tramped in and out of the room, each asking the same questions, each looking at him as if he were some strange animal to be studied. He came to detest them, especially one who called himself Dr. Peyton Edwards and who kept giving him childish tests: fitting square and round pieces of wood into holes in the board and asking him what blobs of ink on cardboard meant. To him, they were simply blobs of ink, nothing more, and he had no intention of playing stupid games. Not when they refused to answer his own questions.

Only Dr. Dailey seemed to understand his torment and would sit and talk with him as if he were a person and not something under a microscope. But Dailey wouldn't talk to him about the murder ten years ago. He said he didn't know anything about it.

Ryan had to know. His mind had been primed by the television shows—news whenever he could find it—he watched nearly twenty hours a day. He would put the pill they gave him in his mouth, then spit it out and turn the television back on. He had an insatiable need to learn, to understand, to regain years he had lost.

He still remembered nothing of his life before the accident, but he discovered he still retained skills. He'd counted the money the doctor had pulled from his pocket and had a knack for math and remembering numbers. He'd found he could read and understand even complicated material, including a medical textbook Dr. Dailey had brought in. He remembered phrases and words, but he remembered nothing of the past. He didn't know whether he had a family, or where he was born or the names of friends.

He touched the phone again. *If there is anything I can do for you, please let me know.*

He hadn't kept the card Julie Farrell had pressed into his hand, but he *had* looked at the number, and he remembered it. He needed to call before they took the phone away. He knew that was coming. Just as he knew there was a fight going on as to how long he should stay here.

This time, he dialed.

It was late, and Julie took one last look at Nick. Prissy, their calico cat, had wrapped herself inside his arm, and the two of them looked content with the world. Earlier, she had read him a story, then stretched out next to him. She wanted him close to her, wanted to satisfy herself he was there. She didn't want to go to her own room and go to bed. Too many terrifying nightmares. Fire was in each one of them, its flames reaching out toward Nick, toward her.

But she knew she couldn't live in fear. She finally went to her own bed and read until her eyes couldn't focus any longer, then turned out the light. She started to doze off when the phone rang, startling her to wakefulness.

She looked at the clock. One in the morning. That usually meant trouble. She picked up the receiver.

"Mrs...Farrell."

She recognized Murphy's voice immediately. It was deep, rumbling. Slow, as if he measured every word. Although she had not seen him since he had ordered her from his room, his face, and voice, had been a constant in her mind.

"Yes, Mr. Murphy?"

A long pause followed.

"Mr. Murphy?"

"I didn't know...who else to ask. You gave me a card."

She could feel his hesitancy, his diffidence. She wondered whether he had any idea of the time. *He* certainly didn't sound sleepy. "What can I do for you?"

Another long pause. She could almost taste his reluctance and so she knew how important this was to him. She swallowed hard, suddenly wanting desperately to do something for the man who had saved her son.

"Information," he said after a moment.

"Information?"

"About what happened...ten years ago."

She juggled the telephone in her hands, remembering the articles. Why would he want to know? Wouldn't it be better...? But then she knew it wouldn't. She knew she would want to know if she were in his position. She would want to know everything, no matter how much it hurt.

Or would she? Would she really want to relive that day she found her husband in the den, his blood soaking the carpet? Would she want to remember the following days when the devastating realities of her marriage unfolded one by one? Would she rather they disappear in a gray haze, never to surface again?

But *she* wasn't going to prison for something she didn't remember. Wouldn't she want to know why?

All those thoughts rampaged through her mind.

"All right," she finally said. "I'll have to get permission from the district attorney to visit again—"

"The one who convicted me?"

"You appear to have convicted yourself," she said.

He was silent, then added, "A family...do I have any family?"

"A daughter, I think."

Another silence. Then, "Thank you, Mrs. Farrell."

She heard the click on his end, then slowly, she settled the phone in the cradle.

Julie called Dan the next day, asking that the district attorney's office pave the way for another visit with Ryan Murphy. She prepared herself for the lecture that came.

"Julie," he said with a sigh that she knew was a mixture of resignation, concern and exasperation.

"I want to see him again," she said, knowing she didn't have to identify the him. "The doctor said it was all right."

"Why?"

"Because he's all alone, and I owe him."

"You don't owe him a damn thing."

"Dan, please."

There were a lot of silences on the phone these days. This was a particularly long one.

"I'll think about it."

"Thank you." She paused. "Does Jerry Kidder still work for your office?"

"He started his own P.I. firm," Dan said. "He's listed in the telephone book."

"Thank you."

"Julie," he said, "I know how tenacious you become when you've fastened your teeth on something, but this is a dead end."

"Murphy's new parole hearing must be coming up soon," she said.

"As a matter of fact, it is, and this office has already gone on record opposing it."

"Dan, the doctor in charge of Murphy's case says amnesia sometimes changes the complete personality of the affected person. All his memories are gone. He starts with a clean slate. He wouldn't be the same man—"

"No, Julie," he said. "I've also talked with his doctor and with some others. There's no way to be sure he really does have amnesia, and I'm not going to risk letting a killer back on the street. And if you're wise, you will drop this. Now. Remember the last time you thought you were so damn sure of something."

That was a low blow. Dan Watters knew exactly where to aim when he wanted something. It was one of the unattractive things about him, but then most prosecutors developed that particular skill. She'd once honed it to a fine art. That was before she discovered that life was not all black and white but an assortment of grays.

"I'll be cautious," she said. "You know that."

"I used to know that."

"Dan, I just need to do something to pay him back. Even if it is just showing him a friendly face."

She could hear his sigh over the phone.

"The prison authorities have control over his visitors, but I'll talk to them. Again. I'll call you when it's arranged. But this is the last time."

But it wouldn't be. Not if what she had in mind worked.

"Thank you."

"I hope I won't regret it."

She hoped he wouldn't, either. She hung up before she uttered her doubts and stared at the wall of her study. Dan, who was a good twenty years-plus older than she, had been her mentor and substitute father. He and his wife, Sandy, had often invited her over for supper and holidays. But after she had left her job, she'd wanted no reminders of those last two years in his office, nor of the ugly publicity she'd brought down on his head. She'd also been fully occupied with Nick, trying desperately to be two parents to him, as well as the provider. She had no time for social activities, not even supper with an old friend.

Two more phone calls. One to Caldwell, Michaels, Evans and Cagle to tell them she was ready to return to work. She immediately was asked to review the Crispen appeal that Mark Haley had prepared in her absence.

Her second call was to Jerry Kidder. He answered his own phone. "Julie?" he said with surprise. And warmth. He had asked her out to dinner several times before she'd married, and he'd never quite concealed his interest in her. Still, he'd always been highly professional.

"I want to hire you," she said. "It's not much of a job, just gathering some information."

"I'm at your disposal," he said. "I'll even give you my friends' rate."

She suspected that the friends' rate would be little or nothing. "No," she insisted. "The regular rate or I'll find someone else."

"You drive a hard bargain," he said, and she could almost see the grin on his face. "Go ahead."

"Do you remember anything about the case involving Ryan Murphy ten years ago?"

"The guy who saved your life? I read about it. Also read he's claiming amnesia."

"His doctor's convinced he really does have it. He doesn't remember anything about his past."

"You aren't getting mixed up with the guy, are you?" The warmth in his voice faded into concern.

Not him, too.

"No, but I do want to help him. He asked for some information about his past, and I feel that's little enough to do after he almost died saving my son." She heard the exasperation in her voice and regretted it.

"What kind of information do you want?"

"Where he was born. Family members who are living. I understand he has an ex-wife and daughter. I want addresses. I want to know about his years on the police force."

"Piece of cake," he said. "You could do that."

"But I don't have time, and you can talk to people I can't. Officers he used to work with. I want to know what they thought of him." She hesitated. "Had you ever met him?"

"Yep. Arrogant bastard. I didn't much care for him, but I never pegged him for being dirty, either."

"Get some other opinions," she said.

"Yes, ma'am," he replied. "You sound like the old Julie Farrell."

She ignored that comment. "As quickly as possible."

"Yes, ma'am," he said again.

"And send me the bill."

"Yes, *ma'am.*"

He hung up, and she was grateful he hadn't asked her whether she was sure or mentioned the possibility she had gone wacko.

Trying to curb her impatience while waiting for Dan's call about a visit, she turned on her computer and accessed the law firm's files for the Crispen appeal and the briefs supporting it. And tried to concentrate. The firm had been generous about giving her medical leave. Now she felt a customary guilt that she was not acting the responsible associate. Guilt had always been a huge part of her makeup. She'd always wanted to be perfect. the perfect daughter, the perfect student, the perfect lawyer, the perfect wife. When she felt herself falling short, she would work even harder at perfection, knowing she could never quite achieve it. The consequence was never feeling adequate.

The brief could be improved. She tried to concentrate. But she couldn't reach beyond dark bewildered eyes, the legal questions tumbling around in her mind and Dan's comments about Murphy's parole hearing. Georgia law allowed parole after serving seven years of a life sentence. Murphy had already served ten, which meant he'd already been turned down at least once. That would not be unusual, especially with this type of crime. Denial of early parole was routine in murder cases, especially when the prosecutor's office opposed it.

Could she talk Dan into withdrawing his opposition?

Unlikely. She needed more information than that offered by the newspapers. She needed to know everything she could about Ryan Murphy and his past. She needed to talk to all the doctors who had seen him.

Whoa, girl, she told herself, but her mind was already racing ahead. She stopped any pretense of reading the Crispen brief and started making notes on what she knew about Ryan Murphy. What she needed to know. Three hours later, Dan called and said a visit had been arranged.

Ryan Murphy looked at the dollar bill dropped in his hand, then back up to the woman standing beside his bed. Her dark hair was pulled back into a twist, emphasizing those wide gray eyes he remembered. They were blazing with a passion that seemed directed at him.

"That's a loan," she said.

He looked at it.

"Now give it back," she said.

He hesitated, not sure what she wanted.

"You don't have an attorney of record," she said. "I checked with the prison authorities. When you give me that dollar, I will become your lawyer."

He still wasn't sure what she was saying. "Why would you want to do that?"

"You asked me to get some information?"

He nodded.

"If I'm your attorney, you can tell me anything and I don't have to reveal it. I can find what information you need and bring it to you without sharing it with anyone. I can see you more often. Now I have to ask permission from what seems a dozen people, and some don't want to give it."

"All I have to do is give you a dollar?" he said suspiciously. He had regretted calling her almost as soon as he had hung up last night. He desperately wanted information, but something inside had balked at asking for help, of involving someone in his problems. One of his guards had sneered after she'd left the first time. "Some women can't stay away from cons." Even he grasped the fact that being involved— in any way—with him would bring trouble.

"That's all," she said.

"Why?"

"Because you saved my son, and he's the most precious thing in my life."

"Then forget it," he said rudely. "I don't even remember it. I'm sorry I called you last night."

She ignored his apology and dropped a package in his lap. "These are articles about your case. I have someone else searching for any family you might have."

He slowly opened the manila envelope, staring at the pile of papers in his lap. Information. He stared at an old picture of himself. He had seen himself in the mirror when a guard allowed him in the bathroom. There was gray in his hair now, and lines around his eyes. Had he ever been as young as the man in the photo? Had he ever looked that confident? He swallowed hard and put both hands over the packet. He wanted to read alone.

"Thank you," he said gratefully, then suddenly was humiliated to realize his eyes had moistened, and he turned away. His life was in those papers. He felt the woman's compassion as he'd fingered through them, and he knew a yearning so deep he could barely contain it. Some part of her had reached out and touched a place he had tried to isolate this past week. He'd learned he couldn't feel, or want, or even dream, because he was worthless, nothing. He'd been caged like an animal for the past ten years and would return to a cage. Even Dr. Dailey mixed wariness with professional concern.

"The dollar," she said, holding out her hand.

He slowly picked it up from where it lay and handed it to her. Their fingers touched and something like electricity ran through him, a hot intense shock that made every nerve tingle. But the connection was even stronger than physical. Her touch was warmth to his chill. She didn't pull her hand away, but he felt it tremble.

Almost involuntarily, his fingers caressed hers in his need to experience human contact, a moment of intimacy with someone who did not look upon him as a monster. He didn't look at her eyes. He couldn't bear seeing pity there. But finally he looked up, and he didn't see pity at all. He saw understanding, and it filled him with a hope he hadn't allowed himself before.

He reluctantly withdrew his hand, "I'm sorry," he said.

She just looked at him for a moment, then moved away. "I'll file papers with the court. I hope to have some more information soon."

She reached the door, then turned again and met his eyes directly before pushing it open and disappearing through it.

Chapter 4

Julie's hand burned from his touch. She almost dropped the dollar bill she was clutching once she'd reached the hallway.

What in the blazes was she doing?

For a moment inside, she'd frozen. No, that wasn't right. There was too much heat and electricity to freeze. She'd been stunned by that one moment when he'd touched her.

Even Douglas had never affected her that way. She'd been dazzled by her late husband, swept up by his charm. She'd never had a serious relationship before; she'd been too intent on her studies and career, and she'd never been pretty enough to capture the attention of the kind of man she thought she'd wanted: someone ambitious and as passionate about the world as she.

Douglas had been labeled one of the city's most eligible bachelors. He was wealthy, charming and at the peak of his career as one of the city's most successful defense attorneys. They'd met at a bar association gala, and he pursued her as no other man in her life had. She'd believed herself in love with him, and he with her. But after a whirlwind courtship and marriage, she slowly began to realize it hadn't been love at all, that he'd grabbed for some anchor in a deteriorating life while she'd been caught up by the idea of love. She'd never really known him, but she tried to make the marriage work, tried to understand his mood swings, his disappearances, his abject apologies afterward. She'd continued with the district attorney's office, although he constantly asked her to resign and stay home "as a good wife should."

She'd worried about his extravagances, especially when she received overdue bills on the large house he'd insisted on buying, the Porsche sports car he gave her as a gift, the speedboat they never used. He made very good money, but he spent more than he earned. His disappearances grew longer, his explanations shorter or nonexistent. But by then she was pregnant; leaving the marriage was unthinkable. His smile seldom faltered, but his natural exuberance became brittle, his eyes sometimes desperate.

His legal brilliance never faded, but she felt as though she was living with a mannequin. He never really talked to her, always turning a serious conversation into a joke, or changing the subject to someone else's problems.

And then she came home one day to find him in his office, dead of an apparent self-inflicted gunshot wound to the head. The next day she received a visit from two D.E.A. agents who said they had been investigating her husband for money laundering. Knowledge of that investigation apparently led to the suicide. Public exposure for Douglas would have been worse than prison.

Familiar sadness washed through her as she thought of Douglas Farrell and the waste of all that brilliance. She'd learned later that he had seen a psychiatrist, that he was manic depressive, and she'd known a terrible guilt that she had never recognized the symptoms. She'd also had to pick up the pieces. She sold the house she'd never liked, exchanged the sports car for a used midsize vehicle and still ended up in debt.

The publicity had hounded her for weeks. It was a good story: a well-known defense attorney, involved in drug trafficking, who was married to an assistant district attorney. When it was discovered two years later that she'd convicted an innocent man on the perjured testimony of a police officer, the publicity started again, and she'd resigned. She'd wanted peace, and she'd buried herself in the intellectual exercise of legal argument.

So what was she doing now? Taking on the case of a former police officer, a man convicted of murder? A man who had saved her life. The press would have a real heyday.

That was bad enough. But now, God help her, she was attracted to him as well.

How could she be so stupid? What was wrong with her?

She almost marched back in the room and handed him back the dollar. He would look at her with those dark blue hooded eyes and say nothing, and she would never forgive herself for not doing what she felt was right, regardless of the cost.

The dollar bill fluttered to the floor.

The call came sooner than she expected. It came, in fact, that night, five hours after she informed prison authorities she would be representing Ryan Murphy at his parole hearing. Caldwell's sources were very good. She anticipated a call from Dan next.

"Julie," Mr. Caldwell started. "I heard some very disturbing news from Judge Llewellen. He said you were representing..." He stopped as if he could not even mention the name.

"Mr. Murphy," she said helpfully.

"Murphy. Yes. Murphy. I thought you understood *we* do not represent criminal defendants."

That was a matter of opinion. She kept that thought to herself, however. "I'm not representing him for the firm. I'll be glad to make that clear."

"We've been very pleased with your work, Mrs. Farrell," he said, suddenly turning formal. "But as I said earlier, our firm cannot be associated with any scandal."

"I don't intend it to be," she replied, trying to swallow the rock suddenly crowding her throat. "I will only represent him at his parole hearing. He *did* save my son's life. And mine."

She was getting tired of saying that. But no one seemed to understand that she valued both highly.

"You won't reconsider?"

"No," she said, realizing that she had already considered losing her job and had resigned herself to it. She had some savings. She had Dan's offer, although he might jerk it back now. She could always open her own office, though she knew the financial instability that meant.

"How is the brief coming?" he asked unexpectedly.

"I'm making a few additions. I'll send it to you tomorrow."

"Good," he said, then paused for a second before continuing. "We don't want to lose you. Can you handle this discreetly?"

"I'll try. I don't like publicity any more than you."

"We'll go on as usual then. For the time being. But if this...Murphy matter becomes disruptive, then we will have to review your employment with us."

"I understand. And thank you."

"Goodbye." The phone clicked as he hung up.

She went into Nick's room. He'd gone to bed thirty minutes earlier and was already deep in sleep. She bent down and pulled the quilt around him, then leaned over and kissed him. There could be no sweeter sight, she thought, than a sleeping child, no feeling as tender as the one she hugged to herself while she watched him. She loved Nick with all her heart and soul. She touched his cheek for a second, pushed back an unruly lock of fine taffy-colored hair. She wanted him this way forever, safe and protected and happy.

Was she robbing him of some of that protection by helping the man who saved his life? Or was she hopefully teaching him a lesson of compassion and honor and loyalty? She hoped the latter.

The soft ringing of the phone in the other room pierced her mood. She would bet almost anything that it was Dan. She sighed, then went to pay the piper.

Ryan read the newspaper headline with a sinking heart:

Attorney Saved By Convict
To Represent Him At Hearing

Local attorney Julie Farrell, who along with her four-year-old son, was rescued from a burning car four weeks ago by Ryan Murphy, former police officer convicted of killing his partner ten years ago, has been listed as attorney of record for Murphy's latest bid for parole.

Mrs. Farrell is a former assistant district attorney. She resigned three years ago after a man she prosecuted was found to be innocent. Her husband, prominent attorney Douglas Farrell, committed suicide five years ago during an investigation linking him to a money laundering conspiracy.

Ryan read on, but he felt sick inside. He'd known little about Julie Farrell, though he'd sensed a sadness about her. Now he knew why. And he felt sick that because of him her life had become public fodder. He folded the paper and allowed it to fall on the floor. Dammit.

He was still fuming when Dr. Dailey entered his room and gave him more bad news. "I'm being pressed to release you," the man said. "The prison authorities want you."

Ryan was silent. He had been expecting the news for several days. He'd been conscious now for two weeks and could have been released a week earlier, according to the doctor treating his physical injuries. Only Dailey's fascination with his amnesia had kept him here this long.

"I'm fighting to keep you a few more days, but I think you should be prepared to leave by the end of the week.'' He paused. ''They're sending you to Reidsville.''

Ryan's gut tightened. He had nearly gone crazy being chained to the bed, and the thought of being caged behind bars was devastating. But he apparently had survived ten years of it and could do it again. He tried to shrug indifferently. ''Thanks for everything you've done.''

''I'll be sending along all your medical records and some recommendations. Dr. Edwards is doing the same. You'll be all right.'' It was as if he were reassuring himself rather than Ryan.

The end of the week. It was Wednesday now. So he had two days at most. Would Mrs. Farrell come by?

''You still don't remember anything? Anything at all?'' the doctor said hopefully. He'd predicted that Ryan would start remembering bits and pieces.

''No,'' he replied, seeing the doctor's disappointment. Minutes later, Dr. Dailey left, leaving him alone again.

He didn't want to think about losing the one thing that gave him hope: Julie Farrell's visits. He'd seen her only once, and briefly, after the time their hands had touched in an explosion of heat. She had been very careful not to allow contact that next time. She stayed only long enough for him to sign a legal paper, which apparently concluded the process of making her his attorney.

He hadn't had to ask how to spell his name. He'd just been able to write it, though neither writing it or seeing it created any sense of familiarity. He wrote it again when she had left, staring at it, willing a piece of memory back. Who was he? What was he? What kind of man had he been?

What kind of man was he now?

Only Julie Farrell seemed willing to help him find those answers, answers that might confirm his worst fears that he was a cold-blooded murderer and drug dealer. She should run like hell. He really didn't understand why she hadn't. He couldn't even understand why she felt she owed him anything when he couldn't remember a damn thing.

But then, he didn't understand much of anything. He kept grasping for something. At times he felt near to clasping a piece of information, a bit of himself, but then he came up empty yet again, the feeling of frustration overwhelming him. And that damn loneliness that left him gasping for breath.

He had read the clippings about himself; he knew he had fathered a child. He wondered bitterly what she thought of him. Did she know her father was a convicted killer? Had she ever come to see him?

Why couldn't he even remember his own child?

None of the clippings gave him much more information than he'd already learned from his guards and doctors about his crime. But reading that he had admitted in open court to killing his own partner made it somehow more real. Still, he didn't feel capable of it.

Or had he become a completely different person? Dr. Dailey said it was a possibility. But even he had sounded none too sure.

The questions in his head wouldn't go away. They pounded at him day and night.

He had to have answers or he would truly go crazy.

Most of all, he felt he had to have some before he was returned to prison.

He was reading, his mind preoccupied with hopes that Julie Farrell would visit, when he heard a knock before the door opened. Julie?

But instead, a man in a suit appeared. Dressed in slacks, coat and a tie loosened at the throat, he strode over to the bed and thrust out his hand.

"Jack Banyon," he said, light blue eyes studying him.

Ryan wasn't sure what to do with that hand. No one else had offered a hand to him before. Finally, he stuck out his own, and his visitor's hand tightened around his.

"You don't recognize me," the man said.

Ryan shook his head.

"I'm Jack Banyon, lieutenant with the police department. I used to work with you. I was a friend. I never did believe that garbage about drugs." His eyes seemed to watch Ryan carefully. By now he was used to scrutiny. Everyone looked at him as if he were hiding something. He wished to God he was.

"I seem to have pleaded guilty," Ryan said.

"You don't remember anything? You really don't?"

"No," Ryan said flatly.

"They wouldn't let me in to see you before now," Banyon said awkwardly. "But I just wanted to tell you not everyone believed you went dirty."

"Why?"

"Just out of character, buddy," Banyon said.

Ryan looked at him just as carefully as Banyon had studied him. He was a big man, but Ryan didn't think any of the bulk was fat. His movements were curiously graceful despite his size. His blue eyes were shrewd, and little real warmth accompanied the friendly words. And yet, in the four weeks he had been in the hospital, this man was the only one from his past to visit him.

He was grateful. Grateful but wary.

"Did you know my wife?" he queried.

"Mary Elizabeth? Hell, yes." Banyon's eyes narrowed. "Do you remember her? I was told..."

Ryan shook his head. It was as if the question came out of thin air. And he knew just as suddenly the reason for it. A friend would know his wife. He didn't know, though, why he had asked it of this particular person.

Banyon pulled something out of his pocket. "Brought this for you. Remembered you used to like them on stakeout."

Ryan took the package. It was filled with wrapped candies.

"Butterscotch. Nothing but butterscotch," Banyon reassured him.

Ryan stared at the small wrapped candies. Butterscotch. It meant nothing to him. Even a flavor of candy meant nothing, recalled no warm memory. Not even a cold one. "Thank you," he said.

"Thank you?" Banyon mocked. "That must be the first." He studied Ryan with hooded eyes. "I don't think I ever came across anybody who had a real case of amnesia before. Heard of temporary amnesia, but the doc said you might never get your memory back."

The reminder was like a knife in the gut. God knew he had heard the diagnosis before. Knew it as well, or as little, as his own name. Yet he hadn't realized how much he'd hoped, expected, that something would come back, some flash of familiarity.

He said nothing.

Banyon hesitated, then said, "Heard your attorney's gonna try for parole. Don't count on it. The district attorney's fighting your parole. So are the police. Ain't gonna happen, buddy, no matter what that woman lawyer tries." He coughed. "Well," he said awkwardly, "I'd better go." He disappeared out the door before Ryan could say anything. He puzzled over the conversation. A friend? A warning?

Julie hesitated outside Murphy's room. As his attorney, she could now see him anytime she wanted.

Dan had been furious when he'd learned that she was now Murphy's attorney of record. "You should have told me what you planned to do," he'd said.

"Then you wouldn't have let me see him."

"You're damn right." It was only the second time she'd ever heard him swear. The first time was when she'd called him after her husband's death. She knew it indicated the depth of his disapproval. "If you think that's going to change my position on his parole—"

"I think no such thing. I do hope you will listen, however."

"We've made our decision," he said, his voice hardening.

"Dan, there was something odd about his plea. You didn't have the evidence to convict him. Even that trace of cocaine could have been the residue from an old bust."

"He confessed, and that's enough for me," Dan said.

"Will you at least talk to me about it?"

"You won't change my mind," he warned her.

At least he hadn't said no. And she hoped Jerry would provide her with enough ammunition to indeed change his mind.

But she could say nothing of that to Murphy. She wouldn't get his hopes up. She had already been told he would be removed tomorrow to Reidsville. That meant a six-hour round trip drive to see him. And she would have to see him often to prepare for the hearing scheduled in late November, just four weeks away.

By then she would have more information. But now she had a little. Just a little.

The officer outside his room had risen from the seat he usually occupied. She had brought him some coffee and a doughnut, just as she had two days earlier. Sugar, she'd discovered long ago, could be a very effective tool. She was now greeted with a smile.

"Mrs. Farrell," he acknowledged. "He's better. Word is—"

"I know," she said. "He's being moved."

"Can't say I won't be pleased," he said. "This is not the most interesting duty I've ever had."

"Well, I'll miss you," she said, as he preened slightly.

"I'll miss you, too, miss," he said as he opened the door.

The beat of her heart speeded as she entered. Murphy was reading a tattered magazine. She saw it was an old copy of *Time Magazine*.

He looked up, saw the direction of her gaze and, without smiling, explained, "Dr. Dailey brought me some old copies."

"How are you feeling?"

His dark blue eyes searched hers. They seemed darker today, almost as dark as his hair. They were also shrouded. The confusion was gone. As were bewilderment and resignation.

"Well enough to leave, I'm told," he said without any kind of emotion.

Self-protection, she wondered. "They're moving you tomorrow."

A muscle moved in his cheek, but he said nothing.

"I have a private detective digging around in your past," she said without preamble.

The muscle moved again.

"He found your ex-wife and child. She married again and lives in

Macon, about seventy miles from here. Your daughter is fifteen." She didn't tell him that his daughter's last name was no longer his.

He absorbed the news without comment. She wondered what he was thinking. She kept trying to put herself in his place—if he truly had amnesia—and she couldn't. She couldn't imagine what it would be like to be told she had a son she didn't remember.

She forced herself to continue. "There's no record of any other family members," she said. "Your employment records say both your mother and father died before you joined the police department. You've never listed next of kin other than your ex-wife."

"That's fortunate," he said.

"I don't think so," she replied.

"How would you like someone like me hanging around your family tree?"

She smiled at the sudden image of him enmeshed in a tree. "It would make for a much more interesting family," she said.

A glimmer of interest suddenly shone in his eyes. "Is yours not interesting?"

She shook her head. "Not big. There's only Nick, myself and my sister."

"Your sister?"

"She lives in Rome, Georgia. It's one reason I moved to Atlanta." She didn't add that they had seen little of each other the last several years. Susan's husband was a consultant who spent months in Germany. Susan was there with him now.

Murphy was watching her intently. He had propped the pillow behind his back, and his fingers combed his dark hair. The hospital gown looked incongruous on him, the worn cotton at odds with strength it couldn't conceal. His arms were lean but muscled, his chest clearly outlined under the thin cloth. A sheet covered his legs, but she could see the length of them. One of them moved, bending at the knee; the other was held stationary by the chain she knew secured him to the bed. She knew the power of that body. It had been strong enough to pull her from the car and throw her well out of the force of the explosion.

And from the moment she had first visited him, she sensed the vitality in him. As his injuries had healed, she had noted his increased restlessness, the energy that he channeled into learning everything he could. Dr. Dailey had told her that he had an insatiable hunger for knowledge, that he continually asked for reading material, that the guards said he watched television far into the night.

Yet despite his obvious need to learn everything he could, there was a dignified reticence about him, a reserve that affected her deeply. She wondered whether he had the same reserve before the accident, before prison. What kind of man had he been then?

She had learned a little more about him. He had been one of the department's marksmen. He was also skilled in the martial arts. His file was filled with contradictions. He had one of the highest arrest and conviction records of any detective, but his record also included negatives: "Doesn't work well with other detectives; disrespectful to superior officers," etc. These were apparently overlooked because of his effectiveness, but they had also stalled any promotions.

Jerry was now interviewing officers who had worked with Murphy. Julie herself intended to talk to his ex-wife. She felt that a woman would be more effective in gaining her trust.

"You played baseball in college," she said as if she were reading a résumé. She had memorized the psychological and physical evaluations of Murphy that Jerry Kidder had found. "You had a scholarship. You were a pitcher, but you broke your wrist sliding into base. Your pitching was never the same and you lost the scholarship. You dropped out of college after your junior year. You enrolled in the police academy, where you graduated at the top of your class.

"Your arrest records were excellent. Your people skills seemed somewhat lacking," she said wryly.

He listened intently, but his face showed little reaction.

"You apparently met your wife at college, but didn't marry until a year after you joined the police force."

He looked expectant, his eyes asking for more.

She spread out her hands. "That's it, Mr. Murphy. That's all I have right now. Did anything ring a bell?" *Mr. Murphy.* She refused to think of him as Ryan It was too intimate, too personal. Murphy was a client. Ryan? She was very much afraid he could become something else.

She sensed his disappointment, but he didn't show it. She sensed altogether too much about him. It was as if some invisible bond connected them. That when he had saved her life, he'd also given her a piece of his soul, or he had taken part of hers. What was it they said about someone who saved a life? That then they were responsible for it forever? Or was the responsibility that of the person saved? She didn't know. She just knew a connection existed.

"Someone came by earlier," he said. "A police lieutenant named Jack Banyon. He said he was a friend, that he never believed I was guilty of the charges."

She was intrigued. She took a pad and pen from her bag and wrote down the name. "Did he say why?"

Murphy shook his head.

"He brought some candy. Little butterscotch balls. He said I used to eat them all the time. I tried one. I hated it."

Her gaze suddenly met his. They weren't shuttered now. Or empty. She saw agony there. Raw pain, and she found herself leaning down and grasping his hand, feeling his fingers lock around hers with a need so strong it made her tremble. It was almost as if she were his lifeline in a rushing, storm-tossed sea.

Just as suddenly as his hand had clasped hers, he tried to let it go, and she found herself clinging to it. A strong hand with callused fingers—long and capable and strong. Just as she found him. Despite everything that had happened to him, despite his confusion and bewilderment or even resignation, he radiated an independence and strength that she couldn't help but admire. He wasn't hiding from the truth, or using his current condition to excuse himself from it. Instead, he was seeking it, and devil damn the consequences.

She swallowed hard to bypass the emotions welling in her throat, the need to comfort even though she realized comfort wasn't wanted. The only thing he had asked of her was information.

She wanted to tell him of her suspicions, that something was very wrong with the plea agreement, that it just plain didn't make sense, but she couldn't raise his hopes, just as she couldn't give him hope about his parole hearing. She was going to try her best, but she was very aware that in today's law-and-order climate few convicted murderers were released early.

"I'll see you tomorrow," she said, releasing his hand. Her own burned from his touch, and she wondered whether he felt that same intense warmth whenever they touched. And it wasn't only her hand. It was her entire body. Her blood warmed, and nerve ends tingled. Every part of her was reacting to him in unfamiliar ways.

"No," he said sharply as if he'd suddenly made up his mind about something. "You've done enough," he said. "You've done what I asked you to do, and I had no right even..."

The object in her throat was growing larger, threatening to choke her. No right? He had every right to ask for everything—and anything—she had.

"I'm your attorney," she said.

"Not any more," he said. "I know you needed to claim that to see me, but now...."

"Are you firing me?"

His determined dark blue gaze seemed to penetrate her heart. "I've been made aware of some facts," he said. "Mainly that I have no chance for parole. I don't want you to waste time on a lost cause."

"Who said that?"

He shrugged. "Seems a common opinion. I've been reading the newspapers."

She had, too. The headline this morning had made her heart sink. She worried about its effect on Nick at his school. Would someone mention his father to him?

And her job? A front-page story was not very discreet. Thank God, they didn't mention the law firm.

But as she read the article and realized the implications, she felt her commitment to Ryan grow even stronger. He was so darn alone. And now even in that isolation that only he could know, he was offering her an out.

"No," she said. "I've done too much work."

"I don't want you," he said stubbornly.

"You want to stay in prison?"

He looked at her with those eyes, and she felt herself melt. He was trying so damn hard to save her again. If she'd ever had doubts, she didn't have them now. And she wasn't going to debate with him.

"I'll be here in the morning," she said and left before he could reply.

Chapter 5

Jerry drove Julie the seventy miles to Macon that night to see Mary Elizabeth Saddler, Murphy's ex-wife. Emily was taking care of Nick.

"Talked to some of the guys who were on the police force with him," Jerry reported as he picked her up.

"And..."

"They didn't have much to say about him. He wasn't the best-liked guy on the force. He never drank beer with them, never shared war stories, never exchanged marital woes. Not one could tell me anything about his private life—whether he had hobbies, or friends."

"Money? Did he appear to have more money than he should?"

"Nope. Lived in a small house in a modest neighborhood. He had an old car. His wife had a newer one, according to the motor vehicle records, but nothing fancy. No smoking gun there."

"No boats, no expensive vacation home?"

"The investigators at the time of the murder looked into all that. They couldn't find anything to indicate he lived beyond his income."

"Curiouser and curiouser!" she said.

"He could have money hidden away anywhere."

"Then why wouldn't he have used it for his legal defense?"

He shrugged. "I don't know why people do anything, Julie."

Neither did Julie. After spending six years in the district attorney's office, human behavior never ceased to amaze her. She'd been fooled enough. Often enough, in fact, and close enough that she knew she should harbor more doubts about Murphy. She just didn't.

"Is she expecting us?" he asked.

"At seven. She was reluctant, then finally agreed because her daughter would be at a play rehearsal tonight."

"I don't know what you expect to learn."

Julie didn't, either. Her excuse was that the more she knew about her client, the better. She didn't want any surprises. But she also had an insatiable curiosity about the man. She wanted answers for him, but she also wanted them for herself.

"Tell me everything you learned about her."

"She's married to an insurance salesman. They live well but not luxuriously. She has a son and a daughter from her second marriage."

Julie wondered again about the ex-wife. An insurance salesman after a detective who apparently walked the edge of danger every day of his adult life? Even with amnesia, Murphy seemed to dominate his surroundings. Even in his confusion, he appeared bigger than life.

"She filed for divorce almost immediately after Murphy's conviction and moved to Macon, where she taught school. She remarried the next year."

"Did she teach when Murphy was with the police department?"

He nodded.

"They should have had a good income then between them," she mused.

"One thing...she never visited him when he went to prison. Neither did the daughter."

"His decision, I wonder, or hers?"

"Perhaps you'll find out," he said.

She changed the subject. "Did you get the police reports on the shooting?"

"Yep. It's real interesting. The investigating officers were very cautious. Isn't often one cop is accused of killing another, much less his own partner."

"You would think a detective would cover his tracks a little better, wouldn't you?"

"It doesn't look as if he had any time. There were police there almost immediately."

"I know, but it wouldn't take long to stick a gun in his partner's hand. Where was his partner's gun?"

He shrugged. "It was never found."

"Now that really is strange. If the gun had been recently fired, it would tend to exonerate Murphy."

"I know. There's a lot of very curious things in the report. But when your client confessed, the investigation was dropped."

"Why was he arrested in the first place?"

"The drug residue. An informant called after the shooting, said Murphy was involved in drugs. His car and home were both searched. Nothing in the house, but his trunk had traces of cocaine. That and the fact that neither officer made a call for backup resulted in his arrest."

"What about his partner? Was his home and car searched also?"

Jerry shook his head. "No mention of it. That doesn't mean it wasn't done. But Murphy wasn't a popular officer. His partner was. The discovery of drugs focused the investigation on him."

"Convenient, wasn't it?" Julie observed. "No gun. Drugs in his car. Then a week later a confession."

"It does happen like that sometimes," Jerry said. "If he was guilty, a deal might have looked real good when the alternative was the electric chair."

"Life in prison?" she said doubtfully. "A cop?"

Jerry didn't answer, but looked out over the rolling Georgia hills as the car neared Macon.

They found the Saddler home easily. An unpretentious but well-kept brick ranch, it was located in a nice residential area near Wesleyan College. She looked at her watch. Five minutes to seven.

"Do you want me to go inside with you?" Jerry asked.

"I'd rather talk to her myself. She might open up more to another woman."

He shrugged. "You're paying the bills."

Julie stepped out of the car, walked up the drive and rang the bell. The door opened almost instantly, and she sensed the woman had been waiting for her.

"Mrs. Saddler?" she asked, holding out her hand.

The woman hesitated, then took it. After that brief pause the handshake was strong. Mary Elizabeth Saddler was an attractive woman, but not a beautiful one. Her light brown hair was short and tousled. Her eyes were probably her best feature. They were hazel, the kind that would change color according to the clothes she wore. Now she was wearing a green turtleneck sweater and matching slacks, both a little large and obviously comfortable, and her eyes looked more green than gold.

A frown crinkled the skin around her eyes, and her lips were set in a tight, straight line as though she was forcing herself to do something she didn't want to do. But despite that, Julie saw a kindness in the

face that provided its own brand of attractiveness. She imagined a smile
would make the woman quite pretty.

"Thank you for seeing me."

"I'm not quite sure why you want to," Mary Elizabeth said. "But
I hope it won't take long. My husband has a meeting tonight, and my
daughter a rehearsal at the school. I have to pick her up at nine."

"Your other children?"

"Playing Nintendo downstairs in the playroom. I don't think we'll
be disturbed." A small, unconscious smile finally relaxed her face as
she mentioned her children. A nice woman, Julie thought instantly.
Even a gentle one. Julie tried to pair her with the portrait she was
getting of the early Ryan Murphy: a loner without friends, at least
without any they had been able to find. And the marriage had been in
trouble before the shooting.

Mary Elizabeth led her into a comfortable breakfast nook and offered
her a chair at the table. "Coffee?"

Julie nodded. "Thank you."

She watched carefully as Mary Elizabeth poured two cups of coffee
and brought them to the table, along with a plate of cookies. She'd
obviously brewed the coffee for this occasion.

"What do you want from me?" Mrs. Saddler said after a moment.

"You've heard about...your ex-husband?"

Her lips tightened again. "Yes. The paper here carried some of it.
A friend sent me the clippings from Atlanta."

"A friend? Was this a friend of both you and Mr. Murphy?"

Her hands seemed to tighten around the cup. "No. Ryan didn't have
time for friendships. He worked long hours."

An intriguing defensiveness mixed with the bitterness in her voice.

"You understand I'm the woman he saved in that car accident. He
also saved my son."

"And now you are representing him?"

Julie nodded. "He has a parole hearing coming up."

"The paper said he was badly hurt." Mary Elizabeth couldn't hide
a note of concern, and Julie felt suddenly hopeful. At least this woman
didn't hate her ex-husband.

"He was in a coma for two weeks. He had a head injury, burns, a
broken arm and ribs." She hesitated a moment, then added, "He has
amnesia."

The hazel eyes across from her widened. "Amnesia."

"He doesn't remember anything of his past. Not why he was in
prison, not that he'd been a police officer, not..."

"Not that he'd been a husband and father," the woman completed for her. "Of course, he didn't remember that before, either." The bitterness was back in her voice, deeper than before.

"You never went to see him." It was both a statement and question.

"In prison?"

Julie nodded.

"I tried. Several times. He wouldn't see me. He returned letters. He said he wanted both me and Laura to forget he ever existed." Weary grief filled her eyes. "Easier said than done. Especially for Laura. She adored him. She sent him birthday and Christmas cards for six years. Each was returned. She finally gave up, and now she never mentions him."

"She must have seen something in the papers about him."

"If she has, she hasn't mentioned it to me," Mary Elizabeth said. "And none of our friends—or her friends—know of the connection. I would like to keep it that way."

Julie felt her heart sink. She hadn't known what she wanted from this visit. She'd prayed she wouldn't learn something she didn't want to know, that he'd abused his wife or something even worse. Now she realized she'd also hoped there might be something she could use in his favor at the parole hearing. But that would mean publicity for the Saddlers and for a vulnerable fifteen-year-old girl.

She adored him. That said a lot right there. Yet he had cut her off cruelly, probably in as heartless a fashion as a father could: rejecting her cards and the heart reaching out to him.

She could see in her mind's eye the look on Nick's face, the shattered faith if she'd rebuffed him that way. A child's heart was so fragile.

The next question was difficult. "Had he been indifferent to her previously?" Children often loved, even when they weren't loved in return.

"I think she's the only person he ever loved," Mary Elizabeth said, the bitterness stronger than ever. "But even with her he held back. As if she were made of glass."

"He must have loved you."

"If he did, he never said so. I hoped, oh how I hoped. I hoped for years. I thought he did...in the beginning. Or I never would have married him. I fell in love with his intensity, perhaps even with the air of mystery around him. He never said anything about his family—not a word. When I asked, his lips would tighten, and he would turn around and leave the room. If for some reason, he couldn't leave me physically, he did it emotionally. Ryan had built a very high wall around himself. I think I knew it when I married him, but like most women

I thought love could tear it down. I didn't make a crack in it. I married a stranger, and he never allowed me to become a friend. I often wondered why he married at all.''

"Could he have been guilty of murder?'' Julie finally asked the damning question.

"Before he admitted it, I would have said no. But the one dependable thing about Ryan was he couldn't abide lies. I can't imagine him admitting to doing something he didn't do, especially if it involved police work. That was his life. It was his life far more than Laura and I ever were.''

"But if he were guilty of being involved in drugs, his whole life would have been a lie,'' Julie said.

A tear snaked down Mary Elizabeth's face. "He compartmentalized everything. And he never let one aspect of his life interfere with another. He never brought police friends home. He never talked about his work. That led to long silences. He was full of secrets. Money disappeared from our account, and he wouldn't tell me where it went. He would receive phone calls and leave without telling me where he was going.''

Her hands were wringing together on the table, and Julie could see the frustration in her eyes, the gradual disillusionment of dying hopes.

She also saw a mirror of her own marriage. The secrets. The disappearances.

"In the end, after I was told he confessed, I had to believe he could have done it,'' Mary Elizabeth said. "I tried to see him, but he wouldn't see me. I wanted an explanation. I wanted a denial. I wanted some kind of remorse for what he had done to us.''

"Is that why you divorced him?'' Julie asked, remembering Dan saying the marriage had already been in trouble prior to the shooting.

"Ryan asked me to. I'd been thinking about it before. I would say we'd had arguments, but Ryan didn't argue. He just tuned out.''

"Did he have *any* friends?''

"Not close ones. Oh, I would invite the neighbors over occasionally, and he would be civil. He could even be charming at times, but his heart was never in it. The only person I ever saw him greet warmly was a priest. We were at a restaurant, and Ryan saw him come in. He got up and went over to him. They talked for several moments, then the priest put an arm around his shoulder. I was stunned. Ryan isn't Catholic. He would never go to church with me, and yet that's the only time I saw him publicly show any warmth.''

"Did Ryan introduce you?''

She shook her head. "They talked for several moments, then Ryan shook his hand and came back. I asked him who it was. He kind of mumbled the name, but I don't remember it. I asked how he knew him, and he got that closed, tight look again. I dropped the subject. Perhaps I shouldn't have, but by then I was tired of trying.''

A puzzled look came over Mary Elizabeth's face as if she suddenly remembered something, then she added softly, ''I did see him again. I saw him at the jail when I went to visit Ryan right after I heard he'd confessed, when he refused to see me. The priest was just coming in....''

''Did he say anything to you?''

''I don't think he saw me. I was crying, trying not...to let anyone see it.'' Her throat was working, just as it must have done on that day ten years ago. Julie could see tears in her eyes. She felt more and more sympathetic toward Mary Elizabeth, whom she'd been prepared to dislike for deserting her husband. It was déjà vu, almost the same scenario that she herself had experienced with Douglas. How long do you hold onto a dead marriage?

And some of her empathy with Ryan Murphy faded. She didn't like the picture Mary Elizabeth was drawing. But it fit with what everyone else had told her about Ryan Murphy.

''I didn't entirely believe the charges until then,'' Mary Elizabeth said suddenly. ''He always seemed so...dedicated to police work. Too much so, for us to have any kind of a future. And he never seemed to care about money. As I said, money would disappear from time to time, but it was always our joint account, the one only he paid into. He insisted I put my own salary into savings in case anything ever happened to him. That was the only thing that saved me when I got the divorce. There was nothing left in our joint account. What bothered me was not that he took money, but that he never had an explanation for it.''

Another puzzle. Another contradiction.

Douglas had had no such scruples. Both their salaries went into one account, and he'd never felt any guilt in raiding it.

Mary Elizabeth apparently interpreted her thoughts from the expression on her face. ''It doesn't make sense, does it? He wouldn't use a cent of my money for his defense. Instead, he used what little he had in the joint account, and after pleading guilty he didn't want an attorney. But Ryan was like that. Full of contradictions. I would catch him looking at Laura with so much tenderness, but he could never express it. I think that look is why I held on for so long. I knew he was capable of loving if he'd ever allow himself that...privilege.''

"He never mentioned that priest again? And you never saw him again?"

"No, he didn't mention him. And I never saw him again after...that day at the jail."

"Did Ryan Murphy ever hit you?"

Astonishment spread over Mary Elizabeth's face. "No, never. He never criticized, either. In fact, he often thanked me for one thing or another. He just...never let me inside his soul. That was the agony of our marriage."

Mary Elizabeth looked at her watch, then toward the door nervously. Julie understood. Her coffee was cold; she'd not taken even a taste of it. She'd been fascinated by the description of Murphy.

"I should go," Julie said. "My little boy will be waiting."

A slight smile came to Mary Elizabeth's face. "You know, I wasn't surprised when I read that Ryan had saved lives. He was absolutely without fear. And despite his detachment, he was very protective of Laura and myself. God help anyone who tried to hurt us."

"A complicated man," Julie observed not for the first time.

"I'm a teacher," Mary Elizabeth said. "I always thought I could reach anyone if I was patient enough. Maybe that's why I was so attracted to him. A challenge. One I wasn't able to overcome." She looked closely at Julie. "Perhaps *you* can."

"The doctors say he may not be the same man he was before. Amnesia can change a personality."

"What is he like now?" Mary Elizabeth asked in a low voice.

"Confused. Bewildered. But still independent. He doesn't like asking for help."

"He doesn't remember anything?"

"No. He can read, write, add and subtract. He doesn't know how he can do these things, but he can do them. The doctor said he could probably remember learned skills. Are there any other skills you're aware of?"

"Mechanics. He could fix anything. And baseball. He played baseball in college."

Julie was taking mental notes. The priest. Mechanics. Baseball. She hadn't wanted to put them in writing, afraid doing so might inhibit the conversation. "What did he read?"

"Everything. Novels. Biographies. Psychology."

"Psychology?"

"He majored in criminology and psychology in college. He was always interested in why people did what they did."

Julie's heart started pounding harder. Suddenly she remembered Dan's absolute pronouncement: *"He's faking."*

She pushed the memory away. She rose from the table. She had what she wanted for the moment. Some places to start. The priest, for one. Why had Ryan not wanted the man to meet his wife?

It seemed one answer led to another question.

"Would you consider testifying for him?"

Mary Elizabeth hugged herself with her arms. "Don't ask me," she said. "It's not fair to Laura. She's forgotten him. She has a father she likes and admires."

"I won't, unless it becomes absolutely necessary."

Mary Elizabeth shook her head, but then whispered, "I...don't hold any ill feelings toward him. I really do wish him well."

"You won't mind if I call again?"

"No."

Julie handed her a card. "And if you remember anything more, particularly the priest's name, you'll call me?"

She nodded again.

Julie held out her hand. "Thank you for being so honest."

Mary Elizabeth took it. "I hope you're successful."

"Would you see him? I'm sure he has some questions..."

"No," she said, dropping Julie's hand. "That part of my life is over. I really don't want to revive it."

"I understand," Julie said, stepping back.

A moment later, the door closed behind her.

They came for him at nine in the morning. Four men in uniform.

Despite his words to Julie yesterday, he had hoped to see her again. She'd probably had second thoughts about representing him. He hoped she had. Still, it would have been nice to see her.

In fact, it would have been more than nice. He'd tried to guard against the attraction he felt for her, the hope she always brought with her. He tried not to want her, not to hope for that occasional touch that made him feel alive and human. He tried not to think of how it would feel kissing her, running his fingers over the fine features of her face, touching her hair.

But perhaps the absence of temptation would reduce the yearning in him. He doubted it, though. He doubted it very much.

The bracelet around his ankle was unlocked and he was given some clothes. The shirt was white, and the trousers white with a blue stripe down each leg. The material was sturdy, even abrasive, but he awkwardly put the pants on without comment. One of the officers helped with his shirt, over his broken arm.

"You know the drill," said one guard who approached, his hands filled with chains. But Ryan didn't. He also knew that with the possible exception of Dr. Dailey and Mrs. Farrell no one believed him. He suspected even they had their reservations.

When he didn't respond, he was jerked to his feet. A chain was fastened around his waist, and then his right hand was cuffed to the waist chain. Another chain ran from the waist down to his ankles where manacles were attached to each ankle. Only his left arm, still held rigid in a cast, remained free.

Humiliation flooded him, and he was glad Julie Farrell wasn't around.

One of the guards pushed a wheelchair up to him. "We have to take you down in this."

He looked around the room. There was nothing of his here. A couple of magazines he'd read. He sat down awkwardly, the clink of chains ringing loudly in his ears. One guard pushed the chair, one went ahead, and two strode beside him. He felt as if he must be very dangerous indeed.

He was wheeled out in the corridor, past a station of some kind. People in the hall stopped to stare at him. The guards moved to a bank of elevators, taking one several floors down. Then he was rolling down another corridor. They were near the door leading outside when he saw Julie Farrell.

She was walking quickly down the corridor toward him, toward the bank of elevators, and stopped when she saw him.

His fingers turned into fists, and his stomach knotted. He hadn't wanted her to see him like this, chained like some kind of mad dog. His head went up and he fixed his eyes at some spot beyond her. He tried to make them emotionless. He tried not to care.

The guards paid her no mind. Perhaps they didn't even know who she was. Even as he steeled himself to pass her, she stopped the guard in front and spoke to him. He shrugged. "Make it quick," he said.

Ryan wanted to look away but he couldn't. Her gray eyes appeared a deeper gray, and they swirled with an emotion he couldn't identify.

"I'm sorry," she said. "I hoped to get here before..."

"Before I was dragged away in chains," he finished bitterly.

She flushed. "I'll get up to Reidsville as soon as they let me. I saw your former wife last night. She really cared about you. She still does."

That was difficult to believe. Just as it was difficult to believe *anyone* could really care about a killer. Being chained like one made him damn well feel like one. For the first time, he felt guilty of a crime he didn't remember.

"You've paid your debt," he said tightly. "In fact, you've more than paid it."

"Sorry, counselor, we have to go," the lead guard said. "The bus is waiting."

Julie's gaze bore into him. "I'll see you in a few days."

The chair started moving, eliminating the need to reply. He kept his gaze averted as a guard pushed open a door, and then he was outside. A cool wind brushed his hair, and moisture dripped from gray skies in a steady drizzle. His chair was pushed to a waiting bus with bars on the window. The doors opened, he stood, then took several awkward steps in the chains. He reached the steps and stopped, not knowing exactly how to mount them. His legs were none too steady from lack of use. He wasn't at all sure of them, particularly with the restraints.

He prayed Julie Farrell wasn't watching.

"Get in, Murphy," one of the guards said impatiently. "We don't have all day."

Unable to grab anything for balance, he took a tentative step. The chain between his ankles allowed just enough slack to make one step at a time. Sweat running off his forehead, he reached the top.

Another guard met him there. He gestured toward a gate set in the middle of a grate separating the driver from the rest of the bus. Six other men were seated inside, each seated next to a window in a row by himself.

"Take the window seat in the front row," said the guard at the gate.

Ryan moved slowly, wondering whether he had ridden on this bus before, wondering whether he had been haunted by his crime, whether he'd felt what he was feeling now: that he was about to visit hell.

He sat down, and the guard regarded him jovially. "You the one who's claiming amnesia?" he said. "The cop who killed his partner?"

Ryan didn't answer.

"You'll remember home when you get there." The guard grinned, turned and went through the gate, locking it.

The bus started out of the driveway onto the road. Ryan looked back. Julie was standing there.

Deprived of memory, of freedom, of dignity, of hope, Ryan forced himself to turn away. He felt trapped in a long, dark tunnel that had no end. And he knew there was no room in it for Julie Farrell.

Chapter 6

Julie watched the bus disappear and felt strangely bereft. She hadn't realized how much she'd looked forward to seeing him, to telling him what she had learned. She'd hoped to see some kind of smile when she told him how well his daughter was doing, that his ex-wife still cared about him.

She'd been too late. And he hadn't welcomed her attempt to speak with him. She wouldn't forget his eyes. She'd thought for a moment they must resemble those of a cornered tiger: proud, defiant, yet terribly anguished at finding itself trapped by something it didn't understand with no way to fight back.

Helplessly, she'd had to stand back as the guards had continued along the hall to the door, and for some reason she'd followed and watched as he'd climbed into the bus. To her dismay, she knew part of her climbed in there with him.

She tried to work on a new brief for the law firm later that morning, but she couldn't stop thinking about Ryan or the trapped look in his eyes. Her mind kept going back to her conversation with Mary Elizabeth as she searched for a key to the old Ryan Murphy. All the riddles had to make sense eventually.

The fact that despite lingering bitterness Mary Elizabeth still cared about him said a lot. That he had thanked her but could not say he loved her would probably keep a roomful of psychologists happy for weeks, if not months. What was so terrible in his background that he wouldn't—or couldn't—speak of it to his wife?

Every time she tried to convince herself he wasn't guilty of the crime, she was reminded of his secrecy, the missing money Mary Elizabeth had mentioned, his unexplained disappearances. She had found dozens of excuses for Doug when the same things occurred. And she'd been wrong.

Was she wrong again? Did she just want Ryan Murphy to be innocent so strongly that she was ignoring the facts and making small inconsistencies appear greater than they were? Inconsistencies occurred in every case. She kept reminding herself of that. There was no such thing as the perfect case.

She shook her head, trying to shake his image away. Worrying wouldn't help either of them. She mentally set Ryan Murphy aside and started to work on legal precedents. But they no longer held interest for her. Mental gymnastics involving a complex legal question didn't compare to the real life tragedy that faced Ryan. For the first time, she realized how much she really missed the tempo of criminal law.

But in the meantime she had a child to support. She went back to work.

Murphy spent two days in the infirmary, spending most of his time taking many of the same tests he'd taken at the Atlanta hospital. It was obvious the prison psychologist didn't believe his amnesia, and Ryan endured the tests only because he hoped to find out more about the other Ryan Murphy. He'd also been warned by Mrs. Farrell to do everything he was told, and do it politely, in preparation for the upcoming parole hearing.

But the damned ink spots still just looked like ink spots, and he said so. The psychologist, Dr. Butler, looked smug. "You said the same thing ten years ago."

He must have been smart ten years ago. "Did I?"

Dr. Butler's demeanor was distinctly suspicious and unfriendly. "You won't get away with this, Murphy," he said. "I don't care what those doctors in Atlanta said. I don't believe you have amnesia any more than I do."

Ryan had a retort, but he didn't think it wise to use it. He'd told himself over and over again to listen, to observe, to soak up information he needed to survive.

More tests. Questions about the government, about current events. Who was president? Who was the last president? What happened to a president named Kennedy? He knew many of the answers because he had read and listened these past few weeks, and his mind was like a sponge. But beyond anything recently acquired, his memory was blank.

He tried to tell Butler that.

The doctor stared back at him. "Amnesia patients have difficulty with short-term memory. They don't remember things they learned the day before. You don't seem to have that problem."

Dr. Dailey had said the same thing and had consulted with other doctors about it. It had been one of the things that troubled him about Ryan's amnesia, had made him doubt the reality of it. Finally, after calling neurologists and researchers throughout the country, he'd been told that insult to the hippocampal system produced highly individual patterns of sparing and loss of memory. Patients differed greatly in the nature of the damage. Ryan didn't think he would try to explain it to Butler, though.

"Dr. Dailey can explain it," he finally said after a dozen questions.

Butler's lips tightened. He looked at a file in his hands. "I see you checked out a number of books on psychology before your...accident."

Ryan said nothing. There was nothing he could say. He remembered nothing.

"Perhaps you were already planning to stage an accident."

His silence obviously irritated the psychologist who shook his head. "I'm having you sent back to your old cell in the protective custody wing," he said. "Perhaps that will help restore your memory."

Maybe it would. Ryan had thought the prison itself might. But the forbidding-looking fortress had induced nothing in him other than the gloom such a facility would probably instill in anyone. Neither had the arriving procedures startled any memories, only a deep sense of degradation. The personal search had been the most humiliating thing he could possibly imagine. He had to undress completely, then open his mouth, allow someone to search. Finally he was told to lean over.

"The hero," one guard taunted as he roughly conducted the intimate search.

Ryan wanted to strike out. He felt rage build inside him even as the search ended. God help him, but it took every bit of control he had to contain it.

Was that where the violence came from? The thought was chilling enough to cool the instinct to strike.

Two days passed, then four, then six, and no word from Julie Farrell. Mrs. Farrell, he reminded himself. He had no right to use her first name. Had she done what he'd asked and dropped the matter? He hoped so. For her sake, he hoped so.

Yet waves of desolation swept over him as he thought about losing her, losing the visits, losing the one bright thing in all the emptiness.

After five days, Julie felt she was making progress in her bid to free Murphy. She had a job lined up for Murphy in the auto garage she used extensively. She hadn't found him a place to stay yet. She'd called on several advertisements, but all balked at renting to a paroled convict.

She knew she needed those two things. A job and a place to stay. The parole board required both. She had avoided thinking about the one possibility that had reluctantly raised its ugly head: her own home had a room over the garage that the previous owner had used as a rental apartment. It had one large room that included a kitchen area, and a nice-size bathroom. The entrance was private.

Did she want to risk allowing a convicted murderer so close to her son? Could she ask some other family to assume that risk if she wasn't willing? She used to enjoy arguing moral questions. This was one she wanted to run from.

Still echoing in her ears was the call two days ago from William Lewis, assistant chief of police.

His message had been short, the warning clear. "You're playing with fire, Mrs. Farrell. Murphy was guilty as hell, and he's smart enough to fool you, me and any doctor I've met. He's ruthless and he's deadly. You've been a former prosecutor. You know how these people use the psychiatric card. Don't let him use you like he used us ten years ago. Think real long and hard before trying to put him back on the streets."

She had. She had searched her conscience and heart and soul. It wasn't only her son's safety that worried her. It was her attraction to the man. She didn't understand it, but it was strong, so strong that her blood warmed whenever she saw him or, God help her, even thought of him.

Had she allowed that attraction to cloud her common sense? Yet she felt gut deep that Ryan Murphy wasn't a murderer and never had been. She wasn't sure what made him confess, but there were just too many questions. The fact that she'd once convicted an innocent man had always weighed heavily on her. She didn't want another innocent man to suffer that way.

She swallowed hard. She knew she wouldn't tell Dan the possibility of renting Murphy her apartment, not yet. Besides, it was a last resort.

But at least she was learning more about Murphy, and none of it was very ominous. Murphy's prison record was spotless, except for two fights in the first year of his imprisonment. He had, in fact, earned his college degree in prison and had done advanced work in literature through a correspondence program.

Jerry had found several people who remembered his college years. He'd been an outstanding pitcher until his right wrist was injured. Teammates remembered an insular man, one who was always civil but who, unlike the others, never shared confidences. He'd been a loner even then; no one remembered him sharing in after-game celebrations, and he seldom even drank a beer. He had been a good student, though, and his grades were excellent.

No one knew anything about a family. All attempts to find any family member failed. There was no birth certificate on file, no next of kin listed anywhere except his wife when he'd been married.

The beginning of a portrait was being drawn. The outline was there but no definition. Shadows without substance.

Much of her time—that not spent on the firm's legal research—was spent on understanding amnesia. But that, too, was like capturing shadows. The one thing everyone agreed upon was that no amnesia case was like another. The doctors could state absolutely that Murphy suffered contusions of both the frontal and occipital areas of his skull, but the memory parts of the brain were still a mystery to researchers. Each amnesia victim was different. Some lost total memory, including the ability to speak and walk; some lost only years. Some victims retained skills; some did not. No one could predict whether memory would return.

Although Dr. Dailey believed Murphy suffered from amnesia, testing showed that his thought processes were not impaired. He could solve intricate puzzles rapidly though he had no idea how he did it.

Finally, she felt she was ready to meet with Dan. After receiving a release from Ryan, Dr. Dailey and two other doctors were willing to discuss his medical condition. Armed with their statements, prison records, inconsistencies in the crime reports and other information, she made an appointment to discuss Murphy's case. If Dan would drop his opposition to Murphy's parole, they might very well have a good shot at it.

Dan listened patiently as the doctors discussed Murphy. He leaned forward as Dr. Dailey finished. "Could he be faking amnesia?"

"I doubt it," the doctor said. "Murphy couldn't have known he would receive a head injury. And he was without memory from the instant he woke from a coma. He wouldn't have had time to concoct such an elaborate ruse, much less keep it up through the excruciating pain he suffered in the days following his emergence from a coma." He shrugged. "It's not impossible, but I would say it was most unlikely."

The other two physicians agreed, although Dr. Edwards hedged more than his colleague.

"What would he have to gain?" Dr. Dailey asked.

"A parole. Maybe transfer to a mental institution which could be less restrictive," Dan replied quickly. "Convicts can be extremely cunning when their freedom is at stake. 'The devil made me do it' is one of their favorites," he said sarcastically. "Multiple personalities is another favorite tactic. I'm not sure whether amnesia has been used recently, but you know by his records that Murphy is certainly clever enough to plan something like this."

"I don't think you can fake the bewilderment I've seen in him," the doctor said. "The struggle to remember no matter the cost."

"You say it could completely change his personality?" Dan asked, his interest piqued now.

"It has, if what I've read of his past is true," Dr. Dailey said. "All the psychological evaluations I've read on him say he's a natural leader who refused to lead—in essence, a loner. This Murphy is quiet, grateful for any help in finding information about himself, cooperative, although he is naturally cautious, considering the situation he's in."

Dan looked thoughtful.

Julie leaped on that moment. "And don't forget he did risk his life to save my son and myself."

"That was the old Murphy," Dan said sardonically. "If his personality *has* changed, then this Murphy had nothing to do with the rescue, just as he didn't have anything to do with the crime. You can't have it both ways."

"Both of them are worth saving then," she said. "And you know you had doubts about his guilt."

"That was before he confessed," Dan shot back.

"I've read the reports. You never would have convicted him if he hadn't."

"Whoever said criminals were smart?"

"Ryan Murphy apparently was. Tell me you never wondered about it."

The doctors and Jerry were listening to the exchange with interest.

"Please, Dan. Just go down and talk to him."

He sighed. "I've already filed our response."

"You can amend it. Say you received new information."

He sat forward in his chair and built a temple with his fingers. "I'll be crucified in the press," he finally said. "Letting a cop killer go."

"He's a hero now."

"For one week. Good story. Convict saving child. But letting him back on the streets? That's a different story."

"Don't promise anything. Just talk to him."

"Now I know why I hated letting you leave my office," he groaned. "You were the best I had in persuading a jury."

"Too good," she said dryly.

His eyes met hers. "Don't let the Corrigan case get confused with this one," he said. "Twelve people reached the same conclusion as you and I had."

"We still sent an innocent man to prison."

"Corrigan never confessed. Murphy did. We aren't dealing with an innocent man here."

"But he *is* a different man."

She held her breath.

"I'll talk to him," he finally said. "But even if I decide not to oppose the parole—and I said 'if'—the parole board might turn him down anyway."

"I know. But it will help."

He stood, ending the conversation. He shook hands with the doctors and walked them to the door. Then he leaned against the desk and eyed Jerry, who'd accompanied her because he now knew a great deal about Murphy's background. "What do you think, Jerry?"

"You know me. I don't think one way or another when I'm on a case. It muddies my thinking. Besides, I haven't seen him."

Julie turned to Dan. "When will you go?"

"Day after tomorrow. I have appointments tomorrow. Hell, I have appointments all week."

"Can I go with you?" Another favor. And she would have to ask still another of Emily. She was going to owe Emily, Dan and Jerry a great deal when all was said and done.

Dan looked as if he was going to refuse, then he shook his head in defeat. "If I said no, you would go anyway, wouldn't you?"

"I'm his attorney."

"Don't keep reminding me."

She reached out for his hand. She was elated, but for some reason she also felt like crying. She'd wanted this so badly. She hadn't realized until this moment how emotionally involved she was. The worst possible thing for a client. And, she mentally amended, for the lawyer. As Jerry said, it muddied the brain.

Julie heard Dan muttering to himself as they waited in a small, windowless interview room for Ryan Murphy. The room's furnishings were minimal: a scuffed table and two chairs. He'd asked for a third to be brought in.

Julie stood silently as they waited for Murphy to be brought in. As Murphy's attorney, she'd insisted on being present, but Dan had asked her to let him conduct the interview *his* way. Since she wanted his help, she hadn't protested.

She watched as Dan stationed himself so he could see Murphy's face the moment he entered the room. He had asked the assistant warden not to inform Murphy about the identity of his visitor. He obviously wanted to see the prisoner's face the moment Ryan saw him.

The door opened, and a handcuffed Murphy entered, followed by a guard. Julie saw his gaze sweep the room, register the presence of Dan indifferently, then move on, lingering on her and they seemed to come alive. Then a strangely flat expression replaced that brightness as his gaze moved away from Julie back toward Dan. She did not see even a flicker of recognition.

Dan nodded to the guard. "You can wait outside."

The guard nodded and left, closing the door behind him.

Murphy stood silently, his eyes watchful but curious.

"Do you know who I am?" Dan asked.

"No."

"Sit down."

Murphy sat, his gaze remaining steadily on Dan's face as if he were searching for something. Other than that one look of recognition toward Julie, who remained unobtrusively in a corner, he'd turned all his attention toward Dan.

"I'm Dan Watters."

"The district attorney," Murphy said flatly. "I read the stories about my conviction."

Julie noted a flicker of uncertainty in Dan's eyes. He'd evidently expected Murphy to deny any knowledge of him. "Mrs. Farrell asked me to see you."

Murphy cut his eyes toward her, then back. Julie was aware of the current between the two of them, a subtle awareness that didn't seem to need words. She hoped Dan wasn't also aware of it. From the frown on his face, he was.

That might have been why he posed the next question. "She saw your wife, your ex-wife."

Murphy didn't blink, just waited.

"Don't you want to know how she is?" Dan asked after a moment's silence.

Something flickered in Murphy's eyes again. A muscle in his cheek jerked. Then he looked up. "What do you want?"

"Julie asked me to see you."

Murphy's eyes again cut toward her. "I asked her to leave it alone," he said roughly. "She doesn't owe me a damn thing." Murphy's eyes glittered, but there was no arrogance in his statement, no bravado, only a raw anguish he tried to hide under anger. He wasn't successful.

"No," Dan agreed. "She doesn't."

Murphy started to rise as if to leave.

"Castilani," Dan said.

Murphy turned, his eyes puzzled. "What?"

"Castilani," Dan repeated and watched Murphy's face. It was absolutely blank.

"That was the last case you were working on," Dan said after a moment. "You were trying to make a case against a man named Castilani. We worked together on it."

"Ten years ago? Why would I remember that?"

Julie wondered too. But Dan's face was impassive. "He's all yours, counselor." Dan paused, then added, "Do you have any idea how lucky you are to have her representing you?"

"Strange," Murphy said quietly as he looked toward Julie. "I don't feel lucky." A muscle flexed in his cheek. "And I thought I'd fired Mrs. Farrell."

Julie saw Dan's face soften slightly, and she looked back at Murphy. She wondered whether Dan saw what she did. She knew he'd been searching for insincerity, cunning, manipulation. But there was none, only determination in those calm, blue eyes. Despite the handcuffs encasing his wrists, dignity and control were reflected by the rigid set of his shoulders, the almost indecipherable working of a cheek muscle.

Dan looked toward Julie. She shrugged her shoulders.

"I'll wait outside," he said.

As the door closed, Julie prepared for a battle of a far different kind than she'd expected.

Chapter 7

Ryan tried to tamp the rush of pleasure that filled him at seeing Julie. He had no right to feel anything. He'd been telling himself that during the time he'd been here.

Perhaps he had grown used to prison before the...injury. He didn't know how anyone could grow used to it, even in the limited experience of his current life. But he must have. He had to have in order to survive. He'd done it once. He could do it again.

But he had to steel himself not to feel. Not to care. Not to hope. Hope was a luxury he couldn't afford. Imagining a different life, like those he'd seen on television, was fruitless. He knew only this one: bars and guards and the thousand humiliations of being regarded as little more than an animal in a cage. And perhaps that was all he was. All he had ever been.

He wanted to remember. And he didn't. Could he face the murderer everyone said he was? Could he face the crooked cop, the man who dealt drugs? Could he face the man who had turned away from a wife and child?

But despite all these questions and doubts, deep inside he yearned for answers. He envied others who knew who and what they were. He even envied the other prisoners who had pictures on their cell walls. He was a question mark. A conundrum. He knew only what others told him, and he didn't feel like the person they described. He couldn't imagine himself doing what others said he had done.

He endured. One day after another. His one escape was books—the cart came by his cell twice a week. But he could have only one book, and that he read in one day. He paced, exercised his weakened muscles and tried to remember. Despite everything he knew about himself, the void stretched endlessly, no beginning, no end.

Who was he? What was he? Were his reactions today what they would have been six months ago? The questions were endless. Maddening.

And only Julie Farrell brought any light into that bewildering emptiness.

He ached to move to her, to touch her, to feel himself being touched. He found himself yearning for something he didn't know or understand.

But she put a briefcase down on the table and sat, her gaze moving toward her hands which were unsnapping a buckle, then opening the case and taking out papers.

She looked up. "Your arm is out of the cast."

He glanced down at his handcuffed wrists. The cast had been taken off two days ago and his arm ached at being held at this particular angle. "Yes," he replied simply.

"Are they giving you any help with your memory?"

"The psychologist? He's convinced I haven't lost it."

"I think you convinced Dan Watters."

"I think you should forget it," he said.

"Do you like it here so much?"

He looked at her steadily. "I've obviously hurt a lot of people. I don't want to include you among them."

"Why should I be among them?"

"I can't pay you anything. You have a child to support."

"I wouldn't, if you hadn't risked your life."

"I told you...you don't owe me anything. It was the other Murphy that pulled you out and he probably had his own motives for doing it."

"Is *this* Murphy giving up? I don't think the other one would."

"He did when he pleaded guilty. He must have been guilty. I'm trying to live with that." And with the loneliness that accompanied the knowledge.

"I'm not so sure he was guilty," she said.

His heart seemed to stop. Breath caught in his throat. He stared at her, barely comprehending her words. *Not guilty.*

For the first time, he felt a seed of hope. But he held it within him. "I confessed," he said.

"And you didn't have to. They didn't have enough evidence to convict you."

"My conscience?"

She smiled. "Murderers and drug dealers don't have consciences."

"Then why?"

"That's the big question. Even if you did do it, why would you confess? You were a detective. You had to know they didn't have enough to convict. Even your wife..." She stopped suddenly.

He couldn't stop the surge of curiosity. "Tell me about her."

"She's very attractive. Light brown hair. Hazel eyes. She's a teacher."

"The...child?"

"Your daughter?"

He nodded. "Did you see her?"

"No. She was out. A play rehearsal."

He wanted to ask more. But instead he looked down at the scarred table.

"It seems a happy home," she said gently.

"I should feel something, dammit." His hands slammed the table in frustration "But there's nothing. Nothing. It's like talking about strangers." He wanted memories. Good. Bad. *Something. Anything.*

He stood, unable to sit any longer. He paced, unable to do anything else. He felt trapped by his own mind.

He couldn't even know what he wanted because he had no knowledge of what to expect, what would make him feel something other than this total isolation. He always felt as if something was tightening around his heart, but he didn't know what would relieve it. He hated his cell. He hated being in a box, but at the same time he couldn't even imagine what something else would be like. Perhaps he would hate freedom, too. Choices. How did one even go about making them?

"Ryan?"

He looked down at her as she said his given name. It was the first time he had heard it from someone's lips. It had always been "Murphy."

And suddenly, he did want something. He wanted to hear her voice say his name again in that same soft way. He wanted her to stay. He wanted it so badly that it took every ounce of strength he had to meet her eyes, to stand casually as if she were a stranger. And he wanted his freedom to discover himself. But he liked her too much to destroy her, and apparently he'd spent his life destroying people.

"I think we have a chance at getting you paroled," she finally said. "Your prison record is unblemished, and you saved the lives of two people at the risk of your own."

Stunned, he sat on the corner of the table.

"I don't want to get your hopes up," she added cautiously. "But we do have a shot at it if the district attorney doesn't oppose it. I don't think he will."

"Why?" he said, not quite ready to accept the words. Parole. He wasn't sure exactly what it would mean.

"Several reasons," she said, avoiding a direct answer.

"I don't think he believed me." He shrugged. "No one does."

"I do."

Her gray eyes were lovely. He'd remembered them as peaceful, but now they appeared more turbulent, almost smoky with determination, even a kind of passion. Raw need kicked him in the stomach. He longed to reach out his hand to her, but he couldn't. He was a convict. She was his lawyer. Touching was impossible even if his wrists weren't still locked together with handcuffs. Caution—or was it honor—was stronger than steel.

He tried to focus on what she was saying. "And if I did get a...parole?"

"You would have to report to a parole officer frequently. You would need a place to live. A job."

"What would I do?"

"Your ex-wife said you were a good mechanic, that you could fix anything. I asked the owner of the garage that services my car whether he could use you. He's always looking for someone. He agreed to try you."

For a moment, the thought overwhelmed him. *Freedom.* He didn't even know what it was. Since he'd first awakened from the coma, he'd been a prisoner, unable to make any choices of his own. "What if I don't remember anything?"

"You can learn."

She said it with such easy confidence that he believed her. Maybe he could.

"What else have you learned about me," he said, aware of greed in his voice. Greed for information. "Tell me everything. The bad as well as the good." He paused, then added dryly, "If there is any good."

She regarded him solemnly. "There *is.* You're exceptionally smart. Prison records show an extremely high I.Q. You were a great baseball player. You apparently were good at anything you tried."

She paused, then continued, "You're also somewhat of a mystery. No one, not even your wife, felt she really knew you. You kept secrets."

"You left out all the good stuff," he said when she finished. "I murdered a friend."

"You weren't necessarily friends." She hesitated, as if reluctant to say the next words, then added slowly, "And I'm not sure it *was* murder. You originally said your partner tried to kill you and you acted in self-defense. It wasn't until ten days later that you decided to plead guilty. And after that you wouldn't see your wife. You asked her to get a divorce.

"It doesn't fit," she added. "Dr. Dailey doesn't think so, either. You were a good detective, one of the best. Good enough and smart enough to cover your tracks."

"Then why...?"

"That's the question," she said. "It keeps cropping up. Nothing in your case made sense."

It didn't make sense to him, either. But he had no parameters to judge by.

"You didn't find any other family?"

"No," she said. "Although you went to school in Atlanta."

"No friends?"

She shook her head. "None that your wife knew about. She said you always compartmentalized your life. But she did mention a priest."

"A priest? Am I Catholic?"

She shook her head. "Not that anyone knows. Your wife said you didn't go to church. You listed no religion when you entered prison. But this particular priest might have visited you in the Atlanta jail. Mary Elizabeth said she saw him there, but she had no way of knowing whether he was there to see you. We checked the jail records, but we can't find him listed as a visitor. He might well have visited other prisoners at the same time so he would not be listed as seeing you specifically."

"My wife," he repeated the words as if tasting them for the first time.

"She loved you. She said you loved your child."

"But not her?"

"She said you never seemed able to express emotion, but you were never cruel. She said you never 'let her inside your soul.'"

He thought about that. In the hospital, he'd watched some afternoon soap operas. Everyone seemed to be in love, whether they should be or not. They said it a lot. What had been wrong with him?

"She still cares about you," she said softly, "so I think there must have been a great deal to love."

His gaze met hers. He saw the understanding there. Not pity, thank God. But comprehension that took away some of the constant raw anguish. For the first time, he no longer felt so damnably alone, a pariah of no value.

But at what cost to her?

Had he considered what his actions cost others before?

Nothing seemed to indicate it.

His gaze fell to the table. How could he accept so much help from this woman?

She moved, came around to him and sat on the table, just as he had moments earlier. Her hand fell on his shoulder. It seemed to burn through the rough cloth. Burned and soothed at the same time.

"She said something else," she said softly. "It hadn't surprised her that you risked your life to save my son and me. She said you were absolutely without fear, that you were very protective of her and your daughter."

He wasn't without fear now. He feared what he was. What he had been.

"And now I can't even remember them."

"That's not your fault."

"But I should," he insisted in frustration. "I should feel something. It's as if feelings had been ripped from me as well as memory."

She shook her head. "I think you feel a great deal."

God help him, but he did feel at that particular moment. He wished he could touch her, that he could feel her body against his, that he could absorb all that faith that she had and he didn't have.

But steel encased his wrists, just as guards and bars kept him from human contact. It was a cold reminder of who and what he was.

But she held out a lifeline. Parole.

He wanted it desperately. He could search for his own past then. He wanted to answer all her questions, despite the answers he might find.

She moved then, and returned to her side of the desk. She reached into her briefcase, took out two books and handed them to him. He accepted them awkwardly.

"I've already checked them out with the guards. You can take them."

He didn't look at the titles. He felt as if treasures had been handed to him. "Thank you."

"I'll see you next week and prepare you for the hearing."

He hesitated, not wanting her to leave. "How is your son?"

"He's doing fine. He asks about the man who saved him and his mommy."

He couldn't find anything to say to that. He didn't remember the boy. He didn't remember the accident. He didn't even remember many of the days that followed it.

Her steady gray eyes studied him. "We're going to get you out of here," she said, then turned and went to the door, rapping on it lightly.

He stood, his hands clasping the books. He wasn't sure whether he believed that assurance or not. But his steps were lighter as he followed the guard back to his cell.

Julie took a deep breath once she stepped outside the building. She needed the air. She needed the freshness of it after the institutional smell that plagued every prison. She also needed it to get her equilibrium back. She had felt herself melting in that room with Ryan, every ounce of control and common sense dissolving into air.

Telling herself the feelings were only the residue of gratitude, she tried to avoid Dan's curious glance. Yet the electricity—the connection—between Murphy and herself remained with her. Her limbs felt weak, her mind slow, and her senses jangled. How could anyone in an ill-fitting prison uniform, his hands chained awkwardly, be so attractive, so compellingly masculine?

He'd moved with the loose-limbed grace of a wild cat. His shirt sleeves, rolled up above his elbows, revealed strong arms and capable hands. His dark hair had been mussed as if he combed it with his fingers; his face, with all its sharp planes and angles, fascinated her. Even more intriguing were the thoughtful silences, the careful search for words, his obvious reluctance to accept favors. Yet he was wise enough to accept what he needed. She wondered whether the old Murphy would have accepted her help. She doubted it. Another sign of change? Or cunning? Those doubts kept creeping into her consciousness, even as she tried to shove them aside.

She'd kept wishing he would smile, though she knew he had no reason to smile. She could only imagine what it would do to that chiseled visage, to that hint of a dimple in his cheek. Just thinking about it created a soft warm feeling in a heart she thought could never be touched again by a man.

Nicholas could make him smile. She would bet on it. His eager, cheerful face could cajole anyone into a smile.

That thought made *her* smile.

"I take it you're staying with his case," Dan said wryly.

Jerked out of dangerous thoughts, she turned to him. "What do you think?"

He looked at her thoughtfully. "I don't rightly know, Mrs. Farrell. He's convincing, I'll give you that."

"You'll support his parole?"

"I won't support it," he said. "Maybe I won't oppose it. Depends on what his victim's family wants."

"They've moved out of state," she said. "I already tried to reach them."

"My people will try harder," he said dryly.

She nodded. That was his job. Victim statements had grown increasingly important in the past several years.

Then she asked a question that had puzzled her. "Why did you mention...Castilani?"

He hesitated for a moment, then shrugged. "That was the last case we worked on together. I wanted to see his reaction." Dan changed the subject. "You know if you keep this case, there will be more publicity."

A shudder ran through her. "I know."

"How does your law firm feel about it?"

"They don't like it," she said honestly. "But for the first time in years, I feel excited about law again."

"That passion used to be turned toward the victims," he reminded her. "Taking the bad guys off the streets, not putting them back on them."

"Do you honestly feel Murphy is a bad guy?"

"I wouldn't have sent him to prison if I didn't," Dan said. "Remember you have a son now. You get involved with the guy and his problems, you're going to get sucked deeper and deeper into his quicksand."

Guilt landed like a boulder in her stomach. She was already spending less time with Nick. Was she also putting him—and herself—in danger?

But she chose not to let Dan know it. "I plan to spend all weekend with Nick."

"I didn't mean time. I'm talking about his safety. Don't let gratitude blind you. That's all I ask."

"You fought hard to get Corrigan released," she reminded him.

"I *knew* he was innocent."

She worried her lip as she remembered the case. Jim Corrigan. He'd been one of her first cases. Charged with arson that resulted in a death. He'd been fired from a lumber company just prior to a fire that destroyed the multi-million-dollar business. A fireman had been killed in the blaze.

Corrigan had a reputation as a hothead, and had been arrested several times for assault. When accelerants were found in his garage by investigating officers, he was charged with arson and murder. Five years later a deathbed confession from the real arsonist, the owner of the business, cleared Corrigan. The resulting investigation showed that an overzealous detective had planted the evidence in hopes of receiving recognition and a promotion.

But Corrigan had always proclaimed his innocence.

Still, it was never easy for a district attorney to admit an error. Many of them, unfortunately, chose to ignore evidence which contradicted their convictions. Dan Watters had never been one of those.

He was stubbornly holding on to his opinion of Murphy, though she sensed she'd made some progress. And she knew him. She knew the best thing to do now was to let him make up his own mind. His inherent fairness would kick in, and he would ignore that protectiveness he felt toward her.

"How is your wife?" she asked.

"Fine. Sandy would love to see both you and Nick. She wanted me to ask you over for supper."

"We would like that."

"Sunday?"

They had reached his car. She hesitated.

"We won't discuss Murphy," he said.

"We would love to come." But she wasn't going to agree not to discuss Murphy.

Julie watched Nick as he craned his neck to watch the huge gorilla groom her offspring. The tenderness between mother and baby was mesmerizing.

Nick stood on the bench to see better, and her hand wound around him protectively. He was so small.

Gazing down on his rumpled hair with love, she shifted her weight from one foot to the other. She planned to spend the entire weekend with Nick. The zoo in the morning. A movie. Pizza. All of Nick's favorite things. Then supper at Dan's the next evening. She'd promised herself she wouldn't even think of Ryan Murphy.

I'm talking about Nick's safety. Dan's words kept echoing in her mind as she tightened her grip. Nick twisted around and looked at her, giving her his most angelic smile. Her heart lurched, expanded. She loved him so much.

Nick pointed at another gorilla loping toward the mother and baby. The animal stopped, gave them a quizzical look, then lumbered over, looking down at them.

"Is he the daddy?" Nick asked. He was fascinated with the idea of fathers. He had only partially accepted the fact that his had gone to heaven before he was born.

"I think so," she said.

"Can I get a daddy?"

"It's not that easy," she said.

"Why?"

"Daddies are hard to find, particularly good daddies."

He frowned, considering that answer, then turned back to the gorillas. The Atlanta Zoo had spent hundreds of thousands of dollars providing "natural habitats" for its animals, and the gorilla exhibit, where the animals were allowed to roam freely in a large open area, was always the most popular. She took Nick to just those exhibits. Somehow, she didn't feel up to seeing any caged animals.

But the zoo was Nick's very favorite place. He loved animals and even now was clamoring for a dog. She wanted to wait until he was a little older, and so far had deflected his requests by telling him Prissy's feelings would be hurt. Since Nick would shed tears at the thought of bruising a flower, he usually went to hug Prissy, explaining that he "loved" her better than "any old dog" even as she saw dogs dancing in his wistful eyes.

They had to stop at the petting zoo, and she watched him happily run his hands through rabbit fur, then feed a small goat. He was weary and beaming when they headed for a theater.

Four years old. Almost five. She wished, in a way, she could keep him at that age forever. But then she thought about him as a young man looking down on his own son, and a sweet anguish filled her. She had these years and she would take advantage of each one of them. Despite her recent vow, she thought of Murphy. His daughter had been five when he went to prison. How had he felt at losing her? At never seeing her again? Or had he felt anything at all?

And why did her thoughts keep wandering back to him. She shook her head, trying to shake him from her mind. It belonged to Nick today. Totally.

But the film was a mistake. A big one. It was one they had selected together, though she had cautiously guided him in that direction. A comedy about Little League. She avoided children's films with death or sadness in them; his heart was too soft, and she wanted these years to be as carefree as she could make them. This movie, about a team of misfits who triumph, seemed the best choice, but all the way through she thought of the man who had been a star pitcher in college.

Damn. The zoo reminded her of him. Now the film. She knew she was really in trouble, though, when they were walking to the car after consuming several large pieces of pizza.

"Mommy?"

She had glanced down at the face camouflaged with red pizza sauce. "What, sweetie?"

"Will you teach me to play baseball?"

"Yep," she said. She had been a fair softball player in high school.

"Can I play in Little League?"

She was beginning to wonder whether the movie had been a good choice or not. "When you're old enough."

"Can I have a glove?"

"Maybe for Christmas."

"But that'll take forever."

"Not quite," she said, tightening her hold on his hand. It would be here much too fast. Days were sliding along rapidly, especially now that she was working two jobs. Christmas? How long? Two months away now.

He looked disappointed. "I already know what I want Santa Claus to bring," he said.

"What?"

"It's a secret."

"Mommies can keep secrets."

He looked at her suspiciously. "Abby says I can't tell anyone or he won't bring it."

Julie bit her lip. Emily's daughter was precocious. Too precocious. "I don't think Abby's right."

But his lips were clamped shut. Well, she had several months to discover the secret and it would probably change ten times during those months.

"Ready to go home?"

He yawned and nodded, his eyes already half closed.

"Have a good day?"

"I had a wonaful day."

"I love you, munchkin."

"Me too, Mommy."

Chapter 8

Ryan kept wondering about his daughter. He wished he had asked Julie Farrell to get him a photo.

He didn't feel like a father. He wouldn't recognize his child. Perhaps he wouldn't feel anything if he did see a picture. But he found himself yearning to see a photo, to find a connection.

His cell seemed to grow smaller each day. Six by eight feet. A metal cot bolted to the floor. A basin. A toilet. A radio. It was all he had.

Despite the continuing pain in his shoulder, he'd started doing push-ups and sit-ups, increasing the number daily. The activity ate up some of the restlessness that was driving him nearly mad. He had one hour a day outside if the weather was good. It had rained for the last week, so he'd not even had that.

Four weeks. He'd been here four weeks, twenty-eight days. Had he really lived this way for ten years with the knowledge that he might live that way his entire life? The very thought suffocated him.

Another week, and he'd have his parole hearing. Two additional doctors, both skeptics, had seen him, presented him with even more tests. Although he felt more warmth from them when they left, he knew they had doubts, and he knew why. He'd read what little was in the prison library on amnesia, and he was only too aware of how rare it was. No wonder no one wanted to believe him.

He finished his thirtieth push-up and fell to the floor, his injured shoulder aching. He didn't want to think about the upcoming hearing. Despite Julie Farrell's optimism, he didn't want to hope, not when his chances were slim to none. He called her Julie in his mind, Mrs. Farrell when he was with her. He'd tried not to think of her as Julie, tried mentally to formalize her, but it never quite worked.

She said she would be here again before the hearing.

When?

Julie stayed away from Reidsville until three days before the parole hearing. The hearing would take place at the prison, as would some twenty others.

How many times had she read the court transcript when he pleaded guilty? Murphy's statement? The statements of prison officials, police officers, witnesses at the accident when Murphy had pulled her from the car?

The most interesting to her was Murphy's statement at sentencing. He had been required in the plea bargain to admit his culpability.

He did it in one sentence. "I'm guilty of the crimes charged."

No remorse, which might have gotten him a lesser sentence. No explanation. No mitigating circumstances. No nothing.

The lack of remorse, she knew, was the greatest impediment to a parole. Parole boards liked remorse. Heck, they nearly always required it.

She had considered strategy carefully. Though she still had doubts about what happened that Christmas Eve night, she wouldn't visit the ambiguities of the ten-year-old case. She decided to stake everything on his act of heroism in saving her and her boy, and the amnesia which changed him into an entirely different person.

She already asked two additional doctors—another neurologist and a neuroscientist who was involved in a research project involving amnesia and memory—to testify. After examining Murphy, both were willing to testify they believed he suffered amnesia and that he could receive better treatment outside the prison system than within.

Dan, after failing to contact Mike Cates's family, had finally agreed not to oppose the parole. He made it very clear, though, that he would keep a close eye on Murphy if the parole were granted.

She didn't know if anyone else would oppose the parole. Her main concern was Murphy himself: how he would comport himself, whether he could handle antagonistic questions. She had felt the tension in him the last time she'd visited. Each day had to feel like a week, a month, to him.

This time she went alone. He was handcuffed when led in, and she asked for them to be removed. After a pause, the guard did so. "I'll be right outside," he said.

She watched as Murphy massaged his wrists for several moments, then he lifted his gaze to look directly at her.

A tremor ran through her. His eyes were so blue, so direct. He looked healthier than he had before. Even with prison food, his body was filling out. His shoulders looked broader than before, and his arms, with the sleeves of his shirt rolled up again, looked muscular and capable.

His dark hair was cropped short but it was thick and had a tendency to curl. Despite the fact that it was early afternoon, a five o'clock shadow was already shading his face. Black Irish. Murphy, with his dark hair and dark blue eyes that crinkled as though he was squinting at the sun, suddenly brought the expression to mind.

She couldn't find her tongue. Her stomach clenched in a reaction she really didn't understand, and her heart seemed to beat faster as she met his steady gaze. She forced her eyes downward. "How are you?" she asked in what she hoped was a businesslike tone.

"I don't really know how to answer that," he replied and she realized she'd forgotten how lazy and deep his voice sounded.

"Most people would say 'fine,'" she said.

"I don't think I'm most people."

He had a point. A very good point. She looked up, wanting to see at least a brief glimpse of a smile. Maybe, she wondered after being disappointed, he didn't know how.

"No," she agreed. "You're definitely not most people."

She sat down. He didn't. Instead, he roamed the room like a caged panther. She didn't like the image. "Sit down. We have a lot to cover."

For a moment, he looked as if he wanted to refuse. Then he sat.

"Good," she said.

"What's good?"

"Doing as you're told."

His lips thinned slightly, and his eyes flared. His hands pressed down on the table and she saw his knuckles turn white.

"You'll have to do that, you know, if you get the parole. You will have to observe a number of rules—I'll tell you what some of those are—and you will have to answer to a parole officer. It won't be easy."

"Do you really believe...?"

"I don't know," she said when he hesitated. "I don't know what your chances are. But I want you to be polite, answer everything calmly. Don't let any of them get you angry. Several will try."

"Why?"

"To see if you will explode, whether you might be a danger to the community. Someone will probably ask whether you regret the crime."

"I don't even remember it."

"Regretting plays a big part in their decision," she said.

"You want me to lie?"

"No," she said. "Just say you don't remember, but that you realize it was a terrible crime and regret any part you had in it."

He nodded. "Do you think they will believe the amnesia?"

She shrugged. "I had a hard time with it in the beginning. Everyone does. We always hear about amnesia, read about it in fiction and watch it on television, but do we really believe it?"

He was silent, listening.

"Here's what I'm going to do," she said, and explained her strategy to him.

"If they grant a parole...?"

"Let me explain what parole will mean," she said. "You won't be able to carry a gun. You can't go in a bar. You can't associate with other ex-convicts. You'll probably have to take drug tests on a regular basis. You will have to keep a job. You can't get in fights. You will probably have to see your parole officer once a week in the beginning."

He nodded, but his eyes were asking questions, questions he wasn't about to verbalize. Questions, she knew, he was afraid would reveal too much.

How would he live in a society when so many pieces of his life were missing? He had made giant strides in the past month. She knew from the doctors how much he was reading, how quickly he comprehended facts and ideas. Yet it must be intimidating not to recognize any faces, places or names, not to know what skills he might have. She expected, in fact, that that would be one of the questions posed by the parole board. If indeed he did have nearly total amnesia, how could he function?

Most people couldn't. But she would bet on Murphy.

She ran him through a number of questions until she was satisfied with his answers. She liked the way he answered. Quietly. Thoughtfully. No touch of arrogance. He didn't avoid tough questions.

After two hours, she felt that she had done as much as she could. The guard had knocked and checked with her after one hour, and again after the second. She knew it was time to go, and she had to get back to Atlanta for Nick.

She finally rose from her seat, and stood with him.

"I hope you are keeping track of your time," he said. "I'll pay you as soon as I can."

She swallowed hard. She sensed he had practiced that promise several times. He might have lost the arrogance everyone remembered, but he hadn't lost the pride.

"I'll keep records," she said, knowing that she wouldn't. He had already given her far more than she could ever repay.

He stood. "Thank you for the books."

"I have several more for you."

The sides of his eyes crinkled and one side of his mouth tugged upward. A shadow of a smile. Maybe only a hint. Her heart thumped more rapidly. She ached to lean over and touch him, but she couldn't. She was his attorney, for Pete's sake.

Instead her hands fumbled inside her briefcase for the books. One was a popular suspense novel. The other was a history of Atlanta. She'd added several recent news magazines to the pile, along with two copies of *Popular Mechanics*.

He looked at her under hooded eyes.

She grinned. "I told Mr. O'Donnell you could fix anything."

"O'Donnell?"

"An Irishman," she said with satisfaction.

"I'll see if the library has a book on car repairs."

She suspected if the library did, Murphy would well fit Mr. O'Donnell's needs. She'd seldom met anyone with a quicker mind.

She knocked on the door.

"Mrs. Farrell?" Murphy's voice was hesitant.

She turned back and looked at him questioningly.

"Do you think you could get me a picture of my...daughter?"

The question was a sledgehammer into her chest. "I'll try."

He nodded, then turned as the guard entered, fitted handcuffs back on him.

His back went a little straighter, but he didn't turn back to her. Instead, he disappeared out the door, leaving the room very, very empty. It wasn't until then she realized how much he'd dominated it.

Julie picked Murphy up at the gates of Reidsville a week following the hearing. After an extremely long and difficult hearing, he had been granted a parole predicated on a number of conditions, including a job and a place to stay. Murphy had handled each question with precision and grace, surprising even her. He had kept his voice even, had expressed regret over events ten years earlier. He'd admitted he didn't know whether he had any skills, but was ready to take any kind of job.

The decision had produced the euphoria of victory at first, then second thoughts. Had Murphy been too good, too prepared. Were Dan and Jerry right? Had she really thought through the implications of her crusade?

She especially had doubts about his living arrangements. She had not been able to find a suitable place for him to live, especially since he didn't have transportation, so she'd offered him her garage apartment. She'd spent the last several days making it habitable: clean sheets and blankets for the bed; towels; food in the old refrigerator left over from the home's previous owner. The space included a bathroom and one large room, one side containing a refrigerator, sink, stove and small table, the other a bed and several comfortable old chairs. The bath had an old-fashioned bathtub sitting on metal feet and a rigged shower above.

The walls needed painting, but she didn't have time to do that. She tried to add some color with a gaily patterned rug and matching curtains. She'd located a bookcase at a garage sale and filled it with some of her own favorite books. Finally, she'd purchased an inexpensive color television.

She had sat down with Nick and explained that someone would be living in the apartment, the man who had helped her and him during the accident. He had been sick, she said, and Nick should respect his privacy.

But Nicholas had been beside himself with excitement at the thought of a new friend, especially the one who had "saved" him. She had worried that Nick would pester Murphy to distraction, that Murphy, a convicted murderer, would be geographically close to her son. That thought had struck her anew during the middle of the night after the hearing.

She felt traitorous even thinking it. Yet it nagged at her. She was a mother, first and foremost. Was she putting her own son in danger? Though she kept pushing the thought away, the possibility haunted her.

She owed Murphy. She owed him more than she could ever repay, but did she owe him enough to endanger her child?

She didn't think he was dangerous. If she had, she never would have fought for him as she had, regardless of what he had done for her. But what if she was wrong? She certainly had been wrong before.

All those questions darted through her mind as she waited one hour, then another. She had brought her laptop with her, knowing she might wait. Bureaucracy, particularly prison bureaucracy, never moved quickly. But she had not been able to concentrate. She was too aware of demons in her head, especially a particularly evil one that reminded her how attracted she was to him.

Stupid, stupid, stupid.

She would just have to find him a new place to live once the publicity died down and he had held a job several months.

Several months!

Jerry had wanted to come with her, but she had demurred. Jerry was openly hostile to Murphy, and particularly to her plan to let him stay on her property. The fact that she had no choice—that he wouldn't be released without an acceptable place to stay—hadn't swayed his opposition one bit.

The gate finally opened. Murphy stood still for a moment, his gaze searching the parking lot, the fields beyond. He was wearing a pair of jeans and a light blue denim shirt that she had bought for him, and he held a paper bag. It was small evidence, she thought, of ten years.

She stood so he could see her. He squinted against the November sun, then walked slowly to the passenger side. "Get in," she said, sensing how awkward, how uncertain, he must feel. She certainly would, if she was going out into a world of which she knew little.

He opened the door and sat inside, hesitating before closing the door. She wondered what it felt like for him, being free. He probably just wanted to stand there, soak in the fresh air without being encircled by bars and fences. It would be a fine feeling to someone who had spent ten years inside, but also to someone who hadn't known anything else.

She wished she could stop hurting for him, empathizing with him. She wished there wasn't this terribly strong connection with him that made it so. She wished he didn't look so appealing as his eyes swept the horizon.

Finally, he turned to her. His eyes were so damned blue, so damned direct. "I'll find a way to repay you," he said.

She could only nod. She couldn't force herself to ask him how he felt. He probably didn't even know how he felt. He was probably assimilating feelings, impressions, as she had seen him do before.

She started the car. The trip was going to be hell. She had never been more physically, sensually, aware of a man before. Her heart hammered and she felt herself grow warm even though she'd turned on the air-conditioning in her new car.

Julie reached over and turned on the CD player. She needed something—anything—to distract her. Unfortunately, the music was Ravel's

Bolero, a particularly sensuous piece of music that did nothing to reduce the heat she felt.

What in God's name had she done?

The silence stretched as they drove through the piney woods of central Georgia. But after the first few minutes it was not awkward. He was absorbing everything. She suspected his eyes missed nothing.

Just outside Atlanta, she stopped at a well-known barbecue restaurant. She realized she didn't know what she liked. Perhaps he didn't, either. He'd had no choices since his injury. But Nick loved barbecue and this meant she wouldn't have to cook tonight.

Murphy—she kept trying to think of him as Murphy rather than the more intimate Ryan—looked at her with those dark questioning eyes.

"We'll go in," she said. "I'll also buy some to take home. Nick loves barbecue."

He unwound his long legs as he left the car, and again she was struck by the athletic grace of his movements. He waited for her to go ahead. Instinctive courtesy? Learned behavior? Would she always question everything he did?

Once inside, she slid into a booth. He was watching every movement, and he followed suit. If he was uncertain, if this was new to him, he showed no sign of it.

He's faking. The demons were at work again.

He carefully studied the menu.

"The barbecue sandwiches are really good," she said. "So are the ribs."

His eyes lifted from the menu so that she was subjected to their full power. They were almost magnetic. Heck, they *were* magnetic. She pitied the poor criminals who had once come under them.

Murphy's gaze went back to the menu, studying it as she had watched him study the fields they had passed.

A waitress came over, her eyes going automatically to Murphy and lingering on him appreciatively. Julie suddenly saw him as the waitress probably saw him.

He looked confident. If he had any fear of the future, he didn't show it. But neither did she see any joy in him, any expectation. Only that infernal watchfulness. Physically, he was very attractive. He'd rolled up his sleeves and his arms were still tan from months on the road gang. His shoulders were broad, and his long legs, which stretched out from under the table, indicated a height over six feet. He had apparently shaved just before leaving because there was no sign of that five o'clock shadow, and his dark hair was mussed as if he'd run his fingers through it. His fingers thrummed on the table with that restless energy she'd sensed so often.

His lips had a crook to them on the left side, giving him a slight perpetual frown. Skin around his eyes crinkled and his heavy dark eyebrows gave him a deceptively lazy look.

She ordered a sandwich and iced tea and listened as he ordered two sandwiches, french fries and a soft drink.

"And pie?" the waitress said, obviously flirting with him.

He nodded.

The waitress turned with a flounce as he studied the interior of the restaurant. It resembled a log cabin, its walls plain as were the tables. Most of the tables, despite the fact it was late afternoon, were filled. Then his gaze settled on their own table, the different kinds of sauces that were offered.

"Hot sauces," she explained. "The more x's, the hotter they are."

"Do you like hot?"

"Yes," she said, but she didn't need anything hot. She felt altogether too warm already.

His gaze bored into her. "I haven't thanked you properly for everything. I meant what I said. I'll pay you back every cent."

"If that's what you want."

"It's what I want."

"I told Mr. O'Donnell you will be in Thursday or Friday. I thought you would...like a day or two to get settled."

"I want to start as soon as possible," he said.

"All right. I must warn you, though, my son is very eager to meet you. He'll probably try to monopolize you. He knows you're the one that pulled him from the car."

Uncertainty flickered across his face.

"You just treat kids like miniature adults," she assured him. "Don't underestimate them."

"I don't even know how to talk to adults," he said, and for a moment she wondered whether he was joking. She couldn't tell, because the expression in his eyes didn't change. The crook of his lips turned up just a trifle, barely enough to notice.

"I think you can manage," she said dryly.

He could probably do anything he wanted, she thought. She wondered how long it would take him to discover that.

When the food came, he ate with precision. Every particle. She tried not to watch, but she did so want him to enjoy it. He'd had little pleasure since the accident, and probably none in the ten years before that. Dear God, she wanted to see a smile.

He was forty-one years old, and many, if not all, had been hard years. Though his dark hair showed only traces of gray, his face showed the wear of those years in the lines that jutted from his eyes, the creases in his forehead when he frowned. She tried to equate this man with the one she had tried to puzzle together. The only common denominator appeared to be his control. Despite his loss of memory, his loss of self, he maintained a tight control on himself, always watching, listening, absorbing.

"Aren't you going to eat?"

She looked down at her untouched sandwich. Where was her own control? She seemed to have lost it the first day she'd visited him in the hospital.

Almost obediently, she picked it up and started eating, forcing her gaze away from him and down to her plate. For some reason, the food seemed tasteless.

His body moved restlessly across from her, and his knee touched hers. Heat and confusion surged through her.

"Sorry, Mrs. Farrell."

She was acutely aware of his deep, lazy drawl through the warm tingling that spread throughout her body. She fought against it. She wanted to tell him to call her Julie, but she couldn't quite force the words from her lips. It would be one more step toward an intimacy that was already beginning to drown her.

She took another bite. The sandwich had gone from tasteless to cardboard. Having him live in her backyard was definitely not a good idea. Yet without an address, he would go straight back to prison.

Her gaze met his again. Damn, did his eyes have to be so blue? Douglas had had blue eyes, but his had been light, not this mysterious deep dusk blue that seemed to see straight into her soul. She didn't want anyone to be able to do that; she wanted her independence. But his every expression, every movement, seemed to imprint itself on her.

He'd finished the pie and she had received her takeout order. She started to take her billfold from her purse, but he was quicker. He took the bill, pulled some money from his jeans and handed it to the waitress.

When the waitress reluctantly disappeared, the side of his lips with the crook twisted slightly. "They said I had two hundred and fifty-six dollars in my account," he explained, holding what he hadn't given to the waitress. "How much were my clothes?"

Two hundred and fifty dollars after ten years! Not much to show for a decade.

She hesitated before answering. She didn't want to take everything he had, yet she knew from the glint in his eyes he was about to insist. She had bought him two pair of jeans and three shirts as well as underclothes. She thought he would want to purchase what else he would need. She wanted to tell him he could pay her later, but he had a stubborn look on his face, and by now she was accustomed to the pride which he'd managed to preserve throughout his hospital stay and weeks in prison.

"One hundred and fifty dollars and some change. I don't remember exactly."

He started to count out the money.

"Make it eighty," she said, "and you can pay me the rest later. You'll need some more clothes, some food."

He opened his mouth, and she knew a protest was coming. "I—"

She interrupted him. "Why don't you work it off? I need some work done in the yard and around the house."

His eyes brightened and for the first time she saw a hint of a smile. "I might just destroy your home." The trace of a dimple in his chin deepened. The tingling in her extremities started again.

"Everyone said you were good at fixing things. Dr. Dailey said you should remember learned skills. And I do have some books. I was going to try to fix some things myself, but after flooding my kitchen with water, I decided to leave repairs to experts."

"I don't think I qualify, but I think I can manage yard work."

"Then it's a bargain."

He looked at her under those heavy brows. He'd been very careful to keep all his actions and words impersonal, even formal, but now his gaze seemed to be seeing her as a woman, and her heartbeat slowed. She felt her face warm under his perusal, somehow feeling wanting. She had pulled her hair back in a clip and, knowing she would be spending long hours in the car, had opted for an old but comfortable pair of slacks and a cotton short-sleeve pullover shirt. Her lipstick was probably long gone.

Doug had always wanted her to look perfect. After his death, she had given most of her dress clothes away, retaining only the business suits she wore to work. Since she did much of her work at home, she'd lived in comfortable sweat suits in cool weather and jeans and over-large shirts in the summer.

Why did she care what Murphy thought? She'd vowed she would never reshape herself again for any man. She'd questioned, in fact, whether she ever wanted to marry again. Eligible men her age were scarce. Most were either married, or something was seriously wrong with them.

Like being convicted of murder.

She stood. "Ready to go?" she asked belatedly, hoping that her legs were steadier than her common sense.

He uncoiled himself from the table, took the takeout package and followed her out the door.

Once outside, she took a deep breath of fresh air, then stepped onto the gravel-covered parking lot. Her thoughts were back at the table, her attention lost in the bewildering attraction she felt for Murphy. Her foot slipped in the gravel, and she felt herself falling. A strong hand caught her elbow, pulled her upright. The other hand went around her to give her balance.

But it didn't balance her at all. Her legs suddenly felt boneless as heat from his touch ignited flames deep inside her. She froze, afraid he might feel her reaction, hear the increased tempo of her heart, of her breathing.

His hands lingered, his warm fingers splaying against her skin.

He was behind her, and her head hit just under his chin, not far from his heart. She thought she could hear it pounding as she felt a sudden pressure in his hands.

She breathed deeply, forcing air from her lungs. *Not a good idea, Julie Farrell. Not a good idea at all.*

She jerked away, feeling his arms drop as she did so. Her keys were already in her hands and almost blindly she made for the car. But she looked down. She couldn't afford to stumble again.

Not in any way.

Chapter 9

How in the hell was he going to keep his hands off her?

He wondered that the rest of the way to Atlanta. She'd felt so good for that fraction of a second. He'd wanted to hold her there, to feel her against his body. He had only reluctantly let her go.

Mrs. Farrell. His attorney. His landlady.

His lifeline.

He really hadn't believed it when the parole board granted his parole, nor was he sure he could function outside a cell, outside of being told what to do every minute of the day. But she had been so sure he could, she'd made him believe he could.

Doubts continued to plague him, however. What if he was a killer? What if that part of him hadn't been erased as thoroughly as his memory had? Could he earn a living on his own? Would he remember any of those skills Mrs. Farrell—Julie—was positive he would?

He still couldn't quite believe he was free. He couldn't see enough of a sky unscarred by bars or fences. He looked at all the people in the cars they passed, and he wondered what they did, who they loved, where they were going.

Freedom. It was exquisitely painful, and he was aware of every sensation: the brush of the wind in his hair, a ray of sun baking his skin, the barely noticeable sweet scent of Mrs. Farrell, the marvelous sound of music, the comfortable feel of clothes that didn't mark him as a convict. All of them made him feel alive, really alive, for the first time since the accident.

After several miles, he had rolled his window down, preferring the rush of air to air-conditioning, the feeling of being closed in. Mrs. Farrell hadn't said anything, so he figured it was all right. He'd taken pleasure in watching her fine hair blow against her cheek. Her gray eyes would turn toward him occasionally, and he thought of how appealing they were.

He ached to touch her, to simply reach his hand over and touch her shoulder. That need grew stronger, more intense with every mile. He controlled that need, though, just as he'd been forced to control all his feelings these past few weeks. Prison required a dichotomy of skills: toughness with other cons and constraint with guards. His control faded quickly as he shared the intimacy of the car with a woman who so appealed to him. He finally rested his head against the seat and closed his eyes, his senses absorbing, memorizing, cataloging every moment.

When they'd stopped to eat, he'd studied the menu, not quite sure what to get until she mentioned her preference, and then he'd enjoyed every bite. Food in prison had been tasteless, but having little but the hospital to compare it to, he'd accepted it as the norm. He wondered how many other foods tasted as good as these sandwiches. He'd tried to concentrate on them, rather than the woman who sat opposite him.

And then she had stumbled, and he'd felt her softness, and something fierce and electric ran through his body. His body reacted, and he suddenly felt a tightening in his groin, but then she'd stepped away and nearly raced for the car. His chest felt as if a belt were tightening around it. He'd had to force himself to get in the car. He rolled down the window further, hoping the fresh air would brush away the cobwebs in his mind, cool the heat of his body.

"We'll be home in an hour," she said, breaking the heavy silence.

Home. What was that? He had not the faintest idea. He hadn't had the faintest idea of where to go or how to find a place when she had offered a part of her property to him. A garage apartment. He wasn't quite sure what that involved, but he also understood that she had tried to find him other places. No one had wanted him.

And now he would be living close to her and her child. His first reaction was to refuse—she already awakened too many emotions in him—but it was soon made clear that he would not be released unless he accepted. He made a vow then and there she would not regret it.

But the long ride with her—with her subtle scent so enticing after the smell of prison—had made him wonder whether both of them had made a mistake.

They were silent as she drove through heavy traffic, then turned off
an expressway to a narrower street. Two more turns and she eased into
a driveway that ran alongside a brick home. She stopped at a gate, and
turned to him. "Can you get out and open it?"

Glad to stretch his legs, he opened the car door and then the gate,
pulling both sides open and watching as she drove into the yard and
parked the car in a garage that had steps running along the outside. He
closed the gates behind her and waited for her to get out.

"It's not much of an apartment," she said almost apologetically,
"but until you find something else...."

After his cell, anything would be a palace, but he didn't say anything. He followed her up the steps and waited while she unlocked a
door and walked in. He followed and swallowed hard when he glanced
around the room. She had obviously taken pains to brighten it. He
walked around it, noted the bookcase filled with books, the television
set. She stood at the door watching as he opened a closet door and
found two shirts and a coat there. He looked at the coat.

"It was my husband's," she said. "I hope it fits. There's another
pair of jeans and some...underwear in the bureau. Extra towels and
sheets are in the bottom drawer."

"Your husband?" He suddenly realized how little he knew about
her although he remembered one news account saying she was a
widow.

"He...died five years ago," she said simply.

He nodded and tried another door. A bathroom. A tub and shower.
Some toilet things had been laid out on the sink. A real razor, shaving
cream.

"I put some food in the refrigerator and cabinet," she said. "You
might want some time alone." She hesitated, then added, "My son
has been wanting to meet you and thank you. Can you come over for
ice cream in—" she looked at her watch "—two hours?"

He nodded. It was little enough after everything she had done for
him. "I'll get my things from the car."

She handed him the key. A key. A small thing. Now a very big
thing. For a moment, he couldn't speak.

She had been watching him. Now she backed away. "If there is
anything you need, just knock on my back door. Otherwise I'll expect
you in a couple of hours. You don't have to stay long."

He followed her out the door and down the stairs. He went to the
car and picked up his bag of belongings, carefully locking the car as
he had seen her do.

"Mrs. Farrell?"

She hesitated a moment, then said, "Call me Julie. We're neighbors now."

"Thank you...for everything."

He couldn't force himself to say her name. They were both walking a tightrope. She felt she owed him because of something another man did. He felt he owed her *his* life, and yet because she was now responsible for him, their relationship was unbalanced; she literally had almost complete control as to whether or not he would go back to prison. It had been her advocacy that had freed him, her promise to find him a job and a place to stay; he was only too aware of the inequality of the...alliance.

Her face flushed a moment, then she turned and went out the gates, closing them behind her. The key clutched in one hand, his bag of belongings in the other, he went upstairs to his new home.

Julie forced herself not to look backward. Nick would be waiting for her at Emily's. She had been ridiculously anxious that Murphy like the apartment. She had even hoped for a hint of a smile.

But he'd been quiet during the entire drive and their arrival at the apartment. She wondered whether he was naturally that quiet, or whether he'd just been absorbing everything. Julie tried to put herself in his position. Because he had no memory, he had no anchor. He didn't know what he was capable of, and what he wasn't. And he had to be the most alone person she had ever met. No family except a former wife, and a daughter who'd apparently chosen to forget him.

She had to give him time. Let him make friends. Find out who he was.

She went past two houses, then turned up Emily's walk, only to find Nick bursting out the door.

"He's been waiting at the window," Emily said. "He saw you drive up. It's been all I could do to keep him in the house." She looked at Julie with anxious eyes. "He's here?"

She nodded. Emily was another friend who had voiced doubts, especially about Murphy moving into the neighborhood.

Emily shuddered. "I really don't think you should have done that. The neighbors aren't happy about having a killer here."

Julie's body tensed. "He's not a killer. Do you really think I would put Nick in danger?"

"I think you've been blinded because...he helped you at the accident," Emily said. "I'm just telling you what everyone thinks."

"Will you at least meet him before making up your mind?"

"I don't think so," Emily said, a hard note in her voice. "And if you want me to drive Nick to preschool, you'll have to bring him over here.''

Not Emily. Although her friend had advised caution in her crusade to get Murphy released, Julie hadn't considered she would be so opposed to him living in the neighborhood. But then she hadn't consulted anyone here. She hadn't thought she needed to.

"Can't he find someplace else to live?" Emily questioned. "A half-way house or something?"

"It's only temporary," Julie said.

"Well, we don't like it."

"Who is 'we?'"

"Nearly everyone on these two or three blocks," Emily said. "Mr. Blalock says—"

"You know Mr. Blalock is a paranoid busybody. I expected something like this from him, but you..."

"My husband and I have our daughter to think about."

Julie knew she should be careful, conciliatory, but she could only think of Murphy, how hard he was working to adjust to circumstances that might destroy lesser men. Outrage filled her. "He's never touched a child."

"How do you know? He dealt in drugs. The paper said so. We don't want people like that around our children. I don't understand how you let him in your house."

Emily's face was set, her shoulders rigid, her spine like a steel rod. Julie thought about trying to reason with her, but Nick was staring up at them both with an anxious look on his face.

"Not in front of Nick," she said.

"Why not? He should know—"

"Goodbye, Emily. I'll take Nick to preschool tomorrow. I'll check in the morning to see whether you want me to take Abby—"

"Don't bother," Emily said stiffly. "I'll take her myself."

Julie took Nick's hand in hers. "If that's what you want."

"What we want is a safe neighborhood."

"Goodbye, Emily."

Julie lifted Nick and gave him a big hug, then put him down and walked back to her own house, mentally cursing the story that appeared in the paper immediately after the hearing. A spokesman for the parole board had announced Murphy's release and the conditions. It had, of course, been front page news.

Former Assistant D.A. Shelters Killer Cop

The newspapers loved that label: Killer Cop. She wondered whether they would ever weary of the story. Probably not. Even she understood the drama of it.

"Why is Miz Richards mad?" Nick asked.

"She doesn't think Mr. Murphy should live in the garage." She had already explained to him that the man who had saved his life would be living behind them. He'd been excited beyond words.

But now his face puckered up as he tried to understand. "Why doesn't Miz Richards like him?"

"She thinks he did something bad a long, long time ago."

He puzzled that out. "Did he have to sit in a corner?" That was his punishment when he was bad.

"Something like that," she said.

"You always love me after I sit in the corner."

"I love you even when you sit in the corner," she corrected.

"Then why is Abby's mommy angry?"

Why? Why? Why? Nick's favorite word. Her heart cracked. Was he going to pay for her decision? Abby was his very best friend.

"Because she doesn't understand. But I think she will." Julie crossed her fingers. She hoped Emily would. Surely when she met Murphy...

She unlocked her front door. Her refuge. It had been that, and more, these past few years. She loved this house, far more than she liked the large, showcase home she'd shared with Doug, perhaps because this was *hers.*

Julie regarded it lovingly. It was a small brick bungalow with lots of character. Built in the 1930s, it had been remodeled by the previous owner who'd built bookcases around the fireplace in the living room and enlarged one bathroom to make it almost luxurious. The floors were hardwood, the ceilings high, giving it more spaciousness than indicated by the square footage. She had placed plants everywhere, and she loved the flowery smell each time she entered. Best of all, it had cost one-sixth of the price of her previous home, and she'd found a low mortgage rate.

The garage apartment had been a bonus. She'd originally intended to rent it immediately, but she had been in one of her burrow moods. Except it really wasn't a mood; it had become a way of life. Ever since she'd left Dan's office, she'd consciously avoided other people. Heck, she'd run as fast as she could from any involvement with anyone. Nick had become the center of her life. He had become her *whole* life. Because her computer was connected to the law firm's computers, she did much of her work at home except for meetings.

Now she'd opened her refuge to Murphy, a man who threatened all that safety she'd woven around herself and her son. He didn't threaten their physical safety—she was as sure of that as she was that the sun would rise every day—but today she'd realized the depth of his threat to her emotional well-being. Just sitting with him in the car had altered the calm, predictable world she'd tried so hard to build. That world tilted crazily now.

"Where is he?" Nick demanded.

"I think he's resting," she said. "But he will be over for ice cream soon."

Nick beamed, forgetting the tension he'd left some seconds ago. "Will he like me?"

"Of course. Who wouldn't?" she said.

"And he saved me."

"Yes, he did."

"I want to give him a present."

"I think a picture would make a perfect gift."

Nick loved to draw. He grinned happily and ran off to find paper and crayons.

She poured him a glass of milk and made him a sandwich of the barbecue she had bought. She put both it and potato chips on the kitchen table, then poured herself a glass of wine. When he returned, he sat on the chair, devoured the food, then leaned over a blank piece of drawing paper. "What do you 'pose he likes."

"Woods and trees," she said.

"And a house?"

"Probably a house."

He didn't say anything but bent his head and started drawing.

She took a sip of wine. Let Murphy like it, she prayed silently. She couldn't bear to see Nick's disappointment if he didn't.

Ryan explored every cranny of the apartment. The bureau contained two additional shirts, a white long-sleeve shirt and a pull-on sports shirt. The refrigerator had milk, orange juice, butter, eggs, soft drinks and some sliced meat. The cupboards had also been stocked with coffee, cans of soup, sugar, salt and pepper, bread.

A surfeit of riches. Too much, at the moment, to digest. Too many choices.

The bookcase was the true treasure. Biographies, history, fiction, a set of encyclopedias. He suspected she had selected carefully. He took out each one with worshiping hands, wondering how he could go from hell to heaven so quickly.

He owed it all to one woman.

He looked at the clock on the table next to the bed. Almost seven. Probably an hour had gone by. He would go over to the house at eight.

Ryan leafed through several books but couldn't concentrate on any one of them. Restlessness filled him. No more locked doors. No more manacles. He wanted to explore his freedom. He went to the door and stepped outside, looking at all the trees that shaded the neat mostly brick homes. They were bare of leaves now but still starkly beautiful in the deep dusk of evening. A cool breeze rustled through the branches. He breathed it all in before closing the door behind him without locking it. He never wanted to hear the sound of a lock again.

He heard a sound in the trees and looked toward the sound. A squirrel was jumping from branch to branch, then ran down the tree and scurried across the yard. Something like elation filled him. He soaked in the sights, the sounds, the smell of freedom. He looked up at the sky. The moon appeared a transparent globe in the intense deep blue of an evening sky.

Unable to resist, he walked down the drive, then opened the gate. He didn't have a coat, but he didn't need one. He relished the cool feel of the air, the small bite that made him feel alive. His strides lengthened and he reached the end of the block, then another. Finally, he turned and retraced his steps, though he felt he could walk forever.

Eight. It must be close to that. And he wanted to shave and take a shower, wash off the prison smell. The least he could do for this great gift was be on time.

Julie tried to calm her nervousness. Perhaps he wouldn't come.

Nick was finishing up his picture, carefully inserting colorful flowers. She thought it wonderful for an almost five year old. He had a knack for drawing things in perspective, something she'd noticed few children had.

Still, it was juvenile impressionism at best.

"It's beautiful, Munchkin."

"Do you think he will like it?" His brow furrowed worriedly.

"I think he will, indeed. He needs something for his walls."

"I'll draw another one," he said hopefully.

"Why don't you wait?"

"When will he come? Maybe I'd better go get him."

Anxiety licked at her. He was so expectant. Ryan Murphy was his hero. He didn't remember a great deal about the accident, but he did remember a man who had saved him. And his mommy. His expectations were so great.

A knock came at the door, and Nick gave her a big grin. "Can I open the door?"

"I don't know if he's ready for you or not," she said.

But he was already gone, his hands opening the kitchen door that led to the backyard. When it opened, she watched as he looked up. And up. And up. Until his face was looking almost straight up.

She followed the direction of his gaze. Next to Nick, Ryan Murphy looked like a giant. His hair was wet, but neatly combed, the black practically gleaming under the kitchen light. He had obviously just shaved and he smelled slightly of the men's aftershave she had purchased without knowing his preference.

The shirt stretched across broad shoulders, and its sleeves were still rolled up despite the coolness of the evening. The shirt had obviously been hastily tucked in his jeans, which fit his long legs like a second skin. He radiated male power and grace and suddenly the large kitchen seemed very small.

"I'm Nick," the munchkin said.

To her surprise, Murphy kneeled, his face almost level to Nick's. "I'm Ryan." He held out his hand and Nick's face cracked into a huge smile.

When Murphy released his hand, he didn't get up, and Nick started the speech he'd been preparing. "Thank you very much for saving my life. And Mommy's."

Julie half expected Murphy to deny any such thing—as he had every time she'd mentioned it—which would have bewildered her son. Instead, Murphy said seriously, "You're very welcome."

"I drew you a picture."

"Did you now?"

"Do you want to see it?"

"Very much."

He stood then and Julie felt she was watching a play. He was doing everything right, everything to make a small boy feel comfortable and at ease. He was anything but the cold, distant man everyone had portrayed, or even the cautious Murphy of the past few weeks.

But he still hadn't smiled.

He looked at her. "Mrs. Farrell," he acknowledged. Not "Julie" as she'd asked. "Mrs. Farrell." He was trying to keep her at arm's length. She knew she should do the same. So she merely nodded.

He followed Nick over to the table and took the picture that Nick handed to him with such pride.

Julie held her breath. So far, he had been just right. But would he know how much heart Nick had put into his picture?

He looked at it carefully as Nick watched, then he looked down. "It's the nicest present I've ever had," he said.

It was probably the first one this Ryan Murphy ever received, but Nicholas didn't know that. His grin grew even broader. "Do you play baseball?" he said.

Murphy looked swiftly over toward her.

She shrugged. "We saw a movie about Little League."

"Little League?" He knew the term, or at least he thought he did. But he wasn't quite sure.

"Baseball for little boys. Why don't you sit down?"

He hesitated, then took a chair and folded his long body into it.

"Do you?" Nick persisted.

"I did once," he said.

"Will you teach me? Mommies can't play baseball."

Murphy turned toward her, and, Lord above, she saw a smile play around his lips. "I think your mommy can do almost anything, including slaying dragons."

"Baseball is man's stuff," Nick persisted.

"Man's stuff, huh?"

Nick nodded fervently.

The small hint of the smile widened. It reached Murphy's eyes, then his mouth. She saw the dimple deepen, and the lines around his eyes crinkle. Her heart lurched, then started beating faster as she looked at the two males, one small and one large, uniting in male conspiracy.

She could almost feel the warmth between them envelop her, too.

Cold? Distant?

Had he indeed changed that much? Or could anyone be that facile an actor?

Nick held out his hand, palm straight up like he'd seen on television. Murphy looked over Nick's head toward her, and she pantomimed hitting palm against palm in a ritual peculiar to males.

He imitated her, gently hitting Nick's palm with his own.

"We have chocolate ice cream," Nick said. "Do you like ice cream?"

Murphy nodded.

That was all Julie needed to spur her into action. She went to the freezer compartment and took out the ice cream, putting big scoops in two of the bowls, a small one for herself.

Murphy tasted it. The smile was gone, but he looked more relaxed than she had ever seen him.

Nick was rattling on between bites of ice cream, telling his new friend about the movie they'd seen. He appeared perfectly happy that

Murphy said little. Murphy, on the other hand, was attentive, his eyes filled with a sad kind of longing while he offered enough reaction to keep Nick content.

Once the ice cream was gone, she looked at Nick. "Time for bed."

He looked at Murphy. "Can you tell me a story?"

For the first time, he looked uncomfortable. "I don't know any."

"That's okay. You can read me one."

Julie shook her head. "Not tonight, Munchkin. I think Mr. Murphy is tired."

Nick looked as if he was going to argue.

"*Now*, Munchkin," she said, "and I'll read you one. You go on up and put on your jammies."

Reluctantly, he pulled back his chair. He marched over to Ryan. "It's good to meetcha."

The hint of a smile again. "It was good to meetcha, too."

"I'll see you tomorrow."

"Perhaps," Julie intervened, guiding him out the door, through the hall to his bedroom.

"I like him, Mommy."

"I do, too, but we have to be careful not to bother him."

"I don't think I bothered him."

"I don't think you did, either, but he's going to be very busy."

He started to take off his clothes. "You promised to read me a story."

"Yep," she said. "Just crawl into bed. Count to twenty."

He looked at her suspiciously. "I can't count that high."

"Yes, you can. Practice so you can show Mr. Murphy."

"One, two, three..."

She closed the door behind her.

Chapter 10

Ryan paced the room as he waited for her to return. He had to work off some of the emotions he didn't know how to handle, feelings that threatened to overwhelm him.

The strongest of which was stark longing.

A few moments in this kitchen had made him want the love he felt here, the sense of belonging that teased and seduced. Had he ever felt that with his wife and child? He knew then he had to meet his former wife, talk to her. He had to know more about himself, or the man he had once been.

He swore under his breath, words he'd learned only too well during the weeks since the accident. He had so many questions and no frame of reference to even begin to answer them. He just had a juggernaut of emptiness that pressed into his heart, his mind, his soul. He couldn't afford to care, to love, to even give until he knew what kind of man he was, what he was capable of.

Yet he found himself caring. He had been charmed by the boy, the first individual who had wholly and completely accepted him as he was. Even Julie had had doubts, and occasionally still did. He saw them flare in her eyes when she didn't know he was watching.

But Nicholas Farrell had no reservations.

He found his hands gingerly fingering Nicholas's drawing. He thought it must be very good for a child, but it was the thought and care with which it was created that brought rushes of warmth cascading through him and made him yearn for more. It truly was the first physical gift he remembered, though the child's mother had given him many of another kind.

Just treat them like miniature adults.

That had been easy. He'd found himself relaxing in the presence of others for the first time since he'd awakened from the coma and found himself a pariah. He had reveled, in fact, in Nicholas's open liking. He'd had to hesitate only when the boy had asked about baseball. Would he remember anything about it, as he remembered how to read? How hard was it to throw a ball, anyway?

That damn frustration was crowding him again, as was the obsession to learn more about himself.

He tried to push it aside, concentrating instead on the room. It was a large kitchen, made charming by whimsical touches. Teapots danced across a trim near the ceiling, and flowering plants hung near the windows. A smiling cow held a roll of paper towels on one counter and a fisher boy cookie jar dominated another. The refrigerator door was crowded with colorful paintings like the one he held in his hand, and an oddly shaped piece of pottery was proudly displayed on the table. More work by the boy.

He tried to equate all the whimsy with the practical Julie Farrell who had been so businesslike with him, who had been so efficient in representing him and preparing for his release. But everything about her was softer, more vulnerable in this house. He wandered through the door to what apparently was the living area. Like the kitchen, the room was inviting. The focal point was obviously the fireplace which was flanked on both sides by full bookcases. A television, cornered at one end, looked like an afterthought.

An overstuffed sofa and two chairs, obviously purchased for comfort, furnished the room as well as more plants. Paintings, all brightly alive landscapes, provided a peaceful tranquility. Large windows looked out to a heavily wooded front yard, and an outdoor gas lamp illuminated several bird feeders.

He heard a noise at the door and looked away from the window. Julie Farrell was standing in the doorway, watching him.

"I like this room," he said.

She smiled, a bright spontaneous opening of her face. He realized then how few times he had seen her smile so openly. Usually she was reserved, cautious. The smile was a gift, like Nicholas's painting.

"So do I," she said. "It's not very stylish, but it's everything I like."

It was everything he liked, too. Deep down in his gut, he felt comfortable here, as if he belonged here. It was a dangerous feeling. So was the heat forming in his groin and the ache that made him very aware that he wanted not only that sense of belonging but her. The power of his need astounded him. A piercing stab of loneliness ripped into him as he realized how impossible either was.

"I'd better go," he said.

Her smile faded, and her gaze locked on his. Awareness was like electricity between them, hot and sizzling and every bit as deadly. And numbing. He wanted to force his legs to move, but they didn't obey his command.

"Yes," she whispered, answering his statement. Yet she didn't move either.

A warm glow radiated inside him. She had changed to blue jeans and a shirt, and she looked young and alive and vibrant. And incredibly desirable. Her cheeks had turned red, and her gray eyes, usually so cool, fairly smoldered with emotion.

Six strides and he could reach her, touch her. Kiss her.

He ached to do it. Only caution borne of the last few months stopped him. Ten years. Ten years without...contact with a woman.

Libido? Testosterone? He'd read enough to know the meaning of both. Was ten years of celibacy making him more...aware? Did bodies react to memories the mind erased? He didn't know. Didn't care. He just knew he wanted her more intensely than he could ever have imagined.

Damn. If he...

Then what? What in the hell did he have to offer her? No one would even rent an apartment to him. He was subject to supervision for the next ten years. He couldn't leave the state, nor move, nor change jobs without approval. The list of parole restrictions was staggering.

Today's freedom had been fine, even heady, but all the time he knew how fragile it was.

Yet he couldn't make himself leave as he knew he should. Instead, he took a step toward her.

Her eyes locked with his, she moved forward. The rose in her cheeks had spread, and he knew if he reached out he would feel its heat.

Then she stood directly in front of him, her face tilted up to his, her gray eyes smoky with emotion. Her hand reached out and touched his, her fingers exploring the calluses on his hands with a searching tenderness. He found himself lifting it, the back of his hand caressing her cheek even as he locked her fingers in his. Soft. So very soft. And more. So much more. Sun to a soul frozen by time. His arms went around her, and he heard her slight intake of breath as she stretched against his body, fitting into it as if she belonged there.

The ache inside became a throbbing, insistent thing. He lowered his head and his lips met hers, merely brushing hers at first. Their breath intermingled, and his heartbeat quickened, pounding against its cage. Then, finding response, his lips pressed hungrily against hers. Her arms went around him, and he felt himself exploding with a desire long held in check. His mouth opened, his tongue urging her lips to open to him, and they did. He tasted her for a moment, finding the effects irresistible, his pleasure melting all the warnings echoing in his brain.

Her body trembled even as it fit into his so neatly, so perfectly, and he released her lips. "Julie." His voice was a soft groan that came from deep in his throat. He wanted her so damn badly, but he wouldn't force anything she wasn't ready for.

Something like a purr came from her, and he nearly threw her over his shoulder and carried her to the sofa. Every fiber of his body burned. Every instinct told him to take her, that she wanted him as much as he wanted her.

What in the hell are you doing? The voice that had guided him through the past months was yelling at him. Instinct warred against hard learned lessons, against the self-discipline he'd worked so hard to develop. Summoning every ounce of control he had, he stepped away and swore under his breath. *Remember who you are, what you are. Hell, where he was.* He stood there, his body aching, and his heart hurting, telling himself to leave, but unable to do so.

He saw the anguish in her face. The need was there, as well as in him. He felt his body trembling with it, with the overwhelming power it had. He felt the bulge straining against his jeans, the pain of its urgency, the driving agony of the pressure building inside him.

The scent of desire enveloped him. Its pull drew his hand to her face before falling to his side. With a groan, he moved farther away and went to stand in front of the window, staring out with eyes that saw nothing. Lust and need danced with something even more elemental: the yearning for affection, even love. His body and mind felt like a battlefield. A decimated battlefield full of wounded.

A hell of a gift for a woman. Especially one who had given him so much.

And who held his freedom in her hand.

He felt her presence next to him.

"I'm sorry," he muttered.

"Why?" The simple question surprised him.

"I can think of a hundred reasons."

"That many?" Her voice was low but suddenly he heard a hint of amusement, almost as if she was teasing him.

For a moment, he felt his lips twitch. The irreverent reply was totally unexpected.

He turned to face her. "Probably a few more," he said softly. If only she weren't so pretty, so desirable. If only her upper lip wasn't swollen from their kiss. If only her eyes weren't misty from what could only be described as passion. If only he didn't want to lose herself in her.

If only...

But he knew the realities of his life. And all of them spelled grief for her. Leaving her alone was the one and only gift he could give her in return for all she'd done.

"I'd better go," he said, turning away from her, moving swiftly toward the hall leading to the kitchen. He was aware that she was trailing him. He prayed that the evidence of his erection would disappear, that the pressure inside him would fade, but it only seemed to grow greater.

"Ryan?"

He turned.

She stood still, her face still flushed, but her eyes were clear. "Don't be sorry," she said. "I had as much to do with it as you did." She bit her lip. "I won't let it happen again."

"That might be difficult," he said dryly. Probably impossible.

Nothing's impossible. Dr. Dailey's words. Ryan had tried to believe it. Now he wondered. God help him, how was he going to keep his hands off her? Yet he must. He owed her too much to destroy her life, as he'd apparently destroyed so many others. Even if he had changed, he had far too much baggage to enter any relationship on an equal basis. And he couldn't have any other kind.

"You have to see the parole officer tomorrow," she said. "I'll drive you."

"I can take a bus. I've taken far too much of your time." He forced a coolness he didn't feel.

"I'll give you directions in the morning," she said.

He nodded. He had to get out before he grabbed her again.

At least he had a shower. He needed one. A very cold one.

Stunned by what had just happened, by her own behavior, Julie stood stone still for several moments. One moment she was a sensible mother and attorney, the next she was acting like a lovestruck teenager, unable to control herself.

Shame washed over her. And determination that it wouldn't happen again.

She would just have to find Murphy another apartment. A rented house. A halfway house, if necessary. That last thought was repugnant. She was familiar with them, knew the lack of privacy they offered.

Still, she had to do something. Her body still sang with the sensations he'd aroused. She'd been enveloped in some kind of magical cloud. Heck, admit it. Desire. Plain, unvarnished lust. It had been, after all, years since she'd last made love.

Julie had known she shouldn't have touched him, that she should have run as if the Furies were after her. She didn't know what had happened in the past few moments, only that the attraction that always whirled around them suddenly became overpowering. She had stood at the doorway, watching his eyes study the room with a longing that reached into her soul. He had looked so alone, and yet she remembered his gentleness with her son. He had been exactly right with Nick, and it had not been pretense. She watched and she wondered again how it must be to remember nothing and cope, the inner strength it must take to relearn everything and do it without bitterness or anger.

She thought about all of it, and her heart had cracked. All the physical attraction she'd felt between them exploded into pure need. When he had stepped toward her, she found herself reaching out a hand to him. An invitation...

A muscle had worked in his jaw as he looked at her, his dark blue eyes intense. She felt she could get lost in them, but then his lips pressed down on hers and she could think of nothing but the sensations flooding her. Her blood warmed, moving slow and languidly as his kiss deepened. Her arms went around his neck, her fingers catching a short lock of hair. She felt the compulsive movement of his muscles flexing in response to her caress. Then her hands tightened around his broad shoulders.

She still remembered the feel of his tongue probing tentatively inside her mouth, then teasing, almost seducing. All the sensations she'd previously felt were beggared by the new ones, by the incessant wanting clamoring deep inside.

She closed her eyes, recalling every movement, every warm, glowing moment. She'd never wanted a man as much as she wanted Murphy. She'd never felt this bone-melting way before, not even in those first heady days with Douglas.

Even now, she felt as if she was burning inside. She remembered how it felt leaning against him, how well the two of them fitted. She'd always heard cold showers helped. But for some reason she didn't want one. She didn't want that golden glow to dissipate.

She locked the door, then went back into Nick's bedroom. She opened the door softly. His small body was curled under the covers; Prissy, who had been hiding in the bedroom during Ryan's visit, snuggled next to him. Dragon, his stuffed dinosaur, lay on his pillow. She quietly walked in and sat down on the bed, watching his soft breathing in the light from the other room. Her heart always turned to a puddle when she looked at him. She wanted to give him the world.

She knew how much he'd wanted a father. She'd seen how quickly he warmed to Ryan. Was she setting him up for deep disappointment, for the same kind of terrible loss she'd felt at eight when her father disappeared? She'd waited for him for years to return, running to the door every time someone knocked or to the phone when anyone called. She knew that was why she'd stayed with Douglas, even after she realized the mistake she'd made.

Would he have ever stooped to talk to a small boy?

She doubted it.

She tried to remember his face, but it was blurry. She remembered the impact of his charm, though. He was one of those people who was truly charismatic and when he wanted, he could charm birds from the trees.

Murphy had none of that charm. Apparently he'd never had it. But he radiated a quiet strength that she realized Doug had never had. God help her, she'd been his for the asking tonight, and he'd obviously wanted her, but he'd had the...integrity to back away from a moment that they both might regret.

She had not the slightest idea how she would handle that attraction between them in the future. But she must. For all their sakes. With a groan, she leaned down and kissed Nick, gathering up the blanket around his shoulders. "I won't ever let anything hurt you," she whispered.

She stood and went to the window, where Murphy had stood moments earlier, his eyes staring blindly out. Her haven. Her burrow. The one safe place in all the world.

She wasn't so sure how safe it was any longer.

Ryan spent a sleepless night. The bed was too soft, the room too large. His body had apparently become accustomed to the narrow prison bed with its thin, hard mattress and rough blankets.

He tried not to think his sleeplessness might be caused by something else. Or someone else. He tried not to remember how his body felt when he'd caught Julie Farrell at the restaurant, how neatly she'd fit into his arms. But his body continued to react to the memory despite the cold shower. Despite several cold showers.

He found himself prowling the room and finally indulged himself with a sandwich and milk. It was an extraordinary experience, choosing something for himself. He thought he could grow to like it. Then he turned on the television in desperation, hoping it would lull him to sleep, take his mind from the tormenting thoughts of the woman next door. Instead, he heard a segment reporting his release and Julie Farrell's role in his parole hearing.

"Mrs. Farrell, a former assistant district attorney, successfully represented former Detective Ryan Murphy at the hearing. Murphy rescued Mrs. Farrell and her son from a burning car three months ago.

Positioned in front of the sprawling Reidsville prison, the reporter continued for another moment before the anchorman cut him off to go to a train wreck.

Ryan turned it off. He wondered whether the news stories about him would ever end.

When dawn filtered through the windows, he pulled on the jeans and the same shirt he'd worn yesterday. Maybe he would get some work done in the yard. He opened the door, taking pleasure in that simple act and took the steps two at a time. He entered the garage. The car took up half of the garage. A lawn mower, tools and boxes littered the second half.

He went back outside. The grass was a little long, but he didn't think either Julie or her neighbors would be particularly pleased at his mowing the lawn this time of morning. Trees crowded the yard. Two of them were surrounded by flower beds dominated by weeds. He kneeled and started pulling.

He'd cleared one bed when he was aware of Julie standing at the door. He wondered how long she'd been watching, and even how long he'd been working. Pleasure. It had been pure pleasure working in the dirt, doing something useful that produced results. The November air was cool, the early sun pleasant. The earth felt good in his hands.

He started to rise as she came down the steps and he brushed sweat from his forehead with the back of his hand.

She looked at the neat pile of pulled weeds, the cleared bed. "I didn't mean you should work at the break of dawn. Or have you been here all night?"

"I'm not used to soft beds," he said. "I enjoyed this." He hesitated, then said, "I must have done gardening before." He realized it was kind of a question. He wondered whether she knew much about his other life, the one before prison.

"I don't know," she said. "You did have a home in DeKalb County which is mainly suburban with large yards."

"I want to know more about...Ryan Murphy."

She was silent. She was wearing blue slacks and a turtleneck sweater, and her dark hair had been brushed back and held by a simple silver clasp. If she'd had as bad a night as he had, she didn't look it. Her gray eyes were clear, her skin glowing in the morning sun.

"Can you tell me more than you have?"

"A little, perhaps. But now I have to take Nick to school. And you need directions to the parole office." She turned and headed back toward the kitchen. He put the garden tools down and followed her.

Nick was eating breakfast and he beamed at him. "'Mornin', Ryan."

Ryan permitted himself a slight smile. "'Morning, Nicholas."

"I'm going to school."

"Your mother told me."

"Will you teach me how to play baseball when I get home?"

"Mr. Murphy may not be here," she said. "I told you he's going to work for Mr. O'Donnell."

Ryan was grateful she didn't tell the boy he first had to see his parole officer. He wondered exactly how much she had told Nicholas, or how much the boy understood.

Nick's face fell.

"We'll try," Ryan said, not sure whether Julie Farrell wanted him to spend time with her son. She was decidedly cool this morning. And why not, after he'd practically attacked her last night?

"Mommy?"

"We'll see," she said, not quite looking at Ryan as she found a piece of paper and brought it over to where he leaned against a counter. She put it down, then poured herself some coffee. "Would you like some coffee?" she asked him.

The coffee smelled wonderful. He hadn't been sure how to make any, and so he'd just poured himself a glass of milk.

"Yes."

She already had a cup out and she poured coffee into it. "Sugar or milk?"

"No."

She handed it to him silently, then took a pencil out of a drawer and returned to the blank piece of paper. She wrote as she spoke. "When you go out the driveway, turn left. Go three blocks, then turn left again and go another block. That's Peachtree Road. Go across the road, and you can catch a bus there. Ask the bus driver where to connect with a bus which goes to the Fulton County Courthouse. You had better give yourself two hours. I'm not sure of the schedules.''

He nodded.

''Are you sure I can't give you a ride?''

''I have to start doing things for myself someday. It might as well be today.''

''When you get back, we'll go see Mr. O'Donnell. I'm working here at home today.''

Thank God, she didn't ask him if he had bus fare. He already felt as old as Nick. ''Yes, ma'am,'' he said.

She looked at him sharply, then smiled sheepishly. ''Did I sound that officious?''

He took a sip of the coffee, expecting the same flat metallic taste as prison coffee. Instead it had a rich aroma and taste. He thought he'd never tasted anything so good. But then, he had thought that a lot recently. ''It's good,'' he said, avoiding her question.

She avoided it, too. ''I have to go. Nick and I will walk you outside.''

He took another sip and started to leave the cup.

''Take it with you,'' she said.

Nick jumped out of his chair and went for the door, holding it open. When Ryan passed him, Nick grabbed his free hand. ''I'll walk with you.''

The hand felt very little, and fragile, in his big one, and yet he felt grateful for the trust it indicated. Yesterday's warmth crept back inside as he listened to Nick's chatter, trying to comprehend the stream of consciousness conversation. He obviously made the right replies, because Nick smiled up at him.

When they reached the garage, he opened it. Nick stopped and looked at his mother. ''Where's Abby?''

''Her mother's taking her today.''

Ryan thought he heard a sudden tightness in her voice and he looked down at her.

Her eyes had clouded. He suddenly wondered whether Abby's absence had anything to do with him.

He remembered the television report last night. The story was probably all over the newspapers, too.

Had he harmed her more than he thought?

She flashed him a sudden smile. "Good luck."

He found himself smiling back. His admiration for her climbed. She never gave up.

Well, hell, he wouldn't either.

Chapter 11

Ryan finished the coffee, took a shower, then changed clothes, putting on the long-sleeve white shirt and the clean pair of jeans.

He looked at a letter he'd been given just before leaving prison. He was to report to a man named Davidson at the county courthouse today at ll:00 a.m. Julie—he couldn't think of her any other way now—had told him he would probably have to report weekly.

He hated the idea. He was growing tired of every word, every movement being watched, being judged. Ten years. Ten more years of walking on the sharp edge of a knife, knowing that one mistake could send him back to an existence that wasn't worth living.

Reluctantly, he put a twenty-dollar bill and some change in his pocket, leaving the rest of his limited cash under the third shirt in the chest. Then he took Julie's instructions and started for the bus stop.

The sun was brighter, the day warmer, than it had been an hour earlier, and he didn't need the jacket. He enjoyed the coolness of the day. His cell at Reidsville had been airless and hot; there had been no air-conditioning, no fresh breeze to brush away the odor of hundreds of bodies and the fear and hate and hopelessness that permeated the isolation section.

He bought a paper from a box at the bus stop. His worst fears were realized as he scanned the first page, then the second, where he found what he was dreading.

Parole Board Defends Decision Freeing Killer Cop

The story quoted a spokesman for the board saying a number of factors were involved in granting the parole, including the prisoner's heroism in saving a woman and child, his exemplary prison record, and continuing health problems. The district attorney involved in the case did not oppose the parole.

Above the story was the old photo of him the paper had previously used.

The damn story was going to live forever. And Julie would probably pay for it. He crumpled the newspaper and threw it into a trash bin just as the bus approached. He had the right change out, thanks to Julie's instruction, and he stepped up, asking the driver about changing buses. Armed with that information, he found a seat by himself.

He'd apparently lived in Atlanta all his life, many of them as a police officer. He should know it well. *Something* should trigger a memory. But as the bus passed office building after office building, then entered the downtown area, he recognized nothing. No familiarity. No shadow of a memory.

He had no trouble switching buses, nor finding the Fulton County parole offices. Julie's directions had been specific. He hesitated outside a cubicle a secretary directed him to, steeling himself against a hostility he'd learned to expect. After taking a deep breath, he knocked, then entered at a gruff "Come in."

Davidson was hunched over a desk so loaded with papers Ryan thought it would fall under the weight. He didn't look up from one of them until Ryan was all the way inside.

"Murphy?"

"Yes."

"Yes, sir," Davidson corrected him.

Ryan bit back a retort, but remembered Julie's warning. Do as he was told. But damn, the "sirs" were grating on him.

"Yes, sir," he replied.

"Sit down." Davidson looked at his watch. "You're on time. Good. How did you get here?"

"Two buses."

"No problems?" He looked at Murphy under heavy lids and bushy brows.

"No."

Davidson raised an eyebrow at the lack of a sir, but didn't say anything. Instead, he picked up the file he had been reading and turned his gaze back on it. "Says here you claim to have amnesia."

Ryan didn't reply. It hadn't really been a question.

Davidson looked up, and Ryan studied him. He was a large man, big boned and now a little overweight. Probably approaching fifty or so, he looked overworked and tired even at this hour in the morning.

"You don't remember anything?"

Damn, but he was tired of that question. But this man was all that stood between him and a bus back to Reidsville.

"No." Then after a slight pause, he added, "Sir."

"Did you get away with that in prison?"

Ryan felt his jaw stiffen. No, he hadn't. He'd learned very quickly to say sir. Once when he hadn't said it quickly enough, he'd been slammed against the bars of his cell. It had taken every ounce of his will power not to strike back.

"Murphy?"

"No, sir, I didn't." He kept hearing Julie's warning. *They'll try to make you angry to see what happens. Keep control. Always keep control.*

"That's better." The parole officer continued to study him under heavily hooded eyes. After a moment he handed Ryan two sheets of paper. "Those are the rules you must follow. If you move, if you change jobs—hell, if you sneeze, I want to know about it. I'm sure you're aware that the police can pick you up any time for questioning. You will cooperate. Every time you come here you will also give us a urine sample which will be tested for drugs. I can also show up at your apartment or your place of work and demand a sample." He let the words sink in. "At this point, you have damn few rights. Parole is a privilege." He hesitated. "I'm surprised they let you go at all. Some people went way out on a limb for you. Don't cut it off."

The observation didn't require an answer, but he nodded.

"Mrs. Farrell said you have a job."

"I'm going by there this afternoon."

Davidson handed him a card. "Call me when it's firm. I want to know your hours and how much you'll be making. A portion of your earnings go to the county for your supervision."

So he had to pay for his own humiliation. "Yes...sir."

Davidson smiled but Ryan didn't see any humor in his eyes.

"The secretary outside will give you a cup. Your name is on it. Use the restroom to provide a sample."

Davidson stood. "You really have lost your memory."

Again, it wasn't a question. Ryan stood also, waiting.

"We knew each other ten years ago."

Ryan stiffened. "How?"

"You were after one of my parolees."

"Did I get him?"

"Yes. You usually did, I was told."

"Did I step on your toes?"

"You could say that. But I didn't take offense. You were doing your job."

The parole officer's voice was almost friendly now. As if Ryan had passed some kind of test.

"Call me about the job," Davidson said. "If you get it, you can call me next week. You won't have to come in."

"Yes, sir." It came a little easier this time, but not much.

Davidson grinned. "Detective Murphy would never have forced himself into saying 'sir.'"

"It's not easy for me, either," Ryan admitted dryly.

"I noticed," Davidson said. "But you did it. You might just make it out there."

"I plan to," Ryan said coolly.

Davidson nodded. "You can go. Don't forget the urine sample."

"No," Ryan said. He wanted out. He needed a breath of fresh air. He was so damn tired of subduing his pride. It was necessary to hold onto what freedom he had, but he wondered how long he could manage it.

"Good luck, Murphy." It was dismissal, or at least he took it as such. He walked out, stopped at the desk and as quickly as possible took care of the last requirement.

Julie found herself keeping an eye on the driveway. She needed to keep her mind on her work. She was already late with the appeal, but she couldn't stop worrying about Murphy, especially as the day wore on. Noon, then one. Two. Three.

Had what happened last night, her unforgivable loss of control, scared him off? But then she realized nothing would scare him off. Not after what he'd already been through. Yet he'd been distinctly uncomfortable this morning. Or maybe it had been her.

She hadn't slept a wink. Her body continued to react in rebellious ways with a yearning and need that horrified her. She couldn't forget, not for one moment, how her body felt tucked into his, or how his lips felt on hers. He apparently couldn't sleep either, for when she finally left her bed after lying awake sleeplessly, she saw him on his knees weeding the poor, neglected garden patches. She watched him for several moments, his hands working the earth, before going to wake Nick.

I'll pay you back every cent.

There was certainly nothing wrong with his work ethic, or sense of obligation....

Julie looked back down at her watch. Where was he?

She certainly couldn't call the parole office.

The phone rang, and she answered it quickly.

"Julie?"

She immediately recognized David Caldwell's voice, and her heart sank. She'd read the story in the paper this morning. It had identified her as associated with Caldwell, Michaels, Evans and Cagle.

"Mr. Caldwell."

"How's the appeal coming?"

"I'm almost finished."

"Good. Can you bring it to the office tomorrow?"

"Yes."

"Around ten?"

"I'll be there."

"Good. I'll see you then."

Julie hung the phone up slowly. She'd expected a reprimand, or reminder, that she'd not sacrifice firm business, or reputation, in the cause of Ryan Murphy. The fact that the call came on the heels of the newspaper article worried her. But he'd said nothing, and that worried her even more.

Trying to focus her attention back on the appeal, her eyes returned to the computer screen.

She had to stop worrying about Murphy.

She had to exorcize those gnawing doubts.

Where was he?

His insides twisted into knots, Ryan stood across from the police station, staring at the imposing white building and jail and willed himself to remember. He had worked in this building for years.

Behind him were numerous bail bond companies, their storefront windows garish with phone numbers. He watched as police cars turned into a parking lot, as people hurried into the building. He could pick out the detectives and officers from the lawyers and secretaries. Or thought he could.

He wasn't sure what had prompted him to ask a security guard at the county building for directions. Perhaps hope that the sight of the building would bring back something.

He'd felt so damn frustrated after leaving Davidson's office. He wasn't sure whether the man was an enemy or potential ally. Whether he had been trying to make a point in those first few moments or whether he'd been trying to discover whether Ryan was lying about the amnesia. Since he had no memory to judge people by, he could only call on his instincts. And he didn't know if they were reliable.

He thought about his meeting with Davidson, about the prospect of living for years under his thumb, urinating on demand, always living with the prospect of returning to a cage if he said the wrong thing or didn't show the right amount of respect.

Julie had said once that he might not be guilty of the crime, that something had been odd about his confession. He hadn't really listened; the fact that he had confessed had convinced him of his guilt. But now that he knew the kind of life he could expect, the threat of prison always hanging over him, he wanted to explore any possibility of removing the shroud that threatened to smother him. Hell, he had to.

He didn't know how long he stared at the building, willing some fragment of a memory, but finally he realized it wouldn't come. Not now. He had to find another way of discovering the truth. *The library.* Julie had given him copies of some stories, but he wanted to know everything. It would be a place to start. And Banyon. Jack Banyon. Perhaps he could find out more from him.

He went into one of the storefronts and asked the location of the library. Then he started walking, his mind cataloging everything he knew and questions that needed answering. Julie had mentioned a priest; had anyone found him? His wife. He had to speak to her. His attorney at the time of his arrest. What had he said right after the shooting? Had he made any friends in prison, anyone he confided in?

His footsteps hurried. For the first time since he had regained consciousness in the hospital, he felt a small bit of control over his life. It felt good.

He reached the library and found an information desk. A helpful woman guided him to microfiche and showed him how to access back copies of the newspaper. In minutes, he was scrolling back page after page of newspapers dating back ten years ago to the week of December twenty-third. He read the initial stories. *Detective found dead. Preliminary investigation shows involvement of another officer. Detective suspended.* Then the press was in full cry. The lead story on December twenty-seventh was his arrest, followed by a story in which his attorney denied his guilt. Two days later, another story reported he had been denied bond.

It must have been some Christmas for his wife and child.

He'd confessed a week later.

He kept searching that final story for clues. Why would he confess, even if he had committed the crime? As a detective, he must have been very aware of the weakness of the case as well as the penalty he could expect. Or had he known he was guilty and wanted to avoid the death penalty?

How could he subject his family to the subsequent publicity, the shame of having a husband and father known as a "Killer Cop"?

He glanced upward and saw the clock. Ten after three. He froze for a moment, then turned off the machine and returned the film. Julie had planned to take him in to the garage this afternoon. It would take him an hour or more, depending on the buses, to get back.

Ryan found a phone and called, but it was busy. He swore softly to himself. No telling what she was thinking. He could wait and call again, but that would just make him later. He strode quickly out the door, heading for a bus stop, his mind puzzling over everything he'd just read.

Julie picked up Nick and returned home. Nick in tow, she knocked on Ryan's door. No one answered.

Nick squirmed next to her. "Where's Ryan?"

"Mr. Murphy," she corrected.

"He said to call him Ryan."

"I know," she said, "but I think you should call him Mr. Murphy."

"But—"

"No buts, love. Let's go get some cookies." She needed distraction. She also knew one reason she was insisting on formality was for her own sake. Ryan had gotten altogether too close last night. Perhaps she could keep more of a distance with Mr. Murphy.

Perhaps.

The word "cookies" had magical properties. Nicholas skipped down the stairs and she followed, her keys out to unlock the door. As Prissy happily threaded in and out of their legs, Julie poured a glass of milk and placed a couple of store-bought cookies on a plate.

"How was school today?"

"Fine."

"Did you see Abby?"

"Yep." The reply was almost lost in the mouthful of cookie.

"Did you learn anything?"

"I read a book all by myself."

"That's wonderful."

"My teacher says I read really good."

"I think you do, too."

"Mebbe I can read to Ry...Mr. Murphy."

"Maybe so."

"After we play baseball."

Baseball again. Would his heart be broken if Murphy disappeared? She kept telling herself it was quite impossible. Then the demon intervened. What if he'd never lost his memory? What if he *had* been involved in drugs? Wouldn't he have money squirreled away somewhere?

He should have been back by now.

Or what if he became lost? Or hurt?

She felt a chill even as she tried to concentrate on Nick, keeping a running conversation with him. But she was conscious of the ticking of the clock.

It was well after five when she heard a knock on the kitchen door. Her heart thumped loudly as Nick raced to open it.

Murphy stood there, the sleeves of his white shirt rolled up in a way she now expected. His hair was mussed as if repeatedly combed by his hand and his angular face was shadowed by new beard. Strain showed at the edges of his mouth. He looked dangerous. Dangerous and exciting and incredibly appealing. Her body still hummed from the contact last night.

She wanted to ask questions. She wanted to know where he had been. But she really had no right. She wouldn't even know he'd been gone so long if he'd been able to rent an apartment on his own. She wasn't his mother, or wife, or keeper. His proximity gave her no more rights than any other landlord. She had to remember that. Even more importantly, she had to distance herself from him. She kept her voice even as she asked instead, "How did the appointment go?"

He shrugged, and she knew it had been more than a little difficult. He quickly changed the subject. "I meant to buy a baseball on the way...back, but it was getting late," he said, looking down at her son.

"That's okay," Nick piped up generously, much more generously than if she had admitted something like that. "Would you like a cookie?"

He shook his head. "Not tonight. I need to talk to your mother." Murphy's eyes locked on hers. So intense. She could no more ignore the demand in them than she could breathe.

She looked down at Nick. "How would you like to watch a movie on the VCR?"

Nick looked from her to Murphy and back. "I want to stay," he said stubbornly which surprised her. Nick *loved* movies.

Murphy sat at the table and looked directly at him. "Why don't you watch it, then tell me all about it?"

Murphy certainly had an instinct about small boys, even if he claimed he didn't know anything about them. And she knew that instinct could exist only if he really liked children. It wasn't something you faked. Nor were children easily fooled.

Nick looked at him suspiciously. "You won't leave?"

"Not until I hear the story."

"You promise?"

Murphy glanced back at her as if seeking permission.

She nodded.

"I promise."

Still obviously reluctant, Nick stood and headed for the living room. Julie followed and mused over the choices. "What do you want to see?"

"The Dalmatians."

She sighed. He'd seen it a hundred times, but never seemed to tire of it. She found the video and inserted it into the VCR, turning the sound high so he wouldn't hear them. She lingered until the credits came on, then went back to the kitchen. She would fix supper while she talked. While he talked. Perhaps that would ease some of the tension between them.

Murphy was pacing the kitchen floor when she returned.

"When you didn't get back early, I called the garage and told Mr. O'Donnell you would be there tomorrow morning. I have to be at my office early, so I'll drop you off at the garage at eight."

"I can find my own way there."

"I don't doubt it," she said evenly, "but the garage is on my way."

"I can't keep relying on you."

"You didn't rely on me at all today. And tomorrow I have to drop Nick off at his school. The garage is almost next door."

Julie put three potatoes in the oven to bake, then took lettuce and other salad fixings from the refrigerator. She would fix hamburger casserole tonight. It was one of Nick's favorites and would last for at least one more meal. *Concentrate on the meal. Not on how appealing Murphy looks.*

"Over the weekend," she said, "maybe you would like to try to drive. They say it's like riding a bike. You never forget how."

He was silent so long she finally looked toward him.

He was still leaning against the counter, yet he didn't look relaxed at all. He looked like a jungle cat ready to pounce on something.

But she knew it wasn't her. She hated the disappointment that followed that observation.

"What did you want to talk to me about?"

"You said...you suggested there was something strange about my plea. You said it didn't...fit, that I would have known enough to cove my tracks."

She nodded.

"Do you really believe I could be innocent?"

"Yes," she said flatly. She wondered whether her answer was wi but she wasn't going to lie about it. She'd always had a feeling t something was very wrong about his case.

"You mentioned a priest...?"

"Jerry, who is working for me as an investigator, is trying to him. So far, no luck. He's already called every parish priest in A and asked if they knew you. No luck. Now he's trying to find who were here ten years ago and have left."

"I want to know everything you've...discovered about me."

"I'll get you all of Jerry's reports," she said. "Former l teammates, prison guards, officers you served with." She h d, then added, "You may not like everything in them."

"It can't be worse than killing my partner," he replied dr

She had to smile at that. Gallows humor. Police humor. S ew it well. "No," she admitted. "It's not as bad as that."

"And my...wife. I want to talk to her."

Seeing the determination burning in his eyes, Julie nodde ask her."

He straightened. "I hate to ask any more of you, but. re the only—"

"Source you have," Julie finished for him. She was s meant to say "hope," but she didn't want to hear that word. She d away again and started chopping onions for the casserole, kno er eyes would soon be awash with tears. "Remember the expr l, 'in for a penny, in for a pound'?"

"No," he said after a moment's silence. "But I know it means. Dammit, I have no right to mess up your life like this

"At least I have a life, thanks to you. And you a messing it up." Sure enough, the tears were coming. She cut the s finer, her knife dissecting with a fierceness that had nothing with them. When they were little more than grains, she turned . "Until the accident, I was drifting. I had opted out of life exce Nick. I tried not to feel anything except for him."

"That can't be bad," he said mildly.

"Yes," she said honestly. "It was. I'd lost ever g in me I liked and respected. Now I feel those parts returning. re making me feel alive again."

"Why?" he asked curiously. "Why did you lose them?"

"You know I used to be with the district attorney's office. I sent an innocent man to prison. He was there five years before I found out I'd been wrong." That was one reason. She wasn't ready to tell him the second, the most personal. The most wounding.

He was silent as he absorbed that information. His brows furrowed together and the corner of his lips moved slightly. After a moment, it quirked up quizzically. "So now you're going to save everyone?"

"You're my first," she said lightly.

He studied her carefully. "Tell me about Nicholas's father."

He *knew* there was more to her reasons than a wrongful conviction. Or maybe he just sensed it, as she was able to sense so much about him.

"There's not much to tell," she said stiffly.

"How long ago did he die?"

This question was like a blow to her stomach. It was an impertinent question and none of his business. Yet she certainly knew *his* business. In fact, she knew far more about him than he did about himself.

"Five years ago."

His eyes flickered toward the living room. Nick was obviously around that age.

"He died before Nick was born," she explained without knowing why she was compelled to answer the unasked question.

His gaze met hers. The usual cautious look was gone. Instead, the deep blue was warm with understanding. Understanding and something more. Empathy simmered between them. The sense of awareness grew stronger, irresistible. She had a warm, burning desire to touch him, to feel him pull her against his body as he had last night. Her cheeks flamed with heat as she remembered every sensation she'd felt then. A yearning poignancy filled her as she realized how much she wanted him, needed him, and how very dangerous those feelings were for both of them. They were both too vulnerable now.

She swallowed hard. She wanted him to go. *No, she didn't.* But she should. She didn't want to answer the questions in his eyes, couldn't afford to deepen the intimacy that already swirled around them like a whirlpool drawing them deeper and deeper into disaster.

"Why don't you go and relax a little?" She hoped her voice didn't sound as tremulous as she felt. "I'll gather Jerry's reports. You can join us for supper in an hour and a half if you want." It was a graceless invitation, and she knew it, but it had just popped out that way.

His gaze made her feel like a coward. And she was one. But she couldn't think when they were alone.

Maybe that feeling wouldn't last. But now she tingled all over.

She heard wicked laughter from the other room. The villainess, no doubt. But she felt as if it was directed at her.

"I think I'll skip supper," he said in a quiet, almost lazy tone. Was he possibly feeling what she was feeling? Was he that good at hiding his feelings? But then she saw the pulse in his throat moving slightly, and she knew he was no more immune to what was happening than she. "I'll drop over at seven, if you don't mind," he added. "I...don't want to break my promise."

She nodded. "I'll have the reports ready. Just be prepared for Nick's monologue."

His eyes lit. "I'll look forward to it."

Julie knew from that look he meant it. She wondered if Nick's unconditional, unquestioning acceptance gave him something she couldn't.

Without another word, he spun around and was out the door. It wasn't until that moment she realized that he had never explained where he had been or why he had been so late. *It's none of your business,* she told herself again.

But something had happened this afternoon, something that had made him question his conviction.

Had she set him up for disappointment by expressing her own doubts, her own personal reservations? Had they just been wishful thinking on her part?

She would caution him when he returned. And she would keep Nicholas with them. She no longer trusted herself alone with Ryan Murphy.

But even as she realized that, she thought about the light of battle in his eyes when he questioned her about his possible innocence.

In addition to the warmth already stirring in a sensitive region of her stomach, she felt that old pull of excitement when she started a new case.

She had fought a few battles already on behalf of Ryan Murphy.

But now she was going to war.

Chapter 12

Ryan poured a glass of milk and made himself a sandwich. He'd not had anything to eat since breakfast, and he found himself ravenous.

He would have liked to have joined Julie and Nick for supper. He would have liked it very much. Too much. Which was why he'd refused. He also had not missed the hesitancy in her invitation.

After finishing a second sandwich, he took a shower. Despite the bitter aftertaste from this morning's encounter with the parole officer—or perhaps because of it—he relished the privacy of the shower, the privilege of remaining under the spray as long as he wanted. Hell, he relished all the little freedoms. Making a sandwich. Walking outside to get a breath of air. Selecting clothes. It was all heady stuff, though the meeting this morning had made him aware of how fast it could all be jerked away again.

If only he could prove his innocence. If, indeed, he *was* innocent. He thought of his daughter. The need to see her was growing stronger, but as long as his conviction hung over his head, he didn't feel he had the right to enter her life. He didn't have the right to claim anything.

He toweled himself dry, then shaved. He dressed in the clothes he'd gardened in early in the morning and went back down to work in the yard. Despite the books and the television, he couldn't stay inside. He wondered whether he would ever be comfortable in a small room again, or whether he would get the panicked, caged feeling he fought so hard to contain in prison.

He would have to wash clothes tomorrow. There were many things he hadn't thought about in prison. He'd heard about prisoners who'd become so institutionalized they couldn't function outside prison. Had he been in danger of that happening before Julie's accident? The thought was terrifying.

Dusk had fallen but he would have some time to finish weeding. It was a small way of paying Julie back. A very small way.

He worked until it grew too dark, then went upstairs and washed.

Nick was waiting for him. Ryan listened patiently to Nick's enthusiastic and rambling account of *101 Dalmatians*. Ryan quickly sensed the boy had a devious mind and ulterior motive: he was in full pursuit of a puppy.

His eyes had met Julie's who spread out her arms in weary resignation.

Then he'd left quickly before Nick went to bed. He'd gone back to his room and started reading everything a private investigator named Jerry Kidder had discovered about one Ryan Murphy.

More, really, than he wanted to know. Ryan Murphy was described over and over again as a humorless, arrogant, intolerant perfectionist. He read the comments of the judge at his sentencing hearing and winced at the harsh condemnation in the words and his own lack of response.

How could he be innocent?

He felt as if he were butting his head against a wall. That wall grew thicker all the time.

Still, he wasn't willing to give up hope.

No one had to tell Ryan that Tim O'Donnell was an Irishman. He had red hair, blue eyes, a burly form and hearty voice.

Ryan had liked him immediately. There had been no questioning looks, no doubt in his voice as Julie had introduced them, just a thorough once-over and a firm handshake.

"I'm not sure how much help I'll be," Ryan said after Julie had left.

O'Donnell shrugged. "If you're a hard worker, I can teach you. If you remember anything from the past, so much the better. At first, you'll be changing oil, filters, plugs and other simple jobs. I have one really good mechanic and with you to help he can concentrate on the more complicated jobs. Minimum wage to start but if you catch on quick, I'll raise it and pay overtime."

Ryan nodded. "I'm not sure why you are doing this, but I'm grateful."

Tim looked at him steadily. "Eight years ago my seventeen-year-old son was arrested for joyriding and D.U.I. I thought for sure it would destroy his chances to go into the military, something he really wanted. Julie reduced the charges to a misdemeanor and got him into the Air Force. He's a sergeant now, a jet mechanic with a wife, kids, and real bright future. I believe she saved his life. There isn't anything I wouldn't do for her."

So he hadn't been her first cause. He wondered how many others there had been.

"Come and meet Johnny," Tim said, ending the discussion.

Ryan met the mechanic, then spent the morning watching him. Johnny was garrulous, obviously eager to have someone helping. "I worked fourteen hours yesterday," he griped. "I'd promised to take my girl out and had to stand her up. Last guy here stayed four days. Couldn't get here on time and complained when he had to delay lunch 'cause of a rush job. Didn't come back on the fifth day. Tell the truth, I wasn't sorry to see him go. Had to double-check everything he did."

Ryan wondered whether there wasn't a word or two of warning in the speech. He understood if there was.

"Tim said you used to know mechanics but that you have amnesia. Do you remember anything?"

"I'm not sure," Ryan said truthfully. "I don't know what I know. I didn't even know I could read until they gave me a newspaper."

"Okay," Johnny said. "We'll replace oil. You do it. I'll tell you how. If you realize you don't need help, just tell me to go away."

Gratitude flooded Ryan, especially for the simple acceptance of what no one else had been able to completely accept.

"There's clean uniforms in the restroom," Johnny said. "So is extra-strength soap. It's a messy job." He was silent for a moment, then said, "I understand you used to be a...police officer."

"So they tell me," Ryan said evenly.

Johnny shrugged at his obvious reluctance to elaborate. "Why don't you change clothes and we'll get started."

Several minutes later, Ryan found himself under a car, his fingers working automatically, moving faster than Johnny's explanation. After several moments, Johnny grinned, and made a circle with his thumb and middle finger. "I'm not needed here," he said as he lifted himself up and went over to another car. With satisfaction, and an intense feeling of accomplishment, Ryan went back to work.

* * *

Despite David Caldwell's secretary's instructions to go in, Julie hesitated outside his office. She'd finished the brief in support of an appeal late last night, and she felt good about it despite the distractions. Still, she felt a moment's apprehension. The publicity about Murphy had continued in the paper this morning; in fact, the story pointed out that Murphy was living in an apartment on her property.

She knocked at Caldwell's door. To her surprise he opened it himself before strolling back to his desk. But he didn't sit down. Instead, he leaned against the corner of it.

Julie handed him the hard copy of the brief.

He took it and looked past her toward the door. Her instincts started squirming uncomfortably.

"Julie, you've done good work for us. Very good work. But we discussed the effect of adverse publicity on this firm. I had several calls yesterday from clients asking about your exposure in this case, and whether we were going into criminal law. Of course, I said we were not. Now this business about this...man moving in with you..."

"Excuse me, Mr. Caldwell," she corrected stiffly, "but he isn't moving in with me. He is renting an apartment over a garage that is separate from the house, just like thousands of tenants do throughout the city."

"Still," Caldwell said, "it doesn't look good." He picked up the newspaper. "This isn't going to end any time soon."

Her stomach plummeted.

"Can you put an end to your...association with him?"

"No," she said softly.

"Then we have no choice but to dispense with your services. We will pay you two weeks severance," he said. "Perhaps we can use you on special projects."

She nodded and turned to go. There really was nothing else to say. She certainly wasn't going to jettison Murphy.

"Julie."

She stopped and turned.

"I really hoped this could work out. Perhaps in a few months..."

He *did* look sorry, and he *had* warned her. But she still felt as if she'd been physically struck. She'd never been fired before. She had not expected the sense of failure she suddenly felt.

She couldn't force herself to thank him. Instead, she glanced down at the brief he held. "I hope the brief is satisfactory," she said.

In something like rebellion, she went to the best restaurant in the area and indulged herself in a glass of wine and a good meal as she considered her financial future, or lack of it. After Doug's death, she'd become very conscious of the financial ups and downs in life; she made good money with the law firm, and she'd saved a third of it. She had enough to meet expenses for a year or more, even if she had to tap her precious savings, and in that time she could certainly find another job.

Still, that sense of failure ate into her, making the grouper tasteless, the glass of wine sour.

She wondered how Murphy was doing.

She left half the meal on the plate and drove home. With Nick in preschool, the house was silent. She kicked off her heels and sat down. Prissy jumped into her lap and purred contentedly as she absently rubbed her hand through the thick fur. *When one door closes,* she thought, *another opens.* The adage, though overused, was comforting as she mused over possibilities. There was Dan's office, but perhaps even he wouldn't want her back now, considering the publicity.

She winced at the possible headlines. *Assistant D.A. Returns After Freeing Killer.*

The phone rang and she dislodged Prissy to answer it.

"We don't want murderers in the neighborhood," said a harsh voice before hanging up.

She set the earpiece down gingerly. Emily said the same thing two days ago in only slightly more civilized terms. Now this. She felt sick inside. Was this going to affect Nick? Would other kids at the school mention it? They often echoed what they heard their parents say.

Yet she knew she wasn't going to retreat. In fact, she was more determined than ever to give Murphy his chance.

Still, she had a disquieting feeling that something had just started, something that could grow more ugly. Perhaps it was the call coming so close to her firing.

She knew hers was a dramatic story. So was Murphy's. Together they provided great fodder for a sensation hungry press. She'd known it when she had first decided to act as his attorney. She'd also known she risked losing her job. The reality of it, however, hit her far harder than she'd anticipated.

At least she would have more time to look into Murphy's conviction. She could help Jerry find the priest whom Murphy's former wife mentioned and talk to some of the other officers serving in Murphy's unit. She also wanted to talk to the first officers on the scene when Murphy's partner was murdered. She would talk to Dan again, too. She wanted to know every case Murphy had been investigating at the time.

She went to her room and slipped on a pair of jeans and sweater. She would pick up Nick at preschool and fix them a good dinner. For a fleeting moment, she thought about asking Murphy over to celebrate his first day on the job, but that was probably a bad idea. A very, very bad idea when even the thought sent her heart beating faster.

Instead, she checked the mail. Her hands sorted through the bills and catalogues. Then she saw an envelope without a postmark or stamp. Only her name was sprawled across the front. She stood there in the yard, staring at it. She knew there was nothing good in it, and her first instinct was to throw it away.

Then her legal training took over. She didn't have the name of the person who called, but this was, could be, evidence of some kind. She opened it carefully.

You are harboring a murderer. Your child could be his next victim.

Shudders rocked her body. How could this all be happening at once unless someone was orchestrating it all? She couldn't believe her neighbors would send such a letter. They might protest, as Emily had, especially if someone stirred the pot, but she didn't think they would resort to anonymous phone calls or threatening messages.

Or was it threatening? Was it merely a warning from someone?

Quickly, she walked inside. She wanted to tear up the plain white piece of bond paper with the large printed letters, but instead she carried it inside to her office and put it in the top drawer of her desk. Perhaps that would be the end of it.

Angry and restless, she decided to stop by the grocery store before picking up Nick. Murphy had already said he would walk home, although the garage was two miles away. He probably enjoyed walking. She would, too, if she'd been locked up ten years.

That damned note.

She grabbed the keys and left.

Julie and Nick were halfway through spaghetti when the phone rang again. She hesitated, then went to answer it, expecting the worst.

Tim O'Donnell's voice boomed through the earpiece. "Just wanted to thank you, Julie. Murphy's a born mechanic, and he's a real worker. Heck, he didn't even stop for lunch. I think he's gonna work out just fine. Thought you would like to know."

"Is he still there?"

"Just left. Said he was walking home. Say, I got an old car he could borrow, maybe even buy. He could pay me a little out of his paycheck each week."

"Did you mention it to him?"

"Thought I would check with you first."

"It's his business. But he needs a driver's license."

"I'll talk to him about it," O'Donnell said.

She hung up, feeling better. Then that insidious doubt crept into her mind. *He's a born mechanic.* So was the old Murphy. A quirk of memory? Or something more sinister? She kept telling herself that the doctor had said he might well have learned, repetitive skills. But O'Donnell described a *natural* skill. Would he retain those, too? She made a mental note to call Dr. Dailey.

"Where's Ryan?" Nick asked when she returned to the table.

"Mr. Murphy," she corrected almost automatically.

"But where is he?"

It was the third time—or the fourth—he had asked tonight, she thought with a sinking feeling.

"He's working," she explained again. "And I suspect he will be tired when he gets home."

"But he likes me," Nick complained.

"Everyone likes you," she said, seeking to deflect his thoughts even as she knew the unlikelihood of such tactics. "Especially me, and I thought we would spend some time together watching a movie."

"But..."

The "but" again.

"No buts, Munchkin."

"Awwwwwwww."

She knew he was giving in.

No Murphy tonight. Time instead to think without the distraction of his presence. Yet he loomed large in the back of her thoughts and she pictured him returning to the dark, lonely apartment.

No Murphy tonight, she reminded herself.

Murphy saw the familiar house ahead and quickened his steps. He reached in his pocket for the baseball. He had passed a drug store on the way home and went inside. He'd browsed aisle after aisle of goods, wondering at some of the items, including a miniature color television no larger than a matchbox. Then he'd reached the toys and found the baseball.

As good a way to spend money as any. He could just see the big grin spread across Nick's face. Too bad it was too late to toss it tonight. He was anxious to see whether he could throw or not. Another exploration of his abilities.

It was already getting dark, and he was hungry. He'd gone all day without food. He'd just damn well enjoyed doing something useful. Now he knew he could pay Julie back. It would take a while, but he'd taken the first step. Something like elation filled him. It was a totally new feeling, stronger even than the moment he'd left prison. He'd had so many doubts then, so many questions. Even a fear of failure.

He hesitated at the gate. He wanted to knock at the door, to share with her his triumph, but he hesitated. He had taken enough of her time. Instead he turned toward the apartment, turning the key in his pocket.

He took the steps two at a time and unlocked the door. Once in, he left it unlocked and put the key on the table. He fixed himself a can of soup from the cupboard and a sandwich, then sat down and stared out the window that faced the house. He could see figures moving inside, and the elation he'd felt so briefly was snuffed by loneliness, by the raw yearning to be inside that kitchen, to share the warmth he knew was there.

He took the baseball from his pocket and tossed it in the air, his hand turning slightly as he caught it easily. It was an inexpensive ball, made of cheap materials but it felt natural in his hand. He tossed it again, then again. Suddenly, he saw a ball coming directly at him. A sudden, unexpected flash in his mind. It disappeared as quickly as it came, and as he stood stunned, wondering whether it was even real. Whether it had happened or he had conjured it.

He dropped the ball on the table and sat down in the big, comfortable chair. He shut his eyes and concentrated, willing another flash, another memory.

But there was nothing.

Julie didn't tell Murphy about the phone call, or the letter. Two days went by without additional calls, and then it was Sunday, and Murphy was home all day. And impossible to avoid as she'd tried to do the past two days.

Sundays were always special. She would make waffles, or blueberry pancakes, then take Ryan to Sunday school and church. Usually, they would go somewhere Sunday afternoon—the zoo, or Stone Mountain for a picnic, or Piedmont Park to feed the ducks.

"I bet Mr. Murphy would like pancakes," Nick said as he plodded into the kitchen with sleepy eyes and wrinkled pajamas. "Maybe he would like to go to Sunday school."

"Or maybe he would like to rest," she said.

But Nick was already peering out the window. "Nope," he said happily. "He's outside in the yard."

Julie had purposely not looked outside. But now she did. He was clipping a shrub which had grown in an ungainly way. Did he ever stop working?

"Why don't you go see if he's hungry?" she said.

Nick took off as if he'd been standing barefoot on hot coals.

She looked out the window and watched Nick run over to Murphy. Her son looked so small next to him, so vulnerable. She'd had no idea how much her son had hungered for male companionship until the past few days. She decided then and there to take him over to Dan's home. Or was it just Murphy who was special to him? If so, how had it happened so quickly?

And with someone described as cold, uncaring and arrogant?

She looked down at the batter, realizing she'd already mixed more than enough for three. She shook her head at herself, realizing how much she had missed Murphy's presence in the kitchen.

Julie poured an extra glass of orange juice and retrieved another cup from the cabinet.

Maybe he wouldn't come.

But she saw him follow her son toward the door and in seconds it opened, his tall, lanky form filling the doorway, then the kitchen. His dark eyes had that same quiet, watchful look and his mouth quirked in a particularly quizzical way that was all his. "The munchkin asked me for breakfast," he said, almost as if he thought she would demur.

She noticed he had picked up her own pet name for Nick and she smiled at hearing it on his lips. "You're very welcome. I hope you like pancakes."

"I'll like whatever smells so good," he said in a lazy drawl. He took several strides toward her, and she had to look up to see his face. He smelled like fresh earth and soap with just a hint of the aftershave she had bought. And at her welcoming words, his eyes went from cautious to warm and beguiling.

Suddenly, her throat was so tight she couldn't swallow. Damn, she should have known this might happen. She moved out of touching range. But though she could swallow again, her heart beat at an accelerated rate.

"Is there someplace I can wash up?" he asked.

She turned back to the pancakes, hoping he didn't see the telltale flush creeping up her face. "The bathroom down the hall."

But she'd barely had time to regain her equilibrium when he returned. "Is there anything I can do?"

"You can pour the coffee."

But that was a mistake, too. It brought him much too close to her.

The kitchen was suddenly very, very small. Too small. She stepped away, afraid he might see her hands tremble, and opened the refrigerator door. Almost blindly, she searched its interior, looking for something she'd missed so she wouldn't feel like such an idiot. But everything was out: butter, syrup, milk, orange juice. She closed the door and returned to the stove, hoping he hadn't noticed she was empty-handed. He probably hadn't, since he was carrying two cups of coffee to the table.

Julie scooped pancakes out of the frying pan onto a plate, then poured some more batter into the pan. She turned to take the loaded plate to the table and bumped into Murphy. The plate started to fall, and he caught it, his lips turning into a sudden, blinding smile.

"I *can* catch," he said with such a warm, amused voice that it turned her insides into a knot.

"I noticed," she said inanely. She also noticed other things, like suddenly how deep and smoky his eyes were.

His gaze held hers for a moment, then he seemed to tear himself away reluctantly and went to the table, holding the plate out to Nick who forked several pancakes onto the table. "Mommy makes the best pancakes in the world," he said.

Murphy didn't take one. Instead, he looked toward her. "Let me finish while you eat," he said.

"Do you cook?"

"I've made sandwiches," he replied, and again she heard the amusement in his voice. Had he found a sense of humor? Or was he simply losing some of that caution he cloaked himself in?

"Thank you," she said, "but I think I'd better do it myself."

"I have to learn sometime."

"Not on my pancakes."

He chuckled. It was the first time she'd heard the sound and it crawled inside and wrapped itself around her heart. Every organ melted like warm butter. She watched him as he slid into a seat, folding his long legs underneath. A fork grabbed a pancake and he took a bite with obvious pleasure.

She flipped the pancakes and took a sip of orange juice. She was already much too edgy for coffee.

Several more sips and the pancakes were finished. She slid them on a plate and sat down next to Murphy. It was a mistake. Their hands brushed as she put the plate down just as he was reaching for syrup she heated earlier. Her blood felt like that syrup—thick and warm— as the now too familiar awareness flared between them. She saw it in the sudden flash of heat in his eyes and felt it in the charged air around them. She wondered whether Nick noticed anything unusual, but he was much too busy shoveling in pancake bites.

"Nick was right," Murphy said. "You do make the best pancakes in the world and *you* were right not to let me near them."

"And you have, of course, tasted enough to know?"

The smile disappeared from his eyes, and she could have kicked herself.

"I'm discovering a healthy imagination," he said, taking another forkful. Then his eyes turned serious. "I would like to...talk to you about what happened ten years ago."

She'd known that was coming when he'd asked to see all her files. "All right," she said. "I'm taking Nick to church, but we'll be back at one."

"Ry...Mr. Murphy can go with us," Nick said, gazing hopefully at her.

"Not this morning," she said, catching the startled look on Murphy's face. "I think we should let him get settled."

"We'll toss a baseball this afternoon," Murphy said. "If it's all right with your mother."

"Oh boy," Nick said. "That's super."

In the burst of enthusiasm, Nick had forgotten their regular Sunday excursion. A bittersweet anguish—something almost like jealousy—struck her for a moment until she saw Murphy's face. He apparently took her momentary silence as a sign that she didn't want him alone with her son. The amused warmth in his eyes faded, replaced by a grimness she'd only seen while he was in prison.

She was struck by her own selfishness. Ryan Murphy had so little; surely she couldn't begrudge him a little time with her son. Still, she worried about Nick's wholehearted response to Murphy.

"Of course you can," she told Nick. "I just thought you wanted to go to the park."

"I'd rather play baseball," he said importantly.

"Then it's settled," she said.

But the wariness was back in Murphy's eyes. He finished eating with the precision she'd seen in the restaurant, not the gusto of a few moments ago. That light had gone from his face, and there was no way she could explain that it had been her own possessiveness, and not him, that had caused her hesitation.

He finished his coffee and stood. "I thought I would rake the leaves."

"You don't have to do that. You need some time of your own."

His eyes narrowed, and his expression was enigmatic. "I like being outside. I enjoy the physical exercise."

And he felt compelled to pay her back.

What would he think if he knew she had lost her job? She hadn't told either Nick or Murphy yet.

Her pancakes cooled on her plate. "I'll see you at one then," she said.

"Thanks for breakfast." He was out the door before either she or Nick could say anything more.

She wondered whether she'd imagined those few moments when he'd seemed to forget caution.

"You'd better get dressed," she told the pajama-clad Nick.

Nick obediently scooted out of his chair, and she walked to the front door to pick up the Sunday paper outside. The moment she opened the door, she noticed the sign planted in her yard. Her stomach knotted.

Slowly, she walked down the driveway and looked at the sign.

A murderer lives here.

She pulled it up. She would take it into her office where neither Nick nor Murphy would see it. She'd been right.

It was just starting.

Chapter 13

Ryan raked the yard, neatly packaging the leaves in large trash bags Julie provided before leaving for church.

Then, restless, he went up to his room and read his files again. He wanted to ask Julie certain questions, wanted to talk to people himself. He would have tomorrow—Monday—off since Tim wanted him to work Saturdays when Johnny liked to take off.

Perhaps he could talk to his ex-wife. Or to Jack Banyon. He was growing more and more hungry for information about himself. Okay, he knew he could drain oil from a car, change and rotate tires, install new brakes. What else could he do?

Could he drive? Fire a gun accurately?

The last question popped into his mind without welcome. His police personnel records said he was a marksman. He tried to imagine holding a gun as he had seen actors do on television.

There had been no sudden flash of memory as there had been when he'd tossed the ball, no familiarity. Perhaps if he had one in his hand...

But that was one of the prohibitions that would surely send him back to prison. No firearms. Not of any kind.

When he felt he'd memorized every fact in the files, he looked at the clock. It was 11:00 a.m. He found some coins and left the apartment. A telephone. He needed a telephone. He walked to Peachtree Road where he found a gas station and pay phones.

The directory was torn, pages were missing. He first looked for Banyon, Jack, but that page was missing. He then tried the city police department. To his surprise, he was directed to Banyon, and hope flared. But then a machine answered, asking him to leave a name and phone number. After a short hesitation, he left his name and address, then hung up.

He itched to call his former wife. He'd found her address and phone number in Julie's file and written it down, but he knew Julie had been hesitant when he'd said he wanted to talk to her. Mary Elizabeth Saddler. He tried the first two names on his tongue. He had lived with her for nine years. If anything should be familiar, it should be her.

But all that developed in the vast blankness of his mind was Julie's face. Her quick smile. The way her eyes flashed. The feel of her. Good Lord, the feel of her. The soft yielding of her body, the taste of her lips.

Had he felt the same way about his wife? He looked down and noticed his hands were clenched into fists. Damn, he had no right to pop into Mary Elizabeth Saddler's life. She didn't want to see him. She'd made that clear enough. Had he been so poor a husband? A father?

No, he couldn't just call her. But he would ask someone—hell, there was only Julie—to arrange a meeting. And, God knew, he hated to ask any more of her. He wanted to throw away the crumpled sheet of paper in his fist, but he resisted. Instead, he smoothed out the paper, folded it and put it in his pocket.

Ryan was stretched out on a step of her porch, a book in his hand, when Julie arrived home. She had taken particular care with dressing this morning. She wanted everyone to know she wasn't hiding, that she didn't give a damn what the press said, or what her neighbors said or what the world thought.

She didn't know that many people at church. She attended often because she wanted Nick exposed to the good parts of religion: the kindness, the compassion, the generosity. But she'd never really become a part of it herself, had never allowed herself to really get involved in anything since her husband's death.

Ryan stood when she drove up, and she was struck again by the easy grace of his movements. At Reidsville, he'd reminded her of a caged panther, but now she realized it was more the long-legged grace of an athlete, the same kind she'd noticed among the Atlanta Braves players.

As he sauntered over, she recalled what Tim had said about a car.

Perhaps it was time to discover whether he remembered how to drive. She was sure he did. Still...he would have to obtain a license and he would need practice after so many years. A high school was nearby and the parking lot in back would be empty. It should be safe enough where public streets were not; Ryan did not need a charge of driving without a license.

"Get in." She tried to make it an invitation rather than an order.

He gave her a quizzical look.

"Let's see how you drive."

He gave her that odd curl of his mouth that she hadn't decided was smile or frown. "Trust me that far?"

"If you can fix cars, you should be able to drive one."

He looked at the driver's seat longingly.

"Tim told me he has a car you can use. Maybe buy."

"I have other debts." He meant her.

"You need a car in Atlanta."

"I can't keep taking from you forever," he said slowly, his hand on the door.

"Call it curiosity," Julie said with exasperation. "I want to know whether you *can*."

It was a challenge she knew he wouldn't turn down. He walked over to the passenger's side, opened the door and folded himself in. He looked at Nick in the car seat in back. "You're going to risk him?"

"We'll make it simple," she said.

She drove to the high school and around to the back where they wouldn't be seen, then changed seats with him. She watched him study every part of the car, and suddenly she knew he'd probably been doing the same thing with cars at the garage. She wondered whether he had driven one there. Suddenly she knew he had. He had a certain gleam in his eyes. Even expectation. Amusement.

He was going to enjoy this.

Her heart jumped. The old Murphy was said to be humorless. This one, however, was showing promise.

She crossed her arms as he very neatly backed up, turned and drove around the boundaries with an ease even she didn't have.

"You've been practicing," she accused.

"Johnny urged me to drive yesterday."

"You know if you had gotten caught..." She didn't have to finish. He knew.

"We were careful."

"I don't suppose it took long to remember."

"No," he agreed simply. "Except for all the gadgets. I think they were created to confuse."

She grinned. "So they are."

"What about baseball?" said a disgruntled voice in the back.

"You've got it, pal." Ryan parked, then changed seats with Julie.

"So when are you going to get a license?" She knew better than to offer to help him in that endeavor. She'd already sensed how reluctant he was to ask for any more help than he must.

"Tim knows a driving inspector. He's going to bring a manual to the garage."

He'll master that in seconds. Just as he'd apparently wrapped both Tim and Johnny around his fingers. But then it was difficult—no, impossible—to resist that insistent curiosity and unexpected competence.

When they drove up to her house, he got out and opened the gate as she drove in.

"I'll get Nick," he said when she stopped, his eyes focused on her as she got out of the car.

She was suddenly glad she'd worn her coral suit. It was the one bright outfit in her closet that was otherwise filled with dark power suits and jeans; she'd almost not bought it, but the color had been so vivid she hadn't been able to resist. Now she was glad, as she saw admiration gleam in his eyes.

She also felt awkward under his gaze. "I have to change," she said. "So does the Munchkin if he's going to toss balls."

She gave Nick the key to the house and watched him run up the stairs, eager to change and "play baseball."

"You wanted to talk to me?" she asked now that Nick had gone.

"The priest you mentioned," he said hesitantly. "Have you any more information?"

The humor had disappeared from his eyes. So had the warmth. Instead they were steely with determination.

Though his stance looked lazy, she saw the tension in the broad shoulders, and she was struck with the extraordinary force of his presence, his vitality. Had he the same magnetism ten years go? No one had mentioned that, though almost everyone had recalled his intensity, his drive, even his ruthlessness in achieving a goal.

"I don't think Jerry's had any luck yet," she said. "We'll continue looking tomorrow."

"What about your job?"

Her heart sank. "I just finished a project," she replied.

He stood there, his hands in his jeans but his eyes bored into her. For a moment, she feared he sensed the truth.

"I want to help."

She wanted to ask him when. But she saw that stubborn set of his jaw. He wasn't going to take no for an answer.

"I'll ask Jerry to come over tomorrow night. We can go over everything then."

"The investigator," he recalled. "I've never met him."

"No."

He looked at her curiously, and she knew her answer was flat. Jerry was still skeptical about Murphy, and he'd been particularly opposed to her renting Murphy the apartment.

Murphy seemed to sense her reluctance. "Tell me about him."

"He used to be an investigator for the district attorney's office."

"Was he there when I...was with the police department?"

"Yes."

Murphy sighed. "Then I want to talk to him, too."

Julie nodded.

"I called that detective who visited me in the hospital," he said, and she realized that he had spent the morning preparing an agenda. He wouldn't stop until he had the answers he needed.

Her eyes must have shown surprise because he hurried on as if afraid she might think he broke into her house. "I used a pay phone at the service station on Peachtree."

Darn. She had tried to think of everything for the apartment, but she hadn't thought of a telephone. Of course, he needed a telephone, especially if he was determined to do his own detective work. And she wasn't going to try to stop him. He hungered to know about himself, or at least the man he'd been before the accident.

Under similar circumstances, she thought she would, too. The haunting empathy she shared with him flared anew. That had been her problem from day one, from the first moment she'd seen him in the hospital bed. This man had almost died saving her, and in that moment his life had become linked with hers in some inexplicable way.

What if he had been a cold-blooded killer? Would she still feel that way?

"You need a phone," she said. "I'll see to it tomorrow." She would also order caller I.D. service for herself. If the gentleman with the angry voice called again, perhaps he would not be so anonymous.

Murphy's back was stiffening again. That damned pride of his. He'd been forced to accept her help, but now he was struggling for independence. He was succeeding beyond anyone's wildest expectations, but obviously it wasn't enough for him.

"You pay for it," she said hurriedly. "From what Tim tells me, you'll make enough in overtime to buy the city. But if it's on my account you won't need a deposit. I'll also make that number unlisted. The newspapers hopefully won't find it.''

She changed the subject before he could object. "Did you reach that detective? Banyon?'' She had written down the name and it stuck in her mind, especially since he was the only one of Murphy's former acquaintances to bother with so much as a hello.

"No, but I left my name.''

Just then Nick came bouncing out of the house, his shirt inside out and the fly of his jeans unzipped. He had, however, put on his tennis shoes.

Murphy's eyes went to him. "I'd better get a ball.''

"Can I come with you?'' Nick asked.

"If your mother says so.'' Two pairs of eyes—one dark blue and the other hazel—stared at her.

Julie remembered his reaction earlier when she seemed to hesitate about letting him play with the boy. "Of course.''

She wanted to offer to do his laundry while they played, but she thought she would wait for a better time. So she turned and went inside to change her own clothes. Perhaps she would make some chocolate chip cookies.

She didn't have anything better to do.

Julie's eyes followed her son up the stairs of the garage, and she felt unsettled. Lonely. Even a little forsaken. Her job was gone. Now she was also losing a part of her son to the man who was still a stranger in so many ways.

Pain started to crowd in back of her eyes, and she was conscious of a slight mist blurring her vision.

After a moment of indulging in self-pity, she snapped out of it. *She* was lonely? How must Murphy feel? No one had ever been as alone as he'd been, and she'd never seen even one minute, one mini-second of self-pity. He'd just picked himself up and charged ahead.

Well, dammit, she was going to do the same thing.

She marched to the bedroom, exchanged the suit for her own blue jeans and a warm sweatshirt. Then she ran her brush through her hair. It had been a long time since she'd played baseball.

Ryan concentrated on the ball. He threw it as gently as he could to Nicholas, who tried as hard as he could to grasp it. But his hands were so small.

Ryan moved closer and closer until Nicholas caught it two or three times, his serious face, pinched in concentration, lighting like a lamp turned on in a dark room at every success. Ryan's heart thumped harder every time Nick grinned, at the uninhibited pure joy of the boy. For the first time, he felt truly relaxed, truly content. Then, like a lightning strike, something flashed through his mind like a film clip. A hand coming down toward him. Fear. No, terror. Then whatever it was disappeared, leaving a residue of panic. He'd felt panic before. He'd known it in the hospital when he'd discovered his mind was blank, again when he'd been told who and what he was. But this was different. Soul deep.

"Ryan...Mr. Murphy..."

The note of concern startled him. He suddenly realized he was just standing still, the ball rolling on behind him. Apparently Nick had thrown it. How many seconds, minutes, had he stood there?

He forced himself to move from his frozen position. "It's okay, partner." But it wasn't. The panic was still there, welling up inside his mind. He heard it in the hoarseness of his voice, felt it in the rapid beating of his heart. Where had it come from? That picture?

The other one had been benign. This was not. He felt as if evil had just traveled through his soul.

Nick's face was screwed up anxiously, his wide eyes staring at him.

"We'll try again," Ryan said, fighting to control the demon suddenly loosed inside him. He took several strides and leaned down to scoop up the ball. "Just once more."

He moved closer to Nick and threw it as softly as he could, but even then it had a power he didn't expect. Nick tried to catch it, but instead it hit his chest, and he let out a little oomphhhh and tumbled.

Ryan's breath stopped and, in four strides, he was next to Nick, kneeling, his hands going around the boy. Such a small fellow. "Are you hurt?" He barely managed the words.

Nick shook his head as his lips seemed to quiver.

Ryan picked him up and dashed for the kitchen door just as it opened. "The ball hit him," he explained tersely. "It was my fault."

"Put him on the sofa," she said, leading the way to the living room. Once there, he very carefully set the boy down and moved away for Julie.

She sat on the sofa next to Nick and started a gentle questioning, then opened his shirt. There was a red mark and she touched it gingerly.

"I'm okay, Mommy," Nick said impatiently. "I want to go back out."

She sat back and looked up. "I think you can stop worrying. Boys tumble."

"I threw the ball too hard." He refused to excuse himself. Guilt weighed heavily on him. What did he know about small boys? What if the ball had hit Nick's head? What if? He recalled the fierce pain in his head when he'd first emerged from unconsciousness. That sudden flicker...impression...whatever it was had completely distracted him, and it still haunted him.

"I'm sorry," he said. "I didn't mean..."

She stood, her eyes meeting his. "Of course, you didn't." Her eyes met his, and the tension started to fade from him. They were so full of understanding, so...very pretty. She had looked spectacular this morning in the coral-colored suit, its brightness contrasting with her gray eyes and dark hair combed back into a sleek knot, but then she seemed untouchable, too perfect and too pretty to touch. He far preferred her this way. The jeans were snug but not tight, neatly encasing trim but rounded hips and slender legs. The sweat shirt had a zipper front which settled nicely over well-proportioned breasts. She'd released the hair from the slick, sophisticated bun and it swung easily around her face.

She looked delectable. One kind of tension faded from his body and another replaced it.

But the remnants of that brief hint of memory, the bleakness it had created inside him warned him. Was his memory returning? Or parts of it? And if it was, what if it was filled with that sense of malevolence he'd felt. Could he bring it into this house? To Julie and to a young boy?

His face must have revealed something, because Julie was staring at him. "What is it?"

He shrugged. How could he describe those two odd glimmers of what must have been the past. A baseball coming at him? A hand raised? They'd been so fast that he wondered whether they really had been memories. Or imagination.

But she wasn't going to let it go. "Something's happened."

He wasn't going to lie. "I had a...couple of flashes."

Her eyes riveted on his. "What kind of flashes?"

"Like photos developing in my head. But they disappeared so fast, I'm not even sure they weren't thoughts, imagination. Hell, I don't know what."

"What were they?"

"One was a baseball coming at me."

"The other?"

"I'm...not sure." How could he explain that sensation of dread, of something far more dangerous?

"You should see Dr. Dailey. At least, tell him about them."

He was tired of doctors, weary of their tests and their contradictory conclusions. Other things—like making a living and paying Julie back for her time—seemed more important. His parole didn't include mandatory visits to a psychologist or neurologist, although treatment had been part of Julie's plea.

"They were too quick, more like impressions than anything else."

"Maybe it means your memory is coming back."

Nick had been forgotten for a moment, and he was wriggling impatiently, obviously disgruntled at no longer being the center of attention.

"I think you need some quiet time," Julie said. "Why don't you draw Ryan another picture."

"But I want to play catch again."

"Not any more today, Munchkin."

Nick's face fell.

"And you need more padding," Ryan said. "And a bat."

"For real?"

"For real."

"I don't hurt," Nick said, obviously afraid his tumble might affect future sessions.

"I think you are a very brave boy," Ryan said. "And I *would* like another picture." He hated manipulating the boy, but he was suddenly getting very warm, and he knew he needed to get away. He needed to be alone. He needed to think about what had happened, and what it meant. Just as strongly, he needed to get away from Julie. He wanted her too much. He already felt his body responding to the...intimacy between them. And after this afternoon, he felt stronger than ever that he couldn't bring his baggage into her life. Not until he understood it better. Not until he knew exactly what happened ten years ago.

After they watched Nick trundle off to gather paper and crayons, he turned toward the door.

"It really wasn't your fault," she said.

He just kept going.

Why was it that whenever Murphy left, the house felt suddenly empty? It had never felt that way before. She'd loved every nook and cranny because it had been all hers. But he filled it with an energy and vibrancy that made it come alive, and made her realize how much she'd been using it as a hiding place rather than a living place.

She didn't think she would ever forget the look on his face when he'd brought Nick in, the tenderness with which he held her son.

Julie thought back to her meeting with Mary Elizabeth Saddler. She'd said she thought her daughter was the only person he'd loved. *Even with his daughter, he'd apparently held back. As if she were made of glass.*

Real fear—the kind that came with worry for someone else, not self—had shone in Murphy's eyes. So had guilt, although the ball had barely caused the slightest bruise, and certainly Nick had taken far harder falls in his play with Abby. He'd also been reluctant to talk about that second memory, but it evidently had made some kind of impact.

She went over their earlier conversation, and her mind stuck on Banyon. He'd never cropped up in any of Jerry's written interviews, or with Mary Elizabeth. Yet he had claimed to be a friend, enough of one to ignore ten years of absence and Ryan's conviction when no one else had. He'd had to be a good friend. But then why had he never contacted Ryan in prison? Ryan had had no visitors, according to the records. And then up pops Banyon. Why hadn't she wondered about it before? Perhaps because she'd had so many other things to wonder about. Usually, though, her prosecutorial mind seldom slipped like that.

Yet Ryan seemed determined to meet him, enough to walk nearly a mile to phone him.

She wrote the name down. Maybe Jerry ought to check on him, too.

Then she went in to check on an altogether too quiet Nicholas.

Chapter 14

Ryan was fighting a host of conflicting emotions late Sunday when he heard a knock at the door. Surprised, he went to answer it.

Banyon.

"Hi, Buddy," his visitor said. "Got your message."

Ryan didn't know what he'd expected when he left it. He certainly hadn't expected Banyon at his door.

The detective held a big flat box and a bulging paper sack. "Thought you might like some pizza and beer."

"I can't drink alcoholic beverages," Ryan said as if reciting a page of rules. He'd certainly memorized them all. And surely Banyon, being a cop, should be aware of them.

"You mean you haven't had a cold brew since you got out?" Banyon pushed past him into the center of the room, eyeing it carefully. "Hell, I won't report you."

Ryan didn't say anything, but he had no intention of violating his probation, particularly in front of a police officer, no matter what Banyon said. He wasn't going to let Julie down. Or himself.

Pizza? Now that was another matter. He hadn't had any in either the hospital or prison. But he'd seen the advertisements on television.

"Thanks," he said cautiously.

"No trouble."

Instincts. How much could he trust them? Ryan wished he knew.

He only knew that pizza or not, he wasn't sure he liked the big burly man with the "hale fellow, well met" manner but eyes that never seemed to smile even though the edges around them wrinkled as if he was trying.

Listen. His instincts were also telling him that. Since he didn't have much else to go by, he decided to do just that.

"Have a seat," he said, indicating the small table with its two chairs. Ryan went to the fridge and took out a cold soft drink and sat down himself, noticing how Banyon's gaze studied the soft drink before the man shrugged, and opened the box.

The pizza smelled good. Ryan had to admit that. But he was far more interested in the man across from him as he took a bite.

"You called," Banyon said. "Do you remember anything?"

Ryan shook his head. "No. I didn't mean for you to come out here. I just wanted to know what you remembered about...Christmas Eve ten years ago."

Banyon looked thoughtful, as if he was trying to recall those events. "I arrived after the...shooting."

Strange. In all that he had read, Ryan hadn't come upon Banyon's name. "You were there?"

"Half the precinct arrived after you made an Officer Down call."

"I was still there?"

Banyon nodded. "You were covered with blood. Cates was dead."

"What did I say?"

Banyon's brows furrowed together. "You kept saying Cates shot first. But Cates's gun wasn't out. In fact, his gun was never found. It was finally decided some passerby had picked it up."

"Wouldn't that indicate he'd taken it from his holster?"

Banyon shrugged. "Not necessarily. There was a lot of confusion. Several people tried to administer aid. A number of people could have slipped it from the holster. Some even said you threw it away before making the call so they wouldn't find a fully loaded gun."

"All I had to do was fire it once."

Banyon looked startled. "Are you sure you don't remember anything?"

"No, but I've read the reports. Some of it just doesn't make sense."

"Maybe you didn't have time to fire it."

"But I had time to throw it away?"

"Maybe someone did it for you," Banyon said uncomfortably. "Hell, I don't know."

Ryan tried another tack. "Did I say whether Cates had said anything?"

Banyon stared directly into his eyes. "Not to me."

"How well did you and I know each other?"

"We worked a couple of cases together before you partnered with Cates."

"What cases?"

"Why do you want to know that?"

"I want to know everything about the years before...my injury."

"Damn, Murphy, let it go. You have a chance to start over, and you have a damn fine looking counselor. Real ripe for the picking from what I hear."

Fury rolled through Ryan like a tidal wave. He'd been angry before. God only knew he'd felt like exploding those first few weeks in the hospital, and then at Reidsville. But it was nothing like the white hot rage he felt now. Before, he'd figured he probably deserved whatever treatment he received. Julie, on the other hand, was guilty only of a compassionate heart. He took in a breath of air and slowly exhaled it. His hands were clenched in fists. He used every means he'd learned not to strike Banyon.

Then he wondered whether that was exactly what the man wanted. Hitting a police officer? That would send him back a lot faster than a can of beer.

"Come on, Murphy. How did you get her to let you move in?"

"I pay rent," Murphy said steadily. Then he wondered how Banyon knew to come to the garage in back. Had he mentioned that when he left the message? He thought he had just left Julie's street number, or had he stopped at Julie's home first?

Banyon was on his third piece of pizza and his third beer. Murphy tried to consider the man as a friend. Had he been this arrogant as a police officer? Probably. A lot of people had said so. A shudder ran through him at the thought.

The pizza he was eating went from good to pasteboard.

Banyon apparently sensed it. "Sorry if I said something out of line. She's just real pretty. The guys say she was a good D.A." He hesitated, then added, "Been hearing she's asking questions about your case."

If Banyon wanted him to answer, he would be disappointed. Ryan had no intention of talking to anyone about Julie Farrell. He took a bite of pizza.

"How's the job?" Banyon was trying hard.

"Fine." He wondered how Banyon knew about it, or perhaps it was all in some police file. Privacy, he'd been told frequently, was not one of his rights.

"You remember how to do that stuff?"

"Some of it."

"The sawbones think you'll get the rest of your memory back?"

"They don't seem to know, or agree."

"Crazy thing, the way you can remember some stuff and not others."

"Frustrating," Murphy corrected him, realizing Banyon was far more intent on obtaining information than giving it. Why? Whys were taking over his life.

"Tell me about some of the cases we worked together," Murphy said again.

"Now you sound like a cop again. You were good. Real good. Tenacious-like. You'd get your teeth into something and nothing could stop you."

"We worked well together?" Ryan persisted.

"Hell, no one could touch us," Banyon boasted.

"Can you give me specifics?"

Banyon looked startled. "Well, there was a murder. Drug related. Victim was a young girl who was a mule for some drug dealers. You rousted every street hustler in a ten-block area. Dried up an entire neighborhood until someone started talking. You were hell-on-wheels, Buddy."

"What about a man named Castilani?"

Banyon seemed to choke on a slice of pizza. "Where did you get that?"

Ryan ignored the question. "Did we ever work together on a case involving him?"

"No," Banyon said flatly. "You sure as hell haven't lost your touch at interrogation. You sure you can't remember anything?"

"Nope," Ryan said. He'd hit a nerve. Too bad he didn't know what nerve. Or why.

Banyon rose from the table. "Gotta go. You need anything, you call me. I'll be in touch." He looked down at the mess on the table. "I'll leave those beers here. You might just remember how much you liked them."

What in the hell did that mean? Ryan worried over it. Had he been a heavy drinker? No one else had mentioned that. Another blank. Another puzzle. But then Banyon was at the door.

Ryan thanked him for coming, then shut the door behind him.

Banyon had posed more questions than answered them.

He looked at the three remaining cans of beer. Even the possession of alcohol could send him back to prison. He took the three, snapped the tops and emptied them, then put the cans in a bag and went down to put them in Julie's trash can.

Ryan sat at Julie's kitchen table Monday night with the investigator named Jerry Kidder. He tried to concentrate on Kidder, not on the woman across from him. But his gaze kept returning to her. Julie was wearing a dark blue turtleneck sweater that gave her gray eyes a blue hue and complimented her dark hair. A pair of comfortable-looking worn jeans left little to the imagination.

Nick was in bed. Julie had set the meeting at 9:00 p.m. for that one reason. She said she didn't want little ears listening.

A newspaper lay on top of the table. Ryan had already read it. A headline on the front page proclaimed:

Citizens Petition Against Killer In Neighborhood

The writer reported that area residents were preparing a petition, protesting Ryan's residence in their neighborhood, to present to both the state parole board and the city.

His stomach clenched as he'd read it. What was he doing to Julie and her son? The only thing that kept him there was knowing that Reidsville was his only current alternative. He already knew that Julie had tried to find him an apartment elsewhere, but no one would take him. Neither did he have the money for deposits that, according to the paper, were usually required. He figured it would take no less than a thousand dollars in deposits and even then he would have no furniture. For now…he didn't have an alternative.

Ryan realized immediately that Jerry Kidder was not an ally. But even then he preferred Kidder's open skepticism and honest hostility to Banyon's false heartiness.

Kidder reviewed his efforts to find the priest. He'd been able to track down all but one of the priests who had been in Atlanta during the five years prior to Ryan's arrest. The last had apparently left the priesthood, but Kidder had a name, and he would go back and interview other priests who might have known the missing man or have information about his current whereabouts. He'd talked to police officers who'd first arrived at the scene of Cates's death. There had been four patrolmen and then four detectives. Banyon was not listed among them.

Five of the eight were no longer with the Atlanta police department: two had joined smaller police departments at higher ranks, one had died and two had left the state. Jerry had talked to the three still with the department and the two who had joined other police departments in the state. They'd all told the same story. Now he was trying to find the two who had left the state, though it was obvious he expected little.

The highest ranking officer had been a Captain William Lewis who was now an assistant chief of police, the same man who had called Julie earlier and warned her about Murphy. She had not told either Murphy or Jerry about the call but now she did. "I think that's a bit odd," she said.

Kidder grimaced. "I don't know why. He was involved in the earlier investigation. It makes sense that he felt he knew more about the case and would have reason to be involved."

Ryan looked from Kidder to Julie and back again, suddenly recognizing the look in his eyes. Kidder wanted Julie. Therefore, he wanted Ryan to be guilty.

Julie didn't seem to notice.

Ryan decided to take charge. "Julie said you knew me...before."

Kidder's eyes narrowed. "Yes."

"Did we ever work together?"

"Not really. I was only slightly involved in one case."

Murphy paused. He saw undisguised dislike in Kidder's eyes. "It didn't go well?"

"You could say that."

"Why?"

Julie was listening, eyes going from Kidder to himself.

"We needed the name of a snitch. You wouldn't give it to us."

"Why?"

"You never saw the need to give us reasons."

"What kind of case was it?"

"Drugs." Now Kidder was practically combative. He said the words triumphantly as if it proved a point. "We were trying to make a drug case against a man named Castilani. You were the closest we got to him."

Ryan saw Julie's eyes widen. Castilani again. "How?"

"One of your snitches told you about a drug deal going down, said Castilani would be there. We had men there at the site. No one showed up. Later, we heard it went down someplace else. We wanted the name of your snitch. You wouldn't give it to us."

"Did I say why?"

"You were 'protecting' him. Hell," Jerry said. "We were the good guys."

Ryan was trying to follow the logic. "If no one was at the drug buy, that must mean someone warned them."

"That's what you claimed. We thought the snitch was sending us someplace else as a decoy."

"Who are 'we'?"

"A task force. Dan Watters, top police officers, some feds."

"How long was that before...my partner was shot?"

Jerry shrugged. "Six months, maybe a few months longer."

"Was Jack Banyon involved?"

"Not that I know of. Why?"

"He says he was a friend of mine. Said we worked several cases together."

For the first time, Jerry looked surprised.

Ryan persisted. "Can you find out what cases I worked during the year prior to that Christmas?"

"It will take some time."

That meant money. Everything meant money. How could he keep stacking up bills?

"I might be able to find out on my computer," Julie said.

Jerry arched his left eyebrow, but didn't say anything.

Minutes later, though, he prepared to leave. "Let me know if you want me to track down those cases," he said. "In the meantime I'll work on finding that priest, though God knows what he could tell us. That's a real long shot."

But Ryan hoped not. The priest might have been a friend, and Ryan apparently had damned few friends. If he had told anyone anything, wouldn't he have confided in a priest who could never speak of it?

Jerry looked at the newspaper. "There's gonna be more of this stuff, you know."

Julie shrugged her shoulders. "I expected it."

The detective glanced over at Ryan accusingly. "And your law firm?"

"I just finished a case," she said in a light tone.

Jerry didn't bother to hide his disapproval as he started to leave. "I'll be in touch as soon as I have anything to report." Then he turned to Julie alone. "Call me if you need...anything."

Kidder meant protection, Ryan realized. Protection from him. He stayed at the table as Julie showed the detective out. He was still mulling over what Kidder said about the drug case so many years ago. *Castilani.* The name echoed in his head.

Castilani. Banyon. Dan Watters. Kidder. All were connected in some way, tied together in a puzzle he had to unravel.

He'd been good at puzzles in all those damned tests they'd given him. Why couldn't he figure this one out?

Because he didn't have enough pieces. Not yet.

Julie returned. "Come with me," she said.

He followed her into another room down the hall. A desk with a computer faced a window. A second desk was set at an L-angle. A stack of law books occupied part of it; the rest was clear. A sign of some kind was leaned against the wall. Two chairs sat in front of the desk, one with a seat that was several inches taller than the other. She took that one and motioned for him to take the other.

"Nick likes to play computer games," she said in brief explanation. "Let's see if you remember anything about computers."

She turned it on, and started typing. Then she stared at the screen for a moment. She typed in several words and the computer spelled out "Access denied." She tried something else, and again, "Access denied."

"Da...rn it," she said.

A smile built inside him. She'd meant something stronger and had caught herself in time. He'd had to rein in similar urges. Those weeks in prison had given him a vocabulary he'd soon learned was unacceptable among most people, even if it was colorfully descriptive of some of his frustrations. If she'd worked among cops and crooks, she must have been similarly exposed.

After several moments she gave up her attempt. "I'll have to find the passwords," she said. "Let's try something else."

She showed him how to access newspaper files, national news magazines, and the Library of Congress, then moved over so he could sit at the computer. In minutes, his fingers were moving rapidly over the keys. He went to the newspaper's library and asked for Castilani. In just seconds, the screen filled with a number of stories, including a story about the man's murder three years earlier.

She leaned over and started reading with him.

Castilani apparently owned a number of businesses, including several restaurants. He also owned a multi-million-dollar home in an exclusive northwest Atlanta community. Several stories told of large gifts to charities and contributions to various politicians. Nothing about drugs.

He leaned back and looked at Julie. "You were with the D.A.'s office what...eight years? Did you ever hear of Castilani?"

"Oh yes. He was on Dan's hit list when I was there. I remember when he was killed. He was shot in front of one of his restaurants. It was said to be a robbery, but no one really believed it."

Ryan read all the stories, then printed them out. He searched for "drugs," then started to read those stories. His hands moved swiftly over the keys. Julie had just opened another door, and the room was oddly familiar. He occasionally had to ask a question of Julie, but the steps quickly fell into place.

He probably would have stayed there all night, searching the computer for one thing, then another, but he suddenly realized how late it was.

"I should go," he said, suddenly standing. "You must be tired."

As he moved, his foot caught the edge of the stick of the sign. It started to totter, and he caught it. The face of the sign turned toward him, and he read it. He felt the color fade from his face as he turned toward Julie.

"When did you find this?"

She gazed directly into his eyes. "Yesterday morning."

"What else haven't you told me?" He heard the harshness in his own voice, the anger.

She seemed to flinch for a moment, then stood taller, straighter. "A few phone calls."

"And now the petition," he said. "Anything else?"

Her eyes didn't waver. "No," she said.

"Dammit," he said, turning away from her. One of his fists slammed against a wall.

Then he felt her hand on his arm. It burned down to his core.

"I have to move," he said. "I can't live here any longer."

"No."

He turned.

Her face was set. "No one," she said, "no one is going to tell me what to do, particularly those who don't have the courage to say it to my face."

"Your son...?"

"I want my son to stand up for what's right," she said. "I want him to have courage and loyalty. I don't want him to cut and run if someone says 'boo.'" Her lips trembled for a moment. "I did that once. I cut and ran because I couldn't face what people said. I've been hiding these past few years, afraid I would make another mistake, afraid to trust."

"What if you have made a mistake?" he asked roughly. "What if you *should* be afraid to trust?"

"Then I'll do what you're doing. I'll get up and dust myself off and attack the world again." He saw a tiny muscle move in her cheek. "I won't hide again. Not ever. And I won't let cowards intimidate me."

Her gray eyes smoldered. Color had rushed into her cheeks. She looked like some warrior queen. She looked...beautiful.

He couldn't help himself. His hand went up, touched her face, tracing it, memorizing every delicate curve. She was so damn stubborn. So...gallant.

All the loneliness he'd known, all the need he'd felt these past few days, cracked open the walls he'd tried so damned hard to build. He reached for her, and she came willingly into his arms, her body nestling against his. Even as she leaned into him, his emotions warred with each other—elation at discovering more skills, hope at the growing possibility that he might have been innocent, fear that his past was still ruled by demons he didn't understand.

"Julie," he muttered raggedly and she lifted her eyes to him, looking at him as if he were the finest man in the world. His body ached for her, but even more compelling was the need to hold her, to touch, to care. Dammit, to *live*.

And now he *did* feel alive. Electrically alive. Light glowed bright inside him. Tenderness fought with a hunger that made him want to possess her.

His fingers stroked the side of her neck in gentle movements, and he felt her pulse quicken, her body move further into his. He felt her tremble, and he sheltered her in his arms.

The searing heat of their bodies radiated between them, melding them into one. His lips hungrily traced the lines of her cheek, then her neck before seeking her mouth. Piercing streaks of raw need thundered through him. Not just lust. He could handle that. What he couldn't control was the yearning deep inside to touch, to possess, to...love.

His lips reached hers, moving lazily at first, touching with a featherlike gentleness despite the explosiveness of his own body. He wanted to prolong every moment, every exquisitely painful moment of exploration. He deepened the kiss, feeling her response. Her body snuggled even more tightly into his, and her arms clung around his neck, her fingertips pressing into flesh.

Locked together by her arms, his hands moved from her neck and instinctively began to massage her back in slow movements even as she inched closer into him, their clothes presenting little barrier to the intensity of sensations building in him. As his hands pressed her hips up and tighter against him, she started to move, her body undulating in slow, sensuous movements that made him want to explode. His kiss became greedy, his tongue teasing and seducing and promising....

Tremors shook Julie's body. A hot desire—so intense she could hardly bear it—burned out of control in the very core of her, and she found herself doing things she'd never done before, had never thought of doing. It was as if her body had taken on a life of its own, reacting in wanton ways foreign to the Julie Farrell she thought she knew. She didn't care. She only wanted more, more of the feelings and sensations and emotions that shimmered between them. Desire spread throughout her like a hot summer's sun pooling golden rays on a favored spot, the circle growing wider and warmer, the living things reaching up greedily for its life-giving power. She felt consumed by the glow of light, the warmth that filled her so completely she wondered how she'd ever survived without it.

His hands were touching everywhere, igniting increasingly urgent sensations. She heard her own soft moan, the cry of her body—or was it her soul—to mate with him.

The friction of their clothed bodies was no longer enough. She was consumed with wanting and feeling, the anticipation of something even greater making her writhe inside. "Ryan," she whispered, knowing it was more a gasp than a word.

His lips left her mouth, moved to her ear, where he nibbled on it, his breath sending shivers of pleasure through her. His feathering kisses moved to her neck, to the pulse at her throat, and she thrust her head up, her eyes misting as she felt the tenderness in each caress, the tethered need in each touch. She felt his body shudder with restraint even as its rigidity radiated his passion.

She moved her hands from around his neck, one of them finding his. She brought it to her mouth, her tongue licking the calluses, tasting the saltiness of his skin. She wanted to give him everything—laughter, sweetness and joy. She wanted to watch him smile. She wanted to erase the look of haunting loneliness she sometimes saw in his eyes.

She lowered his hand and, slipping her fingers through his, she wordlessly led him from the office. She stopped at Nick's room and looked in. He was asleep. She closed the door.

Then they moved to her bedroom, closing, then locking the door quietly behind them.

She turned on a night-light. Its soft glow gave them just enough light to see each other. His dark eyes fairly blazed with the flames she felt in her own body. Her hand reached up and touched the corner of his mouth, the side that had that particular quirk, then her fingers traced the lines of his face, the strong lines that seldom broke for a smile. She loved the harsh features. She loved...

Dear God, she loved *him*.

Her fingers faltered, but she was lost in those eyes of his, in the steady intensity with which they probed her. "Are you sure, Julie Farrell?"

Her name was a melody on his lips. A multitextured song. He lingered over it, as if reluctant to let it go.

In answer, she stood on tiptoe and put her lips to his as her hands did what his had done moments before, slowly, sensuously, moving up and down his body, hesitating at the belt of his jeans. She felt the hardness of his arousal, the sudden unsteadiness of his hands on her shoulders. Then he crushed her to him, his voice whispering endearments between kisses.

She felt his hands pulling at her sweater. She obediently lifted her arms so he could pull it up. Their eyes met. His serious, searching. Hers glazed with tears at the enormity of her feelings. Slowly, his hands undid her bra, letting it fall to the floor. Then his hands were touching everywhere, caressing, stroking. His lips followed in the wake of his hands, and every vital organ, including her heart, seemed to turn to melted chocolate. Heat from his body scorched her even as his hands loved her. Her arousal grew irresistibly as his mouth touched the skin over her heart, then moved down to cover a breast, his tongue dancing around and over the nipple until she thought she would cry out with the pain and pleasure of it.

She found her own hands unbuttoning his shirt, then the two of them were unzipping each other's jeans. With a naturalness that confounded her, they stepped out of them and, unfettered by clothes, their bodies met in a primitive mating game, arching and twisting and fitting until they both were on fire.

She felt him lift her, his mouth fastening on hers, and their tongues met. Hers became as eager as his, and shivers of pleasure rolled through her body even as her heart hammered against her rib cage. He gently laid her on the bed and stretched over her, his body balanced on his arm as he looked at her.

He was waiting again for a sign, and she gave it to him. Her hands touched his chest, playing with the pattern of his muscles, with the arrow of hair that ran down toward his arousal. Her heart was a bass drum now, as he lowered himself. His hands went under her hips and she felt him tease her gently, even as she felt his every muscle tense in the effort. Then he lowered himself and she felt him probe, then enter slowly, sliding in and out until she was moist with wanting.

Her breath stopped as she seemed to step into another universe. This one was all sensation, all emotion. He moved deeper and deeper into her with slow, sensuous strokes as if savoring—and memorizing—every step along this amazing, miraculous voyage of pure wonder. He slowed suddenly, his movements becoming more deliberate, prolonging the exquisite pain of expectation, of fulfillment. He exploited every feeling, every sensation, and then reached even deeper as if he wanted to touch her very soul. Her body moved to the rhythm of his in a sensuous dance that grew in intensity and tempo until she felt she was rocketing through the skies. Her legs went around his, bringing him even further into her, as her body built to a crescendo of sensation that exploded into a nova of white hot splendor.

She cried out, then she felt him pull out, felt the hot burst of his completion against her skin, and she knew he was thinking of her, even as she had thought of nothing but the wondrous feelings her body was experiencing. He rolled next to her, pulling her to him, his hands still wandering gently over her body as if he didn't really believe he was here.

She took his hand, winding her fingers through his. His fingers tightened around hers as if she were going to disappear into thin air. She put her head near his heart, and she felt its accelerated beating.

"I should have...gotten something," he said. "I didn't...never could I have thought...imagined..."

The fingers of her free hand touched his mouth, stopping his explanation. Her body was glowing, still quaking with aftershocks from their coupling. The urgency had faded, but a quiet contented feeling of completion, of belonging, of joy lingered. She had never known love could feel like this. Douglas had simply taken. He'd never waited until she had found pleasure.

Then the insidious thought came. Had Ryan been like this with Mary Elizabeth? Had practice or instinct made him such a thoughtful and loving man?

Practice or instinct?

She lay there, listening to his heart, to his breathing, to her own breath intermingled with his. She wondered what he was thinking. Feeling...

Ryan treasured each second, each moment he held her, his hand locked with hers, her head lying so trustfully on his chest. One of his arms curved behind her, cradling her. Tenderness—or was it love—filled him, forcing him to realize how totally alone, and empty, he had been.

He wanted to keep her there forever. He wanted to make love to her again and again, and feel her reach for him.

But it was impossible, and no one knew it better than he. This was a terrible mistake, and yet he couldn't move, couldn't take his hand away. He memorized the honeyed sensation of her head lying on his heart, her body leaning into his.

The scent of sex wrapped itself around them, perfuming the air. He felt himself growing hard again, but he couldn't react to it. It had taken every fiber of his strength, his control, to pull away from her, but he knew the danger of pregnancy. God help him, he hoped there were no other dangers. Had anything happened to him in prison? Surely, he would have been told if he'd carried anything away from it.

But pregnancy was bad enough. He couldn't begin to imagine what his daughter had gone through because of him. How could he, an ex-convict and parolee, bring another life into this world? He had taken a chance of doing just that.

The warmth seeped away, replaced by an anguished melancholy as he looked down at Julie's face. It seemed so at peace. How could it be?

He felt gutted when she smiled.

He moved. "You'd better shower," he said.

"I'd rather stay here with you," she murmured, snuggling even deeper into him.

"I have to go," he said harshly.

"No."

That stopped him. How do you answer such a flat refusal? He could simply push her away.

No, he couldn't.

She started lightly combing his chest with her fingernails and his skin started prickling. Other things were happening, too. "We can't," he said quietly.

"Why?"

"If I hadn't stopped..."

"I could be pregnant," she replied with an equilibrium that was frustrating. It was as if she'd sorted it all out in her mind to her satisfaction. If not his.

"I won't do that," he said fiercely.

"Then one of us can get protection."

"Don't you understand, Julie?" he said, trying desperately to convince himself as well. "I don't even know who I am," he said bitterly. "Neither do you. As far as the world is concerned, you've slept with a killer. An ex-con. Nothing to take pride in. Certainly no one you would stand in front of an altar with."

She sat up, then, and he couldn't miss the sudden anger in her face. "I don't think I've mentioned an altar. And how do you know what I take pride in?"

"It can't be me," he said steadily. "And you're the kind of woman men marry."

"Really? Tell me more about myself."

He was stunned by the fury he was just beginning to recognize. "You're much too trusting for one thing. Dammit, I've already cost you heaven knows how much money. Friends. Neighbors. I'm not going to take away your self-respect, too."

She started to say something, but he stopped her with his own rush of words. "What if I do get my memory back? What if I am a killer? A drug dealer? Will you always wonder whether I would revert back to type? Would you question every time I didn't get home in time if maybe I'm selling drugs? Will you worry that I might do something to Nick, or that he would grow up to be someone like me?"

She started to reach out to him but he stood before she could touch him, before she could spin that web of magic around him and make him forget reality. He found his shirt and pulled it on, then located his jeans and shorts rumpled on the floor. Without looking at her, he dressed.

Finally, he turned. She was sitting up in bed, the sheet pulled around her. "I'm sorry," he said and started for the door before desire again overtook his pitifully inadequate scruples.

"Ryan?"

He stopped, but he didn't turn around.

"I *would* take pride in you," she said simply.

His insides twisted with a sick agony.

If only...

Chapter 15

Julie spent Tuesday going over all the original police reports on the ten-year-old shooting and matching them with the information Jerry had produced Monday night. Word for word, she reviewed each interview Jerry had with officers at the scene. She looked for any inconsistencies.

She planned to drive out to the location of the shooting this afternoon. She wondered whether the bar was still there, whether any of the bartenders had remained over a decade. She doubted it.

She'd wasted part of the morning fending off reporters and several particularly obnoxious New York producers who wanted Ryan to appear on talk shows. Their immediate interests were the petitions and the outcry of neighbors. However, as a sop to Ryan, they pledged to play up his heroism in the car accident.

In their dreams! She'd stopped being polite after the third call.

Another blow came when the director of the preschool called and said they'd had several anonymous calls in the past week. The callers complained that Nick's connection with a "known killer" placed all the children at risk. Because these callers wouldn't give their names, the director said she gave them no credence; however, she thought Julie should know.

After quelling her anger, she'd repeatedly tried to reach Mary Elizabeth Saddler to ask her to meet with Ryan, but no one answered at the Saddler home. Since it was Thanksgiving week, she wondered whether the family might be on some kind of holiday.

Thanksgiving! It had crept up on her this year. It would be Murphy's first Thanksgiving since prison. His first Thanksgiving ever, since he remembered none of the past. Dan and his wife had invited Nick and herself to dinner, but that would leave Murphy alone. She was quite sure the invitation did not include him.

So she decided to cook a Thanksgiving meal herself.

Now she had only to lure Ryan to dinner. She knew he would try to avoid her. Last night had put them in a truly difficult position. She'd known it when it happened, but she'd been no more able to avoid— or stop—those moments of magic than she'd been able to stop breathing. She hadn't even cared if she got pregnant. She hadn't considered it, but when he'd mentioned the possibility, a tiny glow started inside her. She would like another child. She would like a child with his indigo blue eyes, and crook at one side of his mouth, and the barest hint of a dimple.

Everyone had told her what a great catch Douglas had been, how lucky she'd been to marry him. And except for Nick, the marriage had been a disaster. Now she was...involved with someone every friend, every acquaintance, would disapprove of.

Including, apparently, Murphy himself.

She considered Thanksgiving again. On previous holidays, she and Nick had gone to a restaurant, then a movie. It had hardly seemed worthwhile to cook for two.

But now there was Murphy. If he would come.

She finished going through the reports, making notations on additional questions she wanted to ask the officers, then headed for Tim's garage. She sensed Ryan was going to try to avoid her for the next several days. She wasn't going to let him get away with it. It would be a slight detour before trying to find the bar where Ryan's life came to an end ten years earlier.

Tim met her at the door.

"Everything still fine?" she asked.

"Yep. He's one of the best workers I've ever had," Tim said, but a worried frown settled over his face.

"Tim?"

"He's too good, Julie. He's too good to stay long. I can't afford to pay him much more than I'm doing."

"No one else would even offer him a job," she said. "I wouldn't worry about it."

"It's not me I worry about," he said. "It's not fair to him."

Murphy obviously had another champion. "I don't think he believes that."

"Not now, mebbe," Tim said dolefully.

"Ah now, Tim me boy," she said with a mock accent. "It's that Black Irish pessimism of yours that has you worrying. I think he's well content. He told me you've helped him with the driver's license test. And buying a car. I don't think he's a man that forgets a favor."

"He's forgotten other things," Tim said, screwing his face into a frown.

She had to smile, pleased because he was so concerned. "You worried that maybe he couldn't fix cars. Now you're worried because he can." Then she paused. "Have you gotten any calls about him?"

"A couple," he grumbled. "Idiots. You don't have to worry about that. I don't go back on my word, and I like him."

She wondered if that was where his sudden concern came from. "What did they say?"

He shrugged. "It wasn't any of my customers, so I didn't pay much mind."

Her instincts tingled. So she wasn't the only target. Nor was the preschool. Someone was carefully waging an all-out campaign against Murphy. The neighbors *were* involved in the petition campaign, but this was far beyond petitions and, she believed, her mostly civilized neighbors. It just didn't seem right. It was far too organized on too many fronts.

Or was she merely looking for a villain, reluctant to believe that people like Emily could be so vicious as to use her son, and now endanger Murphy's livelihood, knowing well that he had to have a job to stay out of prison.

She soothed Tim with a few more words, then went into the bay area. Murphy was bent over the engine of a car and she quietly stopped several feet behind him, waiting until he was through with whatever he was doing.

"What is it, Julie?" He asked the question without looking up.

"How did you know I was here?"

He straightened and turned toward her. "Your perfume."

She hadn't used any today, but she *had* washed her hair. She didn't debate with him, however. He was as tense as a bow string on a bass fiddle.

"I had some errands to run."

He straightened, and his eyes met hers.

"Do you have plans for Thursday?"

His brows furrowed. "Day after tomorrow?"

"Right. Thanksgiving," she said with some amusement. Ryan was probably the only person in America who wasn't aware of the holiday.

"Oh," he said, looking back at the engine.

"Nick wants you to come to dinner."

He turned back to her, his eyes hooded. "And you?"

"Yes," she said simply.

"All right," he said simply.

She took a key from her pocket. "Here's a key to the house so you can use the washer and dryer. Or the computer if we're gone."

A muscle flexed in his cheek. "Don't you think that's a little dangerous? Handing out keys to strangers."

"You're hardly a stranger. Take it."

He hesitated, then accepted it without comment before turning back to the car.

"Two o'clock," she said to his back. "Thursday."

He nodded.

Julie drove downtown and to the bar. She parked, then drew a little sketch. The bar was closed, a shuttered derelict on a street of derelicts. She wondered whether it closed as a result of police attention following the shooting. Another question to be asked. Where was the owner now?

She wondered whether it would be wise to bring Ryan here. Would he have another one of those flashes.

Julie looked at her watch. Time to pick up Nick.

Thanksgiving.

A word without meaning, without emotion, to him. He knew what it represented, though. Family, home, belonging. He'd tried to ignore it, even as he wondered what it had meant to him in the past. Had he shared big turkey dinners with his wife and child?

His entire life was a question mark.

He finished earlier than usual on Wednesday. It seemed few people were worrying about servicing their cars today. He said goodbye to Tim, who was locking up.

"Have you plans for Thanksgiving?" Tim asked.

Ryan nodded.

"Good. I'll see you Friday. Do you want a ride home?"

"I like to walk."

"When are you going for your driver's license?"

"Monday."

Tim finished locking the door. A lump in his throat, Ryan started walking. Deserved or not, he was touched by Tim's friendliness and Johnny's casual acceptance. Even several calls from his probation officer, including an unexpected visit, had not dimmed either man's outlook.

The wind was cold, but he enjoyed the sensation of it against his face, and even more he relished the tangy, smoky smell of fall. He tried to avoid thoughts of Julie but he couldn't.

Julie. Just thinking about her turned him inside out. He'd stopped at a drugstore yesterday and bought protection, even as he warned himself to stay away from her. He knew just how much he needed to stay away when he had sensed her presence yesterday. He'd lied to her. It hadn't been perfume. He'd simply known. Perhaps because his heart seemed to stop, and the air had become thick, sultry, like before a storm.

A storm that beckoned, cajoled, beguiled. Tempted.

He turned down the street leading to her house. Several people in their yards turned around and went into their homes when they saw him coming. He'd noticed their open hostility before, but he hadn't realized how strong it was until he'd seen that damn sign in Julie's office, the sign that told him he needed to leave the apartment as soon as possible.

Ryan started to cross the street. He looked and saw no oncoming traffic, although there were several cars parked along the curve. He saw Nick sitting on the porch, and realized the boy must have been waiting for him.

Halfway across, he heard a car and turned his eyes away from the boy. A car was speeding down the street, coming from nowhere, bearing down on him. Ryan threw himself to the side, rolling over the curb. He heard the sound of air as the car missed him by inches and went roaring down the street.

Stunned, he remained still for a moment. He couldn't seem to breathe, and he knew the wind had been knocked from him. He was bleeding from several bad scrapes and cuts. His leg hurt and so did the shoulder which had been injured several months earlier. Nothing seemed broken. He painfully sat and watched his bleeding hands shake.

That near miss had been no accident, no hit-and-run. The car had veered right at him when he'd moved to get out of the way. He'd seen that through the corner of his eye, and his mind had registered the fact even as his body scrambled to get out of the way.

He looked around. Everyone had disappeared into their houses when they saw him on the street. No witnesses now. At least none, he suspected, who wanted to have anything to do with him.

"Ryan!"

Julie ran from the house, Nick right behind her.

Ryan stood shakily. He hurt. From head to toe, he hurt, and he felt the wet trickle of blood in several places. He even tasted it and knew his face was bleeding. And his clothes? Well, his wardrobe had just become even more limited. He tried to give Julie a reassuring smile, but he feared it was more a grimace.

"Dear God." Julie breathed the words. "What happened?"

His first instinct had been to lie, to say it was an accident but then he realized if he was in danger, then Julie and Nick might be, too. "Someone tried to run me down."

Her eyes widened, but she didn't ask him if he was sure. Instead, she looked down at Nick, whose face was screwed into a scared mask. "It's all right, Nick. Run inside and get our first-aid kit."

Instead, Nick went over to Ryan and looked up, his eyes anxious.

"I'm all right," he said.

"No, you're not," Julie said. "I'll take you to the hospital."

"No," he said flatly. "I've had enough of hospitals. And nothing's broken."

She looked as if she wanted to protest, then simply shook her head.

"Nick," she said. "Go get some of your bandages for Ryan."

Nick turned and ran inside.

"Did you see the car?"

"Just the front. It was dark green. That's all I noticed."

"I'll call the police."

"You'd be wasting your time. No witnesses except for an ex-con and a four-year-old boy." He shrugged. "Even if the police believed me, they would probably give the guy a medal. So would the neighborhood." He couldn't keep the bitterness from his voice. He didn't care about himself. But he realized the potential danger to Julie and Nicholas.

"Come on, let's go inside. We have to see to those cuts and abrasions."

Painfully, he followed her inside and obediently sat down at the kitchen table, his thoughts running wild. What if Nick had been crossing with him? A shudder ran through his body.

She put a hand on his shoulder.

It was such a familiar, intimate, natural gesture that he started to relax. Nick came running in, lugging a big box. Julie opened it. "Get me some hot soapy water," she instructed Nick, and he ran off again.

"He likes being helpful," she said. But he also knew she was trying to distract her son from what he'd just seen.

"I can't stay over the garage any longer," he said.

She moved around and sat in a chair opposite him. "And where will you go?"

"Back to prison if I have to," he said. "I won't endanger you."

"Whoever did this was after you, not us," she said. "And it wasn't neighbors."

"I won't risk it," he insisted stubbornly.

Nick came padding back with a dish full of soapy water. "It won't hurt much," he reassured Ryan. "Mommy will kiss it."

That certainly had appeal. His gaze met hers, and for a second the grim look around her mouth eased. But then she was all business, her hands very gently swabbing the raw, bleeding patches of skin, then tenderly applying an antiseptic that stung and burned, but not nearly as much as her touch. Her eyes didn't meet his again. Instead she concentrated all her attention on his various wounds.

Nick watched with unwavering concentration, his eyes full of sympathy. He put his hand on Ryan's knee and stood by him, as if guarding him from any harm. "You can have some of *my* Band-Aids," he offered generously.

He looked at Julie.

"How would you like Mickey Mouse all over you?" she asked.

"I think the guys at the garage would appreciate it," Ryan replied. Nick beamed at him.

Despite the bruises and scrapes, Ryan felt suddenly rich. Very, very rich. His heart expanded with his sudden wealth, and his breath caught in his throat from the grandness of it. Yet just as stunning was the accompanying anguish. How could he possibly accept the gift they offered so freely? What price would they pay for it?

He sat in silence as she finished. Then he stood to go. "I'm always thanking you," he said.

"We're going to call the police before you go," she said. "Then I wish you would stay for supper. It's not much...just hamburgers and coleslaw."

It sounded great. Far better than his usual sandwich. Than the loneliness that haunted him, than the frustration of trying so damnably hard to remember more than those two fleeting images that came and went so quickly. But would it be better for her?

"You're still committed for tomorrow," she said as if she read his mind. "I don't think the world will fall apart if you stay for supper tonight, too."

A smile tugged reluctantly at one side of his lips. "You don't, huh?"

"No," she said seriously. "And you would make Nick very happy."

"Please stay," Nick said on cue.

He reached out and ruffled Nick's hair. The fright had faded from the boy's eyes, but it hadn't left Ryan's own heart. What right had he to bring trouble to them both? And yet he needed them fiercely, both of them. They'd colored his black-and-white world with brightness, even radiance.

He surrendered, although he promised himself he would leave before Nick went to bed. "Only if I can help."

"You are among the wounded at the moment," she replied. "Which reminds me..."

She went to the phone and started to dial a number. In two strides, Ryan reached her and took it from her, replacing it in the cradle.

"Think of the publicity," he said. "And you know the police can't do anything."

"It would put them on notice," she said.

"If they believed me, which they won't. You didn't see it. In the meantime, new headlines, more ammunition for your neighbors. I'll be more careful from now on."

She reluctantly took her hand from the phone. He knew how she felt. She was a lawyer. An officer of the court. Lawyers reported crimes. He knew that. But he also knew reporting it would cause more trouble for her. He could take care of himself, and the attack was aimed solely at him.

Her eyes were uncertain as she looked at him, then conviction took over her voice. "We have to. And maybe the papers won't learn of it."

"And maybe the sun won't rise."

She looked at him with those wide gray eyes of hers.

"Please," he said. "It could endanger my parole."

She surrendered then, as he knew she would. He hated using that weapon, pitting her sense of duty against her loyalty to him.

Meanwhile, he would start looking for a new place to live. Maybe Johnny would know of something.

Nick was watching them from the table, although Ryan hoped he couldn't hear the words. His eyes went from one to another as if he felt the strain in the room. Of course, he felt the tension. Remnants of fear probably lingered in his mind, too. The realization was like a knife in his gut.

Ryan wondered whether he should leave then, at that moment, for Nick's sake, but it was as if Julie knew exactly what he was thinking. She shook her head.

So he did the next best thing he could think of. He tried to break the heavy cloak of tension smothering them. He took a seat across from Nick and held out his arms. The boy fairly stumbled to get into them.

"Now," Ryan said, "what did you do in school today?"

Nick screwed up his face, trying to remember. "Pitcher. We drew pitchers. I drew one of a turkey. Wanna see it?"

Ryan nodded, and the boy ran off to his room. He rose, feeling stiff and sore and raw all over. He stood for a moment, then took the three strides to where Julie was patting out hamburgers. He watched her long slender fingers season the meat, then plop them into a hot frying pan where they started sizzling.

Then she turned to look up at him, worry she hadn't shown in front of her son crinkling the edges of her eyes. "Did you mention those flashes of memory to anyone?"

Understanding immediately, he shook his head. He posed no danger to anyone, not that he could see.

"I can't believe an irate citizen would do something like that."

Neither could he. He hadn't even talked to anyone recently except Johnny and Tim and Julie. Except Banyon.

He remembered Banyon's pointed questions, his own evasions. Had the detective thought he'd remembered more than he had? If so, had he told anyone? All of it seemed far-fetched. Maybe Julie and he were reading more into it than the incident deserved. Maybe they *wanted* to read more into it because it might indicate his innocence. And maybe not. Maybe one of his old partners in crime wanted him silenced.

Or maybe it was just an accident. He wished he could believe that.

He tried to twist his thoughts back to the moment. The aroma of cooking meat smelled enticing, at least it would if he weren't so full of doubts. So was the light, flowery scent that hovered around Julie. Her face was close to his, her cheeks red from the gas heat of the stove and her eyes misting from cutting onions. He wanted to lean over....

"Ryan?" Nick's childish voice broke the spell.

Ryan moved away from Julie. Ignoring the bruises and cuts, he picked up the boy who was clutching a large, colorful picture of a turkey. Ryan's arms held him tight for a moment. So small. So vulnerable. So trusting. So prepared to love everyone.

Nick put his arms around Ryan's neck, and pressed his face against Ryan's cheek, hugging tight. The affectionate, spontaneous gesture slid straight into Ryan's heart.

"I don't ever want you to leave us," Nick said, his little fist still clutching his treasure.

Ryan's hands tightened around him for a moment. He didn't *want* to go. He didn't want to leave this house, nor the apartment footsteps away. He closed his eyes, wishing away the emptiness of his mind, the disaster of his past, the puzzles of the present, the uncertainties of the future. He wanted so much. And the hell of it was that the two people he wanted were within reach. But what would his longing cost them?

Obviously feeling left out, Prissy meowed suddenly. Reluctantly, Ryan set Nick back on the ground, and the boy proudly showed him his "pitcher." The turkey was very, very wide in the girth, but Ryan thought it very handsome and said so.

"We haven't had turkey here before," Nick confided. "We went to a rest'rant."

"You did, did you?"

"By ourselves," Nick added.

Why? Ryan wondered. She was pretty enough to have a dozen men pursuing her. And what had happened to Nick's father? She'd said he died before Nick was born, but not how. She'd said very little about her marriage. He'd never even seen a picture of the two of them together.

"Will you watch the parade with us?" Nick's question interrupted that particular thought.

"What parade?"

Nick looked at him in amazement, as if, indeed, he came from a different planet. In many ways he felt he had.

"The *Christmas* parade."

Ryan looked up at Julie who'd turned around to watch them. He felt trapped, and yet it was a silken trap he welcomed, wanted. Hell, coveted.

"It starts in the morning," she said. "Early."

"And we have waffles," Nick said, obviously trying to tempt him.

Ryan's mouth grew dry. The damned lump that too often inhibited his breathing was back.

"Please," Julie said. A simple invitation, seconded by the warmth in her eyes. She really wanted him. And he wanted to come.

He found himself nodding and was gifted with Nick's broad grin and pleasure that appeared in Julie's eyes. The lump in his throat expanded even as he smelled the odor of burning, and Julie's eyes widened with alarm before turning back to her hamburgers.

That moment gave him time to reestablish some kind of internal control.

But then Nick wriggled in his lap, and he was aware of how much he enjoyed that feeling too.

Burned burgers. Wriggling boys. Christmas parades.
He could get used to this.
If only someone wasn't trying to kill him.
If only he knew why.

Chapter 16

Julie looked sideways at Murphy as he helped her with the Thanksgiving Day dishes.

He was wearing the white shirt with the sleeves rolled up. It was tucked in the jeans that fit him all too well. His dark hair was mussed, and the dark shadow on his jaw was already appearing. All the same, he looked more relaxed than she'd ever seen him.

She attributed that to the magic of Nicholas.

She wondered what his former acquaintances would say if they saw him now, his feet propped on a table, a boy tucked within an arm, a soda in the other hand. He had watched the parade with great interest, often asking her questions about this balloon or that one. He carried on secret conversations with her son, especially when Santa Claus triumphantly climaxed the parade.

Only once had she made physical contact with him. That occurred when she was handing him dishes to put on the table. For a moment, their hands touched, and the air became charged between them. Warm, curling feelings did a slow waltz in the core of her body and worked themselves upward to twine around her heart. He looked so serious and tried so hard to be of help.

Arrogance? She didn't think it existed in this Murphy.

He'd eaten hungrily. In fact, he'd seemed to absorb every moment of the day. Several times, she'd caught him studying her, and she had the oddest feeling that he was taking a photo with his mind. He looked at Nick the same way.

She knew Nick had discussed Santa Claus—and his wish list—with him. She would ask Murphy later what Nick had mentioned. So far, she hadn't been able to pull it out of him. There was also a fifth birthday coming up next week, and a party to plan, gifts to get. She suspected Murphy would be first on Nick's guest list.

Murphy finished drying the last dish which didn't fit in the dishwasher. It was nearly six, and a football game had replaced another football game on the television.

He gave a deep satisfied smile.

"Now you know all about Thanksgiving," she said. "Parades, turkeys, football."

"And football, and football."

"I thought all men liked football."

He raised an eyebrow, and she remembered what he'd said before. He wasn't like anyone else. And he truly wasn't.

She started back for the living room. Nick was sound asleep on the sofa and she started to pick him up, but Murphy beat her to it. He did it with such careful tenderness that she thought her heart would burst. Prissy jumped down from the top of the sofa back and followed.

Julie collapsed on the sofa as she waited for him to reappear. When he returned after several moments, he stood awkwardly at the door. "I had better go," he said.

The air sizzled as she stood. His eyes seemed to burn through her. The muscle in his cheek pulsed and his lips settled in a grim line.

She stood, her legs suddenly more like wet noodles than bone. She didn't want him gone, now that she wasn't sharing him with a nearly five-year-old boy. But she also knew he was walking on the sharp edge of a blade.

"All right. Do you need anything?" Suddenly it seemed ridiculous that he would be alone in the apartment and she would be alone here. But there was no denying the set angle of his jaw.

"No." It was almost a bark.

She bit her lip and started to turn away.

"Julie."

She didn't turn.

"This was the best day I could possibly imagine." Despite the words, she heard the bleakness in his voice. She realized he hadn't changed his mind about leaving. As soon as possible.

She turned around. "I'm glad."

He started to say something, then shook his head wordlessly and headed out the door.

The telephone installation man came Friday. Murphy must have left at the crack of dawn for the garage. She'd not been in the apartment since he'd moved in, and she looked curiously around the one main room. It was as neat as if a monk occupied it.

The only decoration was Nick's picture taped to the refrigerator, and that touched her far beyond what it probably should. She stood there and stared at it. Most people, she thought, would probably have tossed it aside after saying the right things. Instead, he truly seemed to treasure it since he'd done nothing more to personalize the room. There wasn't even a shirt thrown over a chair or a dish out of place. Habits he'd learned in prison? But how would he have remembered them except for that month?

She showed the telephone man where to put a jack. She'd already bought a phone, and she watched as he worked. She wondered whether it was all an exercise in futility, that Murphy would be leaving soon.

But then she could rent it to someone else. She might need the money.

The thought was excruciating. Despite the room's barrenness, she felt Murphy's presence. This room would always be his in her mind.

When the telephone man finished, she wrote the number on a piece of paper and tucked it next to the telephone, then went to the door. She looked back briefly, seeing him pace its confines restlessly. Sighing, she closed the door. She had work to do.

Ryan stood at the door of the garage, waiting for Tim to open up. He shivered in his jacket, its collar turned up against the damp, cold wind. The temperature dropped during the night, and frost had covered yards this morning as he'd walked to work.

He knew he was early. But he hadn't slept during the night, and he wanted to leave before the Farrells—mother and child—stirred. The sky had been gray and bleak, as bleak as his own mood. As much as he had savored every warm moment yesterday, it had only emphasized the necessity to leave. He was getting altogether too close to Julie and Nick and, in doing so, he was endangering them in more ways than one.

But now that he'd experienced the miraculous feelings of belonging, of caring, he didn't know if he could bear losing them. Yet he had to. It would have been far better for him if he'd never known them at all.

Just the thought of loss ripped him apart.

He started pacing back and forth. He'd left the house a little before six. The garage opened at seven for those leaving off a car before work. Minutes seemed like hours before Tim drove up.

"Early again," Tim observed after parking the car and unlocking the door. "Never seen a man so eager to work."

Ryan didn't reply, just followed Tim inside. Customers would be coming soon, as would Johnny. He had a few moments to work on the car Tim had offered to sell him. He started to go to the back to change into work clothes.

"Murphy."

He turned. Tim O'Donnell was looking at him thoughtfully.

"You're the first one here and the last one, next to me, to leave. I think you should have a key to the place so you don't have to wait for me. You can also start locking up."

Ryan stood still, stunned by the expression of trust.

Tim obviously saw his disbelief. "I pride myself in judging character," he said. "I don't have the slightest question about giving you a key." He paused. "Johnny also has one." Oddly, it sounded like some kind of reassurance.

Tim reached in the top drawer of his desk and Ryan walked over to him. As Tim extracted two keys, Ryan noticed a gun lying inside the drawer.

Tim apparently followed his eyes. "I work real late some nights, particularly when I'm doing inventory," he explained, then closed the drawer. Ryan noticed he didn't lock it, but then what good was a locked drawer if a robber walked in?

He took the proffered keys and stuck them in his pocket. He wanted to say something, but didn't know exactly what. The simple expression of trust meant too much to express. So he merely nodded, and headed for the restroom to change clothes.

Customers started appearing, and he and Johnny were busy the rest of the day. It wasn't until late that Ryan had a chance to talk to Johnny.

They were working together on a brake job, the last job of the day when Ryan broached the subject he'd been musing over all day. "I'm looking for a new place to stay. I wondered if you might know of anything."

Johnny looked at him with surprise. "I thought you were renting Mrs. Farrell's apartment."

"Some neighbors have complained. They're not happy about having...an ex-con next door or down the block."

"She's kicking you out, huh?"

"It's my idea," Ryan said evenly. "And I think you should know that a number of landlords refused to rent to me."

Johnny busied himself over installing a brake pad. He was silent for a moment. "Can you wait a few weeks?"

"Why?"

"I've been sharing an apartment with another guy. He's getting married in a couple of weeks and moving out. The lease is in my name."

"It could mean trouble," Ryan warned. "My...probation officer can drop over any time. So can the police."

Johnny shrugged. "I need help on the rent, and you seem easy to get along with. We can try it."

A couple of weeks. At least Julie could tell people he was moving. Perhaps that would lessen some of the hostility. But could he wait that long? Could he live so close to Julie and Nick and keep away from them? He was drawn to them like a moth to fire, only the danger wasn't fully to him. He was also exposing them to flames.

But he realized that with his work schedule, it would probably take that long to find a place and even more to obtain permission to move from Davidson. This way, he could go ahead and inform Davidson. He hated the idea of asking the man for anything, especially since he knew the questions that would be involved.

He could never have a life of his own. Not for ten years at least. Which was another reason to keep away from Julie, or any other woman. Hell, he couldn't even leave the state without permission which limited job opportunities, vacations, or anything else. Just being caught in conversation with a convicted felon—another convicted felon—even if he wasn't aware of it would sent him back to prison. His existence outside walls was precarious at best.

"Thanks," he said. "I'll wait." He hesitated, then added, "I won't hold you to it. In fact, you'd be damn smart to reconsider."

"I'll remember that," Johnny said with a grin. "I'll expect your probation officer to call."

Ryan raised an eyebrow.

"I'm familiar with the procedures. My brother was in trouble once. Just some vandalism at school with other kids, but he drew probation. Jimmy almost decked his probation officer."

Ryan smiled slightly. "I'm trying not to do that."

Johnny grinned at him. "You *do* have a sense of humor," he said delightedly. "Good. I don't like dour roommates."

He said it so easily—as if it were a done thing—that Ryan felt a rush of gratitude. Between Johnny and Tim's gestures this morning, he was beginning to feel as if there was hope he could someday lead at least a partly normal life. He didn't include Julie and Nick in that prospect. He was doing his damnedest not to include them at all in his future.

"I'll finish up," he told Johnny. "It's easy from here."

"I'd trust you even if it wasn't," Johnny said. "You have ten years of new auto design to catch up on, but you'll soon know as much as I do." He hesitated for a moment. "You gonna stick with mechanics?"

"Why not? I can't very well go back to being a cop."

Johnny didn't reply, just wiped his hands on a nearby rag. "See you tomorrow."

"Right."

Johnny left. Ryan took his time in finishing, then opened the door to the office. Tim was talking to customers, and Ryan waited out of sight until they left. Then he checked to see whether there was anything else to do on the last car in the four-car bay.

"Get the hell out of here, Murphy," Tim said with booming good nature.

"No place to go. Sure I can't finish for you?"

Tim hesitated, then said, "Why not? Might as well surprise Katy for a change. I've finished everything but replacing the radiator hose on the Greene car. Didn't have one in stock but the supply company is sending it over by messenger. You can install that."

Ryan nodded.

"I told the customer the car would be ready at eight. Can you stay that long?"

Ryan nodded. "I'll lock up."

"Okay. I know Greene. He always pays with a check, and that's fine."

Fifteen minutes later he was gone, and in another five minutes, the hose arrived. Ryan quickly installed it, drove it into the parking lot and closed the bay door, then went into the office to wait for the customer. Until now, he'd avoided the customers. He didn't want anyone to recognize him and place Tim in a difficult position.

So he pushed one of Tim's old caps on his head, pulled it down over his forehead, and hoped no one would connect a grease-stained mechanic with the ten-year-old photo that the papers had used. He picked up a tattered magazine, but his gaze kept going to the top drawer, and the gun he knew was there.

He'd been a marksman, according to his personnel records. He had handled guns daily. Was it like mechanics? Would he remember how to use one? Would holding it bring back memories as the baseball had done?

The door opened and he rose from the seat. The bill was on top of Tim's desk.

"Mr. Greene?"

"Yeah, is the car ready?"

"Yes, sir." Ryan handed the bill to the man, who looked it over carefully, then wrote a check and left without a word.

Ryan watched him drive out of the garage. He locked the door and pulled the shade. Then he went to the desk drawer and cautiously took out the gun, handling it gingerly. His fingers ran over the butt, then the chamber. With ease he checked it, and found it fully loaded. The safety was on.

The weapon felt familiar in his hands, just as the baseball had. He closed his eyes, hoping for a flash of memory, but none came. But then the other two hadn't come on demand. They had been sudden, unexpected and fleeting.

He placed the gun back in the drawer, exactly where it had been, and left. It was a long walk home.

Ryan got his driver's license on Monday. Johnny had driven him to the licensing facility earlier so he was first in line. An hour later he was the possessor of still another freedom.

He returned with Johnny to the garage, although it was his day off. Since Johnny, with Tim's approval, had taken time away this morning, Ryan helped him catch up. He made final arrangements with Tim to buy the car Tim had offered. It was eight years old but in good mechanical shape and at a thousand dollars a good buy. Tim would take twenty dollars a week from his paycheck for a year.

Ryan left minutes later to see his probation officer.

It was sheer pleasure to drive himself. Armed with maps and directions, he had no problem locating the county offices. He didn't look forward, though, to talking to the probation officer.

Davidson hadn't required him to report the previous week, but had wanted him to come in today. His desk was just as messy as it had been on his last visits, and he looked as if he'd already worked twelve hours straight rather than just the morning.

"Sit down," the man ordered.

Ryan sat.

"Have a good Thanksgiving?"

Do you care? Ryan wanted to fling out the words, but instead he said mildly, "Yes, sir."

"Job going all right?"

"Yes, sir." Damn, he hated those "sirs," but he wanted something and he would play the game.

"I talked to...what's his name...O'Donnell," Davidson said as he leaned forward in his chair and peered down into the same file he had two weeks ago. "He seems satisfied with you."

Ryan saw no reason to respond.

"Any problems?"

"No."

"No drinking?"

Ryan remembered Banyon's offer. That had bothered him 'til this day. "No."

"Haven't seen any of your old prison mates?"

"I don't remember any of them, so I really don't know," Ryan replied, unable to keep the irritation from his voice.

"Watch that temper, Murphy."

Ryan felt his hands ball up into impotent fists. "Yes, sir."

Davidson nodded with approval.

Davidson appeared finished. Reluctantly, Ryan broached the subject. "I would like permission to move."

Surprise flickered over Davidson's face. "I thought you were settled."

"My landlady is...being hassled by people who don't want me there. I don't want to cause trouble for her."

"Very noble, Murphy," the probation officer said dryly. "Give me the address, and I'll check it out."

"It's with a John Gavin." Ryan wrote down the name and address. "I wouldn't be moving for a couple of weeks. His current roommate is moving out then."

"He know about you?"

"Yes. He works at the garage."

"Okay," Davidson said. "I'll let you know. Do you have a phone number yet?"

Ryan gave him the new number.

"Good," Davidson said. "Call me next week. I might have an answer for you then. Report back to the office two weeks from now. You can make an appointment the prior Friday." He dismissed Ryan with a movement of his head. "Don't forget the urine sample on the way out."

Forcing his fingers to straighten back out, Ryan rose and left. He supposed Davidson was just doing his job, but he felt like a delinquent boy every time he left that office. He felt diminished, that he had no control, and he was growing increasingly in need of control.

Ryan arrived back home at four and parked in back, leaving room for Julie to drive into the garage. He knew Julie and Nicholas would be home soon and would see the car.

He'd managed to avoid both of them since Thursday. He'd stayed at the garage until late Friday and Saturday, then Sunday walked to Peachtree and took a bus to a rapid transit station. He took the train downtown and wandered over the downtown area, once more returning to the police station. He was drawn to it, as if the answers he sought were stored there. But no sudden light. No flash of memory.

After a few moments, he walked around the downtown area, wishing something—anything—was familiar. He had lived here all his life, yet nothing looked familiar. It was afternoon before he started back, stopping at the rapid transit station at Perimeter Mall. He went into a department store and found his way to its toy department.

He selected a catcher's mitt for a small hand, then a small padded vest. He'd spent very little money so far, but he remembered that Nick's birthday was next week. As much as he recognized the need for distance, he knew he couldn't ignore a fifth birthday. Hell, he didn't want to.

When he arrived back at the apartment, Julie and Nick were gone. He took the opportunity to use her washer to wash clothes, then he retired to his own apartment where once more he looked over the files, wondering if somewhere he'd missed something. As his knowledge—and awareness—of the world and his own skills grew, he hoped to find a missing piece that would answer some of the questions Julie had posed. He kept going back to the articles about Castilani that he'd printed out from the computer. He was the knot that seemed to tie everything together.

Memory playing strange tricks? Instincts he'd never quite lost? Had he hunted the man? Or had he worked for the man? Ryan didn't know. He just knew the name echoed in his mind.

He heard a car arriving. He tried not to go to the window, but his resolve failed miserably and he found himself looking out. He watched her car disappear into the garage beneath him. In another moment, he heard a knock at the door. He opened it to Nick. Julie stood watchfully behind him.

"Can you come for my birthday?" Words rushed from the boy's mouth.

Ryan looked at Julie. She wore a sky blue sweat suit that, though obviously comfortable, couldn't quite hide the swell of her breasts or her firm, rounded hips. He remembered those hips, remembered how they felt in his hands.

"It's Wednesday," she said. "I asked him who he wanted to come for his birthday, and you were his first choice. I'm afraid you'll have to eat pizza and ice cream."

"I *like* pizza and ice cream."

The wary look on her face changed to a grin. "Good. So do I."

They both stood awkwardly, their eyes meeting above an obviously anxious Nicholas. Ryan wanted to turn his gaze away but he couldn't. She looked so incredibly appealing in blue, her gray eyes taking on a hue like smoke against a summer sky. His heart ached with the longing to touch her, to hold her close, to feel the warm comfort of her body.

"Will you come in?" he finally asked.

Nick shot in, looked around curiously, then ran over to where his picture was taped to the refrigerator. His face creased into a huge smile.

Ryan smiled at him. "My favorite possession." He didn't add that it was one of the very few he had. Everything in the room belonged to Julie. Then he turned back to Julie. "I got my driver's license today."

"I suspected as much when I had to maneuver around a strange car in my yard," she replied with a slight smile.

"You won't have to do it long," he said, looking straight into her eyes. "I think I've found another place to live."

Her tongue flicked out, licked her lips for a second, and some of the brightness faded from her eyes. But she merely nodded. She didn't ask the questions he expected.

"Johnny at the garage is losing his roommate," he tried to explain. "I asked my...Davidson for permission to move."

"When?"

"Two, three weeks, if I get permission. Johnny's roommate is moving out then."

"Nick will miss you," she said simply.

He wondered if she would, too. "It's best. I'm one hell of a role model for a kid. And it should get your neighbors off your back."

"Is that the only reason you're moving?"

"That's one reason," he said.

"What are the others?"

"I'm wrapped in a cocoon here," he said harshly, trying to break through that web of intimacy enshrouding them again. "I have to go my own way, find what freedom I can."

Her gaze was steady. Too steady. He felt as if she could see right through him. He would have been more than happy to stay here. In truth, leaving would rip his heart out. No more boy wriggling in his lap or giving him a spontaneous hug. No more brilliant smile from Julie or pancake breakfasts. No more...comradeship in trying to find the truth of his life.

He couldn't even begin to imagine the emptiness in losing those things. The emptiness he felt when he first woke months ago paled in comparison. He didn't know then what he had lost, what he could lose.

He suspected she saw all that in his face, no matter how hard he tried to conceal it.

Their voices had been low, hopefully too low for Nick to hear. But now the boy approached them.

Julie's gaze went down to him, and Ryan saw her expression soften. He hadn't thought he could care more than he already did, but somehow each time he saw her his feelings grew stronger, deeper, more painful.

"We had better go," she said. "I would like to talk to you later at my house. I have some other news for you."

He hesitated. He was only too aware of the effect of her house on him. Each room was so reflective of her, its comfort and personality and warmth like a drug. "What about here?"

She shook her head. "I don't like leaving him alone."

Of course. He should have thought of that. "All right," he said.

"After Nick goes to bed."

"Around nine?"

"That sounds good," she said, then looked down at Nick. "Come on, Munchkin," she said. "Time for supper."

"Ahhhhhhhh, I don't want to go."

"Not even if we have ice cream for dessert?"

Nick looked up slyly. "If Ryan can come."

Ryan was tempted. Hell, he was always tempted. But he couldn't afford it. Nick couldn't afford it. "Not now, pal. I have some work to do."

Nick's face fell so far it almost hit the floor. "Tomorrow?"

Ryan's gaze met Julie's. "If I get home in time." He would make sure he didn't.

But Nick looked happier, even as Ryan's heart crumpled even more. It wasn't exactly a lie, but close enough.

"Come on," Julie urged Nick.

"I wanta give Ryan a hug first."

Ryan obediently stooped.

Small arms went around his neck and a wet mouth planted a kiss on his cheek. It snuggled its way into Ryan's soul. He suspected that hug would remain there a very long time, wrapped around a heart that had no right to it. Reluctantly, he released the boy.

When he stood, he noticed that Julie was looking away.

He closed his eyes for a moment and took a deep breath. When he opened them, Julie and Nick were gone, and the only evidence of their presence was the moisture in his eyes and the click of the door closing behind them.

Chapter 17

Julie sat across the table from Ryan. He was no longer Murphy. She had tried to think of him as Murphy as long as possible. But now he was *Ryan* Murphy. Friend as well as client. More than that. The man she loved.

But from the moment she'd opened the door, she knew he intended to put an end to any additional intimacy between them. She understood why. He worried about her and Nick, about the sign, about the newspaper articles. And probably most of all about the speeding car. Even then, he didn't know the whole of it. He didn't know she'd lost her job. Neither did Jerry. The fact that she'd always worked at least part of the time at home made her sudden freedom go unnoticed.

Still, she had been stunned when he announced his intention to leave. The reality hit her far harder than she'd imagined.

"You have news?" His mouth was grim, his edginess visible.

"Your former wife said she'll talk to you. You can call her during school hours and schedule a meeting."

She saw the intake of his breath. He sat absolutely still for a moment, his capable hands motionless.

She handed him the number. His right hand moved toward it, his fingers touching it gingerly as if reluctant to take it. The pulse moved in his throat.

"I liked her," she said. "You will, too." She hoped not too much.

He'd been attracted to Mary Elizabeth once. He must have been in love since he'd married her. Would he still want her? The thought had nagged her since she'd talked to Mary Elizabeth.

He lifted his eyes from the piece of paper, and she saw pain in them. She couldn't even begin to understand how he must feel. Meeting a woman he'd once loved, whom he felt he'd wronged terribly. Not remembering probably made it worse, not better. She understood the guilt he carried inside.

She knew all about guilt.

"Your husband," he said as if he were reading her mind. "You never talk about him."

He was really asking something else, she realized. He was wondering about the intimacy of marriage, about the feelings he should have.

"No," she agreed.

His eyes met hers. He didn't ask again, just waited.

"He...committed suicide a little more than five years ago."

The statement was like a blow to his gut. He knew Nick's father had died before his birth. He'd thought once about using the computer to search newspaper files for her name, but he'd resisted; he owed her too much to violate her privacy.

"He was a lawyer, too," she said. "A brilliant one, everyone said. He was also a gambler and God only knows what else. After he died, I learned he'd been laundering money for the bad guys while I was out trying to prosecute them." She tried to smile, but it never made it to her eyes.

Ryan felt her lingering sense of betrayal. Why had she ever taken him on after something like that? "That's why you quit the district attorney's office?"

"That and the fact that I convicted the wrong man of murder."

"And why you took my case? Because you're human and make mistakes, and now you're trying to atone for them?" Ryan's voice was harsh.

"No," she said honestly. "Because I thought the man who risked his life pulling a boy and woman from a burning car was worth saving."

"Even if he had been guilty of murder?"

She met his gaze evenly. After a moment, she said, "I didn't believe it was the same man."

"And if it was?"

"Are you saying he is?"

"I'm asking a hypothetical question."

Her eyes were searching his.

"I truly don't know," she said slowly. "My track record's not very good. Maybe I needed something to believe in again."

"And you picked me?" he asked in disbelief. "You do like to jump from the frying pan into the fire."

"Is that what I did?"

"That seems to be the common consensus."

"The common consensus was that I should marry Douglas. Also that Corrigan was guilty. I don't have a great deal of faith in common consensus."

Her eyes were full of sparks again. He wanted to ask more, but she shook her head. "I wanted to talk about you."

"Did you love him?" He ignored her attempt to shift the conversation.

She didn't have to ask him who. "I thought I did."

"Thought?"

She started chewing on her lip as she sometimes did when worrying. "I can see why you were such a good detective. You don't give up, do you?"

He shrugged. "You know as much about me as I do, and I don't know anything about you." But he did. He knew of her kindness, her intelligence. He knew of her stubbornness. But he didn't know why she was all those things, just as he didn't know why he'd been any of the things people had said about him.

"Now you do," she said. "I wanted to talk to you about...what Jerry's discovered. Jerry's talked to the two policemen who moved out of state," she said. "They didn't have much to add to what we've already heard. One, though, said how shaken you were. He said you seemed genuinely, righteously, angered by what had happened, that you continued to insist that your partner had tried to kill you. He said you mentioned Castilani's name. He was baffled when you were charged with the crime."

Julie saw a flame jump in those eyes he tried to keep masked. It flared when she said Castilani's name. "At least someone was," he said bitterly.

"Jerry also got a lead on the man we think is your priest. His name is Sean O'Grady. He evidently left the priesthood because he got in trouble protecting a couple of boys who ended up killing someone. The church decided he would be better suited somewhere else. He disagreed. The church won't give any information, but we're looking."

"If he's working with kids, he should be easy to find. Social Services..." Ryan stopped suddenly, a closed look on his face.

Julie stared at him. He sounded like a cop, just as he had when he'd been questioning her. Disquiet stirred deep inside, but she tried to ignore it. Ryan's comment meant nothing.

"Anyway, he's working on it." She wanted to add that she was doing the same, but then he might wonder about her job.

He stood and paced restlessly.

"Why don't you get us a soda from the fridge?" Perhaps it would help the dryness in her mouth, settle the butterflies in her stomach.

He reached the refrigerator with his easy-jointed grace and took out two sodas, then returned to the table and shoved one over to her. Julie watched as he took a long swallow.

She played with her can, hoping its icy sides would travel through her fingers and cool the heat surging through her. Even if she tried to drink, her throat was so tight she didn't think she could swallow. She was so aware of him, of the mysteries that eddied around him like water in a vortex. The tip of his tongue moistened his lips, signaling his own awareness.

Who was he? Fine question to be asking now.

She tried to swallow, to break through that lump in her throat that threatened to suffocate her. She was aware of wetting her own lips, of his dark eyes on her.

She fought against the spell wrapping itself around her.

She scraped her chair back and started to her feet so quickly that the chair fell backward with a clattering noise. Horrified at her own lack of control, she grabbed for the edge of the table. He moved swiftly to her, his hands going around her waist, steadying her.

Unsteadying her.

He muttered audibly.

She groaned to herself.

"Julie." His voice was a caress even as his fingers pressed tightly into her skin. She felt his breath on her forehead, the slight whisper of a kiss.

Then just as suddenly, he let her go and stepped away. He turned and bowed his head. He looked so in pain that grief washed through her.

She wanted to touch him. But the figure standing there was a fortress unto himself.

"I'd better go," he said Anguish brushed the words.

She didn't want him to leave.

But for him, she said nothing as he disappeared out the door.

Nicholas's birthday was an ordeal Ryan barely survived. He'd not seen Julie since Monday night, though he replayed their conversation over and over. It explained some things about Julie, and he felt more protective than ever before. That meant he had to get as far away from her as he could. She'd certainly been kicked in the teeth before by someone she loved and trusted.

When he reached her half-open door, he heard angry words.

"A few weeks is too long. You've got to get rid of him now," Jerry was saying. "Lewis is convinced he was guilty ten years ago and that this whole amnesia thing is an act."

"Lower your voice," Julie said. "Nick will hear."

"Will you listen to me, Julie? I haven't found a damn thing that doesn't point right to him, and this idea you have about his character changing, well, I just don't buy it. If you won't think of yourself, think of Nick. And this damn party with him," Kidder added angrily. "It's because none of the kids would come while he's here, isn't it?"

"It's because Nick wanted him," Julie said.

Ryan backed away. The two packages in his hands suddenly felt like lead. Had the parents of other kids kept them away from Nick? Had Julie's help isolated her even more than he thought?

He went back to his apartment and stared down at the phone numbers sitting beside it. His former wife's. He'd called yesterday and made plans to see her Sunday; she'd insisted the meeting be away from her house.

Finally, he heard Kidder's car leave. Ryan would have left, too, but Nick was expecting him. Because of him, there was but one guest. He had no right, no matter how much he wanted to run, to disappoint the boy. He picked up the two packages he'd wrapped so carefully the night before.

This time, he knocked. Julie opened the door, and he saw her cheeks were red, her eyes angry. But they softened when they saw him, and especially when they went to the packages in his hand. "You didn't have to do that."

He felt big, and awkward. Damn, he felt like a fraud standing in the kitchen with gifts, just like any law-abiding citizen. Jerry Kidder's warning had told him only too clearly that people regarded him as a threat. He'd been lulled into thinking otherwise because of Tim's trust, and Johnny's acceptance, but they were clearly the exception.

Two more weeks. He would be out of the Farrells' lives. He could give them no greater gift.

As Julie took the packages, she smiled, though her eyes looked embattled.

"Nick's playing a new game on the computer," she said. "Before I call him, I wanted to ask you something."

"What is it?"

"You and Nick were whispering at Thanksgiving. Did he tell you what he wanted for Christmas?"

"A puppy," he said. It was one of two items Nick mentioned. He wasn't going to mention the other.

"I was afraid of that."

"You don't want one?"

She chewed on her lip. "It's not that. But he'll be in school all day next year and I...well, it's unfair to a dog. Prissy doesn't mind being alone, but a dog...needs attention."

Had he ever had a dog? A cat? He liked Prissy, who occasionally condescended to allow him to stroke her. Did he like dogs? He thought he would. He wondered whether he would go through life wondering about his likes and dislikes.

Nick burst in then, Prissy at his heels.

"Ryan," he said happily and Julie raised her eyes in desperation.

But Ryan stooped and gave him a hug. "I'm ready for that pizza and ice cream you promised."

"Me, too," Nick said, but his eyes went covetously to the colorfully wrapped packages on the table. "Can I open them?"

Julie shrugged. "They're from Mr. Murphy. It's up to him."

"Can I, Ryan? Can I?"

Ryan nodded.

Nick climbed up on a chair and took the smallest package first, shaking it carefully, before tearing off the paper. He broke into a big grin when he saw the glove and pulled it onto his small fingers.

He then opened the other, finding the little chest protector. "Look, Mommy, just like a 'lanta Brave." He climbed down and gave Ryan another hug. "Let's go play catch."

Ryan looked up at Julie.

"Go ahead," she said. "I'm calling now for the pizza. It'll take thirty minutes or so."

Ryan found himself trailing Nick. In one way he felt very successful. Nick obviously loved his gifts. But at the same time, he realized that in another two weeks, he would be gone. Nick would have his old friends back.

He wished he didn't feel so empty at the thought.

As he waited in a fast food restaurant four days later for his ex-wife, Ryan thought of Nick's birthday. It made him think of all the birthdays he'd never shared with his daughter.

How could his wife and daughter not hate him?

Mary Elizabeth had asked that they meet away from her home, away from their daughter, and had selected an easily located waffle house. Her husband had insisted on accompanying her.

Ryan arrived early and took a booth where he could watch the door. He had not the slightest idea what she looked like other than what Julie had told him. Slender. Pretty. Taffy-colored hair. He drank a cup of coffee, then another as he studied the entrance. What would she tell him? What *could* she tell him?

His mouth was dry when a couple hesitated at the door, then entered. He knew immediately from Julie's description that the woman was Mary Elizabeth. Her eyes swept the interior, then she whispered something to the man with her. He went to sit at the counter, while she came over to Ryan's booth. He stood.

"Ryan?" she said uncertainly.

How did one address an ex-wife he didn't remember? He nodded. "Thank you for coming."

She was studying his face. "You haven't changed much."

He didn't have an answer to that. He couldn't even offer a similar response.

After a moment, she slid into the booth, and he took a seat opposite her.

"You really don't remember, do you?" she said.

"I'm sorry." Trite word. Inadequate word. He had lived with this woman nine years. He had made a baby with her. He had hoped that on meeting her he would recognize something. Feel something. Instead, she was a stranger. A pretty stranger with wounded eyes.

She opened her purse and took out a small pocket-size album. "Pictures of Laura. I...put one in there for every year since...you went away."

He opened it slowly. A child Nick's size stared out at him over a birthday cake. Pain ripped down his middle. It was so strong he almost doubled over. "She's...beautiful."

"Yes, she is," Mary Elizabeth said softly as he slowly flipped through the other photos. He watched the child grow and ripen into a lovely young woman. In the last photo, Laura was wearing a blue evening gown, a gardenia pinned in long, straight light brown hair. She looked breathtaking. One photo, about a year old, showed her on a high-school stage in a gypsy costume. He noticed the name of the school on the curtain overhead.

"She's in the tenth grade and on the honor roll," Mary Elizabeth said. "She has a wonderful voice and is active in theater and the choir."

His fingers wrapped tightly around the book.

"You can keep it," Mary Elizabeth said softly.

"Does she know about me?"

"Yes. She reads the papers. I've never tried to hide the fact that her father was..."

"In prison?" Was that broken voice his own?

"Yes. She also knows you're out. And why. But none of her friends do. My husband adopted her when she was eight. We sent you papers, and you signed them."

"She doesn't want to see me?"

"No. You broke her heart, Ryan. You never sent her a letter or a card or a present. I pretended for a while that presents came from you, but she found one in a closet before I packaged it. She knew when she opened it that I had bought it, not you. She loved you. She would have forgiven you anything but forgetting about her."

Ryan already knew from his experience with Nick the fragility of a child's heart. He felt now as if the life had been squeezed out of him.

"Why did you come?"

"Because I know you wouldn't have done it without a good reason. I expect you thought it would be better for her in the long run. It's just that you never explained your reasons. Not to me. Not to anyone."

"I never said anything to you about my partner?"

"That he might be crooked?" She was already anticipating him. Because of Julie? Or something she knew?

He nodded.

"No. But you were especially tense those weeks before Christmas. I knew something was up. You always got that way when you were closing in on something."

"Julie said I took money from our account without explaining."

"It was yours. You always insisted I keep the money I earned as a teacher in a separate account. It just bothered me that you never explained why you were spending several hundred dollars at a time. That was a lot of money to us."

A waitress came and she ordered a cup of coffee and a waffle, and he did the same though he'd never felt less like eating.

"How did we meet?"

She had pretty hazel eyes, and they softened. "We had a class together, and I had a terrible crush on you. You were by far the best student in the class, and one day I got the nerve to ask you to help me. We started meeting for coffee, then celebrated my birthday with dinner. You would never tell me your birthday, so I made one up for you and insisted on buying you dinner. You got all quiet and serious, and I sensed you'd not had many birthday celebrations. I think I fell in love with you then and there.''

"When did we get married?"

"After you graduated from the police academy. You called me one day and said you missed me. I had just finished college and had planned to do my practice teaching here in Macon. It's my home. But when you called, I decided to move to Atlanta instead. In three months, you asked me to marry you."

"You weren't happy?"

"I was deliriously happy at first. But you were always quiet, and when you joined the police force...you seemed to draw further and further away from me. You never wanted to talk about work, and I was scared to death every time you left the house. I think you thought you were protecting me, but not knowing—imagining—is always worse than reality. I started nagging and you grew more and more distant."

"And I never told you anything about that night."

"You told me your partner tried to kill you. I think you were stunned when you were arrested. Then you just broke contact with me. You refused to see me or take my calls. You returned my letters. They announced you'd confessed, and I didn't believe it. You were more committed to that job than you were to me. But then Captain Lewis came to see me, said there was no doubt..."

Her voice broke off.

"I'm sorry."

Her husband came over then, a scowl on his face. He looked at his wife. "Is anything wrong?"

Ryan could tell he was ready to do battle for her, despite the fact that Ryan had four inches and thirty pounds on him. Saddler had nice features when he wasn't frowning so fiercely, and his eyes openly adored his wife.

She smiled at her husband and there was no mistaking the warmth between them. "David, this is Ryan Murphy. Ryan, my husband, David."

Saddler's scowl deepened. He didn't offer a hand. "Murphy," he acknowledged curtly.

He was afraid. Ryan sensed that immediately. Not afraid physically. Ryan sensed he would probably take on an army for his wife. But afraid he would lose her.

He slid out of the booth. It was time to go. He would have liked to stay longer, to ask more questions, but he had enough for now. He knew about his daughter, he knew his former wife was happy. He had done enough damage to both. He wasn't going to cause more trouble.

"Thank you for seeing me," he said. "I won't bother you again."

"It wasn't a bother," she said. "Maybe…given some time Laura…"

He shook his head. "It's better this way."

He nodded at David Saddler and left, forcing himself not to look back.

Julie regarded the spruce in the Christmas tree lot critically.

Such decisions were exceptionally important.

"What do you think, Nick?"

He looked up and up and up just as he did with Ryan. Now why did she think about that? This was an escape from those thoughts.

"I like it," Nick said after due consideration. "I bet Ryan will, too."

She sighed. Perhaps it *would* be best if Ryan moved. He was all Nick talked about these days. He'd been bitterly disappointed when Ryan left early this morning. Nick had wanted him to go tree hunting with them, and had even wanted to wait for him to get back home before going. She would have thought it perfectly absurd that someone could make such an impact on a young life in a matter of weeks. Yet she was no better. She too had known disappointment when his car was gone this morning.

A family, complete with father, came to investigate the tree, and she hurriedly told the salesman they would take it. She waited while he chopped off some of the bottom and then hauled it to the car, sticking half of it in the trunk and securing it there.

She selected a wreath for the door, then paid for both. When they got into the car, she inserted a Christmas tape into the cassette player.

"After leaving the tree off, do you want to go see Santa Claus?"

Nick wriggled with excitement. "Maybe Ryan can go with us."

She closed her eyes. Hopefully, Ryan would still be away. She realized only too well why he felt he had to move. She knew he would probably slice off his hand before hurting Nicholas, but each time they did something meaningful together, it deepened bonds that he desperately was trying to avoid.

Maybe he would still be gone. And yet…

Yet…

Ryan reached his apartment in midafternoon. He had mulled over the conversation with Mary Elizabeth the seventy miles home.

How could he have done what he did to his child? How could he have cut her out of his life so heartlessly?

He had no place to go for answers.

Except Banyon. Banyon had said they were friends. They had been partners. Had he ever said anything to him about his wife and daughter?

Ryan took the stairs two at a time, unlocked the door and, leaving it open despite the cool temperatures, went directly to the phone and called Banyon. He had the man's home number now, and he dialed that number.

Banyon answered and Ryan heard the sound of a football game in the background.

"Jack. It's Murphy."

"Ryan. Anything wrong, buddy?"

"No, just...thought I could use a little company."

There was a silence. Then, "Sure. Where?"

"Where did we used to go?"

"A bar on Highland. Harry's. I'll pick you up."

Ryan hesitated. He wasn't supposed to go into bars.

"Don't worry about your parole. This place only serves beer, and half its business is food. No different from any restaurant."

"All right. I have a car, though."

Ryan got directions and arrived at Harry's thirty minutes later. The place looked as if it had been there fifty years and hadn't been painted in all that time. But every stool at the bar and all but one of the booths were filled. All faces were riveted toward a television hanging in a corner, probably the same football game he'd heard earlier over the phone.

Ryan looked around for a moment, located Banyon who half stood from the booth he occupied. One empty beer bottle and one half full stood in front of him on the table. Fast drinking since they'd spoken only a half-hour earlier.

Ryan slid into the booth and a man who looked at least one hundred years old came tottering over to ask what he wanted.

"A cola."

The ancient looked disbelieving, as if no one had ever made such a request before, and tottered back off.

"Still being a good boy?"

"Wouldn't you? If ten years in prison depended on it?"

Banyon regarded him quizzically. "How does it feel, being out?"

"Better than being in."

Banyon chuckled. "I bet." Then his eyes took on a gleam. "Heard you were moving. Things not working out with that woman attorney?"

Ryan's stomach clenched. "Where did you hear that?"

"The police department's interested in you, buddy. Word gets around."

Davidson. The information had to have come from the probation officer. *The police department's interested in you.* Why? Why bother with a ten-year-old crime? And why was Banyon so ready to meet him on a moment's notice on a Sunday afternoon?

The detective was still waiting for an answer to his question.

"It's just time to leave," he said simply.

"Remember anything yet?"

Banyon had asked that before. Suddenly it was very important to know why.

"Yes," he said.

Banyon's eyes narrowed. He leaned forward in his seat. "What?"

"Just flashes right now," he said. "My wife. My daughter. More and more things are coming back," he lied, surprised at how easily it came. Yet Banyon's interest intrigued him. Something told him to feed it.

"Anything about that night?"

"What night?"

"The night Cates was killed," Banyon said.

Ryan shrugged. "I'd rather talk about my wife and daughter. You said you knew my wife. Did you ever meet my daughter?"

"Yeah. Pretty little thing. Have you talked to her?"

Ryan shook his head. "I saw some pictures. She still has the same dark hair." He wanted to know whether Banyon really had met Mary Elizabeth and Laura.

"Yeah, just like yours."

Except Laura, according to the pictures, had light brown hair, just like her mother.

"Not surprising since Mary has dark hair, too," Ryan said. He held his breath. He doubted now that Banyon had ever met either his former wife or daughter. Why would the detective pretend a relationship that never existed? Ryan didn't like the only obvious answer.

Banyon nodded. "I remember it. Real pretty lady, your wife. Any flames still there?"

So Banyon knew about the visit this morning. He could know only if Ryan's phone was tapped or if he'd been followed. Ryan felt cold, as if his blood had turned to ice water.

His cold drink came. He tasted it, trying to digest what Banyon had just said. Why so much interest in him? Why had his probation officer been talking to the police? Why was he being followed?

"No," he said softly.

"Had any since you got out?"

Ryan knew exactly what "any" meant. "No," he lied again.

Banyon finished his bottle and signaled for another one. "I know some women if you're interested."

"Thanks but no thanks," he said.

Banyon shrugged. "Your loss."

Ryan took a sip of the tepid drink, his thoughts tumbling over each other. "Why the interest in me?"

Banyon looked startled. "What do you mean?"

"You said the department was interested in me."

"Hell, you used to be one of us. It's natural."

After ten years? Interested enough to contact his probation officer? To follow him? Ryan doubted it. He looked outside. The sky was darkening. The clouds were dark, ominous. Bleak.

He tried one more tack. "You remember any more about Castilani? Whether I ever mentioned him to you?"

Banyon paled just as he had before, then blustered. "Why should I?"

"Just thought you might," Ryan said, shrugging. "Can't seem to get that name out of my head."

Suddenly Banyon seemed anxious, jittery. Anxious to go.

Ryan felt a moment's satisfaction. He'd struck someone's gong.

"I gotta go," Banyon said. "You learn anything, let me know."

"I'll do that," Ryan said drily as Banyon rose, seemingly unaware of the irony in Ryan's reply. The big detective threw several bills on the table.

Ryan stood and followed him out the door. He'd invoked some kind of reaction. He only wished he knew what it was.

Ryan held Nick as the boy very carefully attached an angel to the top of the tree, then slowly lowered him.

"That's my special Christmas angel," Nick confided. "Mommy says she makes wishes come true."

If only she did. Ryan had several wishes he wouldn't mind coming true. But he doubted if a Christmas angel involved herself in those kind of dreams. They were pretty heavy duty for a delicate crystal fairy.

"Mommy says she winks when she grants a wish," Nick added, just a little dubiously.

"I thought angels rang bells," Ryan said, then wondered where that idea came from.

"That's only in movies," Julie said with a throaty chuckle. "My angel is unique. My mother bought her when I was a child, and she always told me Francesca winks. She said I didn't look quick enough to see her.

"Francesca?"

"Francesca," Julie said firmly.

Ryan couldn't stop looking at the way her eyes sparkled. He'd been captured by the boy just as he arrived back at the apartment and shanghaied into helping put up the tree. From the moment he'd entered the house he'd felt transported to a magical land. The house smelled delectably of hot chocolate and freshly baked cookies and spruce, and he'd drunk it in like an alcoholic who'd just had his first drink in months.

As he helped string lights and attach little ornaments to branches, he couldn't help but contrast the small dingy bar to the warmth of the room. Or to the loneliness he knew awaited him once he left the apartment.

"Now stand back," Julie ordered after he and Nick had placed Francesca in her place of honor. She stooped and attached an extension cord to the outlet. The tree suddenly sparkled with hundreds of tiny blinking lights, like stars in a clear sky. At the top, Francesca's wings shimmered. She *could* very well wink, Ryan thought. The lights inside her could easily give that impression.

The lights on the tree reflected in Nick's eyes. Julie's cheeks were pink and her eyes bright as she looked at their handiwork. Ryan's heart ached as he fought the feeling of belonging.

"It's beautiful," Nick said. "Don't you think so?"

"I do," he said, but it was not as beautiful as Julie. She looked extraordinarily pretty with the delighted smile on her lips, the glow in her eyes. It was obvious she loved Christmas.

Christmas. Ten years ago he'd killed a man on Christmas Eve. He'd tried not to think about Christmas. But Nick had met him when he'd arrived home from Harry's and pulled him over to the house.

So now he sat in her living room as she brought in a tray of hot cocoa and cookies while a Christmas carol played softly in the background. Had he been a masochist in his other life? Had he sat in a living room longing to be a part of something but never quite able to belong for one reason or another?

"It's beautiful," Nick sighed as he snuggled on a sofa next to Ryan and stared at the blinking lights of the tree. Prissy the cat was marching around the bottom of the tree, occasionally batting a low hanging ornament and swishing branches with her tail.

Ryan took a cup of chocolate and a cookie decorated with colored sugar even as his heart ached. "Yes," he said, but his eyes were on Julie.

He sat there listening to carols, munching cookies, hearing Nick's tale of his trip to Santa Claus. Memorizing moments he might never have again.

Chapter 18

Julie found the priest! Or thought she had.

She had assumed the job of trying to find O'Grady from Jerry, who was busy on another case. After innumerable delays and transfers and dead ends, she'd finally located a Sean O'Grady who ran a shelter for runaway boys in Oakland, California.

She dialed his number, but the person who answered said he was out of town seeking funds from a state agency. She left her name and number, and a message asking him to call, that it was urgent.

Nick was in school. Ryan was at work. She had a million things to do, including Christmas shopping. There were only fourteen days left, and she had bought no presents. She still didn't know exactly what Nick wanted, at least his heart's desire. A puppy, yes, but there was something else he wasn't talking about...the big secret that wouldn't come true if he told her.

But she had difficulty focusing on Christmas. Ryan would be moving out the next week if he received his permission from Davidson. So far, it had not been forthcoming.

Part of her, the selfish part, wished it wouldn't come. She couldn't even think how suddenly bereft this house—her life, and Nick's—would become. He had given it substance, and strength. He had filled the empty parts.

More important, he had made her believe in herself again.

Which made her realize she would have to start job hunting after Christmas. Perhaps she *would* work for Dan if he still wanted her. By then, the publicity would have cooled. But even the thought of a new challenge was dulled. Everything dulled at the prospect of not having Ryan around.

She wanted to pick up the phone again and call some more of her old friends in Dan's office; she'd been trying to find out more about Castilani these past few days especially after Ryan told her about Banyon's reaction. She sought rumors, links with any law enforcement personnel, supposition, anything.

She was on her fourth fruitless conversation when the call-waiting beep sounded. She quickly said goodbye and took the other call.

"O'Grady here," said a gruff voice. "You called about an urgent matter?"

Breath caught in her throat. Let him be the one, she prayed silently.

"I'm Julie Farrell," she said. "Are you the Father O'Grady who was in Atlanta ten years ago?"

There was a short pause. "Yes, I am."

She knew her sigh must be audible over the phone. "I'm an attorney. I represent Ryan Murphy. I understand you know him."

"Ryan?"

She knew instantly that she had the right person. He'd said the name with recognition, even affection.

"You did know him then?" she insisted, wanting to hear it from his own mouth.

"What does he say?" came the cautious answer.

"He doesn't know," she said. "He has total amnesia."

There was a silence as the man on the other end apparently evaluated the information. "Is he still in prison?"

"He's out on parole, and he's trying to find out what happened ten years ago," she said. "I think you should also know that he saved my life and my son's. He was working on a road gang when someone ran into me and we were trapped in the car. Mr. Murphy pulled both of us out. He was badly injured when the car exploded."

"That's how he got amnesia?"

"Yes. And he wants to know more about his...life. His former wife said she saw you at the jail. We thought he might have told you something about what happened, something about his background."

"How is he?"

"Physically, he's fine. He has a job as a mechanic." She hesitated, then added, "But I think someone is trying to kill him."

She heard a swift intake of breath on the other end of the line three thousand miles away.

"Will you talk to him on the phone?" she said.

"Better than that, Ms. Farrell, I'll fly out there."

"You liked him?" she said.

"I loved him," the answer came gruffly. "I have to clear up some things here, but I'll be on a plane Thursday or Friday."

"Let me know when, and I'll pick you up."

"No need to do that. I'll rent a car. I'll call you as soon as I know something."

"Thank you," she breathed into the phone. She heard the line go dead on the other side of the country.

"Phone for you."

Ryan wiped his hands off on a nearby rag and headed for the phone. He cradled it near his ear as he leaned against the wall. "This is Murphy."

"Daddy?"

He stiffened.

"Daddy? This is Laura. I need help. Can you come to Macon?"

He was too stunned to say anything for a moment.

"Daddy?"

"Yes," he finally managed, his heart thudding.

"I can't tell Mother, and you can't, either. You can't tell anyone. I need your help. Someone is…threatening her…and me."

His heart pounded so loud he thought Tim could hear in the other room. "Where are you?"

"I'll be in the same place you met Mother. In two-and-a-half hours."

"You know about that?"

"I heard Mom and Dad talk about it."

"Are you in danger now? Can you go to the police?"

"No. Please come." The phone line went dead.

He felt his hands trembling. Should he call the police? But he didn't trust the police. He really didn't trust anyone but Julie. He went over to Tim. "I have to go."

Tim looked up sharply from a catalogue of parts, took one look at his face. "Okay," he said.

"I'll be in early tomorrow morning."

"You already worked through lunch. Don't worry about it. We're pretty well caught up."

Ryan nodded his thanks and hurried out to the car. His heart still pounded at an accelerated rate. If anyone hurt his daughter...

He looked at the clock when he left. Two o'clock. He should be there by five.

His daughter.

Julie felt her heart contract as her mind echoed Father O'Grady's words. *I loved him.*

He'd said it so simply, so naturally. Would a priest say that about a cold-blooded killer?

The phone rang again and she ran to catch it.

"Mrs. Farrell?" The voice was panicked, almost hysterical.

"Yes."

"This is Susan at The Learning Center. Is your son there? Did you pick him up?"

"No," Julie said, and she knew her voice was close to a scream. "He isn't there?"

"I...I can't find him. He was outside with the other children and..."

"He was left outside alone?"

"Just for a moment while one of my employees was called to the telephone. The area's fenced, and she thought...well, she's new and didn't think. When she returned to the yard, she counted the children and one was missing. We looked all over for him, thought he might be playing hide-and-seek, but..." Her voice trailed off. "One of the children finally said a man with a badge came for him, and told them not to say anything."

"Call the police," Julie said. "I'm coming over."

She grabbed her keys and her purse and ran out the door. She looked up at the garage apartment, but Ryan was at work. She would call him from the preschool. He could stay at their house in case someone called while she looked and talked to the police.

He's so little. Dear God, don't let anything happen to him.

Numb with anxiety, she pressed her foot hard on the gas pedal.

Police were already at the center when she arrived. She gave them a description and pulled a photo from her wallet. Then the questions began.

"Could a friend or relative have picked him up?"

She started to shake her head when Susan, the director of the school, broke in. "We've received some calls about Mrs. Farrell's son."

"What kind of calls?"

Susan looked uncomfortable. "Several callers didn't like the fact that Nicholas's mother is associated with, well, a convict."

Two pair of eyes narrowed and sharpened as they pierced through her.

"Who?"

"Ryan Murphy lives behind her. He's been paroled."

"Murphy?" the oldest cop said. He turned to the other. "The dirty cop that's been in the paper," he explained before turning back to her. "Where is he now?"

"At the garage where he works."

"What's the number?"

She gave it to them, and the older one headed for a phone. The other didn't say anything, just waited.

"He's not there. Left about two hours ago," said the patrolman as he put the phone back in the cradle.

Julie's fear mushroomed. He *had* to be there.

"You got any reason to believe he would take your kid?"

"I know he *wouldn't*," she said.

He stared at her for a moment, then picked up the phone again. "I want an APB posted on Ryan Murphy." He peered at her.

She stared at him in disbelief. "Someone tried to kill him in front of my house a few days ago. I tell you it wasn't him."

"Did you report it?"

She swallowed hard. "No."

"Did you see it?"

"My son..." She stopped suddenly. Julie's heart stopped. She could barely breathe. Had she been wrong? If she was, what had she done to her son?

But she would never believe Ryan would do anything to her son. Maybe Ryan had just reached the house. Maybe he was there now.

"I want to go home," she said.

"A squad car will go with you, Ms. Farrell."

She nodded, realizing it would do no good to protest. And she wanted to get there. Maybe Nick was at home. Maybe there would be a phone call.

Please let him be there.

Ryan waited one hour, then another in the restaurant. No fifteen-year-old girl. He looked in his wallet at the most recent picture of her, the one he'd taken from the album. No one even close to the description had come in the doors.

The waitresses were looking at him impatiently. Several people were waiting for the table. He finally rose, left a couple of dollars tip for a cup of coffee, and left.

He went to a service station next door and called his wife's home. She answered on the third ring. "Mary Elizabeth?"

"Ryan?" Surprise tinged her voice.

"Is Laura there?"

"I thought you weren't going to try to contact her."

"She called me this afternoon, said there was trouble and asked me to meet her."

"It wasn't Laura," she said. "I picked her up at school and we went shopping for her dad's Christmas present. We just got home."

"Nothing was bothering her?"

"No. Didn't seem to be."

"Has she said anything about me? Did she know we met?"

"No."

"She couldn't have overheard you?"

"David and I have only mentioned you when she was out of the house."

A warning. Ryan felt his stomach clench. Someone was telling him his daughter wasn't safe. He felt the earth giving way under him. Or were his legs unsteady?

"Watch out for her, Mary Elizabeth," he said.

There was a silence. "Do you think she's in danger?"

Not as long as he stayed away from her. "No," he said, "but look after her for me."

He hung up the phone, hoping to hell he was right.

Police cars and revolving blue lights crowded the driveway as he drove up. He jumped out of the car and took the three steps of Julie's porch in one leap. He didn't bother to knock.

A crowd of men and several women were in the living room, but his eyes went directly to Julie. She was standing in the living room, her face pale. She looked ten years older than she had a few days ago.

In two strides, he was in front of her. "Nicholas," she whispered. "He's missing."

Before he could take her in his arms, two men closed in on him, one on each side.

"Murphy?"

He knew immediately what they wanted. Suspicion gleamed in their eyes.

He nodded.

"Against the wall."

He tried to tell Julie with his eyes that he had nothing to do with Nick's disappearance, but he was pushed toward the wall. He obediently assumed the position, leaning against the wall with his arms while one of the detectives frisked him. "He's clean."

Another man in plain clothes, which meant he was a detective, moved inches from his face. "Where's the kid?"

"I don't know," Ryan said evenly.

"How did you get here?"

"My car."

"Parked outside?"

"Yes," he said, keeping his eyes on Julie. Now he knew why he received that phone call. It wasn't a warning. It was a trap.

"What does it look like?"

"Green sedan. It's parked just behind a squad car."

"Keys."

"I left them in the ignition when I saw your cars."

The detective nodded his head at another man in plain clothes. "Check it out, but be careful. Use gloves."

Ryan started to move toward Julie, but the detective who appeared to be in charge, stepped in front of him. "I'm Lieutenant Kale. You want to tell us where you've been?"

"Macon."

"Your boss said you left your job suddenly."

There went his job, he thought. As well as his apartment.

"That was a question, Murphy."

Murphy closed his eyes. If he told them where he went, they would call his former wife, probably talk to his daughter.

"I went for a drive."

"You can do better than that."

A stone lodged in his throat. He *was* a Jonah. Julie was looking at him with so much fear in her eyes. He wondered whether there was also accusation in them. He didn't think he could bear that, though he would understand it.

He ignored the detective and looked at her. "I didn't have anything to do with his...with Nick's..." He couldn't continue. He hurt too much. He *did* have something to do with it. Just his living here had something to do with it.

"I know," she said, but her voice sounded defeated. He knew she was standing just by sheer force of her will. He wanted to go to her. He wanted to fold her in his arms and comfort. But he saw the hostile faces around him, and he knew it would only stain her, perhaps even make the police wonder whether she herself had something to do with the disappearance. Pain roared through him like a roaring inferno, only it didn't burn down to embers. It continued to rage.

"Let's go to the station, Murphy," one of the detectives said.

"You have no cause," Julie protested, but it was weak at best. He didn't know whether it was because nothing mattered except her son or whether she believed he could somehow be involved. The inferno was even fiercer. He couldn't avoid the fact he *was* responsible. He would bet ten years of freedom that his presence here had something to do with the kidnapping.

"We don't need a cause, ma'am. He's a parolee."

"It's all right," he told her. He turned to the detective. "Want to search my apartment?"

"We already have." Kale turned to one of the detectives. "Take him downtown. See if he can't do better with an alibi."

The detective took out a pair of handcuffs, and locked Ryan's wrists behind him. He took one last look at Julie's pale face and haunted eyes, and turned toward the door, all the recently acquired faith fading into hopelessness.

They released him at dawn.

He'd spent the night in a small interrogation room being asked over and over again, "Where's the kid?" Detectives were augmented by F.B.I. agents. The first question varied only with a second one, "Where were you?"

He'd finally just stared at them, even when they said his lack of cooperation would be reported to his probation officer. He thought about telling them about the phone call. But where would it lead? Except back to his daughter, interrogation of her about a father she despised and headlines that could destroy her life.

Finally, his frustrated questioners let him go after warning him not to leave the city. They didn't offer to drive him back although they gave him back his keys. He took a cab.

Police cars were still in the driveway. He asked one patrolman whether there had been any word on the boy. When told no, he went directly to his apartment. He didn't think he could bear seeing the grief and fear, and even suspicion, in Julie's eyes, particularly when he couldn't do anything to alleviate it.

The apartment was in shambles. Sheets had been torn from the bed and were crumpled on the floor. Cans of food had been tumbled from the cabinet. Clothes lay on the floor. Apparently the police cared little about the possessions of an ex-con. He sat at the table and stared at the phone. What could he do? Where could he turn? But he had to do something or go crazy.

He finally showered and shaved, and changed clothes. He had to tell

Julie, if no one else, about the phone call, and he wanted to do it without the odor of jail hovering around him like some evil smog. He was just about to leave when the phone rang.

Ryan hurried to it and answered curtly, "Murphy."

"If you want the boy, you'll do as you're told," said a muffled voice.

"I'm listening."

"Meet me in thirty minutes. Be alone or the boy dies."

"Where?"

He was given a set of directions. He knew exactly where it was: a storage facility several blocks from the garage where he worked.

"We'll know if you say anything to the police."

And he knew they would. Otherwise, how would they know about his daughter? Hell, about everything he was doing? After all, wasn't he himself a prime example of police corruption? "I'll be alone," he said.

He wondered briefly whether his phone was tapped, but then why should it be? Any ransom demand would go to Julie, and he'd been in custody until an hour ago. His caller must have known that.

He knew he had to leave without anyone seeing him. He slipped his keys in his pocket and went outside. The one policeman was still standing outside.

Well, no one had told him he couldn't leave.

He sauntered out, nodded at the man, hoping he had no idea who was doing the nodding. He reached his car. A different car was in front of it now, probably the F.B.I. by now.

Ryan quickly stepped into the car and took off, hoping that the uniformed policeman wouldn't pay attention. Unfortunately through the rearview mirror, he saw the man stepping quickly toward the door to Julie's house.

He put his foot on the gas pedal and sped off toward the garage, toward the gun in a top drawer. He hoped like hell Tim wouldn't be running early this morning.

He wasn't. Ryan unlocked the door and quickly found the gun, tucking it in the back of his jeans as he'd seen in a television show. Or had he just known? It didn't matter now. Nothing mattered but Nick.

He was just leaving when Tim drove up. Knowing Tim would find the gun gone, that he had just lost any chance of staying out of prison, Ryan didn't bother to speak or even nod. He'd just lost any right to respect.

Fifteen minutes left.

Following the directions precisely, he drove to the storage facility. He found a key taped behind a sign just as he was told it would be, and he unlocked the gate and walked inside, looking for the unit mentioned in the call. He moved the gun from the back of his trousers to the left side, where it was still hidden but he could reach with one easy movement. Instinct again. Or knowledge. Damn, he was tired of those questions.

He used the key to open the bin. For a moment, he couldn't see anything in the darkness. As his eyes grew accustomed to the darkness, he saw a man in the shadows.

"Are you alone?" Banyon asked in a conversational voice.

Ryan stepped out of the light and into the shadow. Just as the dim light startled him, the sudden infusion of light must temporarily blind Banyon. Ryan pretended to stumble, and in doing so, took the gun from his waistband and aimed at Banyon who himself was holding a gun.

"Where's the boy?" Ryan asked.

Banyon looked surprised as he saw the gun. "It's a violation of your parole to carry that gun."

"It's against the law to kidnap children."

"I didn't," Banyon said easily, obviously thinking he had the edge. "*You* did. You also killed him. I followed you here. Too bad I was too late to save him."

His gaze went to a bundle against the wall, and as Ryan's followed his, Banyon fired. Ryan instinctively moved, firing as he did so. Banyon screamed and clutched his stomach as his gun went clattering to the floor.

His heart in his throat, Ryan kicked Banyon's gun away and walked over to the bundle against the wall, kneeling down to check the boy. He was breathing but unconscious, or drugged.

Ryan returned to Banyon's side, noticing that he was bleeding badly.

"Telephone...in car," the detective said. "I...need help."

"Why?" Ryan said. "Why the boy?"

"She wouldn't stop...the questions. Please..."

"Who else?" Ryan persisted. "Who else is involved?"

"Dammit, I...need...hospital."

"First, who?"

Banyon looked up with pleading eyes, then said reluctantly, "Sandy." His eyes closed and Ryan knew he'd lost consciousness.

Ryan stared at him. What in the hell should he do now? If he called for help, Banyon would accuse him of kidnapping and it would be a cop's word against an ex-con. At the very least, he'd fired a gun and would go straight back to prison; at worst, Banyon would die and he would be tried for murder.

But neither could he leave the man here to die.

Ryan picked up the boy and ran outside, finding the unmarked police car. He put the boy inside, then used the car radio to request help and tell them Nick was safe in the car. He locked Nick inside and threw away the keys. Even if Banyon could reach the car, he wouldn't be able to get inside.

He had five minutes at most.

He ran.

Chapter 19

Julie concentrated on keeping herself together, to keep from screaming, and screaming and screaming.

She had protested any accusation that Ryan might be involved, and yet she didn't understand why he couldn't, or wouldn't, explain where he had been. His eyes had cooled as he'd been questioned, then searched and finally hustled out. The old mask replaced the caring vulnerability she knew.

Dan had appeared after Ryan had been taken to police headquarters and in a moment alone she asked that he do everything he could for Ryan.

"Are you sure he didn't have anything to do with it?"

"Of course he didn't. He had no reason."

"I heard he was moving out. Maybe he was angry."

"It was his idea, not mine," she said impatiently. "He read the papers about the petition, he knew I've been getting complaints. He didn't want Nick and me hurt."

He'd finally agreed to have him released, but then Ryan disappeared again, and there was another APB out on him.

Dan stayed with her, answering the phone. Jerry dropped over, and muttered about Ryan. When the phone rang an hour after Ryan disappeared, Dan picked up. She knew something had happened by the changes in his face. Relief. Concern. Anger.

He turned to her while still on the phone. "They found Nick. He's on his way to Memorial Hospital, but he's all right. No injuries."

He talked for several minutes longer, then hung up. Julie stood still, awaiting more information before she started for the hospital.

"Are you sure he's all right?"

"Medics just wanted him checked out, but everything looks good." Dan shifted on his feet, then said, "A detective named Banyon has been shot. He says Murphy shot him, that he found Murphy with your son."

"Banyon?"

"Do you know him?"

"He visited Ryan in the hospital, then at the apartment in back." She raised an eyebrow. "Some coincidence, huh?"

Dan didn't look at her. "The police have no choice but to bring Murphy in."

"He wouldn't have just left Nick alone."

"Someone—a male—called the police dispatcher from Banyon's car and told them where they could find Banyon and Nick. He didn't leave a name."

"Ryan. Why would he do that if he'd kidnapped Nick in the beginning?"

"I'm interested in that myself," Dan said. "Come on. I'll take you to the hospital."

Ryan drove to Rome, a city some seventy miles north of Atlanta, and hunted for a pay telephone. He called the Atlanta newspaper first to see if they had word of the kidnapped boy. He was given the name of the hospital. He then called the hospital, claimed to be a reporter, and was told the boy was in good condition.

He slowly relaxed. Then he headed to the outskirts of Rome until he found a dilapidated motel that looked as if its owner didn't particularly care who its guests were. He needed rest before he decided anything else, before he made a mistake.

Ryan woke the next morning after a restless night, then went out early for a newspaper. He found an Atlanta newspaper, and opened it, only to find his picture on the front page. He was wanted for questioning in the shooting of Jack Banyon and the kidnapping of Nicholas Farrell. No more than he expected.

They would have his license number. He backed the car up to his room so the license plate wouldn't be immediately evident. Then he went inside, washed and showered. He had to reach Julie. He had to tell her he had nothing to do with Nick's kidnapping, but he couldn't do it from here.

Ryan drove to a pay phone, then called Julie. No one answered. He would try again. He went to the market, bought some doughnuts and a screwdriver. He would exchange license plates. It might buy him a day or two.

But eventually he knew he would be caught. He'd learned a lot in the past month, but he was no match for the police, or the F.B.I. Nor did he have enough money to go more than another day. After the past few days, he didn't hold much hope for his survival in the hands of the police department. Someone wanted him dead, and he was afraid they numbered more than Banyon. But first he had to reach Julie. He wanted to know exactly what was going on.

Julie sat next to Nick's bed, watching him as he slept. And he slept a lot. The doctors had released him this morning after keeping him overnight because his system was full of drugs. He was still sleepy, and the doctors said he might continue to be that way for the next couple of days.

She could barely keep her hands off him. She kept reaching over to touch him and reassure herself he was there.

If only she knew where Ryan was.

None of what she'd heard made any sense. Why was Banyon alone with her son? If he had learned where Nick had been taken, why had he not called for backup? During a few moments of consciousness, Nick had been asked who had taken him from the preschool, but he couldn't remember anything but the "bad smell."

An FBI agent had asked repeatedly if Ryan had taken him, and Nick had given him a disgusted look. "Ryan wouldn't hurt me," he insisted.

Julie hadn't liked the relief that had flooded through her. Had she ever seriously considered the possibility of his involvement? But why wouldn't he say where he had been, and why had he gone after Nick alone? Doubts bedeviled her. She kept remembering how little she'd really known about her late husband. She knew even less about Ryan Murphy.

The phone rang, and she prayed there wasn't still a tap on it. She had requested that it be lifted after Nick had been found. A technician said it had been, but she knew the police might have asked for a court order for a secret tap. Still, she didn't think they would have had time.

It rang again and she reluctantly left the room and headed toward her office.

"Mrs. Farrell?"

She recognized the voice immediately and went still.

"I'm from the Associated Press and would like to ask you some questions."

"I don't talk to the press," she said.

"I understand Murphy worked at a garage. Can you tell me how to reach it?"

She knew immediately what he wanted. "Sorry," she said and hung up. Julie picked up Nick. She wasn't going to leave him alone again. Not for a moment. He mumbled, but then leaned his head against her shoulder. She went out the back door, and started the car. She drove several blocks, looked around. She didn't think she was being followed, but she made several more turns before heading toward the garage.

When she arrived, she roused Nick and together they walked in the office.

Tim appeared almost immediately. He looked at Nick, then summoned Johnny. "Why don't you show Nick here your truck."

Johnny looked from Tim to her, then down at Nick. "Come on, little guy," he said, leading the way out of the office.

Julie silently blessed them both. Ryan had two good friends, that much was sure.

"Have you heard from him?" Tim asked.

She studied him. "You know he didn't kidnap Nick, don't you?"

Tim nodded. "I think you should know a gun I kept in the desk is missing."

"Did you call the police?"

He shook his head. "No. I might have just misplaced it."

But she knew he hadn't "just misplaced it," and she was grateful. "I think he'll call here," she said. "I think it might be wise if you're someplace else and don't answer it."

Tim nodded and left the office to go into the bay.

The phone rang. She picked it up and answered as she'd heard Tim do a million times. "Garage."

"Julie."

Her hand trembled as she held the phone. "Are you all right?"

"Yes. Thank God you understood my call."

"The police are looking for you."

"I know. How's Nick?"

"He's fine, thanks to you. That *was* you who called in about Nick?"

There was a pause. "He wouldn't have been in danger were it not for me. They wanted to frame me for his kidnapping. If anything had happened to him..."

"What happened?"

"A muffled voice called me at the apartment and told me to go to the storage locker if I wanted to see Nick alive again. Banyon was waiting for me. He shot at me. I didn't have a choice."

She was silent. It sounded familiar. Too familiar. A chill ran through her. What if...?

"Julie?" His voice sounded defeated, and she knew he read something into her silence. "Someone other than Banyon is involved. They knew that I was planning to move. They knew I had seen my wife. They knew about...my daughter. A girl, or woman, claiming to be my daughter called me at the garage and asked for help. I drove to Macon, but she didn't show up. She didn't even know about it. That's where I was when Nick was taken, but I couldn't tell the police or they would have gone straight to her." There was a pause. "I'm sorry, Julie. I just wanted you to know I had nothing to do with it."

Julie was digesting everything. Her hand shook as she slid down in the chair. "I know," she said softly, then, "What are you going to do?"

"Good question. I just thought it wasn't a good idea to hang around with a nearly dead cop at my feet."

"Did he say anything?"

"I asked him why. He mentioned a man named Sandy. Does that ring any bells?"

"No." She swallowed hard and made a decision. He couldn't make it on his own, not with amnesia. It was a miracle he was still free, and if what he said was right, someone else in the police department wanted him dead.

Could she permit any more risks to her son?

Could she live with herself if Ryan were killed?

He'd asked nothing of her. He merely wanted her to know the truth, to make sure her son was returned safely. She thought of him out there alone: hunted, friendless, handicapped by limited knowledge. She shuddered. She knew the feeling too well. She'd experienced the feeling of being hopelessly trapped when her husband had died, when she was besieged by reporters and law enforcement officials. She'd felt like a rabbit harried by hounds. Even so, her life had not been endangered.

But didn't she owe her son more than the man who so explosively entered their lives months earlier? A man who might have killed his partner? A man who'd critically wounded a police detective?

The man she loved.

That same man had twice come to her rescue without a thought for his own life. If he was apprehended, he might well die in police custody. Could she let that happen? Yet as an attorney, an officer of the court, she knew the penalties for aiding a felon. What would happen to Nick if she went to prison?

Time. She needed time. Time to see whether Banyon survived. Time to hear what Father O'Grady had to say. He could be the final piece to the puzzle that was Ryan Murphy and what happened ten years earlier.

"Julie, I have to go."

"Where are you?"

He hesitated.

"General area?"

"Rome."

"Drive south on I-75 to the Kennesaw exit." She described a motel at the exit. "Wait in your car."

"No, I don't want you involved. I'd rather turn myself in."

"I found the priest, Ryan. He called early this morning. He'll be here tomorrow. Maybe he can answer some of your questions. Then, if you want, you can do whatever you wish."

There was a long pause.

"If anyone sees us," she said, "I can say I was meeting with you to get you to surrender yourself."

"All right," he said finally, reluctantly.

She hung up. She didn't give him a chance to change his mind.

Minutes later, she was back home getting Nick ready for the trip. She also packed a tape recorder, and tucked several extra tapes in her pocket. After making sure she wasn't followed, she went to a bank teller machine and withdrew a thousand in cash, then drove to a small grocery store where she quickly bought milk, cereal, bread and cold cuts.

North of Kennesaw was a cabin owned by Dan Watters. She had been there several times. A key was always taped beneath a bird house. No one would look for a fugitive at the summer getaway of the district attorney.

Ryan waited in his car. This was a very bad idea, and he would tell her so when she arrived. He'd even thought about not showing up, but then she would probably wait in the cold, drizzly weather all night.

What a mess he'd made of everything. He should have just waited at the storage locker. His life wasn't worth hers. And yet he wanted—no, *had*—to find out what happened ten years ago. And so he'd pulled her into his life again.

After an hour or so, he saw her car. He got out and she drove in next to his car. Glancing inside, he saw a sleeping Nick in the back seat. His heart cracked. He remembered seeing him yesterday, so still. So quiet.

"He's all right," she said softly after rolling the window down. "Come on, get in," she said.

"I think you should go home."

"Not without you." Her chin had that determined set to it. "And we can't argue out here."

He went around to the passenger's side, prepared to argue. But once he slid into the passenger seat, she backed out and drove out of the parking lot. "Where are we going?"

"A place they will never find you."

He must have slept a while, because she felt him jerk awake when she stopped. Neither of them had said much after he had told her everything that had happened.

Julie took the flashlight and found the key that was always kept taped under the birdhouse for various visitors offered the cabin from time to time. She had been among them. But she didn't think anyone else would be here this close to Christmas and in this drizzling, cold weather. Minutes later they were inside a rustic log cabin, and Nick was settled down in one of the bedrooms. She turned up the heat, blessing Dan for keeping the utilities connected year round.

Ryan was watching her. "Is this yours?"

"The district attorney's."

He started at that. "I take it he's totally unaware that he has guests?"

"He is."

"He leaves the key under a birdhouse?"

"Better than under the mat or in the flowerpot," she said, trying to force a note of lightness into the moment, even though she winced at her betrayal of both herself and Dan. An officer of the court. A friend. She was abusing both. But she hadn't been able to think of any place else.

He was staring at her with disbelief. Then the side of his eyes started crinkling, his dark, brooding eyes lightened, and his lips twisted into a wry grin as he shook his head. He took a step toward her, and she was in his arms, his mouth pressing down on hers with a desperation and passion that reduced her to bone melting imbecility.

She'd been cold, but suddenly she turned to fire. Her body melded into his, and her arms went around him. An urgency she'd never known before consumed her. She knew it consumed him as well. Her arms tightened around his neck, and he drew her so close only their clothes kept them from being one. Together, without thought or words, they made their way to the other empty bedroom. She locked the door, knowing she would hear if Nick needed anything.

In seconds their clothes were gone, littering the floor.

He leaned over her, when something—caution—shaded his face, and he went back to his jeans. He pulled out his wallet, then a small package. In a moment he was over her, his hands touching her face, her hair, her breasts. His lips followed, trailing kisses with barely leashed intensity that was equal parts violence, desperation, yearning. She felt all of those when his lips met hers, and his tongue plundered her mouth while his hands stoked her body until she felt she would burst with the growing need inside her.

Bad idea. Worse action. But she didn't care. She didn't care about anything but responding to his hands, tasting his mouth, feeling his body tease hers until she was wild with want.

Then he plunged into her without his previous foreplay. Her body rose to meet his and they met in a crescendo of need and want and...caring until every nerve, every sensitive part of her, exploded with exquisite sensations. She heard her own low cry of fulfilment, then his moan of release as he collapsed on top of her for a moment, then rolled over on his side, carrying her with him.

She felt his chest against her ear, heard the beat of his heart as he put his arms around her and cradled her. Then she felt a wetness and looked up. Tears shone in his eyes. She put a wondering hand up to them, her fingers brushing one away with a tenderness that came from so deep in her heart that she trembled with it.

They were silent for a moment. She recorded the moment, the richness of the feelings, her wonder at the purity of them.

Her hands moved over him as they would some infinitely precious treasure. She wondered if she could ever get enough of him, if these overpowering feelings could ever fade. He didn't bother to wipe away the wetness on his face, but his fingers moved along her face, loving it in a way that far transcended words.

Julie didn't know how much time passed. They were lost in a magical web of discovery, of mutual love and caring.

It was Ryan who finally broke the silence. "Whatever did I do to deserve you?" he whispered into her ear.

Her hand caught his and brought it to her mouth. She loved him so. She loved everything about him: his tenderness, his gentleness with her son, his sharp intelligence, his courage to confront what would have defeated so many others. No doubt remained. Not one. And that reminder made her move away from him, even as she felt grief at the loss of his body in hers, that intimate connection that made them one.

But she held on to his hand, her fingers tightening around his. "I have to go before long. I want to get home before dawn in case anyone comes looking for me. I'm sure there will be more questions."

He didn't say anything, but she felt the warm pressure of his fingers.

"Father O'Grady is flying in today," she said. "Maybe I can learn something from him. And we have to know what happened with Banyon." She was quiet a moment, then added, "We have to find out who Sandy is."

"I want you out of this," he said. "I'll turn myself in."

"No," she said. "Not yet. Give me a couple of days. At least until you talk to Father O'Grady."

"You can be charged with harboring a fugitive, obstruction of justice, and God knows what else," he said in a broken voice. "I can't..."

"Do you have any idea what my life would be if you were killed?" She heard the tremor in her own voice.

"You have Nick to think about."

"Yes. And I would think he would want me to do what's right. Maybe not now, but as he grows up." She met his eyes. "A few days. Just a few days. No one can find you here."

He was silent. "They were willing to kill Nick, Julie. What about him?"

"I won't let him out of my sight. I have a gun. I know how to use it."

His eyes opened wide.

"When I was with the district attorney, I received threats," she said. Then she added, "Please, Ryan. Three days."

His hand ran through her hair. "All right," he said. "Three days."

Ryan prowled both the cabin and the woods around it. He'd wandered down to a short beach on the edge of a lake, and stared out at the rippling gray water. Seized by restlessness and fear for Julie and her son, he almost hiked to the nearest road to hitchhike into Atlanta. But he'd given his word. He could only wait in an agony of worry.

It was late afternoon when he heard a car driving up. He waited behind some trees, hoping his dark clothes blended into late afternoon shadows, until he recognized her car and saw her step out, followed by Nick and a man in his late fifties or early sixties.

The priest. It had to be the priest.

Nick ran toward him, and Ryan leaned down and picked him up. He received a big hug and Ryan studied every inch of him to make sure there were no lingering effects from the other evening. The boy looked tired but no worse for wear.

"I missed you, Ryan."

"I missed you, too, munchkin."

"When are you coming home?"

"I'm not sure."

Julie interrupted and took Nick from him, setting him on the ground.

Ryan forced his gaze away from them and toward the stranger. He saw the man's face crease with recognition and a smile. Then suddenly out of nowhere came a flash streaking through his mind. A younger man in black, a catcher's glove on his hand and a grin on his face. He stopped still, stunned.

Julie's hand reached out, her face worried. "Ryan?"

He shook his head as if to shake the image away. "It's nothing," he said, as he studied the face of the newcomer, once more searching for recognition. The flash of memory had disappeared so quickly he wasn't sure this was the same man.

A hand came out toward him. "Sean O'Grady," said the visitor.

Ryan took it. He felt the strength in it, and even more the warmth, as if O'Grady were greeting an old friend. Suddenly the man let go of his hand and gave him a bear hug. When he was finished, he stood back and grinned. "That was for me," he said. "Mrs. Farrell said you had amnesia. I hoped that you might remember something when you saw me."

Ryan had. At least he thought he had. But he wasn't sure. "Thank you for coming. I...suppose you know I'm wanted."

"Aye, I do, Ryan."

"You could get in trouble."

"I'm used to trouble. And Mrs. Farrell said I might be able to help."

Julie interrupted. "Let's go inside. I'll make some coffee."

Ryan fell into step alongside the priest, or former priest or whatever he was. He kept fighting to remember, to recall that one enticing instant memory.

Once inside, the two of them sat at a table while Julie went about making coffee. She'd brought a coloring book and crayons with her and she found Nick a place in the corner far enough not to be able to hear low voices, close enough to keep an eye on him.

Tension radiated inside Ryan as he looked across the table. "What can you tell me? How did I know you?"

"Everything?" O'Grady looked up at Julie who sat down with them.

"There's nothing to hide from her," Ryan said. He lowered his voice so Nick wouldn't hear. "She knows the worst—that I was a killer who apparently dealt in drugs—and that didn't stop her."

"Where do you want me to start?"

"How long did you know me?"

"Since you were seven."

"How? Were we members of your church?"

"No. The police brought you by my office. They caught you stealing food. It wasn't the first time." He looked at Ryan with eyes that were sad and infinitely weary as if he'd told the tale before. Too many times. It might not have been Ryan, but it had been others.

"Go on," Ryan said harshly.

"I don't know who your father was," O'Grady said. "Your mother was a drug addict and prostitute. She didn't look after you. You looked after her. You stole and cheated and lied to get food for her."

Ryan felt the muscles in his cheek flex. His fingers curled into a ball. He didn't know what he expected. But it hadn't been this.

"I helped a little, got you interested in our youth baseball team. Half the time you didn't show up because your mother was sick or in trouble, but you came when you could. I think it took your mind off her. She died of an overdose when you were nine, and I found a foster family in my parish to take you in. They moved out of state when you were seventeen, and you moved into a room in the church so you could finish high school where you had been playing baseball. You did odd jobs. You always had a knack for fixing things.

"I was so proud of you when you finished high school, then went to college. But never more so than when you graduated from the Police Academy. You...were like a son to me."

"Why didn't I see you after I married?"

"You did. You always made a point to meet somewhere away from your house. You told me you didn't want your wife to know about your mother, about that part of your life. You kept all that in a little box in your head, just like...you kept your feelings in boxes. Perhaps because your mother took so much of your heart, you were afraid to risk it again."

"In other words, I was a cold bastard."

"No," O'Grady said softly. "You gave me money for my boys. For boys like you. There was one in particular. You helped put him through college, although you never let me tell him who was providing the money. You cared, Ryan. You cared about your wife and child. You cared about boys like you. You were just afraid of being vulnerable again."

Ryan's fingers uncurled, then curled again. The money. The money his wife had mentioned. Not gambling debts. Not drugs. He looked at Julie and saw tears in her eyes, and her hand stretched out to him. He took it, his fingers wrapping around hers almost desperately.

O'Grady smiled.

Ryan forced himself back to the story. "Do you know anything about my shooting my partner?"

O'Grady's smile faded. His face suddenly looked older. "No. I saw you right after it happened, and you told me you'd shot in self-defense. A week later you confessed. You wouldn't tell me why." He fumbled in his pocket. "You gave me a letter, though. You told me that if anything happened to you, I should give it to your daughter on her twenty-first birthday. I think you were afraid you might..."

"Die in prison?" Ryan finished.

O'Grady nodded and pulled a folded letter from his pocket and shoved it across the table. Ryan stared at it as if it were a snake. The letter was addressed to Laura Murphy in bold black letters.

Ryan was conscious of two pairs of eyes on him as he slowly took the letter, turning it around several times in his fingers. He swallowed through a growing lump in his throat. The letter held answers. Were they answers he wanted?

He finally opened it.

Dear Laura,

I have asked Father O'Grady to give this to you on your twenty-first birthday if for some reason I cannot.

I do not want you to go through life believing that your father was a murderer, and probably worse. I do not want you to ever think I did not love you, and your mother, more than life itself.

I know you must have wondered why I broke all communication. It is not because I do not care. God knows I do and always will. But it was for your own protection. I believed—whether rightly or wrongly—that a total break was better for you. Your mother could get on with her life, and you could forget me.

I have never been involved in drugs. Your grandmother died of a drug overdose, and I joined the police department in part to fight those who deal with and sell drugs. At the time of my arrest, I was getting close to a man named Castilani through an informant who worked for him. On Christmas Eve, I received a call from the informant saying he feared he had been discovered. I drove out to meet the informant and found him dying. He told me he'd also called Mike Cates, my partner. One of Castilani's men tortured him and left him for dead, but not before mentioning Cates's name.

I was angry. Beyond angry. A man died because of me, because I'd trusted Cates. I went after him, and found him outside a bar he frequented. I accused him and he pulled his gun and fired. I fired in self-defense. Within minutes, a captain appeared and took me off to talk. When I returned to the scene, Cates's gun was gone. Three days later I was arrested at the direction of Captain William Lewis and jailed without bond. That night you barely escaped being hit by a car that didn't stop.

I was told by one of Castilani's men that it was a warning, that if I didn't plead guilty, you and your mother would be killed.

Laura, I had no way of protecting you from jail. I knew what he had done to the informant. I didn't have anyone I could trust. I knew there had been leaks in the task force formed to investigate Castilani, but I hadn't suspected Mike. I didn't know who else was involved. Perhaps the captain. Perhaps even the district attorney himself.

I couldn't take chances with your life, or your mother's.

By now, the major players are probably dead or retired. I am not sure who exactly from the police department and D.A.'s office were involved, and I don't have any proof that would stand up in court. I hope you will do nothing with this letter, except realize that I have always loved you and tried to protect you in the only way I could. It is something I did gladly and without regret.

But I wanted you and your children to know the truth. I never wanted you to feel you had evil in your background.

Be happy, my daughter, and know I will always be watching over you.

> Your father,
> Ryan Murphy

Ryan slowly put it down. He could barely breathe.

He had his answers. Colliding emotions rampaged through his mind. Relief. Anger. Regret. Hope.

He pushed the letter over to Julie, then stood and walked out the door without another word. He needed time alone to absorb what O'Grady had said, what the letter had explained.

Cold. Arrogant. He'd been all of that. But he'd been more, too. He'd loved his daughter and wife. He'd loved them enough to spend his life in prison.

He leaned against a tree, his body bracing against the cold rain which was falling steadily. He blinked to drive the rainwater from his eyes. And the tears. Not for himself, but for the man he'd once been.

Chapter 20

Julie watched Ryan leave, then looked at the letter he'd pushed over to her. She scanned it, then carefully read it again.

Her heart broke for Ryan and the choices he'd felt he had to make ten years ago. Maybe someone else would have made a different one. Maybe someone else would have trusted the system.

But Ryan had trusted no one but himself. And because of Sean O'Grady, she knew why.

She hurt for the small boy struggling to care for a drug-addicted mother, the boy who'd gone to a foster family and been abandoned a second time. Father O'Grady had apparently been his one ally, but he'd also been a reminder of what Ryan had wanted to leave behind. Yet Ryan had gone back time and time again to help others like him, and he'd become a police officer to prevent what happened to him from happening to others.

She thought she would have liked the old Ryan.

She liked the new one better. This one wasn't shaped by the tragedy that had built unassailable walls around him. He had obviously loved his wife and child; he'd just never learned how to show it.

Except by giving up his life, by spending years behind bars for a crime he hadn't committed.

Sean—he had asked her to call him that on the drive from Atlanta—had finished reading the letter and he stared sightlessly at the wall.

"He should have told me," he muttered. "I should have insisted. I knew something was wrong. Holy Father in heaven, he couldn't have done it."

"I don't think it would have helped if you had insisted."

She rose and went to the door. She looked outside and saw Ryan standing in the rain, his hands in his jeans. He looked like the loneliest man alive. But he wasn't. Not any longer.

Julie went out in the rain. She worried that he wanted to be alone. She was sure the old Ryan Murphy would spurn company, understanding, compassion.

Love.

Instead, he turned to her and opened his arms. And she ran into them.

He held her tight, as if his life depended on maintaining his grip on her.

Seemingly out of nowhere, she heard a hard, curt voice, "Get away from him, Julie."

Ryan recognized the voice. Jerry Kidder. Julie's detective. He turned and saw the man holding a gun and started to let her go, but she took his hand and held on tight before turning to face the newcomer.

"Jerry? How did you find us?"

"I've been following you since you got home early this morning. I tried to call you last night. When you didn't answer, I was afraid Murphy had involved you in some way. When you arrived home early this morning with Nick, I was sure of it." He shrugged. "I followed you to the airport, then up here. I lost you for a while, but then I remembered this place. I decided to try it. Very smart."

"What do you want, Jerry?" Her voice was steady, and his hand tightened around her fingers. He remembered her telling him Kidder had once worked for the district attorney's office. His fear was far greater for her than for anything that might happen to him.

"Banyon died," Jerry said. "Murphy's wanted for murder as well as kidnapping."

"He didn't kidnap Nick," she said.

"He *did* shoot Banyon. He's dangerous, Julie. He's always been dangerous."

Ryan listened to the conversation as if they were talking about someone else. He was numb from revelations. Numb and drained. And he knew Kidder wasn't going to believe him. Hope sifted from him like sand through fingers.

"Come inside," she said. "I want you to meet someone and read a letter."

"I'm taking him in," Jerry said stubbornly. "I'm not letting you risk your life and future for him."

"A few minutes, Jerry. Please."

Kidder hesitated, then reluctantly said, "Ten minutes. Does he have a weapon?"

"Ask him," Julie said.

Ryan thought about lying, about keeping some kind of edge. But he was tired of violence and puzzles and lies. He was sick at the trouble he'd brought upon Julie and her son. He wouldn't bring more. "It's in the pocket of my jacket in a closet."

Jerry looked at Julie as if she was out of her mind. "Julie, you come over with me. Murphy, face the tree. Do anything stupid, and I won't hesitate to shoot you."

Ryan nodded and stood still as Kidder patted him down. Then, at the detective's gesture, he walked to the cottage. Kidder stopped when he saw O'Grady. "Who are you?"

"The priest we were looking for," Julie said. "Sean O'Grady."

"*Former* priest," O'Grady said. "I wasn't very good at rules. Who are you?"

Still keeping an eye on Ryan, Kidder ignored O'Grady and went to the closet. Looking inside, he found the jacket, then the gun. He glared at Ryan as he tucked it into the waist of his trousers, keeping his own aimed at his prisoner. "You've broken enough laws to never see the light of day again."

Ryan didn't have a reply. Possession of the gun was enough to send him back to prison for life. "I shot Banyon in self-defense," he said finally.

"Just like you shot Cates?"

Julie was glaring at Jerry now. "Will you just sit down and listen?"

Reluctantly, Jerry sat down. "Eight minutes."

Julie pushed the letter over to him. "Father...Mr. O'Grady was given this letter by Murphy two days after he confessed. He wanted it delivered to his daughter on her twenty-first birthday."

Jerry read it once, then again. His right hand continued to hold the gun when he looked up. "Tell me what happened with Nick."

Ryan repeated everything that had happened, from the phone call to his decision to run.

When he'd finished, Jerry looked over at O'Grady. "You came all the way from California to deliver the letter."

"Ryan's one of my boys," the former priest said simply.

"Maybe he lied in the letter," Jerry replied. He was obviously reluctant to give up his suspicions.

"A man who killed his partner wouldn't care what his daughter thought sixteen years later," O'Grady said slowly.

"There's more," Julie said. "Sean, tell him about Ryan's mother, the money he gave you."

After listening for several more moments, Jerry lowered his gun and set it on the table. He swore softly, glancing at O'Grady as if expecting condemnation. "What did you plan to do now?" he finally asked Julie.

"Talk to you," Julie said. "Do you know who Sandy might be?"

Jerry was silent for a moment, then said slowly, "Chief Lewis. I knew him when he was a detective. They called him that because of his sandy hair. Then he was promoted and his hair turned white prematurely. Everyone just called him 'the old man.'"

"Except for close friends," Julie whispered.

Jerry nodded. "But there isn't enough here to convict him or prove Murphy innocent." He added, "I'm not even sure he is."

"Yes, you are," Julie said with just a hint of a grin.

Jerry shook his head. "What do you want, Julie?" Then he sighed. "What in the hell am I saying? I can lose my P.I. license just by being here, and you and the good father here could go to jail. We're all crazy."

Ryan watched the detective's eyes flick from him to Julie. He was obviously in love with Julie, had come charging in like a white knight, only to find he was expected to help the dragon rather than the endangered maiden. Kidder wasn't a happy man.

Could he even accept help? Could he endanger all of them? He started to voice his belief he should just turn himself in, but Jerry stopped him in midsentence. "Forget it, Murphy. You can't stop Julie once she makes up her mind, and she's right about one thing. She and Nick are in danger now, and will be until this comes to an end. They have to believe she knows too much, and they have to worry that Nick will recognize Banyon's photo."

It was the only argument that could have pierced Ryan's determination to surrender and end Julie's involvement.

They spent the next two hours plotting.

Julie called William Lewis the next day. O'Grady would stay over and look after Nicholas for the next several days. He was an old prize fighter as well as a baseball player, he said. God help the man who tried to hurt the boy, and Nicholas had taken to the older man with twinkling eyes as readily as he had to Murphy.

When Lewis accepted her call, she knew the battle was half won.

"I've discovered information that will exonerate Ryan Murphy of his partner's death," she said. "Since you were his captain, I thought I should bring it to you."

"Where is he?"

"I can't talk over the telephone," she said. "Can you meet me tomorrow for lunch? I don't think it's wise to talk at the station."

He suggested a downtown restaurant and she agreed. It would be a lifetime. She knew the police were combing the city for Ryan, and she couldn't call him. She could only visit him in her mind and hope that Jerry had some luck in investigating Lewis.

Once convinced of Ryan's innocence, Jerry had thrown himself into the project. He contacted a P.I. friend who was a computer wizard and the two were trying to access Lewis's financial records. Jerry had also instructed her on the surveillance equipment and the wire she would wear. He would listen from a delivery truck.

Julie could do nothing more now. Just wait.

The restaurant was a trendy, overpriced, expense-account establishment in downtown Atlanta. Julie arrived early and experimented with the wire from a rest room. Even then, Lewis was late. At thirty minutes past the meeting time, he walked in and greeted her with profuse apologies.

He was a handsome man in his fifties. His white hair was obviously styled and he wore an expensive suit. He greeted her with a wide smile. After they were seated and exchanged a few pleasantries, his manner turned serious. "So you have news about Murphy?"

She handed him a copy of Ryan's letter to Laura, then watched his face as he read it. Nothing changed in it. When he finished, he handed it back to her. "I'm sorry, Mrs. Farrell, I don't know what that proves. He could have written it anytime. Yesterday. Today."

"I have a witness—a priest—who will testify that he has had it in his possession since the day after Ryan confessed."

His face paled slightly, but he quickly regained his composure. "It still means nothing. I wish you had more. I liked Ryan. He was a good cop until..."

"You framed him," she finished. "Banyon told Ryan you were behind everything, that you were Castilani's protector, that you ordered him to kidnap my son, then kill him." Her voice hardened.

"You can't prove that, Ms. Farrell. It's one hell of a fairy tale, but you're wrong."

"We'll see," she said. "Ryan's regained his memory. All of it. He has enough details to interest internal affairs and the district attorney. Dan is already interested," she said, purposely using his first name. "As you know, he decided not to oppose Ryan's parole. He smells something too, and we have enough information to put him on the right scent."

"Then why haven't you gone to him?"

He was very careful not to say anything incriminating, she noticed. Well, she had expected that. "Ryan is wanted for Banyon's murder," she said. "We both know he won't have a chance to present new evidence before being slapped back into prison. I'm sure you can appreciate the fact that his experience with the law has not led him to believe it—or you—can be trusted.

"All he wants," she continued after a brief pause, "is enough money to flee the country."

"You're crazy," he said, but she saw fear in his eyes. "Tell him to turn himself in."

"Angry is the word," she said. "I'm angry, not crazy. I would prefer to go after you. But he's tired. He wants some peace."

"That doesn't sound like the bastard I remember."

"Prison does that to a person. He doesn't want to go back. I don't suppose you would like it either."

"Just out of curiosity, Ms. Farrell, how much does he want to get out of the country?"

"A million dollars."

He looked at her in stunned silence. "I don't have that kind of money."

"Yes, you do," she said. "Someone who is very good with computers has accessed your bank account and found a very nice balance indeed. Now that alone wouldn't be suspicious. Good investments. But you made a mistake of transferring a rather large sum from a Caribbean bank notorious for hiding funds." Jerry had stumbled on that yesterday. Once he had a name, he and his fellow investigator, who was a whiz at breaking into so-called protected computer systems, had successfully accessed Lewis's bank records. The results had been better than she'd ever expected. Lewis had been careful, but not quite careful enough. Apparently he needed funds fast at one time.

If Lewis had been stunned before, he was obviously shocked at this latest revelation. Still, he struggled to control himself. "That's blackmail," he said quietly. "Aren't you afraid I might be taping this conversation?"

"Neither of us have anything to gain. I'm sure you don't want anyone to know about that bank account. Still, you bring up a good point. I think we should end this conversation now. I'll call you later."

She rose and left without another word.

She'd given him enough to stew about.

That afternoon, O'Grady took Nicholas to a hotel. And at four o'clock, Julie called Lewis.

"He needs the money tomorrow," she said.

"I can't get that much."

"He'll take two hundred thousand as a down payment, then two hundred thousand each month for four months," she said. "By the way, all the information has been outlined in a letter being held by an attorney. If anything happens to me, Dan Watters *will* receive it. If you don't show tomorrow, I'll take Ryan to Dan."

A long silence answered her. "Where...do you want me to take it?"

"Tomorrow you drive to a service station off I-75." She gave him the address. "I'll call you there at the pay telephone at exactly 2:00 p.m. and give you the final directions."

She hung up and called Dan.

Ryan paced the floor. He didn't like it. He didn't like any of it. But Julie had called from a pay telephone and told him she thought Lewis had taken the bait, mainly because of Jerry Kidder's work last night. She had also talked to Dan Watters. He'd been angry, she said, but he'd finally agreed to her plan.

He could imagine how angry Watters was: one of his former assistants involved with obstruction of justice and harboring a fugitive in the district attorney's own summer home, though Watters didn't know the latter part yet. They'd decided together that no matter how good a friend Dan was, or how honest a D.A., there could be leaks in his office. Watters's people would be brought to the cabin by Jerry two hours before Lewis's scheduled arrival.

A few more hours. A few more hours, and he would be either dead or back in jail. With luck, he wouldn't be there long.

He heard a car outside and he peered out the window. Julie. Ryan unlocked the door and waited as she climbed out of the car. Then they moved toward each other. He took her in his arms, then walked with her inside.

He didn't ask her if she was sure she wasn't followed. They had already discussed that. She suspected a transmitter would be planted, so she had changed cars at Tim's garage.

"We have some time," she said.

"Julie, you are...remarkable," he said, still in awe at how much she was risking for him.

"So are you," she said. "You saved my life, remember."

"It was probably the best thing I ever did."

"I think you spent your life doing good things."

He settled his chin on her dark hair. "You're the only person who believes that."

"Because you always concealed that part of yourself."

"I really cheated Mary Elizabeth, didn't I?" He moved so he could look down at her.

"Yes," she said simply. "But it wasn't your fault. You didn't know how to reach out."

"That's an excuse," he replied. "God knows what they thought, my wife and daughter."

"But now you have a second chance."

"With my daughter, anyway," he said. "Maybe. Maybe she'll never want anything to do with me."

She leaned against him. "I think she will."

She tilted her head up, inviting a kiss. He obliged. He loved her so damn much. And the future was so uncertain. This could be the last time he touched her. The last time he kissed her. The last time he could dream.

His kiss deepened, and he could think of nothing but her. They moved together toward the bedroom. He felt whole for the first time since he woke from the coma. Their other lovemaking was always shadowed, haunted by ghosts of the past, by his own belief that he had been a killer.

He was free of that, at least, but in hours he might be back in prison.

Ryan felt the urgency in her, the same quiet desperation that flowed through him. His body shuddered, reacting, hardening with a need that went far beyond lust or passion. He forced himself to stop, found the small packet in the drawer in the bedside table and slipped it on. Then he entered, deep and throbbing, and he felt her wrap around him, clasping and wanting. Loving. He savored and collected every touch, every feeling. He took his time, stroking to provide the greatest possible satisfaction but then the rhythm became frenzied and chaotic, and their bodies were reaching beyond familiar feelings, exploding in white hot splendor.

"I love you," he said as he relaxed slowly, his body still fused to hers. He hadn't meant to say the words until he had a right to say them. But they refused to stay inside. He was exploding with them.

He had apparently loved his wife, but he couldn't imagine ever loving anyone as much as he loved Julie.

Her fingers twined themselves in the dark hair that formed an arrow on his lower chest. Then she leaned over and gave him a kiss so long and sweet and lingering that his whole body seemed to sing with exquisite pleasure. Then his hands went up and down her body, memorizing every curve, the satiny feel of her skin, the scent of her. The thought of losing her was agonizing.

They lay there together as minutes ticked by. Love was thick in the air. And so was apprehension.

They finally dressed and went into the other room and waited. Julie made the call to Lewis on her cellular phone. He was at the station, as directed. Curtly, she gave him directions and hung up. "He took the bait," she said.

Quietly, they waited. This time, they were both silent. Soon, they heard the sound of cars and Julie went to the window. She nodded and went to the door, opening it.

Jerry walked in first, followed by Dan Watters and five police officers.

Watters looked at Julie. "*My* house?"

"I couldn't think of a safer place."

Watters then looked at Ryan, his gaze long and searching. "You'd better be right," he said, his comment directed toward Julie.

A man with Watters installed a listening device in each room, then all of them fanned out. Two headed for a storage shed where they would put the listening equipment, two drove the cars away, the others found posts in the surrounding woods where they could watch the front and back doors. Dan hesitated at the door, looked at them both, and seemed to want to say something. Instead he turned and disappeared with the others.

Ryan watched Julie, saw the distress on her face. Although Watters hadn't said anything, his silence had been condemnation. Watters had been her friend. He was learning what that meant.

"I'm sorry," he said, then added wryly, "I wish I didn't have to keep saying that."

She looked at him and put a finger to his mouth. "You *don't* have to say it."

"It seems I do," he said simply, and sat down. The next few moments would be the hardest in his short life.

At exactly 4:00 p.m., they heard another car. Once more, Julie looked out. Ryan went to stand next to her. A tall, gray-headed man stepped out, and a second man stepped out but stood near the door as the first approached.

"That's Lewis," Julie said. They both waited until Lewis reached the door and knocked. Julie answered it.

Lewis stepped in and waited for them to close the door. "Murphy," he said.

"Sandy," Ryan acknowledged.

"So you do remember."

"Yes," Ryan said curtly. "You bastard."

Lewis ignored him and walked around, opening every door and checking every closet before returning to stand in front of Ryan. His hands reached out, unbuttoning the shirt and running his hands up and down Ryan's body, then he did the same with Julie.

Ryan had to restrain himself as Lewis touched her. He kept seeing that letter, realizing that this man was, in part, responsible for almost running his daughter down, for threatening his family. He wanted to put his two hands around the man's throat. But he could do worse, much worse. He could make sure the man went to prison.

Finally satisfied but still wary, Lewis stared at Ryan. "I want the original of that letter."

"The money first," Ryan said.

Lewis placed a briefcase on a table and opened it, displaying packs of bills. "Now the letter."

Julie handed him an envelope. Lewis opened and skimmed its contents, then pocketed it. His hand then seemed to slide along his waist and suddenly there was a gun in it. He pointed it at Julie. "Did you really think you could blackmail me?" he said. "I don't leave loose ends."

"Loose ends like I was ten years ago," Ryan replied.

"You wouldn't give up on Castilani," Lewis said.

"So you ordered Mike to kill me."

Lewis gave a short laugh. "He was glad to oblige. And it wasn't hard to convince everyone else that you murdered Mike Cates in cold blood for trying to interfere with your drug business. You were always an arrogant bastard, Murphy, and you had damned few friends in the department. Everyone got a good laugh thinking that, maybe, you didn't have much cause to be so self-righteous after all."

Two days ago, Lewis's assessment of Ryan's character would have fueled the fires of his self-doubt. But now it didn't matter. Inside, where it counted, he'd been a decent human being.

"Was Banyon working on your orders when he kidnapped Nick Farrell?" Ryan wanted as much information as possible on tape.

"What difference does that make now?"

Ryan shrugged his shoulders. "Curious."

Lewis smiled coldly. "Damn fool messed it up. We didn't think you would have a gun. Where is it now, by the way?"

"I threw it away."

"You did one smart thing. Now you can stand a little closer to Mrs. Farrell."

"How do you plan to explain...?" He couldn't say the words.

"That's easy. I was following a hunch. You see, I've suspected for some time now that Mrs. Farrell's interest in you was of a...personal nature, shall we say? Women can be such fools. I thought she might be harboring you, and so I followed her. And here you are. But you wouldn't surrender peacefully. You fired on me, and I had no choice but to fire back. Too bad Mrs. Farrell was caught in the crossfire."

Ryan gave a disgusted snort. "Who will believe you came out here alone?"

"I'm not alone," Lewis said smugly. "I've got my driver who's a trained officer and this was just a guess. My man will swear to anything I tell him to say. Enough money buys a lot of loyalty.

"As for why I came rather than send a squad to arrest you—" Lewis shrugged "—well, maybe I got a little over-involved. But I think the Chief will understand, considering that you did serve under me. I felt a sort of personal moral duty to put you back behind bars. I'm only disgusted they ever let you out, because I sure as hell thought you would be there for good." He shook his head. "I have to say, though, I didn't think you'd be this easy to take down. Guess prison must have dulled your edge."

"Probably," Ryan admitted as he moved casually away from Julie, drawing the assistant chief's gaze with him. "Then again, maybe it's you who's lost the edge."

Lewis looked around suddenly, his expression changing from smug to wary. At that instant, two men barged into the room through the back door, both holding guns. Lewis turned and fired at one.

Ryan dove at Julie, knocking her to the floor and covering her with his body.

The detectives shot back at Lewis as he ran toward the door, jerked it open and raced for his car. Ryan jumped to his feet and followed the detectives who headed out the door after Lewis. Two detectives emerged from the trees to join the fight. For several seconds, the woods echoed with the sound of gunfire until both Lewis and the driver fell. A uniformed officer also lay on the ground.

Julie appeared and stood alongside him as they watched Dan Watters stoop next to Lewis, then the driver. Another detective used Lewis's car radio, probably to call an ambulance. Watters and a second man approached Julie and Ryan.

"Sorry," Dan said to Julie. "We have to take Murphy in. He's still wanted and he's violated his parole in God knows how many ways."

Julie started to protest, but Ryan shook his head. "It's all right," he said.

"I'll have you out before Christmas," she said.

He nodded, though he didn't share her optimism. He'd stolen a gun, shot a detective and become a fugitive. He'd known this would happen. Had to happen.

Ryan stood stoically as he was ordered to put his hands behind him. He felt the grip of metal, heard the metallic click as the cuffs closed around his wrists. He remembered the biting feel of cold steel. But Julie was safe. Nick was safe. And that was all that mattered.

Julie waited for Ryan at the door of the jail. It had been eight days since he'd been arrested. Eight days to maneuver through the bureaucracy and paperwork. She'd finally gotten him released on bond. She expected either a pardon—or a reversal of the conviction—within a few months.

The wired conversation might have been enough, but Lewis's driver, faced with multiple charges including attempted murder, turned state's evidence and implicated Lewis and Banyon. Lewis himself gave a deathbed confession. Ryan had apparently gotten too close to charging Castilani, who'd been paying off Lewis, Banyon and Cates for years. After Ryan's informant was killed, Castilani had ordered Cates to kill Ryan, and Lewis had positioned himself nearby so he could take control of the investigation and exonerate Cates. When Ryan killed Cates instead, Lewis easily slid into a second plan: framing Ryan. Castilani ordered the attack on Laura, and one of his men passed along the message to Ryan in jail.

Banyon, according to the driver who had passed on orders from Lewis, was responsible for the anonymous calls and the attempt on Ryan's life. He'd also tapped Ryan's phone. No other officers had been involved, either ten years before or now....

Julie checked her watch. Four o'clock. He should have been released an hour ago, according to Dan.

"Where is he?" Nick asked for the tenth time in less than thirty minutes. Nick was beside himself with excitement, had insisted on coming with her. Today was Christmas Eve, and he was getting the best present of all: his friend, Ryan.

The door leading to the jail finally opened, and Ryan emerged. His hair was mussed; he'd been running his fingers through it again. His shirt sleeves were rolled up, and his jacket was slung over his shoulder.

He had that five o' clock shadow that made him look as villainous as any of the desperadoes being brought into the jail.

Nicholas flung himself at him. Ryan leaned down to pick him up.

"It's Christmas Eve," Nick announced.

"I know," Ryan said, looking hungrily at Julie. She took his hand while the other continued to hold Nick.

"Let's go home," she said. "We'll be there just in time for Santa Claus."

Nick looked at Ryan. "Do you think...he'll remember?"

"I think so," he said.

Ryan was silent as they drove through the streets, still busy with last-minute shoppers. When they reached the house, Nick pulled him to the tree and showed off all the Christmas gifts lying underneath. Ryan's name was on a number of them.

She saw the stricken look on his face. She lifted up on her tiptoes and kissed him. "Your freedom is the best present I've ever received," she said softly. "And Nick, too."

Ryan looked dubious. "I'm a darn poor bargain," he said. "I don't have much. In fact, I don't have anything."

"Oh, Tim is clamoring to have you back at the garage," she said. "He was even making noises about maybe retiring and taking you on as a partner."

She saw him swallow as if something very thick clogged his throat. After a moment, he straightened his shoulders and took her hand. "You wanted to know what Nick wanted for Christmas?"

She nodded. It was too late to get anything else, but she wanted to know. Nick wouldn't be too disappointed if he didn't get everything. Ryan was here, after all, and a Sheltie puppy, now boarding at the home of a very abject Emily, awaited him in the morning. "What?"

"A father." He looked into her eyes. "I think that requires a husband."

"Yes," she agreed solemnly.

He seemed to hold his breath. "Will you? Will you marry me?"

"Oh yes," she said and kissed him long and hard.

"Mommy?"

She remembered Nick. She turned to him. "You're getting your wish for Christmas."

"I knew it," he said, dancing around like an inebriated elf. "I knew if I didn't tell you it would come true."

Ryan looked down at him with a kind of wonder. Then he grinned. He couldn't ask for a finer present.

"Welcome home, my love," she said, her hand locked in his. Then she looked toward the top of the tree.

Francesca stared back, then winked.

Epilogue

The wedding was to take place on a sunny Saturday afternoon in late March.

In ten minutes, in fact. Julie knew she should feel nervous, but she'd never felt so calm in her life. She felt such a sense of...rightness about this marriage.

Ryan's daughter, Laura, looked at Julie critically as she took one last swipe at her hair with the brush. "You look beautiful," she said in an awestruck voice.

Her *stepdaughter*. It was amazing. The two of them had gone shopping together for her wedding dress, and it was Laura who'd found *the* dress, a light blue silk with short sleeves and a fitted waist and swirling skirt. That shopping trip had deepened their budding relationship; Laura previously had stayed several weekends with her in an effort to get to know her father, her "other" father.

"I never really believed that anyone looked as if they had stars in their eyes, but now I do," Laura continued.

"Do you?" Julie replied. "I really want you to be happy about this."

Laura grinned. "I am. I get another whole family."

In the beginning, Laura hadn't been so sure she wanted a new family. Julie still remembered the awkwardness, the guilt so evident on both parts at the first meeting between Ryan and Laura. Thankfully,

Laura's mother had paved the way, explaining to Laura how much her father had sacrificed for the two of them, but having a father—especially one she'd tried to hate for ten years—thrust at her had not been easy.

Laura had expressed deep guilt that she'd refused to see him earlier, and also that she'd felt so much anger toward him. Ryan, on the other hand, had worried out loud that perhaps he could have handled things better ten years earlier, that he shouldn't have just blocked both of them out.

Julie knew *this* Ryan wouldn't do that. This Ryan was the strongest man she'd ever known—he'd certainly been tempered by events of the past few months—but he also had a tenderness and sensitivity that never ceased to amaze her. He demonstrated it with the slow, careful but loving patience he had with Laura. He hadn't demanded or expected love but had offered friendship instead and taken care to treat his daughter as an adult, just as he treated Nick as a person who just happened to be small. After Laura's initial hesitation, she'd responded eagerly to him, and now seemed well pleased with both her new father and her prospective stepmother.

"Here," Laura said, and shyly handed her a box. "I knew you had something blue and new. I didn't know whether you had anything old and borrowed."

Laura carefully opened the box. Nestled in cotton lay a lovely silver heart on a silver chain.

"Mother told me my...father bought that for me when I was born. She said it was the only sentimental thing she'd known him to do." Laura bit her lips and tears shone in her eyes. "She had kept it for me but then..." She tried a trembling smile. "He really did love me, didn't he?"

"He does love you. More than life itself," Julie said.

"And now he loves you the same way. I'm so glad."

Julie reached out and hugged the girl as tears welled in her own eyes. She loved this Ryan, but she thought she would love the other one, too. The old Ryan made the ultimate sacrifice for his first family. The new one had done the same for hers.

She would have married either one months ago, but Ryan had wanted to wait until he was totally cleared. The conviction was officially reversed last week. In the days following Lewis's confession, the press had turned from condemning Ryan to practically deifying him. Ryan had been offered numerous jobs, but he'd chosen to stay at the garage where Tim had offered a partnership. Johnny had never wanted any part of management, and Tim wanted to retire in another year. Maybe Ryan would stay; maybe he wouldn't, but he owed Tim, and he enjoyed working with his hands. He had no desire, ever, to go into police work.

He'd had no more mental flashes. He was resigned to the fact he might never regain his memory. But neither of them cared about that. They knew what they needed to know.

A knock came at the door.

Julie sniffed. "I think it's time to go."

"I checked on Ryan—" Ryan and Laura had agreed on using his first name "—before I came to see you," Laura confided.

"You got him out of jeans?"

Laura grinned. "Yeah, and he's baaaad."

"Meaning cool?" Julie obviously would have to learn an entire new language. The thought was daunting, yet really quite wonderfully challenging.

She and Laura walked out of the dressing area and down to the sanctuary of the small church she and Ryan attended. Nick, dressed in a suit with his hair slicked back, met them, his face alight with excitement and pleasure. Laura leaned over and in a big sisterly way straightened his tie. Nick beamed at her. He'd been overjoyed to discover he'd have a sister.

The organist began to play "When I Fall in Love," a song Julie had chosen. As guardian of the rings, Nick started down the aisle first, followed by Laura, her only attendant.

Julie waited, looking over the few people they had invited: Mary Elizabeth, her husband and two other children; Jerry Kidder; Dan and Sandy Watters; Tim and Johnny from the garage; Dr. Dailey and his wife, and, finally, Emily and her husband, both of whom had come over to apologize for their initial attitude toward Ryan. Their daughter, Abby, looked longingly at the natty Nick as he almost skipped down the aisle.

Then Julie's eyes went to Ryan, who stood at the front of the church with Sean O'Grady who'd flown back to Atlanta to be his best man.

As she started down the aisle, her gaze never left Ryan's face.

His features were still, solemn. He did look extraordinarily handsome in a dark blue suit, white shirt and blue tie. His dark hair was neatly combed—obviously no fingers this time—and his indigo gaze, as he watched her approach, seemed to reach out and embrace her.

When she reached him, he held out his hand. She took it. Then he smiled, a breathtaking smile that told her—and the world—how much he loved her. He leaned over and brushed her lips with a kiss, oblivious to the fact that custom said that gesture came last.

He was marching to his own drummer as he apparently always had. But now that beat included her. Nick. Laura.

Her fingers tightened around his as they turned and faced the minister, even as she heard his whispered words, "I love you."

* * * * *

SILHOUETTE SENSATION®

AVAILABLE FROM 24TH DECEMBER 1999

THE TOUGH GUY AND THE TODDLER
Diane Pershing

Within weeks Jordan Carlisle had aided in the rescue of a kidnapped child, begun a flirtation with intensely sexy detective Dominic D'Annunzio…and learned that her own son might be alive. If they found her toddler, would her tough guy stay?

LIKE FATHER, LIKE DAUGHTER
Margaret Watson

Not a night passed that Becca Johnson didn't dream about one long-ago summer and a certain handsome wanderer. Now, finally, he'd come home, but things were different. She was a confident alluring woman with a child to protect—a child with his blue eyes!

THE MIRACLE MAN Sharon Sala

Heartbreaker

Antonette Hatfield wanted a baby, but Mr Right had never come along. Then US Marshal Lane Monday was washed ashore—the answer to her every prayer… But Lane didn't want to get involved—pleasure without price wasn't his style…

ONCE MORE A FAMILY Paula Detmer Riggs

Grady Hardin made it his mission to reunite his family—he was determined to bring back his abducted son and reawaken the love of the only woman he'd ever wanted. But he'd forgotten the intense passion and deep emotions his ex-wife Ria had always aroused in him…

9912

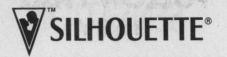

FOLLOW THAT BABY

Everybody's looking for a missing pregnant
woman in the exciting new cross-line
mini-series from Silhouette®.

THE DADDY AND THE BABY DOCTOR
Kristin Morgan
November 1999 in Silhouette Desire•

THE SHERIFF AND THE IMPOSTOR BRIDE
Elizabeth Bevarly
December 1999 in Silhouette Desire

THE MILLIONAIRE AND THE PREGNANT PAUPER
Christie Ridgway
January 2000 in Silhouette Desire

THE MERCENARY AND THE NEW MUM
Merline Lovelace
February 2000 in Silhouette Sensation•

FREE
2 BOOKS
AND A SURPRISE GIFT!

We would like to take this opportunity to thank you for reading this Silhouette® book by offering you the chance to take TWO more specially selected titles from the Sensation™ series absolutely FREE! We're also making this offer to introduce you to the benefits of the Reader Service™—

- ★ FREE home delivery
- ★ FREE gifts and competitions
- ★ FREE monthly Newsletter
- ★ Exclusive Reader Service discounts
- ★ Books available before they're in the shops

Accepting these FREE books and gift places you under no obligation to buy; you may cancel at any time, even after receiving your free shipment. Simply complete your details below and return the entire page to the address below. *You don't even need a stamp!*

YES! Please send me 2 free Sensation books and a surprise gift. I understand that unless you hear from me, I will receive 4 superb new titles every month for just £2.70 each, postage and packing free. I am under no obligation to purchase any books and may cancel my subscription at any time. The free books and gift will be mine to keep in any case.

S9EC

Ms/Mrs/Miss/Mr ....Initials................................
BLOCK CAPITALS PLEASE

Surname...

Address...

....

....Postcode ....

Send this whole page to:
UK: FREEPOST CN81, Croydon, CR9 3WZ
EIRE: PO Box 4546, Kilcock, County Kildare (stamp required)